George E. Spencer

Salt-Lake Fruit

George E. Spencer

Salt-Lake Fruit

ISBN/EAN: 9783337054076

Printed in Europe, USA, Canada, Australia, Japan

Cover: Foto ©Andreas Hilbeck / pixelio.de

More available books at **www.hansebooks.com**

A LATTER-DAY ROMANCE

BY AN AMERICAN

BOSTON
Franklin Press: Rand, Avery, and Company
1884

THE MOTIVE.

HE incidents written within this book are not exaggerated. Those facts upon which the romance hinges are more hideous in their naked truth than thus clothed in fiction's drapery.

Human nature, weak, erring, is prone to sin. But ever between temptation and sin stand the two sentinels which guard civilization, and keep open the road to advance.

Law and religion oppose their mighty front to man's brutality. To his better nature they lend their force. For his errors they mete unto him punishment, they waken shame for past falls, resolution for a better life. Even though he believe not the tenets of any faith, even though he be so unfortunate as to thrust aside all creeds that cannot be proven by human rules, yet will cling to him those lessons of morality learned at his mother's knee, yet will he feel disgust at his own and others' relapses into sin, and, unbidden, rise shame's blush to his cheek as memory brings back scenes and deeds he would forget.

But let any man, knowing his own nature, put himself in the place of Mormon youth; let his first lesson be selfish gratification; let his law and his religion counsel immorality, glorify human sacrifice, — and where comes the end of crime?

Fathers with young daughters, clasp tight to your bosom these tender lambs. Strain them close, — close, until their hearts cease to beat, their breathing stops in death's awful calm. Better thus to end their heart-aches, than consign them to such a fate as may await them, if, unchecked, this frightful anaconda stretches its slimy length across the continent.

Why women speak not, God alone knows who made these mysterious creatures, — these beings who, at rare intervals, surprise a world by their daring heroism, and then amaze it at their long, silent, uncomplaining submission to some frightful fate. Some of Utah's women religious fanaticism holds in terror, — that fanaticism which has made the mother tear from her breast her suckling babe, and cast it into flame before some graven image. But did the world stand by, and cry, "Well done"? No. Civilization rushed in. Its strong hands held her feeble ones, its clear voice rang through her world of darkness and ignorance, and, bidding her look upon her deed, branded it as crime, punished it as crime, and protected from another mother's madness the helpless child.

Some women in Utah are held in silence by domestic tyranny; some by hope, through their zeal, of gaining influence paramount with their husband, and thus, pandering to his vice, obtain mastery of him. Disgrace to woman that thus it is! and yet is it truth.

But to you, men with daughters, those silent tongues speak with eloquence beyond all words. To you these miserable women hold up the daily, hourly torture of their disgraced lives. Help them, or perhaps your own ewe lamb may one day be crushed in the horrible folds of that most hideous, most powerful serpent. Do not deceive yourselves. Do not believe Mormonism is content to rest in Utah. Slowly, surely, the monster is stretching abroad its horrible body. Cautiously those small green eyes, full of cunning, are watching each opportunity for advance; and from its fanged tongue drops the poison of its accursed creed. The power of its institutions is more wonderful, more absolute, than was ever the Inquisition. Its perfect organization excels any known government. No Russian serfs were ever more completely subjected than are its followers. Cunningly it defies, overcomes, and subserves to its own ends, the laws of the United States. By great majorities it carries every election. Its men call upon their creatures for support; and those who would, *dare not*, disobey. We are told that blood-atonement does not longer exist. We are told that the Mormon law is dead, which, for disobedience, took to her open grave the wife, and, first bidding her look therein, cut her throat, and, holding her over the yawning hole, let her know her own blood was moistening the ground where soon would lie her body. But do we know it is a fact? Do we know that law is dead? What do we ever know of the secrets hidden in the folds of that powerful organization? Do we not know that persons in Utah who mysteriously disappear are never found, — are rarely looked for? Do we not know of the murder of a noted physician in sight and sound of passing Mormons? Yet those very men, under oath, declared they had seen nothing. Those living in Utah have known how criminals are shielded by Mormon authorities. There is in Salt Lake a journal that cries aloud to all mankind, bidding them wipe out the lawful immorality of Utah. Undismayed by fears of assassination, that one man holds up daily astounding facts that are unnoticed by the eyes looking at the stock-quotations. His alarum falls unheeded on ears listening to the click-clack of the busy market-reporter.

Fatal indifference, bearing baleful fruit in the not too distant future. And the money, in whose gain he forgets all else, — perhaps one day it will help to buoy the Mormon government, fill the Mormon coffers when that government shall have substituted a Mormon saint for Liberty's statue, and wiped out this we proudly call the great republic.

It is no idle threat. It is a foreboding of what will surely come, unless now, in her might, Liberty puts her heel on the serpent's head, and crushes it. No intermediate legislation will avail. Exterminate, or be exterminated. Forever destroy polygamy, or, like Cleopatra's asp, it will fasten upon this goddess who smiles down on us, stretching out her arms to homeless exiles, and, lo! Liberty, beauteous maid, lies a pale corpse!

Great is thy enemy, O peerless maid! Therefore, now, while life is still left, raise your voice, and call unto the hearts of men. Thy enemy advances: among its minions its purpose is avowed, — thy assassination! Its rulers wary, capable, unscrupulous; its power immense; its discipline perfect. So thorough is its system, that, at its bidding, its ploughman turns his plough into a bayonet, and stands ready to cut thy white, white throat. For the love of God, for the love of offspring, for the preservation of thy fair life, O Liberty, let not the monster grow!

Look not abroad for enemies. Here in thy camp lies this hideous reptile, fattening on thy provender, strengthening under thy protection. Crush it, exterminate it, make polygamy a dead issue, or, into the grave it is digging, Liberty will fall, and the battles of our ancestors, the name of Washington, the glory of our land, will become but as thin, unsubstantial shadows.

CONTENTS.

CONTENTS.

SALT-LAKE FRUIT.

A LATTER-DAY ROMANCE.

CHAPTER I.

T was spring-time in the valley of the Jordan, — that fertile plain for which Nature had done so much that it needed but the hand of man, directing its irrigation, to make it, as it stands, verily a garden-spot.

Every thing was in blossom. The season had been favorable, and all Nature was in her freshest, loveliest garb. The river went smiling on its way, reflecting back the sunlight in a thousand ripples of brightness.

The birds filled the air with song as they flitted from limb to limb of the orchard-trees, laden with treasures of white and pink, that sent out sweetest perfume.

All was an intoxication of beauty and gladness. Beneath those trees stood a youth and maiden, — another Adam and Eve in their paradise. This was told by their glistening eyes, their flushed faces, his pleading tones, and loving words.

One arm was thrown around her, drawing her tenderly to him. Half yielding, half repelling, she stood listening and hesitating.

It is written, "She who hesitates is lost." And who, looking on those dark, liquid eyes, half hidden by drooping lids, her parted lips and heaving bosom, but would feel a surety of her soon yielding to the pleader whispering in the delicate ear that was turned towards him?

"Christine, I love you." His breath was on her cheek, his hair mingling with hers, his arms holding her close to his breast that rose and fell in a tumult of passion.

He was standing back of her, — so near, and yet not able to look into her face that filled with wondrous light as he said "I love you."

The birds seemed to take up the refrain. The apple-blossoms breathed it, the very air was laden with it; and her heart was throbbing with wild gladness, that the one it owned as "lord" was, if but for a moment, all her own.

Trembling, overpowered, she half sank into his arms, all resistance seemingly over, when suddenly, as if awakening from a trance, she tore herself from his embrace, and stood trembling, loving, but determined not to yield.

He, hurt and offended at the very moment when he felt all gained, drew back, giving up the tender pleading; while his eyes darkened with an anger he dared not speak.

Standing thus apart, face to face, the contrast between them seemed greater.

He was strong and fair. Clustering curls covered a well-formed head. Full lips, blue eyes, both beautiful with the coloring and freshness of youth, but in both the possibility of cruelty and selfishness. And, over all the handsome figure, an air of self-indulgence and animal spirits.

She, tall, slender, and graceful, more tender than beautiful, more intellectual than passionate. Yet now, as she rested against the

gnarled trunk of an old apple-tree, one hand clinging to it as if for
support, the other pressed on her bosom in the vain effort to quiet its
heaving, the dark lashes hiding eyes from which tears slowly fell over

"SHE STOOD LISTENING AND HESITATING."

cheeks grown pale with emotion, she was fair enough to tempt a man
to peril his soul for her sake.

So thought her lover, while he gnawed savagely the red lips that
had but an instant since been pressed on her silken hair.

Neither spoke. He was full of rage; she, of some earnest feeling that could not yet command the trembling lips to interpret. At last he said, conquered by his love and passion, —

"Christine, you do not love me."

At this she raised her tear-filled eyes, and looked at him from the depths of her soul.

Trembling with exultation, he fell at her feet. Kneeling there, he once more threw his arms around her, and pleaded in quick whispers.

Again she seemed about to yield, so much did her body and heart plead for him, giving his words tenfold power.

But once more the earnest and better part, the indefinable something called conscience that in some women will rise above even the scorching fire of love, awakened her to her danger.

"Listen, Malcolm." She spoke with difficulty ; those dewy, trembling lips, even now burning with his last kiss, proving but poor allies in her hour of need. "I love you. You cannot doubt it." And again her glorious eyes looked into his. "I love you; but I cannot, I never will, make a Mormon marriage. You were born here : I was born in the far North beyond the seas, where one woman suffices to fill the measure of one man's life. I came here a child, but each year I live makes me feel the horrors of this belief. Friendless, except my grandfather, I cannot escape. Nor would I escape if I could, and leave him, in his old age, alone. Were I not sure I could trust you, I would not dare speak thus my thoughts of this land's religion. But while I must refuse your love, that my heart, alas ! returns tenfold, it will comfort me all my life to know that you did love me."

Her voice died out. The birds were still. The sun was hidden by the mountains. The chilly evening mist of the brightest of spring days was covering the picture that had so lately glowed with warmth and light.

The chill seemed to strike to the girl's heart. She shivered as, with bended head, she turned to leave the place where love and conviction had fought the hard fight.

Her movement awakened him into action.

"No: by Heaven, you shall not leave me!" He sprang to his feet, catching her in such a close, strong clasp, that, had she loved him less, she would have cried out with pain, as, drawing her face to his, he covered it with kisses.

After the first bewilderment and — must it be written ? — heart's joy at being again thus close to him, she struggled to free herself.

Then this other Faust, finding the Marguerite he desired too strong, too pure, to be easily won, and feeling thus near to him her lovely form, held as naught any sacrifice that would win her.

"Listen, cruel girl!" he said, while his eyes and lips feasted on her sweetness. "For your sake I will forswear the faith in which I was raised. I will proclaim my father an adulterer, my mother a victim. Do you become my wife, and your own grandfather shall marry us fast and strong. He is a minister of your faith. Let him bind us, that neither heaven nor hell can separate you from me. I will be true to you, so help me God ! faithful to you, and to you alone."

The moon rose over the mountain-tops, its light falling like a blessing on the pair. She rested in his arms, trembling, happy, beautiful. Their eyes drank love from each other. There was no need of speech. It was a moment of supreme joy.

Could some power have stricken them dead, as they stood thus clasped together, they would have gone down to all eternity a realization of joy and love.

But lives must be lived, sorrows borne, ills atoned ; and the happinesses are but as brief moments.

Shine on them, O moon! Move slower in your course, that the joy may endure but a little longer.

CHAPTER II.

MATTHEW.

ATTER, patter, patter! A handful of gravel on her window awakened Christine from dreams of love and happiness. Springing from her bed, she hastened to throw open the casement, and smiled down on her grandfather.

"Good-morning, father."

"And to you, my child, God's blessing. But hurry down, my birdling. See, the sun has kissed all the dew from the flowers, and you are a laggard."

"I'll be with you in a moment." Then, closing the casement, she made a hurried toilet; while the old man walked around the garden, the smile still on his face with which he had greeted his grandchild.

He was a tall man, with clear-cut features, blue eyes, and white hair falling on his shoulders. He had a noble face and a kindly expression. It was a face that a beggar, in appealing for help, would have picked out of a crowd.

Tender and loving to every thing, he was even now most carefully avoiding a little butterfly that had been hurt, and lay fluttering on the path.

"Poor wee creature!" he said, as he picked it up, and gently put it safe among the flowers. "Thou hast not many moments more of life, but those shall be undisturbed."

While he was still watching it pitifully, his granddaughter stole up behind him, and slipped her hand in his arm.

Turning, he folded her to his heart, and, with eyes lifted to heaven, silently prayed for his darling, then kissed her on the forehead, and told her the day was brighter since she was with him.

It was with affection like this Christine's life had been blessed. She was the only child of an only son,—a sailor, who, just before her birth, had been lost at sea, near the bleak shore of his native Norway. His young wife soon followed, seeking her husband in that land where parting and sorrow are no more.

Thus, in his old age, Matthew Kleigwald found himself left alone with a baby, who cooed and smiled at him as she lay in his arms.

Father, mother, nurse, every thing to the little girl, who daily grew more and more into his life and heart. In her childhood they were playmates ; and, as she older grew, her grandfather was her sole teacher. An earnest nature, enthusiastic and religious, he lived a life quite different from the ordinary Scandinavian peasant.

A life of arduous toil, and yet about it a certain poetry that made him and his Christine seem characters out of some idyl. Hard working himself, he dreaded, as he kissed the slender fingers of his grand-child, and looked into her sensitive face, to think how toil would affect the life he was shielding. And yet, what else could he dare hope ? For with short summers, and the long, cold winters, scanty crops and arid land, he could scarcely now keep the wolf from the door. While thinking of his darling day by day, and growing more and more hopeless of her future, there came to this remote village a Mormon missionary,—a man of fiery eloquence, who taught of love, faith, and hope ; making them seem practical realities as he told of the colony of saints beyond the seas, who, with fertile lands for endowing their toil-worn brothers, stood, arms open, ready to fold them into their blessed community.

No word was said of polygamy, or the many demands and taxes that would be laid upon the converts. Only love, plenty, and peace were preached to men, who, year after year, found the hardest labor but sufficed to keep their little ones from starving.

Among the first to catch the fever was Matthew. He gazed at the wild mountains, so dear to him, that had looked down on all of his

THE MORMON MISSIONARY.

life, and felt he could not leave them. Then, turning to his Christine, and seeing for her only toilsome years, there arose a longing to reach that land of plenty.

Then, too, the religious element in his nature was awakened to wildest enthusiasm, when one evening, after preaching to the listening multitude, the missionary, John Smith, called out, in a voice as tuneful as some sweet instrument, —

"Bring to me the sick, that I may give them relief by laying on these hands that the Lord has blessed."

"Take my child, and ease his pain," cried a woman's voice.

The crowd parted ; and, bearing in her arms a half-grown boy moaning with rheumatic fever, the mother advanced.

Kneeling beside the sufferer, while his eyes burned like fire, John Smith passed his hands rapidly and frequently over the boy's head, throat, and body, until gradually the moaning ceased ; and the mother, with grateful tears streaming down her face, looked on her child peacefully asleep.

Half fearful of awakening him, she grasped the preacher's hands, and covered them with kisses, while she whispered words of deepest thanks.

"Speak aloud!" cried John Smith, whose voice rang out like clarion. "His sleep is God's gift. Man's voice cannot disturb it. He will awaken cured! And now, O ye men of stone! with this testimony to my words as a reproach to ye, why will ye longer delay? Come to the land that holds plenty for ye! Come to the brothers whose arms are held out to ye! Come to God's city, where the saints are your friends, and Heaven's peace is waiting for ye!"

Hundreds rushed up to sign their names to the roll of the elect, among the others Matthew Kleigwald.

Then came a hurried gathering together of household goods, a quick sale of houses and lands, — for Smith was too capable a missionary to let enthusiasm grow old, — and, before Matthew had fairly weighed the consequences, he found himself parting from his home and fatherland, and, advanced in years, going to a foreign country.

When the last "good-by" was spoken at the little graveyard, and Matthew knelt to kiss the earth that covered the dear young wife he had lost in the first year of their marriage, only God knew his bitter pain.

Almost fainting, he felt he could not live away from his beloved surroundings ; but, raising his eyes, he saw the pale face of Christine, who was kneeling by her mother's grave. Rising, he took her in his arms.

"For your sake, my child, I leave the land of my birth. The spirits of those we love will be as near us there as here. Thou, my Christine, wilt have a home of plenty. And, when God shall call me to himself, I can close my eyes in peace, knowing my birdling is safe from the cutting blast of poverty."

Then they walked quietly and sadly to the little church, where the peasants were assembled to say farewell to Matthew, who had been their preacher for many years. Without pay, he had read the baptism, marriage, and burial services for them, teaching them as best he could. And now he was about to leave them! Tears and blessings fell around him. Some old peasants threw their arms about him, and wished him "God-speed" in the new land where they were too infirm to follow him. The younger men crowded near, and said, when he wrote for them to start, they would join him in the New Jerusalem.

Being thus a man of influence in his village, Smith treated Matthew with especial consideration, lessening for him, as well as he could, some of the discomforts of the long journey.

After a quick voyage the converts landed in New York. The authorities of the city, and the officials sworn to protect the rights of helplessness and ignorance, although aware of the arrival of Mormon converts, remained perfectly quiescent. And the "Land of the Free," that had called forth a deluge of blood to wash away that other slavery, quietly smiled while hundreds were hurried across her broad acres into a moral slavery whose existence must ever dim the bright stars of her banner.

Every thing went smoothly. At the appointed place Mormon authorities met the emigrants with deeds for lands, and took from them bonds for the payment thereof, and also of interest moneys that would fall due. They were apportioned to different localities. Being accustomed to hard work and frugality, they would have been useful citizens anywhere. For themselves, finding the land easy of cultivation, they felt few repinings. Most of the men took quietly and contentedly to polygamy. Self-indulgence is always easy to inferior natures, and men are not all superior. As for the women in this land, poor slaves! they had no hearing.

Their heart-aches, their repinings, are among the untold agonies of this troublous world. And yet, perchance, these silently endured griefs may spring into vigorous, avenging life.

Matthew's pure soul was shocked at the moral condition of this New Jerusalem within whose strong walls he had brought his grand-child.

It was easy to enter, but how to escape?

His little money all spent for lands, which yet he only dared call his as long as he was able to pay the interest moneys and the tithing moneys, and outwardly, in a measure, conform to Mormon rules. For, looking at his deeds, he found himself so bound that there was noth-ing else possible except to stay and work, and hope, with favorable crops, to raise and save enough to take Christine away from the coun-try he had sacrificed so much to gain. His age protected him, and Christine's youth was in her favor. Then, too, having more intellect-uality than physical beauty, she did not seem so much desired by the amorous Mormon. And John Smith befriended him. Perhaps a twinge of his almost inane conscience at deceiving so noble a man, made him protect Christine from the hasty Mormon marriages of which young girls, willing or unwilling, were made the victims.

Through his influence, Matthew and his child were sent from Salt Lake to the interior town of G——, where, the land apportioned to the old man being really fertile, and, as she grew older, having no demands for Christine in marriage, they settled down into a peaceful, quiet life. Loving each other, they could easily make a home together; and, known as the *protégés* of John Smith, they escaped many annoy-ances.

Ten years had passed, and Christine was twenty-four. Her face and form, matured into too noble a beauty to attract the average Mormon, must awaken, sooner or later, strong love in some man.

Until a few months before, that man did not seem forthcoming; and Matthew, proud and happy in the loveliness of his child, was lulled

into content and peace. He led a useful life, helpful to all around
him, trying to show to sorrow-darkened eyes, that, even when injustice is permitted, there is a merciful and just God who looks down
on all.

It is a hard doctrine to believe when hearts are breaking ; but,
like a compass on a stormy sea, it is all poor humanity has to steer by.

Then, Matthew, having prospered, and spending little for his own
and Christine's simple needs, was able to do many kindnesses for the
unhappy, until, between him and his poorer neighbors, there had
sprung up, in some instances, true affection. Near him always, as his
twin spirit, was his Christine, sharing every labor of love and mercy.

Intense and poetic by nature, yet Christine was happy in this
useful life, nor seemed to long for that dearer companionship so need-
ful to most maidens.

The light of her grandfather's life, and the friend of those who
needed her, the girl seemed to wish for nothing more.

But there came an awakening from the maiden's peace.

O peace ! Beautiful peace ! Like some white-winged dove, once
let thee fly out of our souls, and never more canst thou be enticed
back again !

John Smith, who never lost his interest in Matthew, and remembered Christine as a fair girl, with fancies sweet as spring-flowers, had
occasionally visited them. The last time he came, he brought his
nephew, Malcolm Smith, a handsome young fellow, light-hearted, and
merry of disposition. He left him to spend some months with
Matthew, "To improve his ideas of farming," he said. But, if Matthew
had noticed his earnest look at Christine the evening before departure, he might have imagined another motive.

Who could not foretell the result of two young and unfilled hearts
brought thus in close communion ? Nature, too, in her early spring-
time, each day blossoming into fresh loveliness. And so, as they

wandered forth together in these lovely spring days, their hearts were blossoming into life's summer; Malcolm listening while Christine talked, telling sometimes of her own imaginings, sometimes bits of her neighbor's history; and every thing she spoke, so full of beauty and poetry.

To some is given the peculiar power of earnest and forcible expression. It was thus with Christine. Listening to her, being so constantly with her, Malcolm seemed to grow in intelligence, and lose somewhat the commonplace in his nature. Her aspirations wakened echoes in his soul; and, long before he knew he loved her, he felt himself a better man through her influence.

To her, love came very soon. And yet she knew it not as love. She only knew, that, to be near him was happiness. To touch his hand, even by accident, gave her exquisite pleasure. And so strong was this physical influence, that, before she heard his voice or step, she would know he was approaching by this same sweet thrill.

She had not desired marriage, since to her a Mormon marriage was impossible. And she did not imagine the possibility of other in this land. So she had grown to hold herself apart from any realization of a dual life. Not longing for it until of late, since Malcolm came, a certain dreaminess had fallen upon her.

The days passed; each one budding into fresh spring beauty, and each one bringing the two hearts closer and closer. They did not question each other or themselves. Only they saw every object fairer because of the other eyes that were looking at it; and in the slightest accident they would find cause for mirth, because of the other laughter that would ring out in unison.

The moon arose in her beauty to add fresh loveliness to an existence that, until her coming, did not seem to lack any thing. And as Malcolm would sit gazing on Christine's sweet face, listening to her pure, rich voice as she sang old ditties to her grandfather, he

could not think of a life without her. He would feel a frantic desire
to grasp the slender hand that lay in the old man's, and set it on fire
with the kisses that were burning his lips, and to wake from its holy
calm the face uplifted to the moon's rays.

So the world stood with them when a letter came from John
Smith, recalling Malcolm to Salt Lake.

He was in the orchard reading it, and feeling his heart like a
millstone within his breast, when the light tread of the feet he loved
aroused him from his reverie.

Christine was coming towards him. She was clad in drapery of a
soft gray color, her face all aglow, and the beautiful eyes, like stars,
shining on his soul. In her hand, a red rose. The sweet lips parted
with smiles, as if the words already had passed to him.

"It is the first of the season. Is it not beautiful? Will you
have it?"

Springing to his feet, he took it, and kissed it with the passion she
had called forth.

Her eyes grew misty, a deep flush rose to her cheeks; and, like a
charmed bird, she stirred not.

The blue sky shone through the apple-blossoms, and the girl's
lovely, changeful face seemed a part and parcel of the exquisite
spring-time.

"I am going away," said Malcolm.

"Going away!" Did she speak? The words sounded but as the
echoes of his own.

Only that the large eyes dilated, and the sensitive face paled to
ashen white, Malcolm would scarcely have thought she had heard
him, so still she stood. Then, turning to leave him, she would have
fallen, so faint she grew, had not his strong arm upheld her; and,
drawing her to his breast, he poured forth the love that burned within
his heart.

For the time she seemed of all earth the only one he loved. And how the story of his love prospered, we have already heard.

They stood under the apple-blossoms, wrapped in each other's arms, until, Matthew's voice calling out for his child, they bade "good-by" to those moments of delight; and Christine had her first secret.

All during her songs her heart kept throbbing with joy, while the slender hand rested in the gentle clasp of her grandfather's. Then came the hour of prayer, the good-night; and then she hastened to her room, where, leaning out of her window, she smiled at the moon that had looked down on her happiness.

Until the dawn was breaking she sat thinking, and trembling at the great joy within her, and then, throwing herself on her bed, fell asleep while smiling.

So it was that the morning sunlight peeped in, and found her still in dreamland, and the call from the dear grandfather was needed to awaken her.

And now, near him, with her hand on his arm, and her secret trembling on her lips, she stood like a guilty thing, until Matthew, wondering at her silence, said, —

"What ails my birdling?"

"O grandfather, I am so happy! Malcolm loves me, and, for my sake, will have a Christian wedding. For my sake he will hold to the laws of our church, and have no other wife than your own Christine."

Why is it that the happiness of some makes the misery of those that love them?

Looking into the face that made his world, Matthew felt the morning grow black, and his heart most heavy. Like a great cloud-burst, these tender words from his Christine seemed to have obliterated what was most lovely in his life. Keeping the smile on his face needed a

greater effort than he would have felt to walk to his death. And
yet he made the effort, that he might not mar one atom of her happiness.

"Are you sure of him, my darling? Are you sure of him?"

"As of my own soul. Nay, more. And I love him, I love him, as
he loves me."

The argument was made, the case won. And the old man, who
felt his priceless treasure taken from him, would have lain down his
life to keep her lover true, from the moment when, avowing her own
love, Christine had thrown herself upon the faithful breast that had
ever given her readiest sympathy.

"Lift up thy face, my darling," he said, tenderly raising her, and
kissing the dear eyes. "If thy Malcolm be a true lover, he shall
have my child, and all my earthly goods. But what will he do? And
where does he wish to live?"

"He will tell you," answered Christine: then, blushing, she drew
down the dear father-face, and whispered, "He is even now coming."

Turning, Matthew saw the lover of his child. With the sunlight
full upon him, his face radiant with the brightness of youth and
beauty, he looked a man to be loved and trusted. So Matthew,
suppressing a sigh, held out his hand.

Malcolm, grasping it, said, —

"Christine has told you. Give her to me; and, as we both believe
in a God, I will be true and faithful to her."

"Darling," said Matthew, "go, see the breakfast is made ready,
while I speak with Malcolm."

She left them with one pleading look that fell on her grandfather's
heart.

For a full half-hour they paced up and down the garden-walk,
talking earnestly. Christine watched them with eager eyes. Then
she saw her grandfather extend his hand, saw Malcolm fall on his

knees, and kiss it reverently, while the old man, placing his other hand on the beautiful young head bowed before him, seemed praying a blessing on it.

And Christine knew all was well for her.

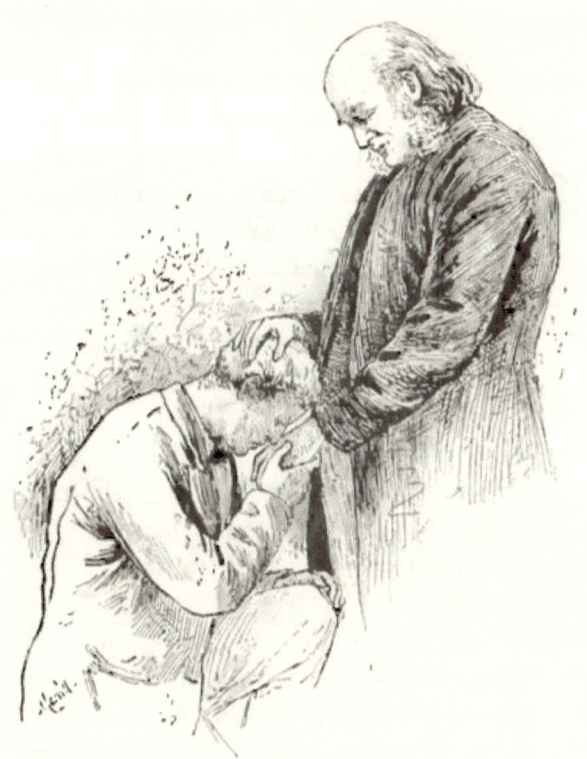

"SHE SAW MALCOLM FALL ON HIS KNEES."

CHAPTER III.

TABITHA'S GARDEN.

MALCOLM had gone. After much consultation, and many objections on the young man's part, Matthew's judgment had prevailed; and Malcolm was to seek his uncle, telling him every thing, even the resolution to have but one wife, before the marriage would be consummated.

Malcolm gone, and the old life to be taken up again! The life and duties, so happy and blessed only a few short months ago, how barren and irksome now! But, spite of aching heart and wakeful nights, Christine kept her eyes bright, and her smile ever ready for the dear grandfather whose life was bound up in hers. His tender love never guessed of the many anxious hours passed by the girl, sitting at her window, watching the road Malcolm had taken when he parted with her.

Love is ever fearful, is ever anxious, creating dangers and troubles for the beloved absent one. In the stillness of the night, Christine would start trembling from her bed, thinking, perchance, Malcolm was ill, or in danger. It was poor comfort to know he was young and strong. She longed to encircle him with her love, to be near him.

"Life is so uncertain," she would murmur. "Perchance we may not meet again."

"Not meet again!" The ominous words echoed and re-echoed in

her heart, until, falling on her knees, with arms outstretched in the darkness, she would cry in bitter pain, " Not that, O God! not that. If it be not for his happiness to wed me, fill his days with blessings, and make him forget me. But, oh, let me once more gaze on that beautiful face! Let me once more look into those eyes that I love, that I love!" And the proud, tender, and lovely Christine would wet the floor with her tears, while her grandfather slept peacefully.

His heart, too, had its care. But age mellows and softens the intensity, if not the tenderness, of feeling. And praying for his child, thinking of her as the honored wife of the nephew of John Smith, he grew calm in the belief of her happy future. He no longer dreaded the day when he must leave her, unprotected, in a land where her sex, and the little property she would inherit, would only the surer make her the prey to rapacity.

After a few days, there came for Christine a letter from Malcolm. Her first love-letter! How wonderful it seemed to her, each word burning itself on her memory.

SALT LAKE, April —.

MY DEAREST, — I arrived safe and well, filled with loving thoughts of you. I seem to see your face forever before me, and hear your dear voice in every sound. So full is my heart of you, that I find myself constantly doing just the things I think you would do. I smile at every little child, and have made one friend since my return, — a cripple-boy who sells papers, and, in some measure, reminds me of your little favorite. I have seen him at his stand for many months, but did not go out of my way to brighten his life, until taught by your sweet example. When you are mine forever, I will grow into a nobler manhood through you. I have seen my uncle, and talked with him about our future. He does not oppose my determination. He smiles when I speak of you, and says, " Time is a moderator of strong affection." But he could not even fancy this possible had he looked, as I have, upon your sweet perfections. Present my deepest respect to your grandfather, and believe me, for all time and eternity,

Yours, and yours only,

MALCOLM SMITH.

Write soon. Oh for one glimpse of the old apple-tree, with you standing under it! Just for one look of those tender eyes, one kiss of those sweetest lips! Farewell. I dare not even think of this, or I would break my promise to Matthew and my uncle, and, forgetting that cruel months must pass before I again behold you, hasten to your side, and clasp you to this heart that is longing for you.

Under the very tree where he had told his love, Christine was reading his letter. The blossom-leaves fell around her in showers of fragrance as the wind gently stirred the branches. Over and over again she read the sweet words, caressing, as if a living thing, the bit of paper that had brought her such joy. To be assured he loved her and longed for her, seemed to take the bitterness from her pain at this separation. While she was still reading, her grandfather came to join her. She sprang up, and, handing him the treasured letter, said, —

"Father, read what he says, and I will go to Tabitha's for an hour. I've not been there for more than a week, and I fancy little Christie is wishing for me."

"Go, my child: I will meet you. We can walk home in the twilight. How lovely the days are! To me the spring was never so beautiful or seemed so peaceful as now."

The old man looked up to the blue sky through orchard-trees planted and fostered by him, glanced at his little cottage, gleaming fresh and white amid its garden of sweet plants, and then back at the face of his Christine, glowing with the tender beauty of a pure girl's first love.

Truly, his "lines seemed cast in pleasant places." And blessed peace shone in his eyes raised in thankful prayer.

It was so Christine saw him, as she turned to throw him a kiss before the trees would hide her from him. He waved his hand in answer, and stood where she had left him. He was thinking of her, praying for her, ere he read the letter open in his hand.

Christine, with happy smiles curving her lips into new beauty, hurried on to the outskirts of the village, where stood a small cabin surrounded by a large and flourishing garden. In the cabin lived Tabitha White and her three children. The garden was so large that it seemed hardly possible it was tended only by one woman and a girl. Yet so it was; for Christie, poor little man, crippled from his birth, could not help. And what with small profits, and paying tithes, their gains were so little that Martin, the eldest, had to seek more arduous labor to supply even the few needs of this frugal household. Where was the head of this family, the father of these children? Dead? No. In the finest house of the whole county, surrounded by the comforts and luxuries of wealth, lived the man who was responsible for the lives of these

"CHRISTINE WAS READING HIS LETTER."

children, and the husband of the toil-worn woman standing at the cabin-door. First smiling a welcome on Christine, and then turning her face, she called in the house, —

"Christie, here is a friend come to see you."

The sound of crutches on the wooden floor; and, a moment later, framed in the doorway, stood a child of eight years or more, with a face beautiful as an angel's, but two useless little legs, that had never been strong enough to support the frail body.

"Christine!" His sweet voice trembled; and, dropping the crutches, the child threw his arms around her neck, hiding the great, wistful eyes on her breast as she stooped to greet him.

The poor, thin arms did not seem capable of the strength with which he clung to her, as he half sobbed, —

"I have looked for you each day and hour. And yet the sun has said good-night ten times since last you came."

Christine, filled with self-reproach, soothed the child with tender words and caresses, until gradually the face left its hiding-place, and the large gray eyes, with dilating pupils, were fixed on hers in half-adoring love.

Sitting on the door-step, holding Christie, talking to Mrs. White, and answering, every now and then, some question from a girl's voice inside the cabin, Christine felt more peace than she had known since Malcolm left.

"Come, Patience," said Tabitha White, calling to her daughter. "Rest for a while. Martin will soon be home for his supper, and Christine may not be able to spare us many moments."

"What, mother! you counsel self-indulgence?" And the owner of the fresh young voice came to the doorway, adding a rosy, dimpled face, framed in sunny hair, to the group that the setting sun was flushing with his parting glory.

A sweet, girlish face and form. One of those sunny creatures who seem born for gladness. But her dimpled hands did heavy work, and even now were busying themselves trying to furbish an old tin pan into brightness.

She sat down on the floor, her hand keeping on with its work as she said, —

"It is good to see you, Christine. Urged by Christie, I would have run down to your place, only this dear old mother of mine has so much to do, she cannot easily spare even these lazy fingers."

Tabitha caught the pretty hand, as Patience was speaking, and held it for a moment in her own. How white and soft it looked in her brown one! Gently pressing it, she let it go.

"It is not lazy or idle, but does its full share, in spite of its fairness."

"SITTING ON THE DOOR-STEP, HOLDING CHRISTIE."

"Ah, Christine!" Patience cried, springing from her lowly seat, "you must take home a basket of my berries. My own raising, aren't they, mother? And such fine ones! I've watched and tended them as a hen her chicks. And I doubt if any old hen is prouder of her young than I of my beauties."

Going into the house, she came to the door with a little basket. With a light spring, jumped across her mother's lap, saying, —

"I couldn't disturb your first rest of the day, dear mother."

And then, swinging her basket, she tripped along to a large hot-bed, where flourished the patch of berries. With the light wind ruffling into curls the sunny hair, and snatches of song coming from the red lips, as she stooped gathering the fruit, she was an ideal of girlhood.

Of all the friends Matthew and Christine had made, there were none so dear as this family. Tabitha strongly interested Matthew. He knew her history, and how she came among the Mormons. He pitied and helped her as best he could.

Years ago Tabitha Simpson was a girl living in a quiet New-England town, — a restless, ambitious girl, full of energy, endurance, and intelligence, qualities that, with opportunity, might have made her independent anywhere; but, surrounded by the bigotry and nar-row-mindedness more peculiar then than to the New England of to-day, these qualities were like enemies turned upon her own soul. No opening outside of the beaten path of labor, trodden by mother and grandmother, no freedom of thought, or occupation for mind, the life was trying beyond measure to the girl, feeling her ability, and full of a blind faith in herself.

It was thus the Mormon missionaries found her, as they came seeking converts. These Mormon missionaries are carefully chosen. They are generally men of education, gifted with the tongue of eloquence.

They pictured the bliss and beauty of the city of the desert, where saints flourished, and men met prophets ; where was held sweet communion with those who had seen the vision of God. To the ambitious they spoke of worldly advance ; to the lonely, of love and companionship. Thus they preached to hungry and dissatisfied hearts, winning them to their own destruction.

O cursed apathy of a land that claims to be the birthplace of freedom ! To sit with folded hands while sinful eloquence converts, to immorality and slavery, the innocent and ignorant! Where is the mother-love of its protecting laws that permits these human sacrifices, and hides the crime beneath the sham mantle of "religious freedom"?

Deep in Tabitha's soul sank the Mormon teachings. To her they seemed of heaven itself.

Leaving home and kindred, with the exultation of a spirit that has at last found the light, she joined the band of converts, in charge of the missionaries, who were starting on the journey across the continent to the "city of the elect."

All dreaming their own dreams of the promised land, they reached Salt Lake as summer was in her first smiling. Tabitha was sent to this interior town, and, told she was thus approaching nearer the longed-for heaven, was given in marriage, or the ceremony so called, to Bishop White, the richest man in the province.

She was given to the bishop an enthusiast. She became his wife, fearing herself a dupe.

When she looked into the sad face of the first wife, and felt the bitter wrong done to her, the faith for which she would have been martyred was shorn of its glory.

It is difficult to see the glory of a creed that teaches cruelty and selfishness. And, from the hour of her marriage, the injustice done the first wife embittered Tabitha's life. Taking the first place in the bishop's household, she still felt herself an intruder. It was only when given charge of the dairy, which formed an extensive part of Bishop White's property, that her energy and capacity for work made her life endurable. Here her country education, and her experience in butter-making, did her good service, rendering her so valuable to the bishop that he seemed quite contented.

Only for a time, however. Too quickly came the change over his fickle nature. Harder and harder Tabitha tried to satisfy his changing fancy. Children had come to her, one after another, filling her empty heart with love, and torturing it with anxiety. For their sakes she would have held fast to the man who was their father.

Little by little the first wife and Tabitha had become friends. The children were the first bond between these two so strangely allied, drawing them closer and closer with their loving, childish ways, until, at last, when the later fancy of Bishop White put them both aside, they fell into each other's hearts, two lonely, miserable women.

With anxious eyes peering into the possible future of the dear children, they made common cause against the impending advent of the new wife. But to what end? What woman can stem the torrent of man's passions when his law and his religion give full license to self-indulgence!

It was the old story. Finally the day came when Tabitha, blinded by tears that dared not fall, was forced to stand beside the father of her children, and sign her acquiescence in his brutal selfishness that was breaking her heart.

This trial she endured alone ; for, shortly before the day Bishop White decided the Lord called him to take a new wife, his first wife closed her eyes on earthly things. Resting in Tabitha's arms, she floated out on the boundless waters of eternity.

After the new wife's home-coming, Tabitha found herself of no further use. Even the charge of the dairy-farm was taken from her. How often, with her baby on her breast, and her two little children clinging to her side, did the lonely woman walk to the graveyard, where a white, painted head-board marked the resting-place of her only friend. What a bitter mockery the inscription, telling of the husband's grief! — a husband who, at that very moment, was gloating over the buxom charms of the new one he had taken to wife.

It was at the grave that Matthew found her. Here he became her friend. From the moment he looked at her weary face, and marked the tender care of her children, he knew the curse of Mormonism had fallen heavily on this woman ; for she had a heart to suffer.

To this last resting-place of her friend, the old man came as often as he could spare the time, trying to whisper words of comfort to his sister in trouble ; for, to suffering humanity, Matthew was a true brother. He brought his Christine to help cheer this drooping heart. Into her arms the baby was placed by the mother, half won to smile as she looked, while the fair girl petted and coddled him in a motherly fashion inborn in some women. This was about ten years ago, and shortly before the morning when, in a furious rage at some childish misdemeanor of Tabitha's eldest boy, the last Mrs. White demanded that the children and their mother should go to another house.

Tabitha, sent away from the house that for twelve years she had called home, was given this little cabin, and large, uncultivated piece of ground, from the proceeds of which she must earn the support of herself and children.

A wife, a mother ! Yet a castaway on the great ocean of life, her breast full of bitterness at her own and children's wrongs. No help, no hope ! For where in all Utah did a woman's wrongs find voice or righting ?

What mattered it to the rulers and elders that a mother and her children had been driven from the roof that should have sheltered them, to a life of toil ? It was the husband's will, and submission was the wife's portion.

Shame, anger, jealousy, all raged within Tabitha's breast, as, holding her sleeping babe, she entered the cabin-door, and looked around on the desolation within. One small window let in the sunlight, which rested on two wooden chairs, one table, one bed, on which were thrown some blankets that had been hastily put in the wagon with the few things that the reigning wife had decided necessary to send for her fallen rival.

The two older children, a boy of eleven, and girl of eight, years, were playing outside in the fresh air, enjoying such freedom as had

been unknown to them for many months. The mother glanced at them as they ran about among the weeds and briers that filled the field around the house. Still holding her sleeping infant, she sank into a chair, and, leaning her face on the table, shed as bitter tears as human heart can yield.

She was thus when a gentle hand was laid upon her shoulder ; and, raising her eyes, she saw Matthew gazing at her.

"Sister, do not despair. God has not left you friendless."

She heard the tender voice, saw the eyes saddened at another's woe, and looked in the doorway at her two children, Martin and Patience, who were eating hungrily of some lunch Christine was serving to them. In her hour of desolation these friends had come to her.

"A GENTLE HAND WAS LAID UPON HER SHOULDER."

So truly, in his noble humility, did the old man look a saint, that she would have fallen to the ground and kissed his feet; but he caught her in his arms, as, from her half-wild expression, he divined her intention, and, gently reseating her, took from her almost powerless hold the baby, whose great eyes were beginning to wander around the strange scene.

For a few moments a merciful stupor overpowered Tabitha. And while Matthew tried to force some drops of water between the closed teeth, and bathed the deathlike brow, Christine, giving the baby to Patience, and telling Martin to gather some sticks, and kindle a fire, hurriedly arranged the bed, and hung some cloth as curtain to the window, thus giving to the barren cabin something of a homelike air.

When, at last, poor Tabitha came back to a realization of troublous life, she saw a fire brightening the empty fireplace, a bed turned down to receive her, and Patience by her side with a cup of warm tea; while Christine walked up and down, cooing and talking to the baby, who seemed never tired of gazing at her; and Matthew, smiling as lovingly at the weary woman as if he were an angel sent from God to comfort her.

Thus, ever after, he seemed to this woman. In her darkest hours the memory of this good man would stand between her soul and utter despair.

When she had grown calmer, he placed her baby in her arms, and, taking Christine's hand, said, in a voice tremulous with emotion, —

"God of all mercy, have pity on our sufferings. Teach us to bear them for thy love. Make us feel thy divine charity for the sins against us, and give us to know, that, even in our desolation, thou art near, and lovest us."

In these few simple words, condensing all the long sermons of Christianity, the old man blessed the sorrowful woman, calling her again his "sister," and, with his child, bade good-night to the tired little family.

Ten years had passed since that sad evening. In all these years Matthew had stood as a bulwark against the troubles that seemed often about to wreck this struggling family. He it was that suggested the cultivation of berries and vegetables. His hands helped in the clearing of the weeds and briers. A skilful gardener, he taught Tabitha the most improved method of vegetable culture. Being full of energy and perseverance, she made an apt pupil.

And the result of her labors lay smiling before her as she sat beside Christine and Christie, watching Patience pick the berries, and glancing ever and anon up the road for the home-coming of her boy. After a little, the faint sound of a whistle growing nearer, a quick step, and, in a few moments more, Martin White stood before them, — a great, tall fellow of twenty, with cheeks pink as a girl's, blue eyes, light hair, and wide, happy mouth. He kissed his mother, took Christine's hand affectionately, then, holding out his arms to Christie, said, "Well, little man, don't you want a trot down to Patience, and back again?"

So contented was the loving child, that he fain would rest near Christine; but, when the kind brother's face bent over him, he smiled his consent.

With dexterous touch Martin put the little fellow on his broad shoulder, and trotted off as light of foot as if he had not worked ten hours that day, nor walked two miles to reach his home.

Down to Patience and back again, with the girl hanging on his arm; her sweet laugh ringing out in the soft spring air, as she strove to keep step with his great strides.

With the last rays of the setting sun, Matthew joined them. The light fell on his snowy hair, and around his whole person, like a halo.

He smiled, and a blessing seemed to descend on them.

Looking at him, a brother of God's own giving, and then at her children's happy faces, her garden blooming luxuriantly, Tabitha's heart thrilled with gratitude. She put out her hand as Matthew came near.

"To you I owe all this. You are indeed father of the fatherless, helper of the helpless."

"No, sister. Not to me, but to Him of whose love for the unfortunate mine is but the shadow."

And so, with holy words, and holier thoughts, with love for all, and malice towards none, this man of simple character stood, an image of the Godhead.

Like a finger pointing to an unknown road, his bare existence was more powerful than argument to prove there must be a God to have made so noble a creature.

CHAPTER IV.

A MEMORY.

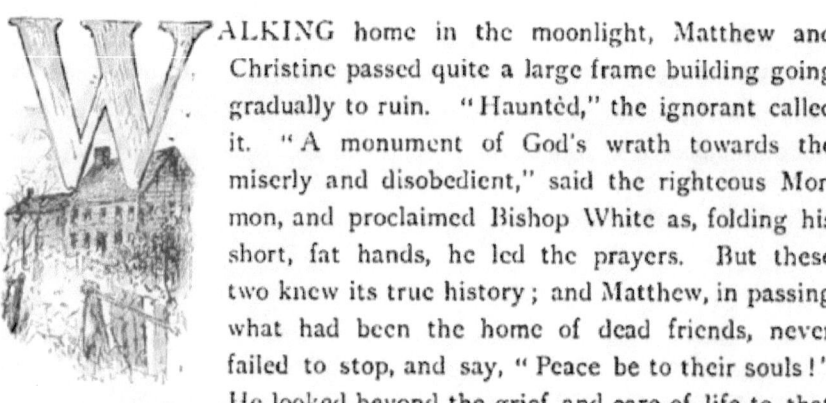

ALKING home in the moonlight, Matthew and Christine passed quite a large frame building going gradually to ruin. "Haunted," the ignorant called it. "A monument of God's wrath towards the miserly and disobedient," said the righteous Mormon, and proclaimed Bishop White as, folding his short, fat hands, he led the prayers. But these two knew its true history; and Matthew, in passing what had been the home of dead friends, never failed to stop, and say, "Peace be to their souls!"

He looked beyond the grief and care of life to that other world where sin is not, and joy abounds. Whatever the pain he felt for another's woe, this belief brought strength as it annihilated bitterness.

Christine, with her hand through his arm, and her head leaning on his shoulder, saw beautiful peace shining from her grandfather's face, then looked on the deserted shell of what had once been home to a simple, honest family. The moon's brightness, through broken windows and fallen door, streamed on the odds and ends of household ware.

The curse of the church had saved, even from the needy, what was now useless to the dead. She sighed as memory brought back the sad details of a family's fate. Thinking of them, she could almost see the master and head of the family, — a great, sturdy fellow, thick-set and strong, with heavy features and colorless skin, while ever between his teeth the pipe, sending forth clouds of smoke. And his wife, fair and ruddy, with her children around her, and always a baby in her arms. They were Germans, living in one of the Southern States. Well-to-do in their adopted country, they were tempted by the promise of gaining wealth in a land where the Church itself looks after her children's welfare. Converted, their goods sold, they emigrated to Utah. They were liv-

ing in the village when Matthew arrived with his granddaughter, and, during the first few weeks of discomfort in settling matters, were kind and neighborly. Of cheerful, happy temperaments, which in Anton was descending into true German phlegm, that, with fat, seems to be a consti-

ANTON.

tutional matter. But, despite phlegm, Anton was sharp, shrewd, and, while perfectly honest, rather close.

"I likes monnish," he would say confidentially to Matthew. "It ish a goot ding to haf in a vamly."

The part of Utah's government that particularly fretted him was the tithing; and, whenever the day would come for its payment, Anton would fume, worry, and even occasionally let his pipe go out. Still, things prospered with him. While not growing rich rapidly, he managed to do quite as well as he had done in the South.

"But dere is vere de lie comes in," he said one day, leaning on

Matthew's fence, and watching him as he and Christine tended their newly planted flower-garden.

"Dey said, 'Cum, vrend, leave dy slow gains, an' cum to de lan' off de bounteous blenty.' Vell, I don't see de blenty. I tells you, Mishter Mattiew, vat I vill do. I vill not pay de ties next time."

Matthew stopped his work, and, going up to Anton, said gently, —

"My friend, your own welfare depends on your paying the demands of the government. The Mormon rule seems to me more political than religious; since their religion, in its motive, has above all political power and advance. They call this tithing voluntary. Yet do they not threaten ills if it be not paid? It is the great source of revenue, one of the powers of their rule; and, be assured, its payment will be enforced. Consider your wife and children. If you do aught to bring upon yourself the vengeance of this church's government, you will ruin them."

"Vell, dere ish no goot talkin', dough I tanks you. I has said I vill not pay, an' I vill shtick to my vord. Dey can't hurt me." And he drew up his burly form, took his pipe from his mouth, and, with a contemptuous "pish!" once more began smoking.

Again Christine seemed to hear it all, and saw every peculiarity of the honest fellow, even the close-cut dark hair, standing straight up all over his head.

Many visits did Matthew and she make to the family, hoping to induce Anton to change his mind. But he would not. He would laugh a comfortable, jolly laugh, and say, —

"Mr. Mattiew, dey vill do nodding. Dese peoples is all like sheeps. Dey follers just vere de first von goes. Now, Yon Anton is going anoder vay. And you'll see, dey vill be surbrised, dey vill tretten, but dey vill do nodding. Ha, ha!"

Matthew tried to rouse the fears of Mrs. Anton; but she smiled, and shook her head. "Yon knows best. He ish verra vise." She had for so long taken as her own his will, she could see nothing but wisdom in it.

When tithing-day came, Anton refused to pay. In vain the tithe-gatherer insisted and entreated.

" No," said the German. " Dey says it ish a matter fer me to give, or not. I vill not." And then he added, in a more conciliatory manner, " Shust you lets me get a little ahead, an' de nex' time I'll pay."

Then, turning, the tithe-gatherer had cursed him, his family, his cattle, his fields, calling down upon them the wrath of God, and hatred of man.

Christine, who had run over with some home-remedy for one of the children, who was not well, stopped at the gate. Almost fainting at the terrible words, she stood leaning against a tree, where, unnoticed by the tithe-gatherer, she had seen him pass out. Dizzy with the horror of that curse, she ran up to Anton, and looked to see what effect it had had upon him.

Except for a nervous working of his fingers, he seemed the same as usual.

" Did you hear him, little gal ? " he asked. " Did you hear de man ov Gott cussin my vamly ? "

" Yes," she answered, and then, bursting into tears, had begged him to pay the dues. " If you haven't the money, grandfather'll give you what he has to help you. Please, Mr. Anton, please pay it. Don't put yourself in danger."

" My little gal," — and he had lain his great hand on her head, — "does yer b'lieve Gott vill hear de vicked vords ov a man like dat ? No, no. He vas only trying to vrighten me. Ha, ha ! Yon Anton am not so easily vrightened."

Only trying to frighten ! He did more. His curses took actual form. The fat cattle, poor Anton's pride, one by one were found dead, — some with a knife thrust in their throats, some evidently poisoned. His chickens were stolen ; and, though he could never catch the thief, he found, at distances from the house, feathers and heads he recognized.

His potatoes, which had this year given promise of a fine crop, perished. There was not water enough for his irrigation. Although it ran to waste around him, although he offered to pay special rates, the Mormon authorities, owners of the water, refused to allow him a particle.

Of all the neighbors, no one spoke to him or his. Men, women, and children, seeing them coming, would cross the road, avoiding, as if plague-stricken, this unfortunate family. Matthew alone stood by him. Threatened, abused, yet did this great spirit never quail.

"Misfortunes, even malice, we may not escape. But sin we must avoid. And it would be sin to turn away from a brother in trouble. Do you not think so, my Christine?" And, child as she had been, he had thus lifted her to the level of his high Christianity.

The woman, leaning on his arm, pressed it tenderly, and looked once more in his face.

"Poor Anton!" he said, and sighed, as he passed his hand gently over her head.

"Poor Anton!"

He, too, was thinking of the unhappy man ; of the morning when, with frightened face, he had rushed over for him.

"Come quick, Mr. Mattiew, vor de lofe of Gott! Mein frau an' de childer!"

Leaving his plough in the furrow, Matthew hurried to the large house, which, once resounding with children's merriment, had now become the abode of mourning.

On the floor, in convulsions, lay the two eldest children. In their little hands was candy. Who gave it was never known, for the children died without telling the name. Playing down the road, when their mother called them to dinner, they had come slowly homewards. Before reaching the house they began to cry with pain ; and, as they had brought them in the room, convulsions set in.

Neither father nor mother noticed the candy until Matthew drew their attention to it. Taking a piece from one stiff little hand, he tasted it, and, almost immediately after, felt a slight cramp.

"Arsenic," he had told Anton, and tried to produce vomiting. But it was too late. In a few hours the children, who at morn had been full of health, were dead, and the poor mother heart-broken. She never smiled again, lost all strength, and, when the third child sickened with measles, died the day it was buried.

Three little graves, and hers close by, were all, except the baby, that remained to poor Anton. Christine offered to take the babe home, and tend it : but he refused.

" No," he said. " I tanks you, little gal, but he's all I has lef'. All gone, — frau, childer, cattle, garden." And he pointed to the bare, withered potato-stalks, all that remained of the great fields he had planted.

Every day the little girl and her grandfather would visit their poor friend, and every day find him with the failing baby in his arms, walking up and down, trying in vain to quiet its wailing. He fell away to a shadow. His pipe, forgotten, lay on the window-sill covered with dust ; his fire unlighted, except by Matthew, who, to tend this unhappy brother, gave every moment of his spare time.

One night, as Christine was reading to Matthew, a knock came to their door. Opening, they saw Anton. It was the first time, since his wife's death, he had left his house.

"Come in, friend," said Matthew. "Come and share our home. There is a place for thee and thy child." And he had put his arm around the shoulders of the desolate man.

" Nein, nein," Anton answered, slowly shaking his head ; and his heavy eyes were full of despair. "My baby ish gone too. Take de liddle body, Mish Christine. Fix him fer de grabe. I ish got nodding lef', only deat', only deat'." And, laying in Christine's arms the rigid body of the infant, he turned, and, before Matthew could detain him, had left the house.

"I must follow him, darling," her grandfather had

DEATH OF ANTON.

said, striding into the darkness after the miserable man. As he reached Anton's gate, he heard a shot, and, hurrying to the house, saw on the floor, where the little children had fallen in convulsions, the bleeding, dying Anton.

On his knees beside him, Matthew prayed forgiveness for his mad act. Opening his eyes, Anton had gasped, "I hopes Gott vill vorgive, I vas so onhappy;" and then, without another word, passed to the great Tribunal, where judgment awaits the sorrowing and sinful. To Matthew's soul, strong and heroic, self-destruction was a fearful crime; yet felt he nothing but pity as he knelt beside the dead.

"Driven to his death! Forgive the crime, great God, Father of mercy." Thus he prayed.

When giving information of his death, and its manner, no burial being offered, and the Mormon authorities calling it "God's judgment," Matthew made the coffins for the father and his baby. He drove them to the open grave he had prepared for them, and, above their resting-place, read the prayers, while Christine made responses.

Each minutia came back to Christine of that most sad experience. And somehow, with the faces of the dead children, their mother, and the ghastly face of Anton as he gave her the baby, came the face of her Malcolm. Radiant with youth and beauty, it was strangely out of place in that sad group. She shuddered. Perhaps it portended ill to him.

"God save him!" cried her heart. And Matthew asked, —

"What ails my child? Come, let us move on, and enjoy the brightness. God sends that as well as grief. We must take them both from his hands. Only, I pray, if it be his will, my darling's 'lines may be cast in pleasant places.'"

And again he passed his hand caressingly over her silken hair. Slowly they walked on, speaking occasionally, but feeling ever that close sympathy, that blessed nearness, which is love's tenderest guise.

CHAPTER V.

PEACEFUL DAYS.

WO months had passed, and only one more of waiting for Malcolm and Christine. There came frequent letters to the girl from her lover, and sometimes one went from her to him. His were often hastily written, speaking of the pressure of business, but always full of his love for her.

No mention of the Mormon teachings. No expressed desire to extend her range of vision, so that it could admit polygamy. Man is by nature a hunter, desiring that which he pursues; and Malcolm was still in pursuit of the game. Though surrounded by Mormon friends, he seemed quite content with his chosen love. None, however, but his uncle, knew his intention of abjuring polygamy. And that uncle, with the smile of a satirist and a knowledge of what the result would be, listened to the occasional outpourings of Malcolm's affection for Christine.

With Christine the days went quietly by. Since arousing herself from her first pain at Malcolm's departure, she had returned naturally to the duties of her life. And the smile, though coming more rarely, was as sweet as before her lover came a-wooing.

She had been busy helping Patience pack fruit for transportation; for Matthew, insisting on loaning the money, had bought a team and wagon for Martin to carry off to better markets the produce of the garden. It seemed to Matthew so much the better plan for them, thus sooner to realize the fruit of their labor. And Tabitha gratefully accepted from this noble brother his generous advance.

How bright was the morning when Martin, in the glory of his new jumper and overalls, with the broad-brimmed hat so familiar to the neighboring towns of Utah, stood at the side of his team, just ready to ride away with his precious load !

Matthew and Christine had come to assist in loading the wagon, and wish the dear boy "God-speed."

Patience fluttered around from case to case of the luscious berries, giving all sorts of motherly advice to the big brother, who, laughing, bowed at each fresh instruction, taking off his hat as to a sovereign lady.

The mother did not speak, but kept her eyes fixed on Martin. To her the thought of future gain was lost in the sorrow of parting.

He seemed to understand this ; for presently stopping his chaffing with Patience, who, with uplifted finger, was uttering some wise saw, he put his arm around the thin form of his mother.

" Don't fret about me, mother. I will be as faithful to your teachings as if you were with me. I will be as careful of myself as if I were dear Christie. And — I will hurry back in time to bring Christine her wedding-dress," he added, as he saw the mother's eyes filling ; and, feeling a great lump rising in his throat, he knew he would break down unless he said something to divert thought from himself.

Christine blushed, Patience laughed ; and Christie, who was sitting by Christine, took her hand, and pressed it so tight that the thin fingers made red marks on the delicate flesh.

" O Martin !" said the child, " if you pass by a big town where they sell rings, bring me a little one for Christine. Will you wear it ?" he asked, looking up at her with earnest eyes.

" Always," Christine answered.

And so Tabitha's tears were unshed ; and Martin's did not shame the down on his lip as the large, white-covered wagon rolled away from the garden-gate, amid blessings from the little band of friends.

The mother stood watching while there was a glimpse of it shining white in the rising sun.   "Her ship" had gone out to sea, bearing part of her heart in it.

"Her ship." Every hour of the day, and many wakeful ones at night, did she see, with her mind's eye, that great, lumbering wagon, and the bright, boyish face that had looked out to throw her one last, parting kiss.

He had been gone three weeks, and now they were looking for him back. How many times Patience would run up to the turn of the road, and strain her pretty eyes for the sight of the white "sail," as she called it !

"THE WAGON ROLLED AWAY FROM THE GARDEN-GATE."

And the mother would pause, during her daily toil, to listen for the sound of the heavy wheels, — the music her ears were longing to hear.

And Christie, with clasped hands, and great, mournful eyes, would pray for the kind brother, who, in all his life, had given him only love and tenderness.

Christine and Matthew came often to spend the hour of rest with them after the day's labors were over.

Those lovely June evenings, when the fields of waving grain, and trees laden with ripening fruit, bespoke the prosperity of the little colony!

There was, of course, much comment on the sudden rise in the fortunes of Mrs. White, and much jealousy felt and shown. But again Matthew, a pillar of strength, opposed himself to the malice of the community, and kept the greatest share from reaching the ones it was intended to wound.

Who could so easily soothe the angry feelings of the neighboring families as he, who had never refused them help? How many times, before things so prospered with him, had he denied himself to aid those who were hard pressed!

Mothers could recall, when their little ones were stricken with illness, Matthew and Christine would come softly to the sick-room, and, saying few words, take their full share of fatigue, nursing them as tenderly as if they had been their own.

Some of these little ones were lying now in the graveyard, — "God's acre," as the Germans beautifully phrase it. But the mothers remembered those who had soothed their last moments, and their jealous murmurings were soon quieted. There was not one in the village, who had needed help, that Matthew had not served, asking no return. Listening patiently to their tales of sorrow, nursing their sick, and praying for their dying, he was associated with all their trials; so tender to the unfortunate, that he seemed of kin to them.

As for the prosperous, he did not affect them much, nor they him. And to them, that Mrs. White, the put-aside wife of the bishop, was able to send off a team with her fruits and early vegetables, was of little account. The bishop, who represented the Mormon government in the town (for Mormon bishops are a temporal as well as religious body), did not choose to hold any intercourse with the family he had ignored for ten years.

It was only when one more malicious, knowing full well the facts of Tabitha's hard struggle for life, congratulated the bishop on the remarkable skill of his wife as gardener, and complimented him on his children, that he thought, some day, when he had leisure, he would call at the cabin.

Tabitha, ignorant of the interest slowly awakening in her husband, was hopefully looking for her boy. And one evening, just as they had given him up for the night, they heard the sound of distant wheels. Patience fairly flew to the turn in the road ; and Tabitha, carrying Christie, went as fast as she could to the gate. Hurrying his tired horses, Martin was soon with them, clasping his dear mother in his strong arms. And at last Tabitha felt repayment for all the troubles of her life.

First tending to his horses, and then seating himself between his womankind, with Christie in his arms, Martin was as happy as the proverbial " king," who, in this quality, far excels his real brother.

He had travelled more than a hundred miles away from his home ; had met with some kindnesses from Gentiles in the mining-camps beyond the Utah border.

" And what do you suppose, Christie, a little girl gave me for you ? A St. Bernard puppy. He is all wrapped in my blankets, fast asleep, in the wagon. He is young now, but in a few months will be large enough and strong enough to carry you anywhere. The brother of the little girl is twice as large and heavy as you; and he rides the mother of ' Rex ' — that's his name — out over the hills every evening to drive home the cows. Won't it be grand fun to see our Christie sitting in a wagon, and hauled around by a great dog? or else riding on his back, like a man ? You'll cut me out, and soon be head teamster for the dear old mother. And here, my boy, is your ring for Christine," he said, as he drew forth a tiny white box, and, opening it, displayed a ring of glittering gold.

Small and plain it might have looked to others, but very grand indeed to the eager eyes now admiring it.

"Let me try it on," said Patience, slipping it on her finger, and holding up her dimpled hand in high delight. "Isn't it a beauty?" she cried, as, dancing around in the moonlight, waving and kissing the decorated hand, she seemed a fairy sprite, so lovely she looked.

"Just stop your prancing, Miss Vanity, and let that poor hand rest. I've something for you. Not a ring," Martin continued, as the girl extended one finger of her other hand, pretending to be unable to let the ringed one go any farther away from her.

"Oh, oh!" she said half playfully, as, with a little sigh, she put the ring in the box, and gave it to Christie. "What is it, you great bear of a brother? Tell me, or I shall die of curiosity." And, kneeling on the step beside him, she threw one soft arm around his neck.

"Don't strangle me, or I'll die, and never be able to give it to you. Come to the wagon, and help me bring it up." So saying, he put Christie in his mother's lap, and, catching Patience's outstretched hand, they ran off together.

Tabitha watched them; and the first evening of their coming to the lonely cabin flashed back on her memory, when these two, hand in hand, played among the briers and weeds. With a great thankfulness she clasped the little hand Christie had slipped into hers.

Hope was growing stronger within her, — hope for this world and the great beyond. And, pointing to the way, there rose before her the vision of a noble man; and to her ears a voice said, —

"Sister, do not despair. God has not left you friendless."

She was roused from these thoughts by the merry voices of her children, as Martin and Patience, both laden, hurried back to her.

"Look, Christie. He's a perfect love!" said Patience; and, unfolding an old shawl which inwrapped him, she disclosed a fine large pup, soft and black as a piece of silk. The lazy fellow, only half awakened, put out his paws, and gave a great yawn. Then he jumped out of her arms; and, as she began to laugh and run, he caught the infection, jumping, running, barking, while Christie clapped his hands with glee.

"Rex, Rex, my beauty!" cried the girl, stooping and catching him. "There's your master," and she put him close by Christie.

It is curious how animals will sometimes almost instantly attach themselves to persons. From the moment Christie's small hand rested on Rex's head, the dog seemed truly to belong to him. From that moment he never willingly left him.

"See what Martin has brought us, mother!" and Patience tried to snatch a roll of something Martin was holding out of her reach. After teasing her a little, he undid the parcel,—a cheap woollen goods, gray for Patience, and a darker shade for Tabitha. These were Martin's treasured gifts. To buy them he had denied himself every comfort on his long ride. But his privations were forgotten in his mother's smile of thanks, and Patience's delight. She passed her hands over the cloth with the air of a connoisseur, and said it was the prettiest thing she ever saw, and she'd look so grand in it that they would have to tell her every moment she was only Patience, or she would surely fancy herself a great lady visiting them.

Then Martin took from his pocket a well-filled purse, and gave it to his mother, with an account of his sales. She was both surprised and delighted. They had realized more than double the amount they could have made if the produce had been sold in G——. And Patience's bright eyes grew larger and larger at their riches, as the money was counted out, and put away in a small bag that answered as bank for them. It was late when sleep came to the little family, but it was a blessed wakefulness. Each heart was full of gratitude that they had passed through the bitter waters of adversity, and stood now on the shore, whence life was opening in ways of happiness and peace.

CHAPTER VI.

FAIR PATIENCE.

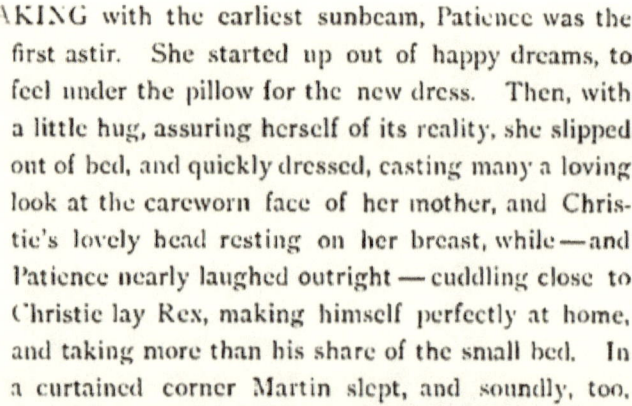

AKING with the earliest sunbeam, Patience was the first astir. She started up out of happy dreams, to feel under the pillow for the new dress. Then, with a little hug, assuring herself of its reality, she slipped out of bed, and quickly dressed, casting many a loving look at the careworn face of her mother, and Christie's lovely head resting on her breast, while — and Patience nearly laughed outright — cuddling close to Christie lay Rex, making himself perfectly at home, and taking more than his share of the small bed. In a curtained corner Martin slept, and soundly, too, Miss Patience felt assured, by his deep and regular breathing. Closing the door, she lit the fire in the small kitchen they had added to the cabin, and, busy as a bee, prepared the simple breakfast for the sleepers.

It was ready almost as soon as they were ready for it. With such happy hearts, it seemed a true feast. After breakfast they all, even including Tabitha, went to see Matthew and Christine. And so early was their visit, that they reached the house before Matthew had left for the fields, where he had already begun harvesting.

Martin carried a large box, which he put at Christine's feet, handing Matthew the bills, and, at his request, opening the box.

"Oh!" in varied tones of delight from Patience, who again, in the fulness of her spirits, executed a *pas seul.* It was one of her merry ways, to sing and dance whenever she was much pleased. She would say, extremes of pleasure paralyzed her tongue, and some fatal accident would happen if her feet did not come to the rescue. And so she laughed, and clapped her hands, and danced around on the nimble feet, as Tabitha gently lifted from the box various articles of feminine attire. And Christine clung to the loving father who had been, as ever, thoughtful of his "birdling." He was murmuring the word over and over again, as he caressed the fair head, that, tall as he was, rested on his shoulder.

He, too, felt an almost childish pleasure in the finery that a little money and a few written words had obtained. And he smiled as he thought how fair and bonny his child would look.

Glancing at Patience, the girl's beauty seemed, for the first time, to fully burst upon him. Of medium height, lissome, and grace itself, with the fair hair hanging down her back in two great braids, and tiny rings, too short to be fastened back, falling over the lovely face flushed with excitement and exercise ; the eyes, blue as a summer's sky, now sparkling with merriment, now uplifted in an ecstasy of delight, as some new bauble was held up for admiration ; the long, curling lashes, and delicate brows, looking almost black in contrast with the blond hair ; and then the hands, soft and dimpled as a baby's ; and the arms, of which just enough were visible to suggest what snowy beauties were hidden, as they curved themselves above the head, or held out the drapery of this Terpsichore, and such a lovely one that the others of the immortal nine would have hung their heads with envy were they to join hands with her.

The smile faded from the old man's face ; and he said, almost involuntarily, —

"What a pity, Patience, thou art so pretty ! "

"Am I pretty ? " and the lovely face flushed to a deep rose-red as these unexpected words fell from lips that, to the girl, were second only to the God he had taught her to worship.

"O Matthew, dear Matthew, do not say it is a pity, since it makes me glad! I love every thing pretty, and pity every thing that is not pretty. And now I needs must love myself; for surely I must be pretty, since you say it." And then, somehow, the brightness died out of her face; and the figure, but a moment since all life and motion, became perfectly still. And yet, still looking at her, Matthew sighed again; for he could not say which was most lovely, the laughing sprite, or this quiet girl, whose unwonted gravity so became her. Sighed; for her beauty was a fatality in this land wherein some lustful man of power had but to desire it, and the young lamb would be sacrificed. And such beauty could not long remain unnoticed.

All through the working-hours of the day, Matthew thought of and prayed for Patience, — prayed she might be saved from the fate of awakening into life the jaded fancy of an old Mormon. He prayed that a haven might open for her as for his Christine, — that a true lover would see and wear upon his heart this beauteous flower. Or that, rather, death would claim her ere to her would fall the sad fate he had seen overtake other maidens as young and almost as fair. And then he bowed his head, and said the solemn words with which he always finished each prayer, "Thy will be done."

"Thy will be done!" sounding first from the shadows of Mount Olivet, and echoing through all the centuries, as strong souls live, to teach the weaker ones the thorny path to bliss.

CHAPTER VII.

GOOD-BY TO OLD FRIENDS.

ABITHA was taking a day of rest, the first for many years. She and Patience were with Christine, putting finishing-touches to the wedding-dress, and packing the modest trunk that would accompany her to Salt Lake; Christie watching them quietly, and Rex sleeping at his side. Lazy Rex! — a regular puppy, large as he was, asleep always, except when eating, or in mischief.

Just now Tabitha was holding in her hand a golden cross and chain. It was the one relic of her girlhood.

An heirloom in her family, it had been handed down from mother to daughter since the Pilgrims had crossed the ocean in their little barks, and landed on the rocky shore of their New England.

"Take it, Christine, with our love. And may it be to you a talisman of happiness!" she said, as she clasped it around the girl's neck, and kissed her tenderly.

Christine had often heard the story, and admired the workmanship of this ornament that had outlived so many wearers. And she knew how dearly it was prized.

"Tabitha," — the girl's eyes had filled with tears at this proof of affection, — "while I thank you, I cannot accept this. It belongs of right to Patience."

"No, no," said Patience, her own merry self shining out in the dimples of her sweet face. "It is much too grand for a simple maiden like me. It suits you. O Christine, take it, please take it ! and then, whenever you wear it, you will think of us who love you." Christine could not resist the pleader.

"I will take it, and treasure it second only to my little ring," she said, smilingly returning Christie's wistful look. Then, while a faint blush stole over the fair face, —

"Malcolm comes to-morrow. Father will perform the marriage ceremony to-morrow night. You are all to come. It will be late, — about ten o'clock. Early the next morning we will start for Salt Lake. Malcolm's uncle will meet us. He knows of Malcolm's abjuring polygamy, and that we will be married according to the rites of the

"SHE CLASPED IT AROUND THE GIRL'S NECK."

Christian church. Once in Salt Lake, Mr. Smith thinks there will be no question of how we were married, and no necessity of going through the Mormon forms."

"Will Matthew remain long away ?" asked Tabitha.

"No; only a few days. He cannot spare time from his harvesting. And, oh!" Christine added, while her voice trembled, and the tears started forth, hanging for an instant on her lashes, and then trickling down her cheeks, "you will be watchful of father's health. If he should be ever so little sick, send for me. Don't ask him, but send me a telegram; and I will be with him as soon as love can bring me."

She turned away her head; for now the tears were raining down her face faster and faster, as she thought of parting with him who had sheltered her whole life.

Christie had never seen Christine weep. He now put out his hands supplicatingly.

"Don't cry, Christine. Your tears fall on my heart."

He was trembling violently. Frightened at his emotion, Christine threw open the window, Tabitha took him in her arms, and Patience bethought herself of Rex for a diversion.

"Up, lazy doggy!" she said, giving his ear such a pinch, that he opened his eyes, sprang to his feet, and barked furiously, while he rushed about the room, seeking the enemy who dared disturb his slumbers. Finally, coming back to Christie, he rubbed his cold, wet nose into the thin hand hanging listlessly over the mother's arm. Such a persistent nose it was, that it kept on poking and poking Christie's hand, until the hand wakened to life, and caressed him.

Christie's delicate frame seemed too frail for the spirit within. Intense emotion generally produced long fainting-spells, in which he would lie like one dead; and each time his mother would hang over him in agonized suspense.

The surety that he would not long be spared to her made him all the more precious to the mother-heart. Now, however, he was soon sufficiently restored to lie on the lounge, and watch the others, while Rex enjoyed a comfortable nap on the floor beside him.

The day passed quietly. Warned by Christie's threatened attack, the girls spoke only on cheerful topics; and Tabitha found plenty of stitches necessary in Christine's finery to keep her busy.

At last it was done, and each article folded away in the trunk;

while lying on a chair, carefully covered, was the soft white dress that Matthew had chosen for Christine's wedding-robe. The golden cross was there too, and on her finger gleamed the little ring she was always to wear for Christie's sake.

The "good-by" was over; and Christine, who had walked with them to the gate, stood watching them down the road. Martin came, just before the hour for leaving, to carry Christie home. He, too, had his parting words with Christine.

"Over ten years ago, Christine, when I was such a little fellow,— nearly eleven, wasn't I, mother?—you first came to us. How I remember that afternoon, when all in white, standing near Matthew, you put out your hands to us, and said, 'Let us be friends!' And friend have you ever been to us,—the dearest, the best. You always seemed an angel to me,—an angel of peace, leaving some of your blessed atmosphere in every home you visited."

This was a very long speech for Martin, who generally was not too quick of tongue. But deep feeling had given him the power of expression, and had called up the tears that glistened in his honest blue eyes. Holding her slender hands fast in his own, he kissed first one and then the other, letting them fall gently, reverently, and said " Good-by."

Then Christie, "Take me in your arms, Christine. Am I too heavy?"

And when she shook her head,— 'twas all the answer she had power to make,— he put out his arms; and she took him to her heart as she had done many and many a time when he was a wee baby. For a moment he kept quite still, looking at her with the old adoring look in his wonderful eyes, too large and bright for the wan little face. He was so small and slight!—eleven years old, but so delicate he hardly seemed half his age.

"Good-by, my Christine," he said. "I will think of you every hour that I live. Kiss my eyes, that when they grow weary watching for you, who may never come again, I can close them, and feel that my Christine's lips have touched them."

Kissing not only the eyes, but cheeks, lips, and brow, she gave him to Martin's outstretched arms, who, starting off with his precious burden, headed the little cavalcade. Then an embrace and a whispered " God bless you ! " from Tabitha, hurrying to catch up with Martin. And a long, loving, sisterly kiss from Patience, whose face, wet with her fast-falling tears, seemed to Christine, even in that moment of parting, the fairest thing her eyes had ever rested on. Tears, so disfiguring to most women, seemed only to add to her beauty. The large blue eyes, brimming over with tears, had never looked more lovely.

" Good-by, good-by, my dearest friend. I cannot fancy what our lives will be without you. But, if only you are happy, we will be content." And then, with one more close embrace, she ran swiftly away, hanging her head like some sweet flower heavy with dew.

How graceful she was, running and springing along ! And then, after she had gone a little distance, turning suddenly, as if for a last embrace, she held out two longing arms to the friend of her life.

And Christine stood, still watching them ; the tears, she had with difficulty repressed, stealing down her face, one after the other, in a slow, sad stream.

Her girlhood, with its peacefulness, was leaving her forever. The quiet life of doing good, wherein she had been so truly loved, would soon seem of the past. And the future, — what did it hold ?

It was thus Matthew found her on his return from the harvest-field

" In tears, my birdling ? " he said, as he folded her in those arms that had loved and tended her from the first moment of her life. " My Christine must not grieve too much at leaving her older friends for a newer, dearer one. Ah, my birdling ! I could not give thee up, did I not see thy own happiness in it. Many a sad hour have I passed, when, as each day seemed to bring new graces to my child, I dreaded lest some Mormon would snatch you from me, and try to force you into this terrible polygamy. But the Lord " — and Matthew uncovered his head — " has rebuked his servant with his goodness. He has sent you a lover, noble and true, whose eyes, touched by the light of your love, can see through the mists and darkness that o'ercloud this unhappy country. He is of influence. He has gifts to command the listening ear of the people of the United States. Who knows but he may be the chosen one to drive the serpent from this earthly paradise? May his voice sound out like God's thunder, and wake to action the mighty power that struck from off the limbs of our negro brothers the cruel chains of slavery! See, even now thy Malcolm comes."

A dust on the road, a rapidly approaching carriage, and, in a moment more, Christine was clasped in the arms of her lover.

CHAPTER VIII.

THE SOLEMN PROMISE.

FTER a little they joined Matthew. Malcolm proposed it. "For was he not to have her for all time?"
he said to himself. And Christine, even in her joy
feeling the loneliness of her father, who was about to
lose the child of his old age, was thankful for this
proof of Malcolm's unselfishness. The three were
sitting at the open door, discussing a subject most
important to all. Malcolm was speaking.

"My uncle says, the sooner we are married, and
away, the better. There will be less time for comment, and a better chance that the manner of our marriage be not
suspected. He thinks it would be safe, once in Salt Lake, that we
should go through the Endowment House, and be 'sealed' to each
other. But," — feeling her hand tremble, and marking the look of repugnance that came over Christine's face, — "unless it becomes a
matter of absolute personal safety, this shall not be required of you, my
darling," he tenderly murmured. "Can we not, however, be married
to-night? Speak, Matthew. Tell her you think it is best."

For a moment the old man was silent. It was only one day sooner.
And yet how hard to part with even one day of his darling's sweet
companionship! But when had he, during the whole course of his
long life, allowed self to influence the least action? Hushing the
voice of his own heart, he said solemnly, —

" If my Christine has fully resolved to be your wife," — and he paused, for his trembling voice told of his weakening self-control.

" If ! " — and Malcolm, who had felt so perfectly secure of Christine, and of late had been growing just a little careless, started to his feet.

" If ! Christine, is there a doubt of it ? Do I not love you utterly and entirely ? For your sake am I not renouncing the religion and laws of my childhood, and perhaps my best chance of worldly advance ? "

Why, just as he uttered this last, did a half-sigh involuntarily escape him ?

Hearing this sigh, the girl answered it, rather than his words.

" Malcolm," — her tuneful voice, full of emotion, made every word harmonious, — " are you quite sure of your own nature ? You are a man, I a woman. No childish weakness must blind us now, and mar our whole lives. Have you truly, in your inmost soul, abjured polygamy ? Do you really feel its sinfulness ? And one question more. Are you sure your love for me, and mine for you, will satisfy you, and make you cease to desire a foremost place in Utah ? "

Looking at her, listening to her, his passion, like a torrent, swept away every doubt.

All day, while riding towards his love, he had over and over again assured himself he had too easily yielded to Christine's foolish scruples. The marriage by her grandfather was all well enough. John Smith had once told him, half smiling, half sneering, that such a marriage would not be recognized in Utah. That when he grew tired of his new love, and wanted another, he would find it easy to set her aside ; and, being thus married, she could not ask for support. The only trouble would be, that, were it known, each of the contracting parties, and the officiating clergyman, would stand in danger of a visit from a certain arm of the Mormon church that generally leaves behind it unpleasant results.

At the time Malcolm had answered with all the impetuosity of indignant and loving youth. But somehow his uncle's words came back to him, repeating themselves in his memory.

It was a power that John Smith possessed in a remarkable degree. He could so nearly estimate people's natures, that he would, by a seemingly chance remark, touch the inner springs. Thus his words would bear fruit, and such fruit as he had desired when throwing the seed upon its congenial soil.

He knew Malcolm thoroughly. Rather liked him, and intended to advance him on the high-road of ambition. First, he must have more money. And then he thought of the old Scandinavian peasant, who had always seemed to him the embodiment of one of the famous Norse kings of his native land. He had grown rich, and his grand-child would naturally inherit every thing.

Of that grandchild he had only a vague idea. During his short visits, made at long intervals, he had been somewhat surprised at her beauty and grace, and when she spoke, which was not often, by a correctness of expression, and melody of voice, rarely found.

She had a dignity of manner that he thought would impress the fashionables of Washington. And he had decided next term to take Malcolm to Washington with him, if — and he put this proviso to his intention — he could be content with one wife for one winter.

Strange anomaly! In the Congress instituted to change, amend, and extend the laws of the United States, as the liberty and protection of its citizens required, and one of whose laws was the punishment of polygamy, a polygamist boldly takes his seat, sharing with his associates in the deliberations of Congress. And, while some poorer wretch was wearing away his hours in prison for bigamy, this man, who boldly flaunted his bigamy in the very capital of the land, lived openly with the several women whom he called "wives!"

He looked on Malcolm's abjuration of polygamy as child's play.

It rather amused him to see how powerful an influence the passion love could exercise over the young. And one day, when his nephew was telling of his solemn intention never to take any other than Chris-

tine to wife, he had looked up quickly from the book he was seeming to read, and said, —

"Better keep this intention as a simple resolution. It is as well not to take false oaths. And, if such an oath be made, you would surely falsify it. As for the marriage," — and he had finished with the words already told.

"BETTER KEEP THIS INTENTION AS A SIMPLE RESOLUTION."

The whole of this speech lived in Malcolm's memory. And so, during the hours of his quiet drive alone in the carriage that each moment was taking him nearer Christine, he had fully determined on recalling his promise of abjuring polygamy. He had not, however, calculated the magnetism of her presence. And, when he clasped her in his arms, he forgot every thing but her, and his love for her. Even the little sigh that escaped him was rather for what might have been, than that he had the slightest intention of asking release from the given promise. But now, when her voice ceased its music, and the lustrous dark eyes looked full in his own, seeking to read his inmost soul, and he knew he must lose her forever, or forever bind himself to monogamy, he did not feel a moment's hesitation.

"Am I sure of my own nature? Sure your love will satisfy me? Darling, darling, you cannot know what love is, or you would not even ask these questions. Do you think a man who has once loved you could ever waste a thought on another woman? When Matthew marries you to me, and me to you, it is for all time and eternity. Beyond you, I desire nothing. For you I would accomplish any thing a man may do."

How brave and handsome he looked, his face beaming with the earnestness of his words! And, at the moment, he was both earnest and honest. Alas that it was only for the moment! Who could see beneath this beautiful seeming the undercurrents of a capricious and selfish nature? Not the old man watching his radiant face, and dreaming for him and Christine such glorious possibilities. Not the fair woman, whose eyes were the windows of a strong, true soul, and who loved this man with her whole heart.

So, once more secure of his prize, Malcolm resumed his seat, and began urging their immediate marriage.

After a little, it was decided as he wished. And Matthew, rising, said he would tell Tabitha of the change. "You know, Malcolm, we will want two witnesses; and Martin has just attained his majority." He walked away on the road to Tabitha's, leaving the lovers sauntering towards the apple-tree which had first heard the story of their love.

CHAPTER IX.

"WHOM GOD HATH JOINED," ETC.

AN eventful day had gone to its rest, and night's starry mantle inwrapped the sleeping world. In all the little town, there was not a glimmer of light to be seen. Outside, Matthew's house looked as dark and quiet as the rest; but inside, with doors and windows tightly fastened, a man and woman were being bound together for life. They stood in the centre of the room, under a large lamp which shone down on them through the garlands Patience had fastened around it.

"We must make the room look fresh and bright," she had said to Martin, when Matthew had summoned them to the wedding. Whispering to her mother, Martin and she had scampered off, and, plucking every flowery bush they could find, had decorated the sitting-room in Matthew's house, where they had often played as children. They hung blankets over windows and doors, and, covering them with garlands, transformed the little room into a sylvan bower. Then, closing the door, they ran home to make their simple preparations for the wedding of their friend. They had said their farewell in the morning, all agreeing that no word of sadness should mar the first moments of Christine's new life.

At ten o'clock, as quietly as if on a guilty errand, Tabitha and her children came to Matthew's; and at half-past ten the heavy blanket that hung over the sitting-room door was lifted, and Matthew appeared, leading Christine all in white, her only ornaments the golden cross and her own loveliness. As Malcolm beheld the fair vision, there came to his thoughts the lines, —

> " A daughter of the gods,
> Divinely tall, and most divinely fair,"

they so aptly described his bride.

He took her fair hand in his, and together they stood before Matthew in the centre of the room.

How solemn the moment! When the words rang out in the stillness, " If any one knows any just cause or impediment," why did not some angel stay the old man who was wedding his cherished lamb to bitter woe?

The only witnesses were Tabitha and her children, — Martin standing behind her; Christie on her lap, pale and unearthly as a spirit; and at her side, with eyes fixed on Christine and Malcolm, Patience was kneeling. In a plain cotton gown, with a wreath of wild-flowers crowning the blond hair, she looked an Undine, with her new-born soul shining through the beautiful eyes.

" Malcolm, dost thou take this woman to be thy wedded wife?"

" I do." The answer came clear and firm.

" Christine," — a slight tremor in the voice, as, for a moment, the minister yielded to the father, — " dost thou take this man for thy husband?"

" I do."

" Whom God hath joined together let no man put asunder."

It was all over. His for life! And Christine's fate was sealed. Then Matthew touched Malcolm's hand, and said, —

" You solemnly swear to marry no other while this your true and lawful wife lives?"

"I do," said Malcolm.

With fervor he kissed the Bible Matthew held towards him. Even while he was taking the oath, his mind was not on it. He was thinking of what a sensation Christine would create among his friends in Salt Lake. Her gifts of beauty, wealth, and conversation would soon

"CHRISTINE'S FATE WAS SEALED."

make her a noted person. And he felt delighted with himself for gaining such a wife. And yet he looked so handsome, so earnest, as he stood beside her, the solemn pledge seemed to impart its sacredness to his great beauty.

Soon, with loving words and wishes, their friends had bidden them good-night, going quietly homewards through the silent country-town, each thinking of Christine, each praying for her happiness.

In the early morning a carriage waited at Matthew's gate, — the same Malcolm had driven over the previous evening. He stood at the horses' heads, looking a little impatient as Matthew and Christine walked slowly down the path. She stepped on a carpet of flowers. "The dear children!" she said; for she recognized the hands of Patience and Martin in this last evidence of affection. And yet, with all this devotion around her, this woman had given her heart to a man almost a stranger to her, — with him was going away from home and friends. And she was content. Such a mighty power is love!

They were seated in the carriage. A crack of the whip, and they were off, leaving only a cloud of dust to tell of their departure, as the sun rose higher and higher over the waking world, and the town of G—— took up its busy labors of harvesting.

CHAPTER X.

CHRISTIE'S VISION.

WEEK had passed since Christine's wedding. Most anxious days at Tabitha's, for Christie had been ill. As the sun was rising on the day of Christine's departure, he started up from sleep, and, clasping his hands, cried, —

"Mother, mother, she has gone, and I shall never see her again!"

Tabitha, who had been sitting at the window watching for Martin and Patience, started towards the bed, and only had time to reach the child as he fell back in one of his alarming fainting-fits.

So fair, so frail, and Death's own image! the dark lashes resting on the white cheeks, and the nerveless little hands slipping away from Tabitha's, as she frantically strove by rubbing, and other restoratives, to bring back some signs of life.

Martin and Patience found her thus on their return from strewing the flowers on the pathway of Christine. There was little else done all day at the cabin but struggle against the angel Death, whose wings seemed overshadowing the dearest loved of all the little family.

Late at night, while the three still kept sad vigil by the child's bedside, taking turns at rubbing the poor little body, and trying every means in their power to keep the fluttering life that at each faint breath seemed about to pass away, there came a change.

With a smile so sweet, it seemed a glimpse of heaven to the anxious watchers, the bright eyes opened wide.

"Oh, thank you, dear Lord! We are at peace. Dear mother, dear Matthew." And, after a little, "Martin, Christine, and Patience. All together, all happy."

His voice ceased; but the smile still shone on his face, and his eyes seemed looking at something invisible to them. How long he would have so remained, they knew not; for they held their breath, and feared to move, lest he might be startled into a relapse. Rex, however, who had taken his share of watching, refusing to leave Christie's side, when he heard his voice sprang upon the bed, and began licking his face before they could prevent.

"My Rex!" And a laugh came from Christie.

A laugh! It was such an unexpected happiness, that all three, even Martin, fell on each other's necks, and laughed and cried, and then kissed the child, who seemed to have come back to them from a distant land, — that land so near, it is ever touching our own, and yet so far away, so strange, so terrible!

"Mother, I am hungry."

"You dear darling!" cried Patience, as she fairly flew into the kitchen, and danced back with a plate temptingly arranged, and then stood watching while Tabitha fed him. At each mouthful, she and Martin would hug each other with delight.

"Mother, darling," said Christie, resting in his mother's arms, "I have had a vision. So horrible at first, and then so beautiful. I will tell it to you."

"Not now. My Christie must sleep now. To-morrow morning tell us."

Too tired to do any thing but smile his consent, he kissed the anxious, loving face bent over him, and soon fell into a deep, soft sleep. Martin and Patience tiptoed away to their own beds, and, tired

out, were also soon sleeping. But Tabitha, feeling sleep impossible
to her, took her favorite seat on the door-step, and, listening to the
soft breathing of her children, fell into a reverie. There had awakened within her a longing for her childhood's home. Seen through
the vista of weary years, how fair and tranquil seemed the old life !
the farmhouse mid the grand old trees, and the church-spire gleaming
brightly in the sunshine. She even heard the lowing of the cows
coming home to the milking. And tripping down the road, carrying
the milk-pails, was a tall, slim girl, dreaming all sorts of wild dreams
of an impossible future. Was that girl Tabitha Simpson ? Poor Tabitha sighed as the picture faded, and she thought to what a future
those dreams had brought her. But still the old homestead, and the
faces of old friends, came before her. Too late now for her. But her
children might have some chance of a future if only she could get
them there out of this fearful Utah. If it were only possible for them
to escape ! She would consult Matthew, and he would know how much
money they would need to pay their way out of this place. Gradually
the thoughts became confused. Matthew, Christine, and her children
were all with her, all happy ; and the tired woman on the door-step fell
asleep. She slept until the daylight's golden gladness shone full in
her face, and wakened her to life and labor.

There were some busy days for them all ; for, as soon as they
could get him ready, Martin would start away on another trip. Christie's illness had detained him ; but, as soon as the child seemed better,
they concluded Martin had better not wait longer. There was a large
load of fresh vegetables to be packed. "And even a few tomatoes !"
Patience exclaimed in triumph, as she ran exultantly into the cabin,
holding one luscious red "love-apple" in her hand. Taking a large
basket, she hastened back into the garden to gather the ripe ones, and
have them packed before dark. Christie, near the open door, was
in a chair, propped up by pillows. His face, more angelic than ever,

wore an expression of perfect peace. He had not told his "vision," as he called it.

"I will wait," he said, "until the work of packing is over; and you can sit near me, and be at rest."

And now the week was near its decline, and yet the hour of rest seemed distant.

"It will come to-night, little brother," Patience had said, as she hurried past him. "We've only to load the wagon; and, as for the tomatoes, I'll soon have them ready."

Tabitha was getting supper, Martin carrying the hampers and sacks of vegetables to the side of the house where the wagon stood, and Patience in the tomato-patch. Since Christie's recovery, the girl had been so thankful, so happy, that, like a bird, she was constantly bursting into song. How sweet the young voice sounded as it floated through the open door! So sweet, that it tempted Christie into a feeble refrain. So sweet, that the mother stopped her work for a look at the singer. Her sunbonnet had fallen off, her face glowing with health and youth, and the wind playing all sorts of antics with the soft, short hairs that could never be coaxed into smoothness. Sleeves rolled up, showing arms white and beautiful enough for a Venus. On the ground beside her, the basket, nearly filled with the ripe red fruit, to whose numbers the busy fingers were quickly adding; and the sunlight, pouring over all, gave its brightness to the lovely picture. Saying a few tender words to Christie, who was rubbing Rex's great black head, Tabitha went back to her work with a smile on her face, and her breast filled with motherly pride. Suddenly, in a frightened whisper, Christie said, —

"Quick, mother! Here's father."

For a moment Tabitha's heart almost ceased its beating. After ten years he had come, this recreant husband and father! And for what purpose? What motive had brought him here? A nameless dread came over her, and seemed to make a leaden weight of the heart that a few moments since was light with hope. She feared for her children, and, hastening to the door, stood before Christie, as if shielding him from evil. Leaning over the gate was a sensual-looking

"COME AND KISS ME, MY PRETTY MAID."

man, long past middle age. His eyes, half covered by fat, were fixed with admiration on the girl before him, — an admiration that chilled the blood in the mother's veins. Perfectly unconscious, Patience worked on. And the man, absorbed in his admiration, seemed equally unconscious of the eyes watching him, as, with all the persuasiveness he could command, he said, —

"Come and kiss me, my pretty maid, and I will give you a gay bracelet to adorn those snowy arms."

Startled, the girl sprang to her feet. Her nervousness only added to her beauty, as, alternately blushing and paling, she pulled down the sleeves, and concealed the arms that had called forth the unwelcome compliment. She knew who had spoken to her; but, from her first remembrance, her strongest feelings towards her father were fear and repugnance. And now she stood like a frightened fawn, not knowing what to do.

"Patience, kiss your father."

Tabitha's voice sounded harsh and rasping; for her throat felt clutched by an iron hand, so filled was she with dread of evil.

Instantly obeying her mother, Patience held towards her father her dimpled, blushing cheek.

There was a strange look in the little eyes, and a discomfited expression around the sensual mouth, that hardly touched her soft face, as the bishop beheld in the young beauty before him the daughter whom ten years ago he had driven from his house. His injured wife was walking towards him, and now stood beside her daughter, — the mother who had watched over, and worked for, the children he had almost forgotten.

It may have been some glimmer of conscience that drove the color from his face, as he awkwardly extended one chubby hand, and said, —

"Tabitha, dear, I came to see you."

How she loathed him as she took the hand she dared not refuse, and, opening the gate, bowed an invitation to enter!

The bishop, somewhat recovered from his discomfiture, answered that he would surely come some other time, but just now he was obliged to go. So, uttering a few gracious commonplaces, he turned to leave. Looking back, however, and saying, "Patience, my child, you must come to see me," he again bowed farewell, and walked homeward.

A good man! A saintly man! Honored by his State, and fawned upon by his neighbors. He walked on, with head bent down, chuckling at his thoughts.

Tabitha stood watching him out of sight. Feeling a shudder creep all over her, she turned to go to the house.

"Come, Patience, or we'll not have the tomatoes packed before evening."

The girl was standing perfectly still, pale as marble, except a scarlet spot on one cheek. It was where the bishop's lips had touched her, and which, with unconquerable repugnance, she had rubbed until the delicate skin was bruised.

"Mother," — the words came in a low whisper, — "is it possible that man is my father? I cannot recall one moment in my childhood that he was ever kind to me. Whenever I was near him, I felt as if I had seen a snake. And just now, when you bade me kiss him, I grew sick and faint. Is it possible to feel thus to a father?"

. "Alas, my child, that it is true!" answered the mother with a bitter sigh. "I wish Matthew were here," she added, as again that nameless dread overpowered her, and made her tremble. And she longed for the true friend whose guidance and counsel had never failed any needing help.

But, in the busy, work-a-day world, there is not leisure for the indulgence of feeling. One must be "up and doing," though the heart be aching and the brain be whirling. So Tabitha and Patience, each taking a side of the heavy basket, had to utilize the waning daylight, and most carefully pack the tomatoes, or they would be too bruised to sell to advantage.

Christie, who, until his father disappeared, had hidden his face on Rex's head, now looked up and smiled as Tabitha and Patience came near.

"Can you wrap and pack the tomatoes here? I've felt so lonely and cold ever since father came."

So they sat on the step at his feet, and went busily to work. Patience tried hard to call up some of her gay spirits; but the smiles would fade, and the laugh change to a sigh. Presently Martin, who had been out of sight for the past hour, and knew nothing of what had occurred, came to her aid.

"Well, Patience, lazy girl! The tomatoes not yet ready! I'll help." And he sat down beside her on the low step, and, not noticing their anxious looks, began telling how he had packed the different vegetables : thus, in his kind, commonplace way, bringing back their thoughts from phantom dreads to their actual interests ; for, to them, it was of great moment that the more delicate vegetables should be on top, and things arranged to keep in good condition while the long miles were travelled that lay between their garden and the purchasers.

By the time every thing was finished, and the last hamper secured, Patience, with the elasticity of youth, had somewhat recovered her gayety.

"Martin's last supper at home," she said to herself. "He shall not have a dull one."

There was a great affection between Martin and Patience. His amiability would soothe her more nervous and excitable nature : and so, when helping him at the wagon, she had told him about the visit of their father, even of his compliment to her ; and, as Martin did not seem to think any evil would come of it, the dread which had made her sad and nervous lost its power.

"I'm as sorry as you are that he is our father. But he is, and we must try to make the best of it. He has not seemed to think about us for ten years, and perhaps he won't again for ten years more. And say, Patience, I'll tell you a secret, if you'll just keep it to yourself. It has fairly burned my tongue for the past ten days. But I just thought the dear old mother has had hard enough lines already, and I didn't want to raise false hopes for her."

"A secret ! Why, Martin, how could you keep it from me ? Tell me this very moment;" and she climbed upon the side of the wagon, to get nearer his face.

"Well," said Martin, as if to begin a long preamble.

"Not another 'well,' I implore you! But tell me the secret quick!" cried Patience.

"My dear girl," resumed Martin, "unless you let me tell you my own way, I cannot at all. I'm not compressed lightning."

Patience's only answer was, —

"Then, tell it as quickly as you can."

"Well," he resumed, "you remember all about the nice little girl who gave me Rex for Christie, and how kindly the whole family treated me? I was tired out when I reached their town. It is a mining-camp outside the Utah border. Her mother made me stop to supper. Her father told me to put my horses in his stable, and the little girl was as good to me as a girl could be. That night, after supper, they asked me some questions about Utah and the Mormons. They soon found out, that, though I was a Mormon born, I was not of the religion. They continued to question, and so I told them something of our history. All of a sudden the little girl burst out crying, and ran to her father, saying, 'Help these poor people from that terrible place!' Then Mr. Marks asked me if I could leave, and bring you all with me. I told him that disaffected Mormons were watched, and not allowed to go out of the country, but that the families of teamsters sometimes took trips away with them; and that we lived so quietly, being quite poor, that I did not believe it would be at all difficult for us to leave. 'Then, my man,' he said, 'if you can bring your mother, sister, and little brother here by the middle of December, I will promise you work, and four dollars per day, as long as you are honest and faithful.' Think of that, Patience!"

Her only answer was a hug and a kiss. Then, jumping down to the ground, she took his hand, and, pulling him along, said, —

"Now, tell mother every word of this. It will help relieve her mind. Don't you see anxiety for the future is wearing her out? Come, you dear, stupid love of a brother. I believe you just kept this secret to make us feel happy all the time you're away."

So they hurried to Tabitha and Christie with the wonderful hope that had sprung up for them.

"That must be the meaning of my vision," said Christie. "Take me in your arms, mother, while I tell it."

CHRISTIE'S STORY OF THE VISION.

They had been talking around the supper-table. But, when Christie held out his arms to his mother, she took him tenderly on her lap, and the others drew their chairs near. The child began, —

"It seemed to me I was sitting outside Matthew's house, waiting for Christine to come. I knew she was married, and was going away; but I wanted the last look of her dear face. The carriage was at the gate; and Malcolm, so handsome, was standing at the horses' heads. Presently the door opened, and Matthew came out with Christine.

She looked at the flowers strewn on the path, and said, 'The dear children have done this,' and then, smiling, while the tears stood in her eyes, stepped in the carriage. Matthew and Malcolm both got in; but, in a moment, Malcolm's face changed to sullen fury, the horses madly rushed along, and the road seemed one sheet of fire. I cried out, 'Christine has gone, and I shall never see her again!' Then, before I could speak to you, mother, who seemed near me, I felt myself falling down, down, and then awakened on a dark road. Patience and mother were toiling along, and I was on Rex's back. Every thing was dark, and we seemed afraid to speak, when, suddenly, mother snatched me in her arms; and, where before I could not see a single person, there now stood a number of men. Their faces were covered, and they held in their hands flaming torches. Among them, with his hands tied, was Matthew. He stood just like the Saviour he tells us about. He spoke, and said, 'Do not be afraid.' And then, while I was still trembling, I seemed lifted out of your arms, mother, and held tenderly in such strong arms that I looked up, and I saw the most beautiful face I ever dreamed of. It was a man's face; and he kissed me, and said, 'You were patient, now be happy.' Then he put me on my feet. They were strong beneath me; but, falling on my knees, I said, 'O Lord! is it you?' He answered 'Yes,' and smiled upon me. 'Then, Lord, give my mother peace, or I cannot be happy. See, she is looking for me.' Then he smiled, and, holding out his hand, took yours. In a moment you stood beside me, — not pale and thin as now, but bright and shining like a star. Then Matthew came, and, falling down, would have kissed the feet of the Lord; but he smiled again, and, raising him, put Matthew's head on his breast, and said, 'Here is your place, my friend.' Yet I was not happy; for I wanted my Patience, my Christine, and my Martin. I wanted them to be in the beautiful place with us. The Lord knew I was not happy; for he said, 'Why, Christie! not yet content?' —

'Dear Lord,' I said, 'how can I be at peace, when some I love are still suffering?' — 'Child,' he said, half reproachfully, yet so sweetly, 'look!' Down a dusty road, a little way off, was Martin springing along. His face was shining with a glory that seemed to cover him. He held out his arms to me, and said, 'I'm coming, little brother.' And then, farther down the road, were Christine and Patience in each other's arms. They, too, looked peaceful, and were hastening towards me. As they came nearer and nearer, and their faces grew brighter and brighter, I fell on my knees, and said, 'Thank you, dear Lord: we are all at peace, — dear mother, dear Matthew;' and, after a little, 'Martin, Christine, and Patience.' Then I awoke, and saw you all around me."

While the child was speaking, he seemed like one whose life was ending here below, and for whom heaven was opening.

Tabitha's heart ached as she looked at him. Martin had bowed his head on his hands, and Patience was softly weeping.

"Why," Christie said, "I have made you sad!" Then, with a half sob, "I've told my dream badly; for, if you could have seen the Lord's face, you would not feel sad again. Since I dreamed of him, I have not even grieved over Christine's departure. But my heart seems ever beating out the words Matthew always says, 'Thy will be done, thy will be done.'"

He had hardly finished speaking when there came a rap at the door.

"Matthew!" they all cried out with joy as the door opened, and their friend stood in their midst.

He looked tired and dusty; had but just arrived, and, hearing Christie had been sick, came at once to see him. He asked about his sickness, and told the little fellow he was thankful to see him better.

"Yes, you may give me a cup of tea," he answered to Patience's inquiry.

And the girl, delighted to do even this slight service for him, who, serving every one, yet would receive no service, hastened to the kitchen.

She soon brought in some supper, and smiled with pride and happiness when Matthew praised her cooking, and seemed to enjoy it.

After he had eaten, he told them all about Christine, — what a pleasant trip they had, and what a pretty little house, all furnished, John Smith had presented to her. And then, opening a large parcel, he gave each a *souvenir* from the dear, absent friend. For Tabitha and Patience, warm knitted jackets ; for Martin, a pair of heavy driving-mittens ; and for Christie, a soft fur-lined coat that would cover his poor little feet. "She sends you these with her dear love, and begs you will write to her."

In her own happiness she had remembered them, thinking of each one's needs. Her and Matthew's friendship had been the main-stay of this family. And to-night, when the old life of pain had seemed to be nearing them in the strangely awakened interest of Bishop White, these two dear friends were heaven-sent to keep hope alive in their hearts. Looking at Matthew and Martin, while they talked of the morrow's trip, Tabitha was feeling this comfort.

Martin told Matthew of the hope for their future. And the old man, counselling silence, saw in it a happy release for these dear children of his adoption. He would come on the morrow, and hear Christie's vision, he said, as he put his hand on the child's bright head, and blessed him. To him the patient little sufferer ever seemed nearer heaven than earth ; and to his simple, unquestioning faith, there appeared nothing strange that angels should hold converse with him. So, bidding them "good-night," Matthew left them happy and peaceful for his coming.

CHAPTER XI.

"MARRIED AND A' THAT."

IN July, mid nature's bounteous gifts ripening unto harvest, Christine had been married. Through fields of grain, kissed golden by the sun ; of tall, luxuriant corn, whose dark green glistened in the brightness ; past brawling brooks ; past orchards laden with luscious fruit ; past houses with children playing at their open doors, and hiding 'neath shadows of waving branches, — on dashed the train, bearing to her new home Christine and her happiness.

Sweet through car-windows came the breath of the new-mown hay. Lovingly the breeze lifted the soft silk of her hair, and kissed the snow of her brow, lingering on the beauty of her face as if to carry its image to some sick-bed, whose sufferer, dreaming of angel's smile, forgets his weary pain.

Tenderly gazed her grandfather on his child. And her husband, exalted by love's first glory, seemed all that woman desires in man. It is a curious phase of human nature, that a woman like Christine — strong, intellectual, and self-contained — should have given herself utterly to a man greatly her inferior, of whom she knew nothing, except that he was beautiful. And yet every day this phase is seen, and every day the passing crowd wonders at it. Can it not understand, that, of all, a noble nature is easiest deceived ? Can it not understand, that, of its nobility it endows its love, giving to that love its own high attributes?

Christine had wandered with Malcolm midst flowery fields, through shaded paths, with spring's fresh beauty around them. She had talked to him of her spirit's whisperings; and he had listened, smiled, assented. And, behold! to her he stood clothed in each noble thought.

It had not seemed that she had uttered the aspirations that bring poor humanity nearer the Godhead, but that he was the leading spirit; and she loved him, that his beauty was but the outer cover of a noble soul. Strong in her own faithfulness, it had never entered her mind to conceive that his impetuosity could be allied to weaker qualities.

The eyes that looked so frankly into her own in the days of his wooing, that now were liquid with love's languor, seemed to be full of truth's own brightness. Once removed, that first doubt, born of his sigh, was a thing vanished, as the mist of the morning. And, when she gave him her hand, her heart went with it entirely, utterly. The tears in her eyes, as she left her father's house, were more for others than herself, — those dear friends to whom she was so much, who had made her world, until this bright young sun-god had come, and bade her follow him. And follow him she must, — to the world's end, if need be; through misery, poverty, and pain; through every thing but sin. There her feet would refuse to carry her pure soul. But there was no question of sin in the handsome eyes looking at her, and, no doubt, only perfect trust in those dark depths, whose answering glance mirrored her sweet soul.

Faster the houses grew up midst the fields, holding themselves closer and closer together, until, a goodly company, they grew, and grew into a stately city.

Among its brick and stone, man's works of strength, great trees stretched out their branches covered with thickest foliage; and Matthew smiled at these familiar friends as the train stopped: and, at the depot, John Smith was waiting to welcome them.

Malcolm was rather anxious about the effect Christine would produce on this uncle whom he admired, and of whom he stood as much in awe as was possible to his nature.

He could remember him a quiet student, poor, and almost unknown. And, year by year, he had seen him climb ambition's ladder; until now, in all Utah, no man's voice had equal power.

A cynic and a satirist. Yet, at will, he could command eloquence so fiery and impassioned, that it would light the flame of fanaticism till it blazed just as he directed.

As for women, — well, he had married three wives, quiet, ordinary persons, each of whom had brought him a rich dower. To these he seemed most kind and respectful. And they, whether held in check by the same power with which he controlled the populace, or whether really contented with their strange lot, seemed placidly to accept their destiny, and appreciate gratefully the polite attentions of their husband.

But towards other women John Smith's cynicism grew most bitter; and Malcolm smiled nervously, as, descending from the cars, he presented his wife.

Somehow, from the moment John Smith met them at the train, and drove them to the house, which, furnished even with two smiling maids, he presented to Christine as her wedding gift, all she did seemed well done to him. And Malcolm stopped biting his lip, laughing with content at first the interest, then admiration, which brightened his uncle's cold eyes.

He grew more and more pleased with himself and his choice, as, day after day of Matthew's visit, John Smith put aside all business, devoting himself to the pleasure of the old man and his child.

Already Malcolm began to look forward to the effect his wife would produce upon the fashionable Mormon world. She who could so interest that coldest of men would soon be reigning queen of society, and perhaps might even acquire influence with the government if — But that ugly little "if," which, even in these first days, began to obtrude itself, was put to flight by John Smith's laugh.

Never before in his life had he heard his uncle laugh, except that conventional sound, which, through policy, he sometimes gave in compliment to the worn-out joke of one he wished to flatter. Here he was laughing with almost boyish merriment at some bright speech of Christine's, which had made Matthew pat her cheek, and smile in reply.

And Malcolm wondered more and more, and felt more and more delighted with his wife, as he noticed only her comments, her laughter, had power to arouse his uncle. When, out of her happy heart, in these days of Matthew's stay, Christine's laughter would ring like soft bells, John Smith would laugh with her; and, putting off his cold dignity, he seemed to grow in youthfulness of heart.

Each morning his carriage brought him to their house, and waited outside, as some fresh plan he had made for their pleasure was approved, amended, or changed, according to the lights and shades of Christine's face. All this was delightful to Malcolm, until, become quite secure of it, he grew indifferent. He yawned a little as he thought, "he thinks a lot of her;" and then he wished for some new observers to admire Christine's charms, and feel the power of her eloquent thoughts. But of this slight weariness nothing was seen; and the yawns were hid in very charming smiles, that his wife thought brighter than heaven's sunshine.

Delightful trips were made to all surrounding places of interest, — to the shore of the lake whose salt waters are so buoyant that human body cannot sink, and so strongly brine no fish lives under its waves. A phenomenon, it stands memorial to the strength, extent, and power of that debasing creed which is America's shame. That this region, gifted by nature with fertile lands, great mineral wealth, springs of boiling, healing waters, should be the cradle of immorality, the school where young souls are taught to embrace vice, is a shame, a horror, greater than any glory our country can boast !

CHAPTER XII.

VISITS OF INTEREST.

THE day before his departure Matthew expressed his desire to visit the railroad then in course of construction, and also the public schools.

Discourses on doctrinal points had been studiously avoided by John Smith; and, of course, courtesy forbade Matthew making inquiries on a point that to him was of vital interest. He wanted to know how a system called public education, professing liberal religion, could be made to subserve a private tyrannical creed, and thus youth, the strengthening sinews of a state, trained into determined support of the political power of Mormonism, as opposed to the expressed desire of the United-States Government, by which government the school system had been established.

In his own little village, where Bishop White represented both spiritual and temporal power, this had been easy enough. But here, in a great city, a metropolis, where lived Gentiles in numbers, where came and went a travelling public, there must require great management, extensive influence. And from observation, and perhaps some questions to superintendent and teachers, Matthew hoped to glean an explanation.

Whatever John Smith thought of the old man's wish to visit the schools, he showed only pleasure in being able to gratify it. Riding betimes to the door, with plans arranged for their comfort, and some loose flowers for Christine, which he handed her as he joined the little family still seated around the breakfast-table, —

"Don't hurry: we have plenty of time. The horses will go all the better for a longer rest," he had said, as Matthew proposed their starting at once, and not keeping the carriage waiting.

His gracious acquiescence, his evident pleasure in giving pleasure, delighted the old man, and touched his child's heart.

"THE FLOWERS MATTHEW HELD TO HER THROAT."

The girl's face flushed, and the dark eyes raised to her uncle's were full of gratitude. He saw it shining through the tears which had sprung to her eyes, as, handing Matthew his coffee, she had thought with a pang how soon must cease those little services, so dear to both. John Smith felt the soft sadness of her face, the beauty of those unshed tears, as for a moment — hardly so long — he looked at her.

And then, while talking to Malcolm, eating heartily of the tempting breakfast deftly served by the neat little maid, he noticed, without seeming to do so, how vastly becoming to her were the flowers which

Matthew, taking from the table, held to her throat. And she, bending down her head, rested her cheek caressingly against her grandfather's hand.

It was a sweet picture, the two sitting thus close together. And those eyes of John Smith, for all their cold gravity, held it in his vision after he had turned away, and was apparently interested in something else.

They were to ride out as far as the railroad was built. After they had discussed its probable speedy completion to their heart's content, they would lunch with a friend of John Smith's, whose house was near the railroad, and who was one of the school trustees. With him they would return to the city, visiting such schools as he should select.

It was a charming day. The trees, in all the glory of summer. foliage, gave to the broad streets the beauty of a park ; and the little streams, running on each side, between the double rows of forest kings, carried in their swift current much that in other cities make thoroughfares unsightly. This very singular and attractive mode of sewerage is one of the distinctive features of Salt Lake. As it stands embowered in shade-trees, the beautiful natural basin in which it is built surrounded by grand mountains, whose snow-caps rest against the clouds, it is a city to waken delight and admiration in the stranger, and will, in memory, hold clear its place when other cities equally great, but less unique, have faded into general views.

"Even the weather conspires to honor you," John Smith, sitting opposite, said laughingly to Christine, as they rolled along over the smooth paving. And then he thought how much more charming than speech was the smile with which she answered him.

Matthew, next her, had taken in his own the dear hand resting on her lap. He was so soon to leave her! How precious she was to him! He did not speak, but smiled down lovingly upon her. And the dark eyes raised to his were still dewy with the sadness of the coming parting. So much had each been to the other's life, it was no easy matter to separate. Each heart was feeling the void to-morrow would bring, while the man who had won this woman's love was humming to himself as he gazed out of the carriage. And now that they were in the country, without occasional enlivening bow and smile from passing acquaintance, finding the stillness rather oppressive, he glanced at his wife; thought she was "a deuced handsome girl." Then at Matthew, who, in his costume and appearance, carried the country. But it was the pleasantness of the country. There was nothing awkward or uncouth about that noble head and majestic form. Looking at him, one thought of clover-fields waving in summer's wind; of yellow wheat ready for the sickle; great trees shading cool lanes; and rippling brooks, on whose green banks peacefully grazed the patient cow, and gambolled playful lambs, — Nature, beneficent in its goodness and beauty, a sermon more potent than human eloquence. Such thoughts were wakened by the kindly glance of Matthew's clear eyes. Yet while John Smith, cynic and unbeliever, felt it all, and truly honored this simple-hearted farmer, Malcolm, young, hopeful, gay, saw it not.

The calm face, framed in snowy hair, inspired him with no other sentiment than, "If the old cove comes to visit us next winter, we must try to reconstruct his costume. He'd not be bad-looking if he'd wear fashionable clothes."

Then his eyes fell on his uncle; and he wondered how it was he had managed to ingratiate himself with the great Brigham, and make such a lot of money. Then he sighed lightly, and, looking out on the beautiful pastoral landscape, wished the horses would hurry up. He was growing "deuced tired" of riding about to places where there was nothing to interest.

Thus, after all, a great deal depends on the eyes that see. Malcolm's eyes, so perfect in color and shape, saw only a handsome woman and country farmer where those of John Smith's, very inferior in appearance, found enough to interest and fill his thoughts during their long and rather silent drive.

At the terminus of the road was a small frame building.   It served for a temporary office ; and, before it, a long line of men, in single file, were entering by one door, and departing by another.

"Pay-day. I had forgotten," John Smith said, as the bearer of his card returned, and, bowing very low to the great man, invited the party to enter.

The gentleman at the desk suspended his labors to come forward, shake hands with Mr. Smith, and be presented to his friends.

"We will be more comfortable if not disturbing you," said Mr. Smith. "We will wait here a few moments, and admire the orderly manner in which your business is conducted.   Then, with your permission, from your foreman, whom I know, we can gain any information we desire."

"VOLUNTARY CONTRIBUTIONS."

After a few courtesies, the usual commonplaces of such occasions, the superintendent returned to his desk, and the day's business was resumed.

To the left of the desk was seated a small, spare man, who had most obsequiously returned Mr. Smith's bow. This was the tithe-gatherer. He held in his hand a list containing each man's name, wages, and indebtedness to the Mormon church. As each received his pay, the amount he must give to the church was stated to him, and immediately surrendered.

"Voluntary contributions," John Smith said in Matthew's ear.

"Voluntary?" and the true eyes looked steadily down on the uncle of his granddaughter, while to Matthew's mind came the full force of what is called "voluntary."

Let one of those men fail to pay the demand of the tithe-gatherer, and he loses his place. His neighbors refuse him countenance. His property is stolen or injured. For him protection is impossible. The law can not, or will not, find the offenders. If sickness comes upon him or his, yet must he stand alone. Boycotted! Accursed of the church! Avoided by its followers. Is that voluntary, when refusal entails such results? Instance after instance of this oppressive system of taxation came before him. And poor Anton, his destroyed crops, his stolen cattle, his martyred family, and own despair, made darker, more criminal, the cruel law. Again he caught his dying look. Again in his ears sounded the gasping of his failing voice, "I hope Gott vill vorgive, I vas so onhappy." Poor Anton, poor Anton! Was he to be punished? God alone knew. His will be done. Even as his heart ached in pity, Matthew uttered his prayer.

CHAPTER XIII.

A BROTHER'S HELP.

THE perfect system of Utah's tithing, the exact knowledge of each family's finances, is one of the government's great powers. The name of each man, woman, and child is registered, with amount of wages earned, or property owned. The president of the church appoints to each district its tithe-gatherer. To him is furnished the different amounts due from each individual. And, as the non-payment is so surely and swiftly punished, omissions or failures to comply with the Mormon law are rare, most rare. The tithing-money is paid to the president, who does with it — well, it is better not to question what, secretly managed, can never be satisfactorily settled. Inevitable as death is this tithing. No pity or justice stops the demand. By it the poor are made poorer. For it the women toil in fields, and children are put to work, that the unlucky family-mill may grind, grind, until the church is satisfied. Matthew felt the little room oppressive as he watched the faces of the men, and speculated how many absolute needs of each family were sacrificed to the tyrannical demands of Mormonism. Yet was there no escape? The United-States flag protects the Mormon rule. Under its free laws flourishes this perfect system of cruel, oppressive government. The old man was glad to leave the office that for him was filling with painful thought. Out in the fresh air and sunlight he joined Malcolm, who was smoking, and chatting with the foreman. "What pleasant ways he has!" thought Matthew, as he looked at his Christine's husband.

Gay, beautiful, strong. The old man felt in this bright figure a renewal of his own youth. Returning Malcolm's smile, thanking God for his child's happiness, for her blessed, sheltered future, the morrow's parting lost its sting. Could he regret that wherein she so greatly gained?

Never had Malcolm appeared to greater advantage than during these first days of his married life, — thoughtful of those attentions so grateful to the old, full of tender courtesies to his wife, and, to his uncle, deference tempered with merriment.

Truly, there seemed nothing to be desired for that beautiful woman, whose dark eyes unconsciously followed each graceful motion of him she loved. The sunlight was upon her; love and tenderness surrounding her as she stood the central figure in the little group of grandfather, uncle, husband. And who so fitting for her husband, her companion, as this radiant youth, filled with all those gifts that make youth's greatest charm? Who, looking on him, hearing his ringing laughter, would have imagined the courtesies so graciously rendered were becoming rather tedious? And the happy face that made his wife's heart glow was mask to the thought, "I wonder how much of this goody-goody business a fellow is expected to stand."

John Smith marvelled at the change in his nephew. He seemed to have lost the frivolity which had marred his many gifts. "Malcolm may be rich, but never powerful," his uncle had said of him. Yet now he was almost modifying his opinion.

And was it wonderful with such a woman for wife? Strength, truth, intelligence, — all these were Christine's; and adorning them, as the vine a noble structure, grace and beauty. The man of the world, whose life had been one success, sighed heavily, then, as if brushing away some obtrusive thought, turned to his niece, claiming her attention, as, between him and her husband, she walked towards her grandfather.

He was talking with the foreman. Even while Malcolm was jesting with the man, Matthew saw he was in trouble. And trouble to Matthew was a cry for help that never passed unheard. So when Christine and Mr. Smith came from the office, and Malcolm, with laughing remark, joined them, Matthew turned to the foreman, whose sad eyes seemed fixed in painful thought. In voice that could not fail to reach an aching heart, he said, "Friend, you are in trouble. As a brother, I will serve you if I can."

The man frowned, but it was to hide a tear. He bit his lip to keep back a sob wakened by the voice and manner of this stranger. He looked at the benevolent face, from whence shone the true spirit of brotherly love, hesitated a moment, and then blurted out, —

"You may betray me, but I'll risk it. Up to this day I've been a Mormon, in truth as well as word. Believing in its religion, I gave my daughter — my favorite child — in marriage to a Mormon. Against her pleading I did this, deciding it was for her good. And now, under Mormon mummery, she is dying."

"Can I see her?" Matthew asked.

"They will not let me in," the father groaned. "And her husband, the fool, is locked in his own cellar. Sent there to pray, while his wife, and the baby coming, are at the mercy, and under the foolery, of those layers-on-of-hands! If a husband cared for his wife, would he leave her at such a moment without succor?" the man said bitterly. His sun-burned, commonplace features were dignified by his sorrow. And the slow tears, that, unheeded, rolled down his cheeks, seemed the first heavy rain-drops that presage storm.

"Do you not think if I, a stranger, went with you, these people would be shamed into admitting you?" said Matthew.

"Will you go?" the man answered eagerly. And then, "Wait: I will ask leave of absence." Hurriedly he left Matthew, who made his explanation to Christine and her escorts.

"I cannot go with you, my child. There is some one in trouble. Use your eyes for me, love, and to-night tell me of the schools."

To her these words were all-sufficient. Duty ever was Matthew's life's rule. Tenderly pressing his hand, she made no further comment than her simple assent.

John Smith suggested, "Might not the person wait?" And Malcolm, with an expression too bright to be sympathetic, too charming to be unattractive, said nothing, but thought, "What an old softy! He'd rather tag after the lame,

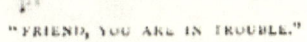

"FRIEND, YOU ARE IN TROUBLE."

halt, and blind, than sit down to a fatted calf." And then, with most winning grace, he helped his wife into the carriage, held the door for his uncle, and, cordially shaking Matthew's hand, hoped he would return to them soon, as neither he nor Christine felt willing to yield too much of this last day.

Christine, turning to look back at her grandfather, saw him walking rapidly down the road in the direction of a little group of cottages clustering under shade-trees.

CHAPTER XIV.

A VICTIM.

ITH quick steps, Matthew and Foreman Renan walked on.

"If any thing happens, I don't know what will become of me. I forced this marriage upon her; and yesterday I went to see her, and found her weeping. It is her first confinement, poor child! Think of her without other help than those layers-on-of-hands! I spoke to that dolt, her husband; offered to pay for nurse and doctor. But his words, 'My mother came through all right : she can run the same risk,' were my only answer. Ah, stranger! faith is a different matter when it must be exercised for your own flesh and blood. At such a time, and not a woman near her!" Thus, in whispers, groaning, and hanging down his head, Renan, in disjointed sentences, poured out his troubled thoughts upon the sympathetic silence of this man, who, from stranger, had now become trusted friend.

"Here we are," said Renan, stopping before a neat little house with clustering vines, its garden surrounded by a white painted fence. But just now, to a stranger, it would have seemed the abode of the insane from the strange noises which proceeded from it. The air was made hideous by loud groans in different voices mingled with curious guttural chants ; and occasionally from the open windows was violently thrown some simple article of household ware, — pans, pots, flat-irons, pillows, chairs, each in turn was dashed away by unseen hands. The grass was literally covered with the inner ware of a modest household.

Matthew groaned in spirit at these evidences of the ignorance and superstition cultivated among people living under the protection of what is called "an enlightened country."

"America the land of advance?" He questioned it, as thus brought face to face with an illustration of superstition equal to the dark ages. He knew by experience what these signs portended. Had he not, in his own little village, known Bishop White and his deacons groan and pray around the bed of the sick, letting the patient die, actually die in torture, when some simple remedy would have relieved, perhaps cured, what was not at inception a dangerous malady?

As Matthew and Renan stood for a moment at the door, waiting response to their knock, and demand for admission, a faint moan mingled with the hoarse voices of men, and a weak cry of "Mercy, oh, mercy!" roused the father to desperation. He dashed himself against the door, bursting it open, and then stopped aghast. "Brother," Matthew had called him. And true brother, ready to help to his uttermost, he stood at his side. But help had come too late!

On the bed lay a young woman. Pretty she might have been but for the drawn look of agony over a face paled with the ashes of death. Her blue eyes open, yet was their sight gone! Her hands extended, held before her, seemed still putting away some object of repulsion. At her side, wailing, was a new-born infant. Uncovered, unwashed, this pitiful bit of humanity moaned its protest to the wrong that had killed its mother. And around the room stood four great, brawny men, who looked angrily at the intruders.

Not seeing them, his eyes filled with something more horrible than madness, Renan gazed on his child. He sprang to the bed, caught in his those clay-cold hands, tense in their dying struggle: he looked into those staring, sightless eyes, leaned his head on the still white breast, and, with one wild shriek, "Dead!" fell writhing on the floor. The layers-on-of-hands, who had used their force on a woman in the throes of parturition, stood aloof from the groaning, struggling man.

Matthew, alone, unaided, held from self-destruction the desperate, unconscious hands. Mighty as he was, the old man was strained to his uttermost. Yet even now, with the sweat of exhaustion starting on his brow, and his breath coming short and quick, he heard above the groans of the miserable man, the feeble cry of that "motherless babe."

"Cover the child, and call a woman to attend it," he cried, as, with all his force, he struggled with the man on the floor. After some time, when Renan's contortions became less violent, and he could for an instant relax his hold, he looked to see if his order had been obeyed. The men had gone. The dead mother, her now silent baby, and that heavily breathing figure at his feet, were all who shared the room with him. Quiet, except for the horrible stertorous breathing, Renan lay, an impurpled image of death. Leaving him, Matthew took in his arms the naked babe. It was barely breathing. Tenderly wrapping it in flannel, he dipped his hands in water, washed the little face, and baptized the dying child. Even as he held it, the poor little mouth opened in a faint gasp, the little body quivered, a gurgling in the baby throat, and on his heart he nestled a corpse.

"Poor innocent," he said, "even as thou camest into the world hast thou returned to the God who made thee." He kissed the cold brow, lovingly laid the dead baby beside its mother, and reverently covered them. As he did so, he heard voices outside.

"You can go in now. There was an evil spirit in the house. It entered the chairs, the irons, and various other things. We threw them outside, yet did it still torment the woman until she died."

" Dead ? And the child ? " said another voice.

" Dead also, we believe."

A step, and Matthew, turning, saw a rather good-looking young man standing in the door. He seemed frightened, advanced timidly, and said, in a hesitating manner, —

" Are you one of the ministers ? "

" No," answered Matthew. " I came here with Mr. Renan."

For the first time the young man saw the figure on the floor, and started back in horror at the purple face, the fixed stare of the dull eyes, and the white froth covering his lips, and lying in flecks on his breast.

" What has done this ? " he asked, shuddering as he turned his eyes away.

" His daughter's death." And Matthew, to give point to his words, and waken from lethargy this man's heart, uncovered the faces of wife and child. The man leaned for a moment over the dead woman, touched his lips to her cheek.

" Poor Rose ! " he whispered. " Every thing was done that could be done to save you."

" Sir," said Matthew sadly, almost sternly, " I do not know your name, but I conclude you are the husband of that dead woman. In her state, nature, strained to its uttermost, is in pain so intense, even barbarians respect the sufferer. A woman needs help, not laying-on-of-hands. Duty is, to God, fuller of prayer than spoken words ; and it is duty, sacred, most high, to minister to the tortured. That helpless infant, unwashed, uncovered, the wind blowing on its tender body, and chilling its feeble life, is as much the victim of neglect as if for days it had been left unfed. To the new-born, warmth is the necessity of life. They are now both dead. Gone to their Creator ! We are powerless to help them." Gently he drew the sheet over them ; and then, in softer tone, turning to the young man who stood as one dazed, " Help me move Mr. Renan from the room."

Nervously, reluctantly, fearful of touching the sick, the young man obeyed. But when Matthew, after making Renan as comfortable as possible, turned to go, with, "I will bring a physician from the city for your father-in-law," he caught hold of his sleeve.

"Let me go, let me go. I will hurry back. I cannot stay here alone with the dead, and that." And he pointed nervously at the unconscious Renan.

Thus Matthew was left, where he had so often been, tending the sick, and watching the dead; the only sounds, poor Renan's awful breathing, until, after a little, some women came in to lay out the bodies in the adjoining room.

Watching the ghastly face of the man so lately in health, Matthew prayed that God would fire the heart of Christine's husband, until, become his apostle, he should glorify his youth by wakening into active life laws whose might and power would stay this downward path of ignorance and sin. Too well did Matthew know the weakness of poor humanity to think that law can wholly conquer sin. But that law's power and that religious force should be used as levers thrusting towards sin, encouraging crime, were considerations that filled this high nature with sadness unutterable.

When the doctor arrived, he pronounced Renan dying. After several hours the heavy breathing grew slower, came at longer intervals, and then was succeeded by the gasps, tremors, and convulsions of death.

Gone! Life with its hopes, its labors, its woes, was over for him. And Matthew, leaving when he could no longer serve, found night had fallen, and John Smith's carriage waiting for him at the gate.

Back into the city, with its lights and bustle, Matthew carried the shadow of those tragic deaths. Yet calm his soul! Though his heart grieved, faith kept ever burning his spirit's lamp. For all this

pain and suffering he could see no object ; of these innocent sacrifices, no results. Yet God knew best. " Thy will be done." And
this holy submission shone from his face on Christine, as, from her
post at the window, where she had been watching for him, she ran
to open the door.

CHAPTER XV.

DIFFERENT THINGS TO DIFFERENT MEN.

THERE was a look of pain in her eyes that made him hold fast the hand she slipped in his as she sat near him ; while Malcolm half rose from the lounge where he had been dozing, and said gayly, —

"We passed such a pleasant day, only regretting your absence ! Mr. Jansen was very agreeable and obliging. Confessed himself so captivated by Christine, that he wanted to show us all the schools in the city. It was very edifying to see so many young-sters, each one, we were assured, fired with the desire of spiritual and temporal advance."

Matthew looked at Christine. She did not echo her husband's pleasure. Had it been such a pleasant day?

"I don't believe Christine enjoyed herself, despite the extreme compliments of our host." And John Smith smiled gently at her serious face.

No, she had not shared Malcolm's enjoyment. On leaving Matthew, they had driven to a house on the outskirts of the city. With its various wings, evidently built at different times, it looked somewhat like a public institution.

"Each wing represents a new wife," thought Christine, and sighed for the unhappy lot of woman. Yet was this better than in poorer houses, where oftentimes the bed of one wife touches that of another ;

as poverty compels the several women belonging to one man to share the same room.

"Why do you sigh?" asked John Smith, who, having taken Matthew's place at Christine's side, caught the soft pity of her breath. Her eyes passed over the house, and then came back to his face. Without other explanation he knew her thoughts. Indeed, most pleasant and strange charm of this new uncle, he seemed always to understand her.

"I would you did not feel thus," he said.

"I would it were not thus," she answered. And then Malcolm, with head leaning back, a sleeping Adonis, the bright light adding to his beauty, started up as the carriage stopped.

"I hope, uncle, Mr. Jansen is prepared for hungry folks. The air has made me ravenous," he said, as, lightly springing to the ground, he gave his hand to Christine. Helping her down, he retained her hand, and drew it in his arm, his uncle preceding them, as a woman's sharp voice sounded from one of the wings.

"Sarah Jane, jest you tell yore father I ain't a-goin' ter hev mutton fer my dinner, an' my chillern's, when Mandy's mother'll sit down ter goose."

A little girl ran out of a door, then, seeing the strangers, ran back quickly. Some words of scolding and urging from the sharp voice, and then a blow, and a child's weeping. But evidently the poor little one would rather face the mother's anger than the strangers' eyes. Malcolm laughed, — a charming laugh, yet it jarred on Christine as nothing from him had ever before done.

"Goose, is it, deary?" And he pressed his wife's hand. "I hope it's well cooked, for I'll do it honor."

Though his voice and manner were tender, yet the flush on Christine's face was not of pleasure. Petty though it was, she pitied the woman who felt her rights slighted; and the perpetual jangling of these creatures, forced into such close proximity, was brought vividly before her.

Their host, and the wife chosen to receive them, were most cordial to John Smith's relatives. But, above their welcome, Christine seemed to hear the sharp voice, and that quick blow to the little child.

The lunch, whereat appeared the goose, fat, and browned to Malcolm's taste, was most excellent. The Mrs. Jansen who did the honors was a pretty-looking Danish woman. Speaking English imperfectly, she atoned for her deficiency by pleasant smiles. Two sweet little girls sat near their mother, so quiet that one would fancy they, too, were foreigners. Christine's thoughts and sympathies were with the neglected wives, sitting in their lonely wings, and feeling themselves slighted. She could not enjoy the viands set before them; could not, except by silent attention, show her interest in the conversation. After lunch, bidding adieu to Mrs. Jansen, whose husband declined for her Christine's invitation to join them, they drove to the city. Charmed with the grace and beauty of Mrs. Malcolm Smith, and accepting her silence as the result of his own brilliancy, Mr. Jansen expanded into the most direct and tiresome compliments. He was a short, stout man, of swarthy skin, and coarse, curly black hair. A thorough egotist. One of those who accentuate their witticisms by winks, motions of fingers and thumbs, interspersed with, "Don't you see? Do you catch it?" and always, by their own laughter, showing their appreciation of home wit, and giving the signal to more obtuse listeners.

Malcolm, pleased with his lunch, and Mrs. Jansen's smiles, and a little flushed with wine, laughed heartily at Mr. Jansen's remarks, — too hearty and prolonged laughter if it had been other than Malcolm. But his face and form were the embodiment of joyousness; and his voice had such a clear ring to it, that Christine smiled, though failing to see the humor which so amused him. And John Smith smiled because she did. When they reached the school selected for the visit, Mr. Jansen, though lacking a half-head of Christine's graceful height, offered her his arm. And she, flushing, not quite used to this manner of walking through a building, seeing her husband's look, accepted it with dignity.

'A man is not great by his inches;" and lack of inches is not felt by either the man or woman when force, physical and mental, makes a woman gladly acknowledge lord and master. Yet if ever a small man, with small traits, shows most to disadvantage, it is when close to a woman whose face, seeking purer atmosphere, is lifted above his own.

But Mr. Jaasen did not feel this. Great in his own esteem, he never doubted the esteem of others, and grew quite confidential to Christine.

"OFFERED HER HIS ARM."

"You see, my dear madam" (and he gave a little snort of satisfaction after the manner of a water-dog), "these schools are one of our cleverest bits of management. The United States insists we shall have public schools" (a quick little shrug). "We always obey the United States" (a knowing wink), "so we have them. The taxes support them; and the Gentiles — those sons of perdition — pay their full share. Officers must be elected. God is just. We outnumber the accursed Gentiles; so, in elections, we have our own way. Good, faithful Mormons are trustees : good, faithful Mormons are superintendents. Mormon teachers are employed. The blessed book of Mormon revelations, given to our most glorious founder, is the Bible for these cells of learning, the guide to the growing youth, who will, ere the century closes, own and govern this great land from ocean to ocean. If for the present we are, by tyranny, forced to bow to that farcical government called the United States, yet, by the power of God, who watches over his saints, we are enabled to turn those very laws to our own use. And by this power we are enabled, with less expense, to educate, in holy Mormon doctrines, the coming rulers of the land."

He had been speaking very loud, as if addressing the hundred or more children, who, over their books, had been intently gazing at the visitors standing in the door-way. Warming with his subject, he had released Christine's hand, seeking his handkerchief to mop his head. Her face had flushed to rosy red. Feeling herself out of place, and misunderstood, thoroughly opposed to every word he had uttered, still she was unable to speak the thoughts that filled her mind. Could she, the wife and niece of Mormons, proclaim her opinion of their church? For the first time, through all her love, she felt the falsity of her position. She looked at the children with a heart full of pity, thinking what future fruit such teachings would bear. Bowing gravely to them, she moved on ; and her down-cast lids hid tearful eyes, — Mr. Jansen at her side, chuckling as at some huge joke, while with nods, winks, attempted nudges, and pointing of fingers, he thought he carried with him the entire sympathy of his listener. Again he offered her his arm. But this time Christine would neither see it nor Malcolm's face. Her husband was pleased with the admiration of Mr. Jansen. Its coarseness and boldness did not offend his delicate feelings. John Smith, on the contrary, resented the familiarity of his so-called friend. Never before had Jansen appeared equally offensive ;

and, as Christine moved away to avoid a more persistent nudge, he clinched his hand so tight that his glove was torn. He said nothing, however; for Jansen was a power in his way, and John Smith preferred tools to enemies. But presently, much to Mr. Jansen's surprise, he found himself talking to John Smith; while Christine walked beside her husband, who, with hands in his pockets, was trying to joke her about her conquest.

"It's slow fun teasing you, dear," he said, after a little; as his only answer had been a pained look from the lovely eyes. And then he thought how good and true she was, — how far above the trifling women, whose vanity, on the alert, catches at every crumb of praise. She was beautiful too: every one noticed that. He was a lucky fellow to have won her. And again she seemed to lift him up from the shallow current of his life, as in those days of sweet-breathed spring.

They drove Mr. Jansen to his city-office, where, with much flourish of compliment, he took his leave; then home, whence John Smith sent the carriage for Matthew. The quiet hour of waiting, John Smith relieved by pleasant converse; not talking too much, but, with introduction of new thought, striving to quiet Christine's flushed, excited face, that moved him strangely. And Malcolm, stretched on the lounge, beautiful, graceful, lazy, smoked and dozed, until, at Matthew's entrance, he sprang up gay and fresh as a boy.

Christine held her grandfather's hand in hers, — old, but firm, and so tender! How long she had clung to it! How faithfully it had guided her! To-morrow she would lose him. To-morrow would break the last link that bound her to her old life, — the natural one. And now in this new life, that to-night seemed so out of tune, she must walk alone. Alone! The thought came unbidden. Like skeleton at feast, it reared its ghastly head, frightening the love that was her bosom's guest.

"Christine!" Malcolm called her. Malcolm loved her! His voice, his look, sent the warm blood surging through her veins, flushing into deeper pink the roses on her cheek, and wakening the lustrous eyes into newer depth and beauty. Malcolm saw it, and drew her down to sit beside him. John Smith saw it, and, with serious eyes, gazed on her; while, for the first time in his life, his heart contracted in sudden, violent spasm of pain.

Matthew saw these two — husband and wife — looking tenderly at each other; and blessing them, praying for them, the old man forgot himself.

CHAPTER XVI.

THEIR MARRIED LIFE.

WHEN, the next morning, Matthew had to return home, and, taking his child in his arms, kissed and blessed her; when Christine, with tear-blinded eyes, that could no longer see the dear old face smiling at her from the car-window, turned to Malcolm in a mute appeal for sympathy, — it was John Smith's hand that clasped her own, and, drawing it within his arm, led her to the carriage as the cars rolled out of the depot.

She was thankful to him, yet grieved that Malcolm's was not the answering spirit, and, looking around to find him, saw her husband's handsome face in a group of other faces, chatting away, and laughing, apparently forgetful of any greater interests. There came over her heart an icy wind, that chilled the soft dew of her tears.

John Smith, watching her, and reading her feelings, was vexed with his nephew. He leaned out of the carriage, and called him. With his quick, light step, and smiling face, Malcolm came to them; and, noticing Christine's tears, he took her hand, and tenderly kissed it. Thus he atoned for his neglect. He had such a tender way of giving even the slightest caress, he did not find it difficult to win forgiveness from one that loved like Christine.

Weeks passed. Malcolm remained more away from home; and the long walks together, which, to Christine, had been such pleasure, came now at longer and longer intervals. Yet would she chide herself for her "loneliness," and find repayment for the day's stillness when evening would come, and, lying on the lounge, Malcolm would sometimes hold her hand as she read or sang to him, while he looked at her as tenderly as when they stood beneath the orchard-trees, and wandered through the country's sweet by-ways. But often, when she would raise her eyes from the book to find response in his sympathy to some thought that had touched her, she would see his eyes, so lately looking at her, were closed in softest slumber, and between the parted, smiling lips came regular breathing, telling of his quiet sleep : then she would reproach herself for the pang of disappointment that echoed through her heart.

John Smith came very often. His wives were still away, as was most of the fashionable Mormon world. Some now were beginning to return ; and Christine had many visits, and some invitations to quiet evenings. Malcolm had looked forward with exultation to the sensation she would make, but was annoyed almost to anger when he saw how quiet and reserved she became in society

Although for years Christine had lived in a Mormon settlement, she had not become socially accustomed to the plurality of wives. Feeling for polygamy the greatest abhorrence, Matthew had guarded her early girlhood from all intimacies that could wash away the blackness of this sin. Tabitha and her children had been her only intimate friends, to whose home she had gone freely and constantly. To all she went with Matthew when need or sorrow called them. When suffering humanity can be relieved, who stops to think of social, religious, or even moral, questions ? Not Christine, nor her example and preceptor, Matthew. And among the villagers, to whom all they had was freely given, it had not seemed strange that Matthew and his child never mingled in their dances and pleasures. Consequently, when, in

Salt Lake, Christine was socially introduced in Mormon families, polygamy had for her all the horrors of novelty.

Mr. Brown and the five Mrs. Browns, or Mr. Jones and his two wives, would, from the instant of her presentation, fill her with grief and shame for an institution that sanctioned such a state, and called it marriage. Intense pity for her sister-women paralyzed her quick ideas ; and, instead of delighting Malcolm's friends by her bright and varied discourse, they saw only a tall, graceful woman, with expressive face, and large, dark eyes, who rarely smiled, and spoke but little. That the smile was sweet, the words apt, did not seem to impress them. Malcolm bit his lip to keep back angry words. Yet for all her sweetness, and that still the glamour of her charms was upon him, he would have spoken his annoyance but for the evidently increasing admiration of his uncle. His appreciation of Christine, his enjoyment of her society, stirred the lagging affection of this beauteous youth, and still kept him from avowing even to himself a slight but growing *ennui* at the quiet domesticity into which he had hurried. Christine, brought up in a life of active good-doing, found her idle days very wearisome to her. Sharing each useful labor with her grandfather, listening to his earnest thoughts, she had known peace and contentment. She looked around, eager to find outlet for all her pent-up activity. But as now, Malcolm having less and less leisure, she timidly wandered forth alone, in all this great city she could find only the street-beggars who wanted any thing of her. Always she gave them something. It was the sole wish of her husband that she had opposed, when, as they walked together, these beggars had thrust their hands before her, and knocked at her tender heart with piteous tale. She had said to Malcolm, —

"Ah ! let me give a trifle, dear. If they are impostors, it is too little to injure any one ; and, if needy, I will not have refused my mite." To which he made no further remonstrance than a shrug, and "Oh, well !"

Soon he did not even notice the old bodies who had become regular pensioners on his wife ; for now he so " rarely had the time for pleas-

"THE BEGGARS THRUST THEIR THIN HANDS BEFORE HER."

ure," he explained to Christine, as, with eyes more than lips, she asked him for what she so dearly prized, — his company.

CHAPTER XVII.

WITH THE MRS. SMITHS.

AND John Smith! How was it with him, — a man long past forty, who had great wealth, and the greatest influence in all Utah, whose life's motive had been ambition, and for whom remained but one higher round on the ladder he had so successfully climbed.

He was studying a new character. This woman, young enough to be his daughter, with her earnest thoughts, her noble aims, her tenderness for all humanity, however fallen, was a fresh experience to him. When he first saw her as Malcolm's wife, their love and interest for each other amused him. It seemed a little drama played for him alone. And he would often wonder, if, in his youth, he had met such a woman, could she have satisfied the cravings of his nature? Would she have filled his heart, and made him happier than the cold goddess, Ambition, at whose feet he had laid every pure and joyous impulse of his life?

On their return to the city, Malcolm and Christine were invited to meet John Smith's three wives. The house was large and handsome, the parlors elegantly furnished. As Christine entered on the arm of her husband, and three ladies rose to receive her, her embarrassment would have been great; but John Smith, with ready ease of manner, came forward, and, leading her to the tallest of the three, said, —

"Letitia, let me present my niece, Mrs. Malcolm Smith."

Mrs. Letitia Smith bowed, and, extending her hand, said she was pleased to see her. Then Christine was presented to the other two Mrs. Smiths, and, by the order of presentation, knew they ranked as one, two, three.

She tried to entertain the three quiet ladies, but seemed to herself to utter only the stupidest commonplaces.

PRESENTED TO THE MRS. SMITHS.

Malcolm, who had quite a respect for the wives of his uncle, was really displeased with the impression Christine was making, then suddenly bethought him of her voice.

"Sing, Christine," he said.

"Will you sing?" John Smith interposed, and, opening the piano, came to lead her to it.

Christine, with grief, had noticed Malcolm's displeasure. She,

who had never met but loving glances, now saw a frown on the face
she most loved.

Timidly raising her eyes to John Smith, she said, —

" I will sing for you with pleasure if you like my voice. But I
do not play. I am so sorry," she added, turning to Malcolm as if in
apology.

John Smith had seen this country-bred girl move and act like a
queen. Always gentle, but always dignified, this timidity seemed
strange in her. And yet she never looked so lovely in his eyes as
now. He did not understand that the mainspring of her gentle dignity was simple truth of character. And always sure of pleasing the
dear grandfather, who had been her only critic up to Malcolm's coming, she had never felt timid.

" I will accompany you on the piano," said Mrs. Smith No. 3.

But John Smith, whose ears were very sensitive, dreaded the
effect of Mrs. Smith's music, and said quickly, —

" Thank you, my dear. But, as Christine generally sings without
accompaniment, perhaps she will thus be more at ease." Then, turning towards Christine, he said, " Will you sing ? "

His voice unconsciously took a more gentle tone in speaking to
her. Like his face, his voice was generally cold. But, at will, the
cold gray eyes would flash, and his voice possess the power and
variety of every human passion.

At these moments the whole man was transfigured. And John
Smith, who ordinarily appeared a middle-aged man of medium height,
and rather heavy build, with intelligent face, and cold, searching eyes,
seemed, by the force of a positive character and the gift of eloquence,
to tower above all surrounding men.

This change he could produce at will. And to this iron will he
made himself, his every impulse, and almost all who approached him,
the mere automatons. He did not use the slightest inflection of voice,

except in obedience to his mighty will. Yet at this very moment, at the timid raising to his of a pair of soft dark eyes, his voice had ceased obedience to its master.

Still hesitating, Christine turned to Malcolm with the question, "Which song do you most like?" trembling on her lips. Ah, how anxious she was to please him!

Seeing her motion, and not understanding, or not wishing to understand, he said impatiently, —

"Oh, do sing!"

Saddened and depressed, the girl's thoughts flew to her grandfather; and she sang one of his favorites, —

" I have left my snow-clad hills."

Her rich voice filled the room, and thrilled the hearts of her listeners. When the song died out, she did not move; the hands, which her grandfather always held while she sang to him, lying idly in her lap; the dark eyes, glistening with unshed tears, fixed on space. Her heart was still with the old man. She had almost forgotten where she was, until she heard John Smith saying to Malcolm, —

"She has a magnificent voice, and sings well. But she must learn the piano, or the effect in general society will be much lessened."

These words broke in on her dreams of home. She moved nearer the three ladies, who, like the three Fates, always made a group together.

"Thank you," said Mrs. Smith No. 1.

And Christine, feeling she had given pleasure, was repaid.

CHAPTER XVIII.

A SOCIAL TRIUMPH.

HE days passed on, each bringing some change. Acting on his uncle's suggestion, Malcolm at once supplied Christine with a teacher of music. Her supple fingers, natural talent, and great application, made her progress in the study appear remarkable. The long, lonely hours of the day she would while away at the piano, which, the morning after her first song for Mr. Smith, had arrived with a card, " From your uncle."

And sometimes, of an evening, when she would play some simple accompaniment to her voice's melody, John Smith would listen, and compliment her improvement, as Malcolm half dozed on the sofa.

While Christine's musical studies were still in their infancy, she scored a social triumph that delighted her husband; as few things she now did seemed to affect him. They were invited to the season's first large reception in the fashionable Mormon world. John Smith showed as much interest in Christine's toilet as if he were father as well as uncle.

When, in soft, pearly satin, with the crimson roses in her hair, at her throat, and in her hands, that he had sent for her adornment, she looked half timidly for Malcolm's approbation, John Smith thought he had never seen lovelier vision of woman. His heart throbbed wildly, his throat grew dry and hard, but his smile and manner were an uncle's calm admiration of his niece's charms.

"You look very well, my dear," he said quietly. While Malcolm, anew impressed with her beauty, kissed her soft cheek.

It was on this evening Christine was introduced to Elder Sanson and his two wives. He was a prominent and wealthy member of the church. The second wife had been but lately "sealed" to him. She was a fresh-looking girl, with an amiable, rather heavy, face, seemingly pleased to have gained the affection of a man in high standing with church and state, and though really young enough to be the daughter of the elderly lady who had for years been chief in her husband's counsels, yet was treated by her with a consideration amounting almost to reverence.

To Christine this phase of human nature was inexplicable. All the more, that Mrs. Sanson, senior, was a woman of intelligence and reading, whose strongly marked features told of resolute character. She seemed to recognize the rare gifts hidden beneath the quiet of Malcolm's wife. Perhaps this proceeded from the fact that John Smith, who introduced his niece to Mrs. Sanson, was an old acquaintance of the lady's.

Determined that Christine should be appreciated by one of the most highly esteemed women of the church, he remained near them.

Exerting his own charms of manner and conversation, he lifted the thoughts of Christine from the tenets and practice of a religion that were forever wounding her tender soul. For the moment forgetting that great moral wrong which crushed her thoughts with the silence of disapproval, Christine spoke as she had been wont. And though, unconsciously, each pure utterance was a reproach to the state of society wherein she found herself, these two pillars of that society seemed in sympathy with her fair thoughts.

They were sitting in a corner of one of the *suites* of rooms thrown open to receive the guests; and, interchanging thoughts and fancies, they found themselves congenial spirits. In all the dreary round of gayeties, wherein her husband's will had led her, this was one of the few evenings for Christine marked as pleasant. Soon after their arrival at the reception, Malcolm, seeing the constrained look and manner, which were the invariable result in Christine of being brought face to face with polygamy, with a muttered excuse left her to his uncle's care. Almost savage with anger, he hastened to another room, where some time later, jesting with some gay companions of bachelor days, the voice of his wife reached him. She was singing a Norwegian ballad of faithfulness and love. Once in those spring-days, which for him were quickly slipping into the sea of forgetfulness, she had given him a hasty translation of the song. And now each word, clear as then she spoke it, fell on his ear.

> " True to thee, beloved, though thy face I no more see,
>   True to thee, and knowing thou art ever true to me.
>   Once living, love cannot die; it is not a thing of earth;
>   From dust that forms the body, it springs to heaven where it had birth.
>   Like star of that bright heaven, it shines down on my soul,
>   Where half of me is waiting for this half that makes the whole.
>   The day is long and dreary, how dark and sad the night!
>   But I know that still thou lov'st me, and through death I'll reach the light."

An occasional chord of the piano reverberated through the rooms, a harmonious accompaniment to the rich voice. Conversation ceased. The melody was within the understanding of all. And the words, — did they touch any hearts?

At the piano Christine sang, her look most perfect illustration of her song. Standing near her was John Smith, quiet and self-controlled. But there was one from whose face those simple words had torn the mask. Mrs. Sanson! Seated in her chair near the piano, she had forgotten place, people, every thing but her own sufferings, and those who had caused them.

"CHRISTINE SANG."

Leaning forward, with one hand crushed against her side, the other raised and clinched as if it held a dagger, her face was drawn in fiercest passion. And, through the teeth, tight closed, with hissing sound came hurried breath. So the Borgia might have looked, as, furious at the insult to her name, she vowed vengeance on her wronger. It was this hissing sound that drew John Smith's eyes from the fair face of his niece. He started slightly as he looked at the woman before him; waited for a moment, half expecting to see in that up-raised hand the gleam of weapon ready to strike a deadly blow. And then he involuntarily followed the intense look of those eyes.

There, in another corner, were Elder Sanson and his young wife. He had evidently made some allusion to the song, and was holding her arm in a manner intended to be concealed. A bland, elderly smile was on his face. He was well satisfied with himself, and this young woman who belonged to him. And she, looking unaccustomed to such gallantries, was yet pleased with them in a good-natured, phlegmatic way. A curious smile parted the lips of John Smith, as, from them, his eyes returned to the intense face of the first wife. Apparently by accident he stepped on her dress, recalling her to herself, and the fact that Christine's hand had struck the final chord ; while in through open doors were crowding the guests, whose departure from the room had left it almost entirely to their little circle. It was then that John Smith had asked Christine to sing for Mrs. Sanson ; adding, as explanation of her lack of proficiency on the piano, " My niece has only begun the study of instrumental music, but we are quite proud of the progress she has made." Turning to Christine, he had said, —

" Sing the ballad you sang last night for Malcolm."

Complying readily and gracefully, her thoughts had been of Malcolm, and those happy days, when, wandering together, tracing the footsteps of beautiful spring in the flowers she had called to life, Christine had wakened to love.

And now the tenderness in her face had set one man's heart a-fire, but not Malcolm's. He felt only pride at the sensation her glorious voice had made. He flushed with pleasure as he saw the crowd surrounding the piano, beseeching new songs. And Christine, looking past all other faces to his, caught his smile of approval, and, with deepening feeling in her eyes, turned to listen to the thanks of Mrs. Sanson.

Perfectly self-possessed now, the lady spoke in her usual measured way, not a trace of excitement lingering in voice or face. John Smith felt a thrill of admiration, as at this moment Elder Sanson, with his new wife, joined the group around Christine, and the older wife moved, and graciously welcomed them beside her.

" Very pretty," said Elder Sanson, whose face bore index to a character that conscience would rarely stir to self-reproach.

" Very pretty," echoed the young wife. " Don't you think so, sister?" And she turned to her partner in the possession of the portly elder.

"Yes, my dear," answered Mrs. Sanson No. 1; and for a moment, in the kindliest manner, she rested her gloved hand on the plump white one of this strange sister. "It is a lovely song, and well sung."

Christine, looking at the two women standing thus in pleasant nearness, marvelled more and more at the powerful influence of Mormon faith over morals and hearts.

She was not, however, given much time for thought; as song after song was entreated, until John Smith, ever watchful of her, to relieve his niece, escorted to the piano a lady, who, shouting an operatic selection in very bad style, was loudly applauded.

THE TWO WIVES OF ELDER SANSON

At the close of the evening, when saying good-night to Mrs. Sanson, Christine was cordially invited to visit her, — an invitation which she returned, and in which she was so ably supplemented by her husband and uncle, that Mrs. Sanson promised to call very soon, and then won a pleased "Do, my dear," from Elder Sanson by saying, "I will not only call myself, but will bring with me my younger sister."

They bowed and smiled, and, with expressions of cordiality, separated. The picture of the two wives to the one elder, with hand clasped in hand, and between their smiling faces his fat one in evident approval of the peace in his household, stamped itself on Christine's memory. Involuntarily she shuddered at the awful power of Mormonism. Leaning on her uncle's arm, and preceded by her husband, she had nearly reached the door, when her sleeve was touched by a small hand, and at her side, in gray silk, stood a pale, timid-looking woman.

Early in the evening Christine had been presented to the lady, where beside four gorgeously dressed creatures, all co-wives of Mr. Berry, a large mill-owner, by force of contrast this quiet figure had attracted her. But, perhaps awed by the husband who stood more over than beside her, Mrs. Berry had only given Christine a quick, nervous bow, and then had looked hurriedly at him.

He was a tall, sallow-faced man, much wrinkled, and, despite his riches (Malcolm whispered, " He's a millionnaire "), having about him tokens either of constitutional ill-health or ill-humor. Christine was inclined to think the latter, as she noticed the frown which was his answer to his wife's timid glance.

His frown instantly disappeared as he smoothed his face into a smile, and spoke to the niece of John Smith, who, after a few moments' chat with the Berry family, had led Christine away. Spending the evening with Mrs. Sanson, she had seen no more of the showy group of women, among whom the pale one looked as out of place as a frightened mouse in a cage of peacocks.

Now, if possible, paler and more nervous, Mrs. Berry held fast to Christine, speaking in quick half whisper, as if anxious to finish before interrupted by her sister-wives, who, headed by their one man, were bearing towards her.

" Mrs. Smith," — the nervous hand on Christine's arm trembled, — " your voice has made me long to know you. Come to see me, at my own house. I live out near the mill, — only come to town when

obliged to do so.   Let me call on you, and take you back to spend
the day with me.   Let me come Wednesday.   I will be alone then.
Pray let me come."

She was so very anxious, was trembling with nervousness, that
Christine felt a true woman's instinct to protect this woman, by some
strange fate placed amid surroundings so unnatural.   Four wives, and
yet that man had to take this other woman!   How horrible was polygamy!   Christine thought of her Malcolm, and was blessed, resting
in his truth, as, taking the hand of this less favored woman, she felt
for her a sister's pity.

" You will not refuse," Mrs. Berry said eagerly.

" I accept with pleasure," Christine answered, "and shall expect
you Wednesday."

" Thanks, thanks."   And Mrs. Berry gave Christine a shadowy
smile.   It was chased away, however, as Mr. Berry came near, and
said in an undertone, but quite loud enough for Christine to hear, —

" Mrs. Alice Berry, you astonish me by your strange behavior in
society.   Could you not have waited for the other ladies and myself?"

Poor little Mrs. Alice made no answer, but timidly fell back, glad
to hide herself behind the gorgeous peacocks.   They fluttered around
Christine, spreading their gay plumage, and talking all at once, except
when their master spoke.   Then they listened in admiring silence,
coming in at the close with a chorus of ohs and ahs, expressive of
the wisdom of Mr. Berry, and their admiration of it.   The owner
of these gorgeous birds seemed much pleased and altogether smoothed
down by their delicate attentions.   For a moment, however, his look
wandered to the nervous gray mouse, that also belonged to him.   He
frowned heavily as he saw she was not even noticing him, or any
thing he said.   Her eyes, with her heart in them, were fixed on
Christine's face.

To the flattering speeches of Mr. Berry and his peacocks, Christine bowed acknowledgment. That their expressed desire to continue the acquaintance "so delightfully begun" was reciprocated by Malcolm, not Christine, and the invitation to call was given by him and his uncle, did not offend. They considered that this country-bred girl was awed by their grandeur and condescension. Then, too, John Smith's cordiality was something worth having. As for his niece, who, by the by, seemed a favorite of his, she was well enough in her way, but totally without style, thought these wise peacocks, as, with waving of plumage, and some extra flutterings of tail-feathers, the stately group moved away. One last look of entreaty the little mouse cast on Christine, and was then marched off in custody of her master ; for his manner of offering her his arm, to Christine's eyes, seemed more like the closing of a trap than an act of courtesy.

The evening had been a pleasant one, Christine thought, leaning back in the carriage, and looking at the silent figures of her husband and uncle. Yet, even as she thought it, she shivered ; for that timid little mouse, with beseeching looks and gesture, kept creeping over her heart, making it echo with pity for her, so young and feeble, in the grasp of the mighty institutions of Utah !

CHAPTER XIX.

A WOMAN'S CONFIDENCE.

WEDNESDAY morning came, bright and clear. Christine had told Malcolm of Mrs. Berry's invitation. He was delighted.

"They are awfully rich people," he said. "I wish you'd cultivate them, darling. They could be made very useful to me in a business way." And then, kissing his wife, he had not noticed the pained look on her face as he hurried off to "business." Christine would not acknowledge it, even to her inmost thought; yet she was often pained at Malcolm's veneration for money. In many ways would he show it. But she closed her eyes. She would not see any spots on the sun of her life. At the window, watching him down the street, she smiled at his graceful figure standing out from the more ordinary ones. How quickly he walked! Anxious to be at work! He was certainly very attentive to business. It was remarkable in one naturally so gay, and something that each one interested in him should appreciate, entailing, as it did, so many sacrifices. Was he not always regretting that he no longer had time for those long walks or talks with his "darling"? and then adding, with his gay laugh, —

"But it is all for your sake, love. I want to make money, so I can have time to enjoy your sweet company."

Truly, she ought to be grateful for such unselfishness. And yet,

what made the tears come to her eyes, and her heart throb with pain?
She brushed the tears away, and bravely hushed her heart. Malcolm
was true, was faithful; and, if she were lonely, she must endure it.
Then she hummed the song of faithfulness until the words soothed
her, seeming almost as if spoken
by Malcolm. Sitting at the
window, she saw pass
the little hunchback
who sold newspa-
pers. He looked up,
and nodded. This
was the boy Mal-
colm had once writ-
ten her reminded
him of Christie. Be-
fore her husband's
pressing business put
an end to his pleas-
ure, one of their
walks had been to
the paper-stand of the cripple. She had said to Malcolm, —

"Show me the child who looks
like my Christie." And they had
started at once. When she saw the
narrow, wizened face of the news-

THE NEWSBOY, — MALCOLM'S PROTÉGÉ.

dealer; when, with a leer intended to be funny, he had looked up at
her, and, in the manner of an old man, had said, "Mr. Smith, you's
got good taste, and knows a pretty face from an ugly one," — she
had felt a shock greater than a blow. He like Christie! And there
rose before her the pure face of her little friend, with its angel eyes

and quivering mouth, as he had looked when, lying in her arms, he had said "good-by."

He was a star that might shine in the crown of God. And this boy! With eyes screwed up in most knowing fashion, he was critically regarding Christine, while Malcolm, at her side, was laughing heartily at his compliment and his old manner. Quickly the woman's soul was stirred to pity as she looked on this unfortunate creation of the streets; necessity, and his surroundings, educating only the inferior parts of his nature.

Shrewdness, cunning, duplicity, all were marked on the little old face, and heard in the sharp, thin voice. His rudeness encouraged for wit, vulgarity laughed at as satire. Who could blame the child? Who could feel less than commiseration for him? Christine spoke kindly to him, in gentle words rebuked his familiarity; and he never more offended. Always having for him a pleasant smile, and patronizing liberally his stand, she became a favorite with this poor little waif. Discussing her with his crony, — a young knight of the ragged order, — he said, —

"She's a rum 'un. One o' yore Sunday-school sort, yet never preachin'. Jest a sayin' things in a soft way as makes a feller wish he didn't lie, an' starts him a-thinkin' 'bout hymn-tunes. She allus comes here. Don't never ferget a pore chap. Buys my papers an' books, an' allus gi'es me a little extra. Don't hev ter cheat her. Lor, no! She's reg'lar prime, she is! Axes arter my healt' as ef I wos the Pres'dent. An' don't like no jokes. She's the wife o' Malc. Smith, the pretty feller, wid blue eyes. They used ter walk out tegither. But now she plays a lone hand. And he!" A knowing wink and a whistle concluded the sentence. And then, a customer coming up, the boy began his jokes and talk, keeping the man laughing until he gained an extra dime.

"Fer my wit?" asked the hunchback. And as the man nodded,

and went on, he turned to his admiring friend, and said, "That's the way I fetches 'em."

The passing face of the newsboy had taken Christine's thoughts away from Malcolm back to her dear father, Christie, Patience, and Martin. Even Rex added his wise head to the loved group. Tender tears were in her eyes, almost blinding her to the sights of the street, when a handsome carriage drove up, and, the footman opening the door, there stepped down a little lady, — Mrs. Alice Berry.

Dressed in rich black silk, with an eager look of expectancy, she did not seem the same nervous, frightened creature as when overshadowed by her household gods. And when Christine, smiling a welcome, opened the front door, her answering smile made the pale face youthful, almost pretty, as she ran quickly up the steps, clasping the extended hand in both of hers.

Together they entered the house and the pretty little parlor.

"Quick! Your bonnet," said Mrs. Berry, in a sweet, girlish voice. "I'll have a day's holiday. We'll drive home, and, taking my boy with us, go to the mills, if you'd like. Or over the country, which, this morning, seems full of gladness for me."

She had a quick, nervous manner of speaking, which her sweet-toned voice, pleading looks, and beseeching little gestures, made very charming. She seemed so eager about this expected pleasure, in such haste to possess it, as if momentarily expecting the descent of the gorgeous peacocks, whose strong beaks would snatch away her crumb of enjoyment. Christine caught the infection, and did not feel safe from attacks from those stately birds, until, seated in the carriage, with Mrs. Berry's nervous little hands holding fast to hers, they rolled down the broad streets with the beautiful shade-trees on each side.

It was a lovely autumn day. As they passed under the great boughs, soft showers of leaves fell to the ground. The wind wafted a leaf through the open window. Mrs. Berry caught it.

"I am like this leaf," she said sadly, as she held it in her open hand. "Born and bred in Utah, nurtured a Mormon, yet is it killing me." Her smiles had vanished, and to the pale face had returned that nervous, frightened look. "See;" and she pointed to a long row of buildings, sitting back of little court-yards. "In those houses adjoining each other, built all alike, women waited day after day. Waited for the coming of that man whose slaves they were. Waited to catch the handkerchief that he would throw. From those windows mothers watched jealously, as caprice would incline him to favor another mother's offspring. Taken up, or cast down, as suited his passing fancy. Wives, mothers, but no sacredness of home, no protection of husband. And then, in later years, all neglected; and from behind their curtains they looked over the way to that handsome house, where, palled with their attractions, his fancy built a gayer cage for his latest possession. The great Brigham Young! The Apostle of Light!"

Her lip curled in scorn; and then more hurriedly, more excitedly, she went on. "How did these women endure this daily, hourly martyrdom of all that was best in them? God knows! Perhaps as I do, with suicide staring me in the face, looking out of every pool, beckoning me from every height." She was trembling violently. Her eyes dilated until the light blue was lost in the black of the pupil. Her hands, loosed from Christine's, seemed putting away some horrible temptation that allured, even as she repelled it. With a gasp of suffocation, she tore the lace at her throat, and called out, as if to actual existence, —

"Tempt me not. I have a child."

What could Christine do, what say in comfort to this woman, so small, so frail, yet torn with mighty feeling?

She put her arms around the slender figure, smoothed the soft hair of light brown; and as, at this tenderness, the slight arms clasped her throat, while sobs burst from aching heart, her own tears, in holiest pity, fell upon the pale face.

"Tears for me? Oh, thank you!" Then, quickly pressing her trembling lips on Christine's, Mrs. Berry smiled through all her weeping, as she said, —

"I shall never feel so desperate again. I have a child and a friend."

After a little, with soft touch of cool fingers on hot brow, and gentle words to divert her anxious thoughts, Christine had calmed the agitation of this sister-woman, who, like bird in fiercest storm, had beaten its wings against her heart, and, opening, the sanctuary had taken her in. Resting on that tender heart, the agitated face grew soft, and a stillness fell upon her wild despair. Presently, in gentle voice, she said, —

"If I might die now, and, with my baby in my arms, float away to that mysterious eternity, which puts the quietus on all our bitter woes! If you knew how I long for death! Is it not curious, frail as I am, I still live on?" And she held out a hand, from which, in her excitement, she had torn the glove. It was delicate and white, with every blue vein standing out under the thin skin. She looked slight enough for a wind to blow away, as she clasped her hands in her lap, and, gazing out the window, said softly, as if to herself, "But I could not die, and leave my child. Do you believe in God?" she asked suddenly.

"I do." In reverent voice Christine's answer came.

"And do you believe in polygamy?"

"No."

"No?" And Mrs. Berry flashed a look of amaze on Christine. "How, then, did you, a woman, marry a Mormon?"

"All Mormons need not be polygamists," Christine answered calmly.

"Need not be, but they are." Mrs. Berry's voice grew bitter as she went on. "Will a man restrain self-indulgence when society and religion urge him to it? when each woman that he takes to wife, binding her to slavery and sin, is counted a jewel in his heavenly crown? You wonder to hear me talk thus, — I, who have a one-fifth interest in a husband." Again scornful curves of her lips, and self-contempt in the face, as, with the two delicate hands, she beat her breast. "I hate myself for being the thing I am. And yet," — turning quickly on Christine, and putting her arms around her neck, she looked earnestly at her, — "and yet I read only pity in those eyes." Then, covering her face with her hands, she cried to herself. Unable to endure the sight of her suffering, and touched to her inmost heart by the loneliness of the drooping figure, Christine clasped her to her breast.

"Mrs. Berry, from my soul I pity your sorrow. I would I could comfort you. But I know not what to say, except that our afflictions, great as they may be to us, are sent by Him who made us. We must endure them, and lead pure lives."

"Pure lives! That is what tears my soul. I loathe this man who calls me wife. Yet, were I his true and only wife, I would endure my life, offering up its sorrow to that God you adore. But to feel each day and hour I am but a thing too base to call the mother of my child, to feel that my innocent babe is doomed to be what will make of other women the thing I am, maddens me."

Again the wildest excitement flashed from her eyes: again the pale face, blanched to marble, seemed to emit rays of white-heat. Her breath came so quick and short, that Christine, fearing each moment death itself would follow in this wild mood, besought her to be calm.

"For the child you love, control yourself," she implored.

"Yes, yes," answered Mrs. Berry, essaying in vain to speak. But from that dried throat, and shaking mouth, only broken words could come.

"I will — I will. Let me — tell you — what is killing — me. Perhaps, at night when — temptation comes, — when leaning over that — sweet face — I pray the eyes — that for me — light — the world — may never open — again, — when for that — angel child — my soul's soul — I see no safety — but in death, — perhaps — to know — there is one — one friend — who will pray — for a soul — in peril — may calm this — fever that — sets my brain — a-fire."

Exhausted, she leaned back in the carriage. Christine was praying for her. Only God could still the tempest that tossed this soul. With clasped hands, and upraised eyes, she pleaded for a breaking heart.

"Praying for me?" Mrs. Berry said in a whisper. And then, "Teach me to pray."

Without answer, Christine uttered the words her heart was sending up.

"O Lord, who made us, and who sees our woe, give us strength to bear it! We may not understand the need of agony. We may, in our sinfulness, feel it unjustly sent. Forgive us, and let us bear our cross as thou didst thine, with pity for another's grief, greater than our own, with forgiveness for the fellow-being who wrongs us. Save us from despair and sin. Open the way, that though in grief, yet in purity, we may walk. Have mercy on us, and give us strength to say, even from breaking heart, 'Thy will be done.'" Like manna from heaven fell the soft words on that famished spirit. Mrs. Berry, calmer, took Christine's hand, and held it to her breast, while down her white cheeks slow tears were falling. Then, with pleading look that made the words entreaty, —

"Are you my friend?"

"Yes." And Christine, stooping, kissed her brow. How hot it was! It almost burned her lips.

"Thank God!" was Mrs. Berry's answer to that little "yes."

Silence fell upon them; and Christine, looking from the window, saw with surprise they were still in the heart of the city. It had seemed hours since she entered the carriage, yet but moments could have elapsed since her pitying heart opened to this storm-driven soul.

"Friend," Mrs. Berry was saying softly. And then she smiled.

"Do you know," — she was speaking now in her natural manner, — "I am twenty-one years old; and, except my boy, I have never had a friend until now! I knew you would be my friend when I first saw your face. I will tell you my life, and then ask you what I must do. I was born here in Utah. My mother was a Mormon convert. God help her, and forgive her! for I know not what lies they told a free woman to induce her to become a slave. My father and she both died with some epidemic when I was a little girl, too young to remember either. I was brought up by the charity of the Mormons, in an institution where, from morning until night, the glories, beauty, and power of the Mormon faith are chanted into innocent ears. The revelation of the new books of the Bible, the visions of the founder of the faith, and, above all, his direct mission from Deity, became actual facts to my mind. If, at fifteen, I had been called on to die for the faith, I would have walked to the scaffold singing hallelujahs. Would to God that had been my fate! But a worse one was waiting for me. Monthly the elders, and other dignitaries of the church, would visit the seminary; and, after their departure, incidents in their lives, examples of courage, nobleness, generosity, were related to us, until, as the next visiting-day would come, I would feel a positive exaltation in breathing the same air with these holy men. Brigham Young, that earthly god, — for so he was made to us, — would sometimes honor us with a visit. Considered a proficient on the piano, and once having pleased his fancy, I was called to him. After a few words he held out his hand. Touching it with fingers still tingling with the melodies of great masters, I bent over that hand, and, as if it could open heaven's gate, pressed my lips to it. Bah!" And she spat as though some disgusting object had found its way to her mouth, rubbing it fiercely with her handkerchief to cleanse it from the stain.

"Among the girls in the seminary I had no friends. Their little schemes and plans pained me. And to them I appeared an enthusiast, too dangerous to be intrusted with their secrets. Oh, could I

"I BENT OVER THAT HAND."

but then have died!" She clasped her hands, gazing in sad regret at such possibility, then, with a deep sigh, went on, —

"One day I was summoned by the head of the school, and told that God, pleased with me, had inspired for me love in the heart of one of the great and good men of the church. I could have fainted from excess of humility. To me it was being allied to an angel. I did not even ask his name, but, hurrying to my room, fell on my knees, and prayed to be worthy of such blessing. The day came. I was taken to the Endowment House. Even that disgusting and absurd formula did not open my eyes. Where my modesty was shocked, I thought it my sinful nature, and called to mind the angels' purity, whose raiment was holiness. But when, with tears of humility, I stood trembling before a tall figure, not daring to raise my eyes; when, in the sacred light of my new home, I fell at his feet, and, not yet looking in his face, said, 'I am not worthy to be the wife of a saint,' a cross voice replied, 'Get up. Don't be a fool. I didn't want an idiot : I've four already. I married you because I believed you had some mind, and might be able to bear me a son, who could be some-body, not a brainless doll like the other brats.'

"If the earth had opened before me, I would not have been so terrified. This cross voice, this peevish face, and, above all, these unworthy words, shattered my faith in religion and man. Was this a sample of the saints I had honored? Was this one of the men whose sanctity, held up as model, I had in vain desired to imitate? Great God, was it all hypocrisy? With beating brain, and bursting heart, I was another being. That man had murdered my true self. I looked down on the corpse of the girl who had entered that room, and turned to fly. But no escape. A little girl of sixteen in the grasp of a man!" She covered her face, and moaned, as if the bare remembrance was intensest pain.

Then, for the first time with a burning flush coloring the pallor of her skin, she went on. "After that hour of horror, torn from the belief which had been the staff of my life, I began to investigate. I looked on the deadly sins of what they called 'God's Church.' I saw the poor oppressed with the heavy tithing they could ill afford to pay, and knew it flowed into the treasury to enrich the already wealthy. I saw girls forced into a bondage they abhorred; saw the actual bar-ter and sale of daughters by unnatural parents; saw the perpetual bickerings and heart-burnings between these *sister*-wives. Oh, satire on the name! I saw the mask of falsehood held over all, by some for fear, by others for gain; saw intelligence crushed, advance opposed, love preached, malice practised; marriage between those so near of kin, that Nature herself marked such unions accursed. And my heart filled with bitterness, as looking on this beautiful world, the grandeur of these mountains, the wonders of this interior sea, I asked, Is there no better teaching, no higher law, than this from which my soul recoils? Once being quite alone, and trembling at my own temerity, I went to the office of the Gentile journal, and, with that sheet hidden in my muff, returned to my house, where in quiet I could read, and then hid my face, ashamed that even the loneliness of my chamber should look on what the world called women like me. From that day I read every thing I could buy, stealing like a thief to stores forbidden by the Mormon church, hiding, like sins, the books and journals, that educating my mind, were pressing daggers through my heart. At last, timid, alone, almost without money, I resolved to leave Utah. Rich as he is, Mr. Berry keeps the purse-strings, making each member of his family dependent on him. But, poor or rich, I could not longer endure the degradation of my life. I was living in Salt-Lake City with the four other creatures called Mr. Berry's wives. They are sisters. Think of it, — sisters! And their constant warfare over each article given or promised to the other sickens one's soul. The children, poor little victims, I pitied them; and they returned my little kindnesses with affection. Yet, incited by their mothers' bickerings, what fearful words and quarrels pass between them, hardly out of swaddling-clothes! The very day when, breathless with the excitement of my hidden purpose, I left the Berry mansion, intending never again to return to it, I heard the voices of those sisters raised in tones and expressions that belong only to the lowest order of creatures.

"I hurried along the streets, overpowered by agitation. At the entrance to the depot, where I intended to buy my ticket, I paused for an instant to catch my breath, and calm myself, that nothing in

my manner would excite suspicion. With veil pulled down, I had
entered the door, when the world seemed crumbling at my feet. I
was clutched in a grasp like a vise ; and a voice, that made my blood
stagnate in my veins, said, very softly, just in my ear, —

" ' Mrs. Alice Berry, you have made a mistake. Your carriage is
waiting for you.'

" Desperate, I looked up and down, to see one human being to
whom I could appeal ; but, except a group whom I knew to be Mormons, there was not a soul in sight. I tried to scream, but, shaking
with nervousness, could not utter a sound. In vain I struggled to free
myself from that cruel hold. I was powerless. Almost lifted from
my feet, he put me in the carriage, closed the door with a bang, and
I was alone with the man who had ruined my youth. He held my
wrists in his hand, crushing them with a malice that made him hideous. Facing me, leaning towards me, speaking in cold, deadly whispers, a passer-by might have thought his manner affectionate. Perhaps
this was intended ; for, as if acting under instruction, the driver was
taking us through all the principal streets. But the words Mr. Berry
uttered are burned into my memory.

" ' Fool, traitor, idiot ! Did you suppose your outgoings and incom-
ings were unnoticed ? If it were not I have hopes the child you are
bearing will be a boy, I'd drive this moment to the boiling spring, and,
holding you over its seething water, let you taste the hell you deserve.
If you are the mother of a girl, I shall confine you for life in the
lunatic-asylum. It is the only safe place for such as you. If a boy
comes, it depends only on yourself whether or not it be taken from you
in its infancy. From this moment you go no more alone on the streets
of Salt Lake. I have prepared a residence for you near the mill. We
are now on our way to it. When you visit the city, you ride, and the
coachman is instructed to inform me of each place you enter. Three
miles is the limit of your country-drives. Beware, for I know how to

punish disobedience! Now, Mrs. Alice Berry, keep my command-
ments. If your child is a boy, such as I desire, you shall not lack
for comforts, and shall remain near him as long as you are necessary
to him.'

"These last words, spoken in a lower tone than the others, pressed
yet more cruelly on my soul. They have created a terror that never
leaves me. As Mr. Berry ceased speaking, he loosed his clasp; and,
stiff as a corpse, I fell back in the carriage. When we reached the
house, which since has been called mine, alarmed at my condition, not
for my sake, but for the safety of the son he desired, he sent for
physicians. He would not trust to the laying-on-of-hands when a possible son was in jeopardy. Ill and threatened as I was, I would have
made an appeal to the doctor, who was a Gentile; but, at each visit,
Mr. Berry sat close at my bedside. I heard the doctor say to him
one day, —

"'The lady looks extremely young. Did you tell me she was your
wife?'

"'Yes, my dearly beloved and only wife,' answered that man I
loathed.

"'Why,' — the doctor looked surprised, — 'I have always heard,
Mr. Berry, that you are a polygamist!'

"'Doctor,' — and lying, basely lying, that man's voice never faltered, — 'the Mormons are much slandered. There are spiritual rela-
tions, which are recognized in a spiritual manner. But most of us
have but one wife.' He dared say this before me, who had lived in
the house with women having as much claim as I to the title of wife,
—women who had borne to him children, as truly his as that baby he
was expecting. I was strangling with horror at his depravity, and
started up in bed, determined then and there I would unmask the
hypocrite. But the doctor, who had thought me sleeping, was alarmed
at my face. He came to my bedside, urging quiet; and over his

shoulder, without making sound, Mr. Berry's lips formed one word, 'Remember, remember!' Could I forget his threat?

"A week after, just nine months from the day I left the seminary, I was a mother. My boy, my beautiful boy, was born. He would have been taken from me, and given to nurse: but thank God,' — and her eyes were raised to heaven, — 'thank God, my milk was plenty and rich; and the doctor declaring a change might injure the infant, my baby was left to me. I saw no more of the doctor,

"REMEMBER!"

but I had my baby. Oh, the delight of his soft little face to my breast! His pure eyes looking into my soul chased away my bitter thoughts. I loved him, until earth, sky, heaven, were centred in that little body; and he loved me. Long before he could speak, his eyes would follow me everywhere. Strange to say, though his every wish is gratified, and though never by word or look have I done aught to influence him, he cannot like his father. Never will he go near him, except at my entreaty; and, from the moment he could walk, I have seen his little hand rub the cheek his

father kissed. His father sees the child dislikes him, and he curses
me for it. 'He has sucked traitor from your breast,' he hissed in my
ear, when first he noticed the baby turned from him. His four wives
see the child avoids his father, and incite him to anger. Mr. Berry
has told me, that on David's fifth birthday he will be quite old enough,
and shall be sent to school, — to a Mormon school, where his mother
may see him only at the will of Mr. Berry, where his soul will be
tutored as mine was, to break his heart, and ruin his life. David told
his father, that, if taken from me, he would never eat again. It may
seem unnatural; but so strong is the character of my boy, that once,
enraged at him for the repulsion the child cannot control, his father,
forcing me into a carriage, took me to Salt Lake, and kept me there
two days. But he brought me back himself; for a messenger came in
haste to say David was dying, that since my departure he had not
tasted food. That was five months ago. Since then, I am not allowed
to take the child to the city; and a watch is kept on me day and night,
lest I should attempt to carry away this boy who is to inherit his father's
name and wealth. In two weeks more my boy will be five years old.
Will he be taken from me? I tremble at every word that his father
speaks, dreading lest it be the sentence that will drive me to despair.
I tremble at every look of the four wives, lest I see in their eyes exultation for what is coming to crush me. They hate me because my child
was the desired boy, and I fear them as I fear every one who wants my
child torn from my arms. What am I to do? Can you tell me?"

With piteous gesture she looked into Christine's face. But what
answer could Christine give? What hand but God's could lift the
blackness that shrouded this life? Christine could only say, "Friend,
we will pray God to show us the way;" could only hold the nervous,
fluttering hands in her own, and, in earnest voice, utter what from such
a woman was solemn promise, — "I know not how to help you; but, if
to you there ever comes a way, tell me, and I will do it."

Just then the carriage drove up before an iron gate opening into a large, carefully tended garden ; and inside the gate, with outstretched arms, and sweet voice calling " Mamma, mamma ! " was a most beautiful boy.   Strong, well formed, tall for his age, with handsome head held proudly up, and bright eyes full of spirit and intelligence, he was a child to waken pride in a parent.   Jumping from the carriage, not waiting for the footman, his mother ran to meet him, and caught him to her heart as he sprang towards her.   From the tenderness of their greeting, they might have been parted months.   But is not every moment an epoch to hearts and lives like these ?   So thought Christine, looking in wonder at the woman's face, transformed into beauty by the rapture of mother-love.

CHAPTER XX.

MOTHER AND SON.

BIDDING the coachman return at sunset, and declaring they would spend the day in the garden, and in the white dust of the mill, David, holding fast his mother's hand, with loving wilfulness guided her wishes. He it was with joyous voice proclaimed that lunch should be served under the trees, and with imperious gesture, softened by natural sweetness, bade the servants do his mother's will. To Christine he frankly held out one little hand, saying, as he looked in her face, "I like you, because mamma does." But soon, when she smiled, sang, and talked to please him, he amended his first greeting, telling her he liked her for herself a "little bit. But my love, you know, is all mamma's. I've none to spare."

The table, spread under a beautiful evergreen, was covered with dainties. First seating his mother, David pulled Christine gently to her chair. "Mamma first, always mamma first," he said as explanation. Then he drew his own chair close to his mother's, leaned his head on her breast, kissing her pale face until it caught some of his own brightness. He laughed as he said, —

"See, mamma, I've brought roses to your cheeks."

His joy wakened hers. Her burdens cast aside for this hour of pleasure, she bloomed into youthfulness. After lunch, hand in hand with her boy, she ran on before Christine, showing her the treasures

of the garden. Her laughter echoed David's. And when, as sudden
cloud overcasts the sunshine, memory and fear would whisper in her
ear, and the brightness pale, David's "Laugh, mamma. I cannot
laugh alone," called out afresh the sweet sounds of mirth.

They plucked flowers for "mamma's dear friend," showed her the
fountain on the front lawn, the trees that David loved. And then, slipping his other hand in Christine's, David, run-
ning between the two, drew
her and his
mother to

the back of
the house.
Here the
grounds, more
extensive, were ar-
ranged in a miniature
park.

"Come see my pretty
well," cried David. "It

DAVID BETWEEN CHRISTINE AND HIS MOTHER.

always frightens mamma, yet it is so wise."

In the centre of a grass-covered mound, with a marble curb around
it, was the well, with water cool and delicious.

"I kneel, for mamma trembles if I stand near the well. But
listen, listen; for my wise well will answer aloud a whispered
word."

Down on the grass he bent his pretty head over, until his mouth
just passed the stone barrier.

"Who do you love?" he said softly. The echo from the well repeating, he shouted out in glee, "My mamma, oh, my mamma!"

Through the sweet voice thrilled feeling too deep for baby years; and as the loud echo took up the words, repeating in goblin tones the child's musical laughter, a strange shiver passed over Christine. The distinct words, unnatural laughter, the boy's bright face and graceful figure, seemed mingled as in a dream, that not fearful, yet produces in blood and nerves the sense of horror. A sound from his mother, and David's laughter ceased. Running to her, he cried, as if in pain, "Mamma, mamma!" he threw his arms around her, caught at her waist, and tried to pull her down to him.

Deadly pale, all her brightness gone, she seemed dragging herself from some influence that forced her forward, where her eyes, in dilated horror, were fixed upon the well. Christine started towards her; when with a shudder, and as if struggling with some unseen power, Mrs. Berry staggered back to the stone bench, to which she clung as to anchor of safety.

Christine had realized the danger, had felt the woman's temptation, and now, with face hardly less pale than her own, sank on her knees beside the child.

"David,"—she spoke from trembling lips,—"as you love your mother, never go near that well, and never let your mother go. It is a dangerous place. Ask your father to have a cover made, with a pretty little boy on it, who can tell you more secrets than ever the deep and terrible well."

"O mamma!"—and the child clapped his hands,—"we'll have a little boy to say good-morning to us when the sun shines."

Mrs. Berry tried to smile in answer to her child, but could not. When he saw her sad look, his lips quivered; and, clasping him in her arms, she burst into tears. Then Christine knew for this hour the tempter's power was gone.

Still holding David, great boy as he was, Mrs. Berry walked slowly through the trees on the road leading to the mill. Christine, at her side, seemed guardian angel, warding off the temptations, that, strong and terrible, assailed the unhappy woman.

"It did me good to carry him," Mrs. Berry said, when, near the mill, panting with fatigue, she loosed her hold, and let David slip to the ground. And, though she was very tired, Christine saw the truth of her words in the softened look that had replaced the wildness of her face.

The mill was an object of great interest to Christine. Her grandfather was the largest wheat-grower in his section of the country; and the improvement in mill-machinery had been of great benefit to all Utah, as wheat had become one of its principal products. At first the machinery was so imperfect, that Utah flour was quoted of inferior grade. But, in the last few years, great progress had been made. The Territory was rapidly advancing, and could now hold its own against the California crop. With this important change the name of Berry was associated, and Christine found every surrounding of interest. The mill was a large stone building, its machinery of the finest, and its capacity the most extensive in Utah. Safely stored, and in great quantities, was the grain in whole; while in a large depot, ready for transportation, were piled hundreds of sacks of flour.

The superintendent of the mill, a pleasant-looking Norwegian, was charmed at meeting a country-woman in Christine; and, with the delight experienced by even the voluntary exile, they began at once to speak the sonorous tones of their Northland. David was so highly delighted with the strange words, that his merry laugh resounded above the whirr-rr of the wheels. The mill was examined: and then they went to the little building, and primitive machinery, that, by Mr. Berry's command, were kept in running order; being the pioneer mill of the Mormon community. After a pleasant hour, Christine, with a hearty hand-shake from her compatriot, said farewell, and, with David and his mother, walked back to the house. In the parlor more wealth than taste was displayed ; the only beauty of the room being a large portrait of David, — lifelike, as at this moment he stood beneath it, the proud head, and bright face with an eager look of expectancy, as if mamma were coming. Upon him the sunlight fell through leafy boughs ; and, for background, the house and mill, to which this boy was heir. In the one picture were united the child's bright beauty and his father's pride.

At the piano Mrs. Berry rendered symphony after symphony in masterly style, surprising in so fragile a creature ; while David, standing near, his little hand resting on her side, watched her with dreamy eyes, whence spoke musician's soul. And Christine, looking at this mother and son, their wonderful love and adverse fate, was to her own heart repeating her grandfather's prayer, stilling her questionings of the incomprehensible with his constant words, "Thy will be done." "The day was done ;" and they were standing on the broad porch, watching the sunset, the carriage waiting at the gate ; and David, holding Christine's dress, was saying in his manner, half coaxing, half imperious, "Come soon again to see my dear mamma," when a horse's hoofs were heard ; and the rider, like a dark cloud, hid sunshine from the face of mother and child.

With pleasant greeting to Christine, and a few words to his wife, Mr. Berry held out his hand to David. How strange to see the little fellow, his face grave as an old man's, walk slowly to his father, and, barely touching the dry, hard fingers with his soft ones, quickly withdraw his hand ! Through even the sallow skin of Mr. Berry shone the hot flush of vexation. He frowned heavily, remembered Christine, and forced a smile. She saw the effort, and was about to make her adieus, when a beseeching look from Mrs. Berry detained her. Again she had become the frightened mouse of their first meeting,

in such terror of this man, her master, and so friendless, except for
the little child holding her hand, that Christine still lingered. And
though her heart was longing for Malcolm, and fearing her absence
might delay his dinner, never did she so exert herself to please. But,
despite her efforts, Mr. Berry looked cross and absent-minded, glancing ever and anon at David, whose little face was drawn in a frown
that produced the first resemblance to his father's.

Who can lighten the oppressive atmosphere of family disunion?
Christine, feeling the failure of her purpose, rose to go. "Good-by,"
she said to Mrs. Berry, tenderly holding the trembling hand. From
her lips, and with her look, the words took deeper meaning. "Good-
by" to David, resisting her desire to kiss the rosy cheek he held up
to her. Then, escorted by Mr. Berry, she walked to the carriage,
dreading the moment, when, closing the door. he would make his farewell bow, and, in his present mood, return to wife and child.

To her surprise, with a strained attempt at gallantry, he said,
"Mrs. Smith, may I see you safely home?" And, to his surprise, she
accepted. Her sweet smile sprang from the thought, that for an hour,
at least, Mrs. Berry would have quiet, and perhaps in an hour Mr.
Berry might be more amiable.

If ever woman could charm away anger, Christine was she. She
spoke of the mill, its improvement, and present perfection; and Mr.
Berry's face lightened. She praised the gardens, the beautiful trees;
and he smiled. From them to David, whose bright intelligence, and
strong character, made easy, almost sure, high predictions for his
future. And then she won his heart, or, rather, his apology for that
truer, better part of man. His face lost its peevishness as he talked
of his plans for the child's future, — how wealth should spread open
for him all the pleasures and information of travel; how its might
should for him make easy the delights of ambition and political power.
Filled with his own ambition, he had forgotten the tender years, and

thousand possibilities, that might arise between the little child and his manhood. To him, David was the embodiment of his own desires; and, wrapped in his future plans, he thought not of the present. Listening to him, as if a picture had been unfolded to her vision, there came before Christine that fearful well, David bending over it, and a few feet off, clinging to the stone bench, his trembling mother. A shudder passed over her.

"Mr. Berry," she said, breaking in on his dreams, "I think you owe it to David's safety to have the well covered."

"My dear madam," — his tone was filled with a species of pity for her lack of comprehension, — "David is no ordinary child. In spite of his years, he has intelligence equal to most men. He would no more lean over that well than I would. It is a remarkably fine well, sixty feet deep." And again the pride, that, for him, was all the pleasure he had in his possessions.

Sixty feet deep! What a fall for human body! Christine blanched at the bare thought, and then with incident of accidents, with her own fears, tried to arouse Mr. Berry to proper care in this matter. "A fall there would be almost certain death, and an accident might happen even to a man."

Mr. Berry moved uneasily. Death associated with David! He looked angrily at the one who dared suggest it. Then, meeting her earnest eyes, and hearing her words, as, unnoticing his look, she was quietly talking, he ended by agreeing with her. "An ornamental cover, with an iron railing on the marble curb, would be an improvement to the grounds, and protect from accident men as well as children."

"I shall give the order as I ride back home," Mr. Berry said; and, handing out Christine, he re-entered the carriage.

She looked up at the windows with an expectant smile. Malcolm would be watching for her! No! Only her little maid, bowing and smiling to her mistress as she ran down to see if there was any thing to be carried in the house.

Mr. Berry drove off : and Christine, in her quiet home, waited for Malcolm until the clock struck seven ; then, taking a cup of tea, she sent away the untasted dinner, listening in loneliness to each passing footstep.

After an hour, John Smith called. He was full of interest in her day, in her description of the mill, and agreed with her as to the intelligence and charms of Mrs. Berry. So fresh and pleasant seemed every detail to him, even the flowers that David gathered, that Christine did not imagine her uncle knew the gardens far better than she, and had always found Mrs. Alice Berry an extremely quiet, uncomfortable sort of a person. It was all changed now for him ; and, had Christine been capable of betraying her friend's confidence of her married life, John Smith would doubtless have pronounced Mr. Berry a brute. Yet Mr. Berry and he had been for years more or less associated in political matters, a connection that would likely endure. Only now, looking at the dark eyes and graceful figure of the woman before him, feeling for her what was a resurrection into new life, other matters, other persons, were of trivial importance.

It was late when Malcolm reached home. He greeted his wife affectionately, was delighted to find his uncle with her, said he was "tired out," and threw himself upon the lounge, where, with flushed face, and eyes unusually bright, he seemed absorbed in exciting thought.

"Calculations," he answered, as Christine, drawing her chair near, slipped her fingers in the hands clasped above his head, and, in voice tender and arch, asked, "What is it ? "

After a moment he rose, and leaned his elbow on the mantel-piece, shook off "business anxieties" with a laugh, and began talking in his gay, careless manner, falling ever and anon into reverie, and always

with that excited look which so became him, and the smile that made
his mouth more beautiful.

Somehow, — she could not have explained it, for no shade of doubt
was on her soul, — the delight that his presence had brought her was
gone ; and over her, like cold mist, came a nameless sadness.

John Smith, saying good-night, took in the group of husband and
wife, — his face, eyes, figure, all full of something that had apparently

"'CALCULATIONS,' HE ANSWERED."

delighted him ; and she, pale, still, with bended head, down-cast eyes,
and the two slender hands clasped nervously together.

"Good-night." And, gently laying his hand on hers in the tenderest caress he had ever permitted himself, he forced her to look at him.
The dark eyes were full of tears : the tender mouth had a droop in
its soft curves that made him shiver. Yet she smiled for answer.
Just then she could not speak without losing self-control ; and John
Smith, turning quickly, laid his other hand affectionately on Malcolm's
shoulder as adieu, and left the room. No one had noticed the hand
that had touched Christine's was hanging at his side tightly clinched ;

and, though first at the hall-door, he waited for Malcolm to open it. For a few moments they stood in the night-air talking pleasantly. Promising, in reply to Malcolm's urging, that he would see as much as possible of Christine, his uncle walked slowly down the steps. As the door closed, leaving him alone in the street, he opened the clinched hand, kissed it passionately ; then, as if he were violently throwing away something it held, he said, in intense whispers, " Fool, fool!" stopped for a moment, raised his hat as though its weight oppressed, and, an instant afterwards, calm, cold, passed on his way, — a man feared by some, admired by many, known by none.

CHAPTER XXI.

A VISIT AND ITS CONSEQUENCES.

FEW days after her first visit to Mrs. Berry, Christine received a call from the two Mrs. Sansons. The elder lady leaned on the arm of the younger, as mother might on daughter. With flattering attention she listened to every commonplace, ill-spoken sentence of this new sister. Looking up quickly, Mrs. Sanson, senior, caught the expression of Christine's face. It was wonder, — wonder that human being could thus completely accept the position forced upon her ; wonder at the harmony existing between women in such strange relationship, all the more remarkable for the natural force and intelligence of the elder woman. With a smile, perfect in its calm, Mrs. Sanson answered her thought : —

"Does it seem so strange to you, my dear, that I should be content, after so many years of married life, to take the second place in my husband's affection ?"

She spoke very quietly, the strongest expression of her face being amusement at Christine's embarrassment. Her face flushed to scarlet, Christine knew not what to reply. She could not speak untruth, nor could she offend good breeding.

Mrs. Sanson waited a moment, and then, with another smile at the blushing, silent Mrs. Smith, went on in serious voice, —

"For us, good Mormons, true children of the true faith, polygamy is the divine right of man. If our husbands will it, we must submit, —aye, joyfully welcome our new sister to our hearts."

Saying these words, this elderly lady took the hand of the second wife, held it for a moment, and, pressing it gently, released it, as turning on Christine eyes more fierce than soft, and with a twitching of her lips that seemed out of keeping with her calm voice, she said, —

"I hope, my dear, when your time comes, you will be blessed with like strength."

Before Christine could reconcile those fierce eyes and nervous mouth with the gently spoken words, before the flush had faded which indignantly rose to her cheek at the bare suggestion of Malcolm's ever acting so cruelly, Mrs. Sanson had lightly changed the subject, and now, with just enough sarcasm to be spicy, was discussing their mutual acquaintances.

She did not speak another serious word until, by some accident, Mr. Berry's name was mentioned.

"A most admirable man, full of ambition and capability. He is one of the shining lights of our church. His first four wives are excellent women, living in that beautiful harmony which is one of the effects of our religion. But the last wife!" — And here, with a little shrug, and a side-glance at Mrs. Sanson No. 2, who was absorbed in looking at photographs, Mrs. Sanson, senior, grew confidential. "The last Mrs. Berry is certainly not quite right. Insane, some call her. Mr. Berry's most intimate friends have advised him to have her placed in some retreat. She has been a great disappointment to all who knew her as a child. She was educated by the charity of our church, given every advantage by its munificence, and had, up to her marriage, shown proofs of unusual ability. Her music was remarkable; and some verses of hers have become standard hymns, so filled are they with zeal and fervor. Yet now she actually lives outside the pale of our holy faith, and once, when spoken to of her religion, dared to say she was no Mormon in belief. It is strange God permits such ingratitude. Ah, indeed is Mr. Berry to be pitied! The only explanation is, the total unsettling of her mind, — the loss of that very intelligence which made Mr. Berry stoop to marry her."

During this long speech, which Mrs. Sanson's voice made harder to bear, Christine had been struggling to control her indignation at this misconception of her new friend. Full of the true character of this woman so misunderstood, yet she dared not express her thoughts, lest she should increase the dangers surrounding Mrs. Berry.

Controlling her excitement, and speaking quietly, Christine replied she had lately spent several hours with Mrs. Berry at her own house, and that never had she met a more interesting or gifted woman. Not allowing herself to be daunted by the raised brows and sarcastic smile of Mrs. Sanson, she then spoke of the Berry mill, and of her own interest in it because of her grandfather's occupation. Thus turning from personal to general matters, she hoped she had not offended this elderly lady, nor made her the enemy of that unfortunate young mother who seemed to have drawn upon herself the dislike of the Mormon community. An audible yawn from the young wife made Mrs. Sanson laughingly remark, —

"Youth's beauty and innocence must excuse its forgetfulness of social law." And then she shook her fingers playfully at her sister's too candid rejoinder, —

"Well, I'm tired."

"Poor child!" as if speaking to her own little one. And then to Christine, with the grace of manner consequent on long experience, she said, as she took her leave, —

"You young ladies must forgive an old one, if, in her own pleasure, she forgets it may not be mutual."

Still leaning on her sister's arm, she entered her carriage. Christine, thinking over the visit, felt it had not been a success; felt that, despite her desire, and Mrs. Sanson's compliments, she had not pleased this esteemed friend of Malcolm's uncle. What a strange hard glitter in her eyes! Had her defence of Mrs. Berry incited anger in this woman of influence among the Mormons? The thought made Christine sick and nervous, made her long all the more for Malcolm. Yet — and with this thought came sadness — she knew he would be vexed with her for her failure in making friends. Presently his step and laughing voice mingled with John Smith's quiet one; and, telling Maggie to lay another place at table, she opened the parlor-door for husband and uncle.

"How pretty you look, love!" Malcolm said.

John Smith said nothing, only bowed and smiled as he took a chair, and looked at her. Then Malcolm continued, —

"I saw the Sanson carriage drive away. Did you have a pleasant call?" And as Christine, with beating heart, grieving to disappoint him, described the visit, Malcolm's face lost its brightness. He frowned, and bit his lip, as, in vexed manner, he said, —

"My dear girl, if you intend to be disagreeable to every one who differs with you on religious belief, you'll be unbearable. For God's sake, Christine, don't become that abomination to God and man, — a bigot!" Then he turned impatiently away, and began to whistle, as if to keep himself from saying more. John Smith, watching his niece, saw her lips part, and a breath or so come quick, as if she were in pain, or had been running. Yet there was no sound, no quiver of the face that had become very pale; and she stood just as when speaking, with her hands held close together. A curious look came over him, and his face grew paler than hers. He took up the battle for her, laughingly, wittily, and, in a few moments, had Malcolm in a good-humor.

Christine heard their voices as in a dream. At Malcolm's words she had turned deadly sick. He had never before spoken irritably to her. In all her life she had never heard an unkind word. She felt no anger at his injustice, no desire to defend herself : only the room grew dark, and her head dizzy. Presently some one took her hand. She felt herself seated in an easy-chair, tasted some cool water, and, feeling better, saw John Smith at her side, and Malcolm standing near, looking as if nothing had ever marred the beauty of his face.

He was telling a funny anecdote to his uncle, who smiled quietly in reply ; but his eyes were on Christine. Meeting her glance, he held the glass towards her. "Another sip?" And, when she shook her head, he put it on a table near, then began talking with Malcolm of things generally interesting, until Christine unconsciously listened, was soothed ; when Maggie, all smiles, announced, —

"Dinner, ma'am."

"I'll yield her to you, uncle," said Malcolm, putting her hand in his uncle's arm, to lead her to dinner. "I can afford to be generous with what is so truly mine, — ah, Christine!" He had changed to gay humor, was so sweetly attentive to her, so pleased that his uncle had come to cheer her during the evening hours he had to be away.

"Only a little while to-night, darling," he said to her. "I shall hurry back." And then she thought he looked saddened that she did not seem happy. Christine blamed herself, struggled with herself, yet could not seem what she was not.

She took her share in the conversation, making the little dinner pleasanter by the presence of gracious womanhood, but could not lighten the weight on her heart. She did not complain at her husband's going, did not urge his remaining, only begged him not to overtax his strength, and wear away his life with work.

"Money is not all, Malcolm," she said half sadly.

"No ; but it is a great deal, Miss Paleface." And he gently pinched her cheek, to bring back the roses that had bloomed there before dinner. She took his hand.

"Malcolm, I don't care to be rich." She spoke so low and gently, it was almost an undertone. But John Smith heard it; and again that curious look came over his face, as with gay laugh, and a merry, "I do, and for your sake," from Malcolm, her husband kissed her cheek. Then lighting his cigar, and bidding his uncle "take good care of Christine," he hurried away. As he closed the front-door, his voice, humming an opera air, came into the quiet room, where his wife, with clasped hands, leaned forward, her eyes fixed on the fire that Maggie had lighted in the pretty little parlor. Its red light fell on her, where, as the darkness deepened, she seemed to absorb all the brightness of the shadowy room. The sadness of her face had changed to peaceful-ness. She was thinking of her grandfather, of his prayers, lessons, life, and his teaching of submission, and endurance of life's trials. She was thinking how, trivial, unworthy as they were, even the heart-aches, that she feared proceeded from selfishness, would be accepted if she but offered them through Christ. She was thinking of Mrs. Berry, her past and her future; and, in praying for this tender soul in peril, her own sadness was lost. She had forgotten her uncle, so swift and strong had been the current of thought, bearing her away from her present. But he, in the shadow, watching her, noting each change in her expressive face, was thinking only of her. When the sweet mouth lost its drooping, and the dark eyes filled with peace, he was so truly thinking only of her, that he lost himself, and sighed. That sigh brought her back. She had forgotten this kind uncle, who was always so good to her, and every one. Ah, how sad he must be to sigh like that! She had never heard him sigh before.

"Forgive me," she murmured. There was the sound of tears in her voice; and the hand she held towards him trembled a little as he clasped it a moment, and then let it go. "Forgive me that I had forgotten you, and you never forget any kindness."

Most unjust praise, most unmerited contrition! Yet both beautiful in their sincerity. He did not answer. By the fire's glow he had seen the glistening eyes. These, and her voice, her touch, were too much for him. He clinched his teeth, that words might not escape. He loosed her hand, that he might not crush it. Of all men, he knew he had not deserved that she should feel she had injured him. Sitting there in silence, watching her, had he not wished the flames might leap out, and consume them both ; or even that thus alone, they two might stay forever, — she in the firelight, he watching her, until both were dead? As no answer came, the sweet, trembling voice went on : —

"You are troubled, unhappy. I wish I could help you. You have been so true an uncle to me, that I " — And then she paused, tried to say something, and could not. The three wives of this man came to her thoughts. If in trouble, theirs the happiness to comfort him. To him who had three comforters, she could be of no help. He waited a few moments, longing, yet fearing, to hear more, — fearing lest this gentle sympathy would madden him into some maniac's act ; longing for another word, as the famished for cool water. Then, seeming to understand the cause of her silence, he frowned heavily, and a moment after, in his quiet voice, said, —

"Let us have some music. Sing me the favorites of your grandfather."

As, in ready willingness to please him, she lit the lights, and went to the piano, he spoke of the dear father with such genuine admiration of his grand simplicity and true nature, that her sensitive face grew tenderer, and the voice singing the old man's ballads came from a heart full of love.

CHAPTER XXII.

DAVID'S BIRTHDAY.

SEVERAL times the Berry carriage, with a note from Mrs. Alice, called for Christine, bearing her away to the beautiful garden, at whose gate, with her boy at her side, the pale mother waited to welcome her.

"Come as often as you can," she had asked Christine. And she had replied, "I will come whenever you send for me. But do not come for me : stay with your boy." So the visits were frequent. To Christine, helping another was helping to bear the ever-increasing loneliness of her life. She felt she could not go too often where she was so much needed ; for, as David's birthday approached, the anxious mother grew more miserably anxious. The possibilities of that birthday ! Would Mr. Berry keep to his expressed resolve ? Would he separate those two lives so bound in each other ? What would be the result ? Christine would start out of sleep in terror, from dreams these fears had created. Despite her self-control, despite the tower of strength she was to Mrs. Berry, Christine had caught the infection of her fears. Kept within her own heart, they grew and strengthened, until she would tremble at the slightest sound, — a nervousness that, unnoticed by her husband, was not unmarked by John Smith, to whom the slightest turn of her head was of moment. One day, when a quickly opening door made her turn pale, and utter a faint "Oh !" he asked, "What disturbs you, my child?" And with a flush, while her frank eyes looked into his, she answered, "I cannot tell you." Small as the incident was, her sweet truthfulness only added to her perfections, only made her dearer.

The glory of autumn's golden haze, its soft blue skies, and gentle breeze, that make this season of decay most beautiful, welcomed David's birthday. Christine had been sent for early in the morning. She was still watching down the street where Malcolm had disappeared, when the carriage drove up; and with kind words to Maggie, whose delight it was to watch her mistress's departure and arrival, she rode quickly away to her friends. The gardens had never looked more lovely. And David, full of life and joyousness, wandered among the flowers, making garlands for "mamma," throwing bouquets at Christine, and filling the air with his fresh young voice. Mrs. Berry, almost as happy as he, seemed to have forgotten her apprehensions for this day. She was dressed in a robe of pale blue, which, while it made her look more delicate, became her greatly; and she seemed hardly out of girlhood with that bright look in her face, and the ready smile coming at her boy's wish.

"Isn't mamma pretty?" David had asked. And then, with the tenderness shown only to "mamma," he had pulled her down, and kissed her, asked her to take him in her arms, and tell him how she loved him. So, holding him to her, she said, solemnly, as if it were prayer, —

"I love you with all my heart and soul. With every breath I draw, with every present joy, with every future hope, I love you."

"And I love you, too, mamma," the boy had said, clinging tight to her, and pressing his face to hers. They were standing under a great tree, through whose lightened foliage sunshine streamed upon them, brightening the mother's pale face, adding beauty to the rosy boy, whose arms were about her neck. Christine, on the stone seat near the well, looked at them through tears. To-day she could not keep back her tears. The gayer the boy grew, the happier in him his

MRS. BERRY AND DAVID.

mother, greater, stronger, became the nervous apprehension that made her steal stealthy glances down the road toward the city. But as the day passed on, and even Mr. Berry did not appear, she grew calmer, and her smiles were no longer forced.

Walking slowly up and down beneath the trees, answering questions from Mrs. Berry, and David too, about the faith and noble life of her grandfather, Christine was feeling the sweetness of the hour. When, on a sudden impulse, David cried, " I will hide, and mamma will find me," he started off at full run. Christine, seated, watched the merry game between the two, smiling in sympathy with their laughter. It was David's turn to hide now ; and, bidding mamma close well her eyes, he ran in glad jumps to the front of the house. His mother waited for his shout, but it came not. Paling a little with sudden fear, she ran to the well-mound, whence she could command a view of the garden. As she stood there, Christine saw her face change, as if turning to stone ; and, starting to her feet, she saw David rushing wildly, followed quickly by his father and a stranger. Hidden by the trees, Mr. Berry did not notice her.

" Stop, David. Come to me this instant, or it will be worse for you."

His voice was harsh, and shaking with anger. He put out his hand to grasp the child ; but, with a spring, he escaped.

" Do not be annoyed, Mr. Berry," said the stranger. And something in his voice made Christine shiver. " Your little son will soon learn the holy law, — obedience." But Mr. Berry did not seem to hear him. Defied thus, in the presence of a stranger, by his own child, he felt bound to assert his authority. Taking long strides, he had his hand almost upon the bright head ; when wild with terror, and shrieking, " Mamma, mamma, save me!" the child rushed up the mound, and sprang into her extended arms.

For less than a second the frail figure swayed backwards with the impetus of that spring. With a smothered gasp, Christine ran towards the two, seeing their danger. But, before she could reach the spot where those figures stood, there was only space. The sun shone upon grass and marble, and a sepulchral splash told where mother and child had fallen. The stranger, stooping over the well, looked down. Cold and dark, it told no secrets. Christine, running quickly to the house, had picked up a coil of rope she had seen on the porch, and, returning, was fastening one end around her body, before the two men had recovered self-possession. Pressing the other end in Mr. Berry's stiff hand, she ran to the edge of the well. Mr. Berry did not speak, — seemed unconscious of what she was doing. But the stranger caught her by the arm.

"You are risking your life," he said. "I will call men accustomed to these things."

"Hold the rope," was her answer; and, shaking off his hand, she took the fearful plunge. How cold the water was! But she was a sailor's child; and the lessons of her youth bore fruit, as down, down she went in that terrible dive. She touched their icy faces, steadied herself, put her arms firmly around them, then, giving the rope a jerk, locked her hands together. Slowly, slowly they were pulled up. As she felt the warm air, Christine fainted. When she recovered consciousness, she was lying on the floor in the parlor, John Smith bending over her, some one feeling her pulse, and a strange voice saying, —

"She will soon be all right."

With consciousness came remembrance. "Mrs. Berry — David?" she said faintly.

"Christine, you must keep quiet." Her uncle's voice was strangely agitated, his face was very pale.

"God have mercy! They are dead! I know it." And, putting one trembling hand to shield her eyes, she wept.

"My dear niece, you will be ill if you are not calm."

His thoughts were all for her. What mattered it to him if the whole world perished, so she lived? What to him were those two

cold forms lying near? Only a woman and her child! While she!
And the room turned black as he once again lived over the moment,
when, talking to a group of gentlemen in the hotel-lobby, a man had
jumped from an exhausted horse, and, rushing to the door, had called, —

"Is Dr. X—— here? Come quick, for God's sake! Mrs. Berry
and Mrs. Smith have been drowned in Berry's well."

Mrs. Smith! That name made his heart stand still. It was only
last evening Christine had told him she would spend this day with
Mrs. Berry. He walked quickly out, took a hack at the door, and,
telling the driver he would be paid treble if he made speed, drove
to the first doctor's. Taking the physician with him, they reached
Mr. Berry's house before the arrival of the other doctor. In the
darkened parlor, on the floor, lay three dripping bodies, the water in
little pools around them, and the terrified servants trying, without
effect, what restoratives they knew. Looking down on his boy was
the father. Not a sound from his lips, not a muscle moved. He was
like one struck dead. Hardly glancing at the others, John Smith,
seeing Christine, was at her side.

"Look first to her," he said to the doctor.

Already she had begun to breathe; and, speaking the words she
had heard, the doctor hurried to the others. He felt the pulse of
each, listened at each heart, and then called, —

"Open the windows. I want air and light."

Bright flashed the sunlight on a sight to make angels weep. With
her pretty dress "clinging like cerement," her delicate arms locked
fast around her child, the mother lay — dead! And the boy, — his
rounded cheek pressed to hers, — was he dead too? It was the
doubt of this that made the doctor call for light. Leaning on her
uncle's arm, with water still dripping from her, through tears Christine looked on those two white faces. No terror in them now. Only
love, sublime, eternal!

Without a struggle they had passed away. God had lifted the clouds which overhung their lives, in his own way. Fearful to human nature, incomprehensible to human hearts, yet must we submit, bowing to his will. So felt Christine, as, after a few moments, the doctor, shaking his head, said, —

"I see no signs of life. It seems a pity to separate them," he added, as if to himself.

And then, in a voice so unlike his own that Christine started, Mr. Berry said, —

"Try every means to restore that boy. Even if you know he is dead, try to restore him."

Dr. X—— arriving, the two doctors labored at the resuscitation of the child. Again and again they strove to bring back life's breath to that little body. Sitting near, wrapped in a warm cloak her uncle had put around her, Christine waited. Time passed. The doctors worked on. But no human power could stir that still body with life's pulses. His soul had fled. Gone with the mother he loved, away from a life so full of difficulties, — a life that would either degrade his fair soul or break his heart.

The doctors ceased. "There is no hope. The child is dead." Dr. X—— was speaking to the father. Mr. Berry did not reply. He gave no sign of hearing, did not seem to see, as, with a touch of nature that made Christine's tears flow afresh, the doctors put the child back in his mother's arms, then, bowing, left the room.

Christine knelt beside the dead, kissed tenderly each face, and then, with a pitiful glance upon him, even him, whose acts had killed them, was led away by her uncle. At the threshold she turned for a last look at those two who had so deeply entered into her life. Oh, pitiful group upon which the sunlight rested! And, gazing down in stony despair, the murderer!

CHAPTER XXIII.

THE FALLEN MASK.

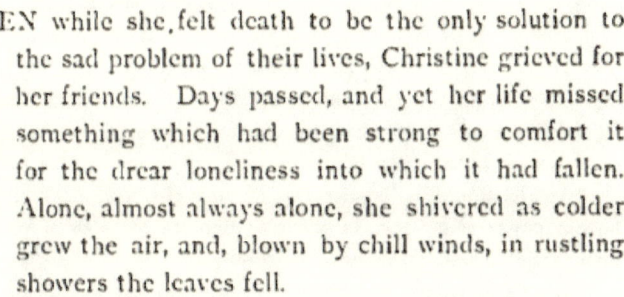

EVEN while she felt death to be the only solution to the sad problem of their lives, Christine grieved for her friends. Days passed, and yet her life missed something which had been strong to comfort it for the drear loneliness into which it had fallen. Alone, almost always alone, she shivered as colder grew the air, and, blown by chill winds, in rustling showers the leaves fell.

Malcolm's "Too bad that Berry should have lost his boy. He seemed to think lots of the child," dried up the tears Christine would have wept on a loving breast.

Kinder and more thoughtful than ever, the good uncle was ready to sympathize with his niece. But sincerely fond as she was growing of him, who seemed more like father to her, Christine was, by nature, reserved. Love alone was the "open sesame" to her deepest feelings. And there was one who loved her even as she loved him. To her grandfather she wrote of her dead friends. In his heart reposed the sacred secret of their lives. His answer came, a part of himself; and sitting by the window, looking through tears' sad mist at the sadness of the autumn day, she turned again to his dear words, that some of his strength might come to her fainting heart : —

"My darling, though human nature recoils in affright, death is not sad. 'Ending the heartache, and the thousand other aches that flesh is heir to,' it brings us to an eternity of brightness. All this we do not comprehend, because earth's dust blinds our eyes. But we must believe. No reasons can satisfy intelligence. Our reasons are so weak, our intelligence so limited, yet each so pride-full, they rise above our praying faith, and demand hearing. But there is a voice, God-given, which answers them, — the craving, the necessity, of our hearts. Without this faith, what are we? Storm-driven birds, wearied of wing, and no shelter near. And with it, serene and safe, we rest upon God's cross, and reach down loving arms to other souls struggling in fierce waves. Without it, our lives are governed but by self-interest, human sympathies. With it, poorly, faintly perhaps, yet do we reflect God's own charity, — love, patience, forgiveness, for friend, for enemy, growing each day nearer the holy, most holy, life of Christ. Thus, seen through faith, death loses its terrors. Were I dead this moment, my spirit would be near you, my child; and then I should not miss you as I do.

"Yet let not this disquiet you, nor mar the happiness of your home. The old have a power of memory as compensation for the loss of youth. And, when I sit in my quiet house, I see my Christine. As a baby, she plays around my feet, and clambers to my knee. She brightens the world for me. Beautiful as it is, I find its chief beauty in my Christine's face.

"Our dear friends are well, Patience studying faithfully. She has not yet ceased thanking me for taking your place as teacher. She runs up almost every morning to see if I need any thing, and, in the evening, comes to recite her lessons. As I see her pretty face bending seriously above her book, I think of another face, and another little maid I've helped, as best I could, over the stony path of knowledge, until, grown learned, she outruns her master. So Patience links me yet closer to my past, and my dear, dear child.

"Tabitha does not look well. She is kept nervous and anxious at the newly awakened interest of Bishop White. He spoke to Tabitha one day last week as he stood at her gate, — said he thought Patience should have the advantage of the Mormon seminary. Patience is frightened at the bare idea. Her father may meditate a rich marriage for her. God save her! Poor child, poor child! I would she were not so fair. Yet am I doing wrong, for beauty is God's gift. He knows best.

"Christie does not gain strength. To please him, and myself too, I've become his teacher as well as his sister's. Twice every week I go to him. His spirit is so bright, and heart so strong! He writes some remarkable things. If he lives, and can go to a country where mind is not crushed, the child will some day be called a genius. But, whatever his future, his daily life is nearer heaven than earth.

"Keep well, my child, and, with your husband, come to us at Christmas-tide."

She was lingering on the dear words, feeling that calm steal over her that to troubled hearts sometimes speaks in ocean's mighty roar, waving forest-boughs, or the restful, restful mountains, whose tops seem whispering heaven of heroes' deeds. Her grandfather's noble face and peaceful smile filled the room for Christine, and took away its oppressive loneliness until Malcolm came home.

He was vexed at something. What was it? With that same dizziness coming upon her, she tried to imagine what could have annoyed him. In answer to her gentle question, his "Nothing," so sharply and significantly spoken, silenced, while it convinced her there must have occurred something really important.

After his hastily eaten dinner, he rose to go. At the door he stopped, bit his lip, hesitated, and then in a quick, impatient way, said, —

"I do think, Christine, you might sooner have returned the call of Mr. Sanson's wives. He was barely civil to me to-day, and, when I asked the cause, said he felt very much hurt that you hadn't been to see the Mrs. Sansons. Both ladies took a great fancy to you. And, what makes it worse, the elder goes away in a day or so. It is rather hard on a man when his wife won't attend to society business."

"Forgive me, Malcolm," Christine had answered. "I shall go to-morrow without fail."

"Go where?" asked John Smith, coming in on his way to a political meeting.

And, when Malcolm explained, his uncle had a plan that called forth a faint smile from his niece. He would call for her, drive her to the Sansons. After the visit, they would stop at the bank for Malcolm, ride out to the boiling-spring, and then stop at an exhibition of art-works that was being held in the city.

"You will enjoy them, my dear," he said to Christine, himself enjoying the momentary brightening of her face.

He could have struck Malcolm when his light words, "Thanks. For myself, I must decline. But Christine will go," took all the light from the dark eyes, and gave to the sweet lips that sad drooping. She did not speak; but, when he called "Christine," she followed her husband to the door.

"Don't be a little fool. You'll enjoy yourself more without me. And now, dear girl, I ask, as an especial favor, that you be as pleasant as possible to my uncle. If he keeps on liking you so well, I shall expect him to settle half his fortune on you. By-by." And, touching his lips to her cheek, he ran lightly down the steps. She stood, for a moment, just where he had left her, holding fast to the knob of the open door. She felt so dizzy, every thing looked so black! Was she going to faint? No: she mustn't do that. A kindly voice at her side, a strong hand closing the door; and somehow, by the half-opened window, she sat in the parlor, holding some roses her uncle had brought to her.

"You didn't notice them when I handed them to you before Malcolm left."

"Didn't I? They are very beautiful." And then she noticed they were red roses,—like the one she had given Malcolm on that far-away spring day; like those she had worn the first evening she had met Mrs. Berry. She did not know her tears were falling until she saw them glistening on the velvety leaves. Only that dizziness was gone; and her grandfather's words, "through death to an eternity of brightness," came to her with the roses' perfume. John Smith did not seem to notice her weeping. He sat at a little distance, not looking at her, as she found by a timid glance when she brushed away the

tears, fearing lest he should think Malcolm had said aught to make
her unhappy. And then she gradually grew more composed, as her
uncle spoke quietly of things themselves indifferent, but to which he
lent an interest. When he rose to go, she looked up with a smile for
him, — a smile that he thought of every moment, even while, at the
meeting, men were shouting in applause as he closed the best speech
of the evening.

The next morning, before Christine had finished her toilet, the
carriage was at the door. John Smith thought she looked most lovely,
as, flushed with haste, anxious not to keep him waiting, she entered
the parlor, ready for the visit. Being rather early for calling, Mr.
Smith proposed a short drive through the city. Past the grand new
temple hastening to completion, its beautiful granite, shot with black,
glittering in the sunlight. Near this noble structure, the older temple, looking small and insignificant. But here, thousands had been
taught a religion degrading to youth and age, — a religion at whose
moral depravity the civilized world stands aghast! John Smith, watching Christine's face, saw deep sadness cover it, and the flush that had
been so lovely fade into paleness. He had seen her steady gaze on
the Mormon temples, and divined her thoughts.

"Thinking of the faith, Christine, which to me is revelation, to
you is pain? My dear niece, our minds are not all constituted alike.
Like maxims, even in religion, will not satisfy opposing natures.
But, of all religions, should not the first principle be charity? Where
you cannot understand, will you not extend that holy virtue?"

He spoke very gently. His gentleness was more potent than argument. But was it right to be charitable to that belief which counselled immorality? Was it charity, God's true love, not to oppose a
religion that forced superstition upon growing minds, and slavery upon
mothers and daughters? How could he, that kind uncle, with his com-
prehensive mind, his great intelligence, uphold a faith so degrading?

Mrs. Berry and her martyred youth came in Christine's thought. Her pale, agonized face, those nervous, fluttering hands, appealed against the belief this man upheld. The hypocrisy of Mr. Berry, his mask of religion, used as step to political power, added blackness to the picture. And, like cherub face, little David smiled on her from heaven. Saved from the future prepared for him, God had helped him at an hour when help seemed impossible. Would he not help the other little ones? Her heart throbbed as she prayed for them, — the little ones growing older, the little ones yet unborn. She prayed for her uncle, that, like Paul, he might become God's apostle, and himself preach conversion to those whom he had led astray. Yet, though in error, at least he was sincere. His intellect was clouded, his judgment warped; but against him there was not the sin of falsehood.

The carriage rolled on under the now almost leafless trees. Yet how beautiful the tracery of their branches against the clear sky! And the mountains surrounding the natural basin of Salt Lake had already donned their caps of snow. A lover of nature, Christine felt its calm stealing over her, as thus luxuriously, in easiest carriage, they rode along; while John Smith, master of the art, touched the keys that brought smiles to her face before they drew up at Mr. Sanson's door. There was another carriage in waiting, which moved on, and gave place to them. Helping Christine out, John Smith, saying his soul was not attuned to harmonious discourse, and bidding her not stay too long, and waste the day indoors, re-entered the carriage to wait for her.

Christine found the door open, and in the hall signs of confusion. To a tidy-looking girl, who came forward to receive them, she handed two cards. "For the two ladies," she said, as the smiling girl, without speaking, indicated an open door. The room was so dark, that Christine could hardly distinguish objects. Almost groping her way, she seated herself on a sofa nearly facing the door, where, by any one entering, she would be soonest seen. So many minutes passed, that, thinking of Mr. Smith waiting outside, she rose to summon a servant, when voices approaching made her resume her seat. A man came down-stairs bearing a trunk ; then Elder Sanson, all smiles and self-satisfaction, with his young wife, attired in travelling-costume. He had her hand, and was talking in that strain, half affectionate, half flattering, that some imagine attractive to the young. It seemed so to this young person, who replied, " Lor' me ! Sech nonsense ! Well, I never ! " and then gave a pinch to his ear, at which they both laughed immoderately. The open door, commanding a long view of the stairs and hall, would have made Christine uncomfortable, had not the presence of the maid, to whom she had given her cards, assured her they were aware of the visitor waiting in the parlor. The maid followed Mrs. Sanson, with travelling-satchel and shawl in her hand. Mr. and Mrs. Sanson stopped for a moment just opposite the door. Christine rose, expecting their entrance. But they did not come. Her face flushed ; as, supposing this was Elder Sanson's way of showing his vexation at her tardy visit, she felt the rudeness with which she was being treated. An impulse came over her to leave the house, and then she thought of Malcolm. He would be offended. Could she not bear a little slight for his sake ? So she again resumed her seat, and looked away from the love-passages of the old elder and his young wife, which seemed given for her benefit, and that of the smiling maid. Presently, taking out his watch, Mr. Sanson said, —

" We've not much time to lose." And Mrs. Sanson called out to some one above, —

" Come and say good-by, and wish us a pleasant trip."

" In a moment, my dear," came the answer, in the voice of Mrs. Sanson No. 1.

Insulted now, for there was no doubt Mrs. Sanson No. 2 did not intend to notice her visit, Christine decided she would wait for a mo-

ment to see Mrs. Sanson, senior, explain the cause of her delay, and
regulate her own conduct by her courtesy or discourtesy.   She had just
come to this conclusion when the senior Mrs. Sanson appeared.   She
looked far from well, but was smiling graciously ; and when her

"I'LL JEST SPARE YOU ONE KISS."

blooming sister kissed her sallow face, and, with loud laugh, held
towards her the elder's coarse mouth, saying, " Now, I'll jest spare
you one kiss," she leaned forward, and touched her lips to it, as if it
were a perfectly natural and agreeable arrangement.   And her words,
in pleasant voice, only added to this marvellous example of Mormon
rule.

"My dear sister, I do wish you pleasure.   Having so often travelled with my, *our*, husband,"—she corrected herself with slight emphasis,—" I know full well my wish will be more than realized."

What religious intensity! What strength of belief! What power the Mormon Church possessed! It annihilated a woman's nature. And yet she must suffer. It was not in created being not to suffer at coldness from one beloved. For giving her a cool marital kiss, and "Good-by, my dear," Elder Sanson, with excess of demonstration, led away his young wife.

A most unwilling witness of this, to her, painful scene, Christine moved forward to greet Mrs. Sanson, senior, who entered hurriedly. Anticipating an apology for the rudeness of the younger wife, and feeling so full of pity for this older one, Christine, with extended hand, had already said, " Pray don't mention it. I "— But Mrs. Sanson did not see her, did not even hear her. She seemed to have forgotten her existence. With the precision of one acquainted with the arrangement of the room, she walked so quickly that her dress, with a "swish!" swung against pieces of furniture, and, with rapid movement, dashed aside the heavy curtain, letting the glare of daylight flash on her face. And what a face! Christine, looking at her, trembled violently, as, fascinated, rooted to the spot, she hardly breathed. The woman's shaking hand rattled the brass rings of the hangings, and the sound seemed unnatural accompaniment to that most inhuman countenance. Eyes glaring like tigress at bay. Her brows so heavily knitted, that her forehead was a mass of wrinkles; while under the thin skin of age, even to her throat, the knotted veins stood out clear and distinct. In hissing gasp her breath seemed gathering force for speech; and from distorted mouth, like pythoness of old, came fearful curse.

"May Heaven blast you! May loathsome disease eat up your skin, and turn to repulsion his fickle fancy! May your offspring be thing so horrible, that it shall sicken the sight of man! Curse you, curse you! You have robbed me of my life."

Christine's tongue clove to the roof of her mouth. She could not utter a sound. Every faculty was lost in horror, — horror at that figure whose writhing mouth seemed, in silence, piling curse upon curse, until, like mountains, they crushed her with their hideous weight. Suddenly the curtain was dropped. The room was in darkness. A hurried movement, and a figure stood in the doorway.

"Are you ill, ma'am?" said a man-servant passing down the hall. And then Mrs. Sanson's voice, in its usual measured tone, —

"Only a slight headache, Thomas. You need not serve dinner. Send some tea to my room." Quietly she moved up the stairs; and Christine was alone in the dark room, which still echoed with those frightful curses. She tried to move, but felt in a nightmare. "Save her, save us all, O Lord!" she prayed; and the spell was broken.

Slowly, languidly, she walked to the door of the room, and looked up and down the hall. Seeing no one, she went to the front-door. Opening it, she met her uncle on the step.

"You were so long, I was anxious. Christine," he exclaimed in sudden alarm, "you have been ill!"

"No," — she could barely utter the words, — "let us go."

Drawing her arm through his, he helped her to the carriage, watching her anxiously, she was so pale, so agitated.

"What is it, my child?"

"I cannot tell you."

She had unwillingly witnessed the tearing open of the hidden page in a woman's life; and, however terrible, it was a sacred secret. Mrs. Berry's words, "the mask of hypocrisy held over all," had sprung to hideous reality. She leaned back in the carriage. Even the kind attentions of the most kind uncle could not exorcise the demon, which, looking from a woman's eyes, had affrighted her.

After a few days, there came to Christine a note of apology from Mrs. Sanson.

"MY DEAR MRS. SMITH, — I have just received your cards, which I learn were left some days since. Our new waitress is a freshly imported German, and cannot speak a word of English; so, if any thing should have been amiss, I trust you will excuse. As soon as I recover from a slight indisposition, I shall do myself the honor and pleasure of returning your call," etc.

But she never came, and so the acquaintance ended ; and Christine, too sad to form new ones, was striving to bear those trials which God was sending. She could hardly tell when it began, the change had been so gradual ; but "business," as Malcolm called it, absorbed every moment of his time, except the hours for meals, or when he slept. What that business was, Christine knew not. To her questions, he returned only such vague answers as, "Nothing that you could understand, my love ;" or, "One can hardly explain business to a woman," or some other equally clear reply, until Christine, grown too proud to question further, made no comment, as, after hurried meal and hasty kiss, he would leave her. Leave her, and to what ?

To listen to the ticking of the clock, and watch the hands, as slowly, wearily, the hours dragged by ; to try to pray, and feel the words, like clouds, rest on her heart ; to know, each day surer and surer, that, where she loved, she was not beloved. It was November, with moaning winds, with damp, cold air, and sad, sad days. Wearied of the loneliness of the house, she would vary it with the loneliness of the streets ; starting back, and drawing down her veil, as some sudden turn would bring before her a familiar face of Mormon acquaintance.

She dreaded a kindly look or word from unloving lips. She feared to break down, and, betraying her secret pain, bring censure on her husband ; for she was in that condition when a woman most needs sympathy and companionship. Her loneliness was appalling. Yet she never complained, — never, even by a sigh, told her need of human tenderness.

Had it not been for John Smith, she would have felt entirely friend-less. He had seen the changing of Malcolm's changeful nature. Busy as he always was, he would come in often of an evening : espe-cially after finding her so much alone, his visits grew even more fre-quent. Sometimes Christine would feel ashamed at her pleasure in seeing this kind uncle, knowing the hours spent with her were robbed from his three wives. Often, blushing as she did so, would she, at first, ask him to bring "the Mrs. Smith" with him. But they rarely called.

"They prefer home-quiet, even to the society of those they admire. And they do admire you, my dear child," he had once added, as he looked into her wistful face.

Except when John Smith came, she had no visitors. Was it a wonder that her smile awakened at the coming of this most kind uncle ? And, for her entertainment, he would talk as he seldom did, except to produce an effect, or score a mark in the game of his life. And she would listen until her listening, sympathetic, inspiring, would lift him out of himself, and, forgetting all his past, make him feel as if but at the beginning of life.

He had ceased to wonder what his life would have been had he earlier met a Christine. For now he lived only in her presence. A great contempt for Malcolm grew up in his mind. A man who had won such a woman, to neglect her !

And for himself, — rage ! rage beyond expression, that he should have planned this marriage, — he who would hesitate at no sacrifice to annul it. And how easily he could annul it, were it not for the purity and faithfulness of Christine.

He would, while seemingly absorbed in some political question, plan various ways to dispose of Malcolm. He could be sent on a

mission, and kept away three years or more ; could be made to think
it best for himself to divorce this woman, and marry a richer one.

And then *her* face would arise from out this turbulent sea of
passionate longings. And the man who had never refrained from
accomplishing his objects, whatever might be the manner, and who
recognized no law but might, would recoil abashed before the power
of a woman's purity. Yet, strange as it may seem, let her be one
whit less pure, and she could not have aroused the dormant heart of
John Smith.

He now went daily to Malcolm's house, and always found Christine
alone, passing the long hours of the evening as best she could. Yet
with all his burning fire of passion, like a slumbering volcano longing
to burst forth, in every word and gesture he appeared but the kind
uncle to the lonely woman, welcoming him with sweetest smile.

Never a word or glance from him that could startle an angel.
And though sometimes, when looking at her, a mad longing would
come over him to crush her in his arms, and die with her, the hands
that would touch hers in the ordinary evening greeting would give
only the cool, kind clasp of relationship. She never complained of
Malcolm's absence, made no mention of her loneliness. But John
Smith could see she was growing paler every day, and her smile had
a pathos about it more touching than tears. Letters from home came
regularly, — one every mail from Matthew, often one from Patience
and Christie, and sometimes a few lines from Tabitha and Martin, —
each full of love for her, of longing for her coming ; and, in her
replies, not one word of how she they loved was neglected here.

"We miss you every day more and more, dear Christine " [wrote Patience in
her last]. " Matthew keeps well, but longs for his ' birdling.' He has had a little
arbor made under your favorite apple-tree, and a wicker chair for you, so you can
read there, and look out over the road. We've all been decorating your room.
Christie is raising mignonette in a box for the window. ' Sweet, like my Christine,'

he says. And did Matthew tell you that your place was laid at table each day, and
by it a little bouquet that he plucks for you himself? We've all chosen a flower to
raise to supply these bouquets. Matthew's are the rose geranium. 'Always good,
fresh, and ready, like my child,' he said. And the ivy-vine you planted, — you remember it, don't you? 'This is like her faithfulness,' he told me one day, when he
laughed a little at me for taking a rosebush as my particular care. 'Why, Patience,'
he said, 'it will be so long before blooming!' — 'But it is like her face,' I answered,
— 'once seen, never forgotten.' So I go on, giving every spare moment to my rosebush, and longing for the first bud. But, oh, a thousand times more do I long for
your face, my dearest friend! I heard some little lines that I always say when I
think of you, —

> " ' Her angels face,
> As the great eye of heaven, shyned bright,
> And made a sunshine in the shady place.'

"I don't know if I have it right. I caught Matthew saying it to himself one day
when I went down to carry him some of the fine cabbages we have raised. I knew he
was thinking of you. He was smiling, and was so absorbed that he did not know I
was there until I touched him. I ran home, saying the words over and over again, not
to forget them. When I told them to Christie he was delighted. He has made up
a rhyme to them, and a tune. Such a sweet melody! He and I are to sing it under
your window the first night you arrive. I hope Malcolm does not object to music.
Christine, Christine, when will you come? Before the snow; or just think how cold
we will be shivering out there, for we've quite determined on serenading you. Rex
sends his love. He has grown so tall you would not know him. Christie rides him
everywhere. The nice soft harness you contrived is just the thing. It is too comical to see Rex come every morning to have it put on him. He's such a wise fellow,
and looks so seriously at me when I say silly things, that I grow positively ashamed.
And, when he's all harnessed up, he is so proud and important, that I feel much
honored when he rubs his nose against my hand. As you directed, we fasten the
collar around his neck, and slip Christie's hands in the little knitted loops. He
guides Rex by a gentle pull of his ears. The broad knitted band that goes round
Rex's body, with the loops for the poor little legs, steadies Christie, and makes him
comfortable. It is much easier for him than the cart. The jolting was too hard for
the dear little man. How good you always are! Our guardian angel, we call you.
Matthew has written Christie's vision for you, and put it in the Bible. Ever since
that night, the dear child seems more frail. Sometimes I fear he will vanish from

our sight, and go direct to the beautiful heaven Matthew tells of. I want him to be happy, but I want to keep him a little longer in this world. It is such a lovely world, with its trees, flowers, the bright waters, and, above all, the ever-changing skies.

CHRISTIE AND REX.

If we might only have you with us, and all of us be together, I think this world would be heaven enough for me. Matthew says we are not intended to be happy here, — that this is only a preparation for the after-life. He must be right; for even

I, who do not require so very much to make this world a heaven, have of late found a serpent in my flowers.

"I have told you, that, shortly after you went away, Bishop White — I cannot call him father — came to our gate. He did not come in, but even the sight of his face seemed to turn me sick. And, when mother bade me kiss him, I felt like fainting. He has often come since. Doesn't speak, but just watches me. Christine, dear, he makes me so nervous by this silent watching, that I can hardly keep from screaming. Mother never leaves me for a moment while he is in sight. If she did, I believe I would become crazy. I think if I could only have a peep at your dear face, it would exorcise that fearful one that keeps grinning and grinning at me, even in my dreams. Matthew says we must love all God's creation, but I cannot love Bishop White. If I pretended it, I should be false to truth.

"Martin is away. The last sales he made were very good. Mother has our little money-bag quite full. She has given it to Matthew to keep for us. She wanted to begin to repay him for the team, but he will not hear of it. He says that will come when we are settled, and Martin is regularly engaged at four dollars per day. Won't that be grand? Martin is now teaming for Mr. Marks. The mill will not be ready for work until the new year. But there was some hauling needed, and Martin was lucky enough to get it. He will be home for Christmas. Will you come too? Surely Malcolm will not keep you always in Salt Lake. We all love and need you; and you would be happy with us once more, if only he would come."

And so the letter ran on, full of devotion for her who sat alone, the tears slowly falling down her face as she read the tender words. Of late, tears often sprang to Christine's eyes; but rarely did she weep as now, while reading the letter of this dear younger sister. It seemed so strange to her, who had ever been loved, that she could not keep the heart of the man to whom she had given her life. Daily she saw it going farther away from her. He was not only indifferent to her, but to that dearer life that now she could feel throbbing near her own. He never mentioned it. She longed to lay her aching head on the tender breast of her grandfather. She longed to clasp the loving hands of the friends who wanted her. She looked around the pretty room, whose every detail spoke of dainty womanhood, and its loneliness made her shiver. She tried the piano for company ; but her fingers would only bring forth wailing minor chords, that made fresh tears fall. Then looking at the clock, and seeing it pointed nearly the dinner-hour, she hastened to make her toilet.

Malcolm had once said he admired a well-dressed woman. And this woman, who loved him, had ever since tried to be well dressed for his sake. This evening she chose a dark garnet silk he had given her in the early days of their marriage. He had liked her in it. The delicate touches of pink, lightening its sombre richness, became her, he had said. And the lightest word he had ever said was treasured in her memory.

She did not blame him for his growing indifference. Even in her thoughts she would not blame him whom she loved. The fact of this indifference filled her with disappointment and grief. But she would defend him even to her own heart, and say, " Love is not within our control." He was never ungentle in his manners, never alluded to the ambition he had sacrificed to her love. And, since she had come to Salt Lake, she had more clearly understood how great this sacrifice of ambition would seem to a young man like Malcolm, to whom the possession of power must be sweet. She saw that the Mormon State required obedience of its people ; that, when it advanced any one, it must have the right to command polygamy. And, generally, this was the first command to an ambitious son.

That Malcolm felt ambition stirring was evident. How eagerly he would listen as his uncle told some incident in his own life ! — told it so well, that, while his auditors were surprised at the power of Mormonism, there never seemed any egotism in it. These topics he generally discussed the rare evenings he found Malcolm at home.

He would speak of the reclaiming of the desert, the advance of the State, the mighty force which held together this people of different nationalities, alluding lightly to polygamy.

Malcolm, with eyes fixed on space, listened to the tempter. Yet so well did John Smith handle his subject and his listeners, that he seemed speaking but his honest convictions. Neither imagined that his motive-power was the hope of modifying and debasing the earnest principles of a noble character. Neither imagined that to his creed he was striving to convert a woman. John Smith's able dissertations never awakened discussion. Malcolm lacked ability, even if he had the will, to combat his uncle's views.

And how could Christine speak against the moral teachings of a church that counselled polygamy, when she must proclaim its sinfulness to this uncle married to three wives? His kindness to her surely was an index of his treatment of them. Thus would she be forced into stillness; but, all the while, she would keep her lovely eyes on Malcolm's face, and from her heart would rise the prayer, " Lord, hold him true to himself."

She did not know John Smith was looking at her, trying to read her inmost thoughts, and puzzled that her face should wear this holy calm at the very moment when he was attacking the bulwark of her happiness. He who could play at will with human passions, and make the entranced crowd do his bidding, was nonplussed by a woman's face. It was not given him to understand, that, while his eloquent words were nerving the arm of her husband for her death-blow, Christine was praying for that husband, and even for him.

She was thinking of these discourses this evening while dressing, and felt thankful, spite of temptation, that Malcolm had kept true to his oath. She was thinking a little of John Smith, wondering how so intelligent and gifted a man could believe in a faith whose teachings were insults to modesty and morality, — a faith that encouraged man's basest passions, and made of women, not helpmeets, but slaves. She did not for a moment doubt his sincerity : she only marvelled how it was possible for him to believe as he professed. And then, looking at herself in the mirror, she hoped she would please Malcolm. With the hope, a soft flush came into the cheeks that had grown so very pale; and then, every moment listening for his footstep, she waited, — waited until her heart beat nervously; and still he did not come. Presently a ring at the door, and a hurried little note from Malcolm : —

"DEAR CHRISTINE, — Don't wait dinner for me. I will be detained until a late hour, perhaps until after midnight. We have a good deal to look after to-night. Don't be worried: I am all right.
"Yours,
"MALCOLM.

"My uncle has stopped in to see me for a moment, and, at my invitation, will dine with you; so you won't be lonesome."

"So you won't be lonesome!" The flush faded from her cheeks, and the tears came back to her eyes. But, at John Smith's step near the door, the tears were brushed away; and the suspicion of them only gave additional lustre to the large dark eyes raised to greet him. He gazed into their sad depths, and would have perilled all his life's gains to have had them once look thus for him.

When he gently took her hand, he was fancying what would be the result if he drew her to his breast, and let the pent-up torrent of his fiery love sweep over her.

What would be the result? He read it in the pure, pale face, the eyes looking trustfully at him. He was not yet mad enough to entirely shut himself out from the little gleam of heaven that came to him each time he looked on her. And so they walked into the little dining-room, where the table was spread for two.

CHAPTER XXIV.

A TRAGEDY.

H E placed her chair, and then took his own, saying, —

"I saw Malcolm for a moment, and he asked me to be his substitute. A poor one, my dear, but perhaps a little better than dining alone: and then, I, too, was left alone; for Mrs. Smith has gone out of town for a few days."

A vague wonder often came to Christine when he spoke of "Mrs. Smith." Which Mrs. Smith did he mean? or did he mean all three? The latter now, she supposed; for he spoke of being alone. He sighed when he said it. Perhaps he felt a little depressed. And Christine tried to put aside her sad thoughts, and show him some return for his many kindnesses.

During the dinner he was as agreeable as it was possible for man to be. He told incidents of travel, and foreign people, — anecdotes full of point and spirit; unselfishly trying to forget his depression, so Christine thought, and was grateful to him. Then when the meal was over, and they were seated in the cosey parlor, he entered the world of authors.

He was a lover of Shakspeare. He had studied that king of writers, and quoted passage after passage to his fascinated listener. Shakspeare was Matthew's favorite book. He and Christine would often read it together, and wonder at this master mind. But never before had his power so awed her as now, when the gems of his thoughts, in clear, correct expression, fell like priceless jewels from the lips of John Smith.

He was quoting from "Othello." As the passionate words came into being, there seemed no longer a friend and uncle near her, but a

"HE PLACED HER CHAIR."

tortured human heart, whose very strength made its weakness. John Smith paused ; and Christine, with a deep breath, came back to reality.

He had not lost one fleeting expression of the sensitive face, and stopped thus suddenly, for he felt a madness creeping over him, the wild jealousy of Othello, to kill this beauteous Desdemona.

Just then the little clock struck seven.

"Christine,"—how calmly he could speak, while even yet that

frantic impulse was firing his brain! — "you have never been in a theatre?"

She shook her head.

"Would you like to go?"

The large eyes were glistening with the past excitement. The charm of the great Shakspeare was still upon her. She did not answer, but seemed thinking it over. He spoke again : —

"Would you disapprove of going, or would Matthew?"

This was the question she had been turning over in her mind.

"I do not think he would object," she slowly said. "He ever taught me that pleasures were not wrong, but blessed favors, except those pleasures that may be sin for us, or make sin for others."

"O sweetest saint!" cried out John Smith's heart. "Would that I were greater saint, or thou wert greater sinner!"

But with his lips he spoke not. He was waiting to see how she would reason out this new matter. She, too, was for a moment silent. Then turning to him with a smile, and extending her hand in gentlest entreaty, she said, —

"Forgive my moment's doubt of you. You would not take me to a wrong place."

Not take her to a wrong place! At that very instant, standing quietly near her, and gently holding the delicate hand, he would have thrown his arms around her, and taken her to a yawning hell.

Anywhere, so she was with him! Yet he only smiled in answer to her, and said quietly, —

"The play to-night is the one we were just reading, — 'Othello.' A great tragedian from the East is here with his own company. You would enjoy it. And " — seeing her eyes turn to the clock — " you will be back long before midnight, so you will be here to welcome Malcolm. We have just time," he added. " Put on your hat, and come as you are."

Mr. Smith's carriage was at the door ; and, in a few moments, they reached the theatre.

It was like a troubled dream to Christine, — the crowded lobby, the glittering lights, the pushing and confusion. But, with the ease of one accustomed to crowds, Mr. Smith, giving her his arm, led her into the theatre. Here was more quiet ; and, the lights being low, Christine had a few moments to regain composure. Mr. Smith had secured the box to the right of the stage. It would be more comfortable for her, he said, than those crowded seats.

After a little the orchestra entered ; and, with a flash, the theatre was ablaze with light.

" Look at the people, Christine, now, before the play begins. Since you have never been in a theatre, the audience is something to see."

He pushed aside the heavy curtain ; and for a moment she leaned forward, looking at a sea of human faces, rising tier above tier, every space filled with a bit of humanity. It gave her a curious sensation, thus opposing her two eyes to the thousands that seemed gazing at her. Every thing was bright beyond her power of endurance ; and she leaned back as the curtain fell again to its place, noticing, as she did so, that the box opposite theirs was dark and untenanted.

After the invariable squeak, squeak, of orchestral preparation, the music began.

It was good music ; and Christine shielded her eyes with her hand while she listened, the tears were so very near those eyes to-night. She was ashamed of her weakness ; but this music unnerved her, and made her think of Malcolm.

" Did he seem quite well when you saw him to-day ? " she asked, leaning towards John Smith, who was sitting a little back in the box, where he could see, neither stage nor audience, only her face.

" Did who seem well ? " He, too, had been in a reverie ; and she had startled him.

"Malcolm," she answered simply.

"Perfectly well. I never saw him look better."

She was relieved of that fear ; and now the curtain went up, and Christine's whole interest was absorbed on the stage.

When the gentle, timid Desdemona bravely spoke her love before the great council, Christine's heart beat in unison with hers ; and as the play progressed, and Iago's poison stung to death Othello's noble nature, she murmured, —

"I would rather be the doubted, injured Desdemona than Othello. Life must be bitter indeed to him who injures what he loves."

The curtain rose and fell ; the players came and went ; and, except those few words, Christine seemed lost to every thing but the scenes before her. Her face expressed each hope, fear, and dread of the hapless wife. And not until the death-scene, when Othello, crazed with jealousy, smothers his faithful love, did Christine look away from the too real acting.

She turned with a shudder ; and, as she did so, a face in the opposite box caught her passing glance, and blotted out every thing else.

It was Malcolm! Malcolm in his beauty and tenderness, — the Malcolm of only six months ago. Thus he looked at *her* as they stood under the apple-tree. Thus he leaned towards *her*, till the brightness of his golden hair had mingled with her own. She could almost feel it at this instant, and his warm breath on her cheek !

And *now!* O Lord, O Lord ! have pity on this woman !

He, her husband, was giving all this to *another!* A fair, rosy face, a very much bedecked young creature, was smiling at him, coquetting with him, taking all his tenderness as her due.

Did she know that man was married ? Did she not feel his wife looking at her ? Was it a cruel dream ? Christine pressed her fingers to her eyes, and looked again. There he sat, laughing and happy, in the full glare of the gas that lit up the box. Just then he was taking one of the girl's hands from the flowers she was holding, and he kept it in his own. They seemed to feel that this earth held but them, and the pretty comedy they were playing, — a comedy that was giving the death-wound to a strong, true heart !

With face turned ashen white, features drawn in agony, and eyes

"THE PRETTY COMEDY THEY WERE PLAYING."

so large, so piteous, Christine's world had narrowed down to those two laughing figures before her.

Looking at her, holding himself in terrible check, John Smith stood forgotten.

She seemed like one who had been turned to stone by some great sorrow. She did not move : she hardly breathed. He was watching to see this sorrow change to wounded love and anger. But no :

she leaned forward, motionless, unchanging. He touched her hand. It was as cold as ice. Alarmed, not knowing what might happen to her, for each instant the red line of her compressed lips grew paler and paler, he put his arm through hers, and raised her to her feet.

"Christine, let us go," he whispered.

Not answering, not seeming to see him. Only by a weak, uncertain movement, as if turning to go, did he know she had heard him. Tenderly he helped her to the carriage. Tenderly he drew the warm robe over her. And yet, loving her to madness, he it was that had bared her bosom to this blow.

Before him came in character of flame her gentle words, —

"Life must be bitter indeed to him who injures what he loves."

He was beginning to taste that bitterness, as he looked at the pale, cold ghost of the woman, who, a short hour ago, had been filled with gracious, graceful life.

What had he hoped to gain, he madly asked himself. Did he suppose wounded love and pride would make her seek refuge in the arms he would hold out to her, — those arms so loving to her, so strong to crush him who had slighted and insulted her? Did he expect *any thing* from her like another woman?

"Fool, fool!" he called himself a thousand times as he sat looking at her motionless figure.

They reached her door. She held out her hand, and tried to speak good-night. No words came, only a gasping breath. And, with that frozen look of piteous woe on her face, she was passing away from him, into the dark and silent house. He could not have it so.

"Christine," — and he caught the ice-cold hand in his, detaining her, — "if there is any thing under heaven that your father might do for you, tell me, and it shall be done; for no father could love you more tenderly than I."

He spoke so gently, and looked so true, that the poor girl tried to make some answer. She opened her lips to speak, but again only a gasping sob came forth. And then, to show her thankfulness to this good uncle, she pressed her lips to his hand, and, closing the door after her, vanished from his sight.

He stood for a few moments, half tempted to break down this slight wooden barrier, and be near her. If *that* would have really brought him near her, he would have broken it into fragments. But he knew too well the woman he loved. He dared not remain longer; for his coachman was watching him, and doubtless wondering at his delay. John Smith understood human nature too well to look upon servants as machines. He knew them as severe and often just critics of those who paid their wages, and he took care not to give his a chance to criticise him. Even now, in the midst of the storm of passion, remembering the man on the box waiting for him, he took out his watch as if marking the hour, then came leisurely down the steps, stopped on the sidewalk as if deliberating, again took out the watch, and then saying, "Well, James, I think we'd better drive home. It is rather too late for the office," stepped slowly into the carriage, and pulled the door to with a snap. And James, touching the whip to the horses, said, as if to some one near, —

"Well, I never! He's a cool one! From the way he was bowing over her pretty hand, I thought he felt something; but it's no more to him than saying good-night to one of his own old ladies."

"A cool one!" Most astute James! You are all wrong this time. A seething caldron was more calm and cool than this man's brain.

Reaching his home, he said good-night to his coachman. Civility to servants being one of his minor rules, even now he did not depart from it. Seeing no light from any window but his own, he walked quickly up-stairs, and closed the door.

What would she do? What would come of this? Would Malcolm reach home, and, after a lovers' quarrel, would they make it up again? No: there could be no quarrelling with Christine. In her face there had not been one trace of anger.

He who had travelled the world over, and had seen the greatest masters' greatest works, who had stopped spellbound before the sorrowful face of the Mater Dolorosa, had never beheld such sorrow as in that woman's face to-night.

"If there were a God and a heaven, I should think her an angel grieving for a lost soul."

Was there a God, an all-powerful being? The doubt of what he had long ago taught himself as certainty made him pause an instant. Then, holding up his hand as if taking a solemn oath, he spoke aloud. "If, in the universe, there is a Supreme Power, give me but Christine, and I will be its slave."

He stopped and listened.

No sound but the ticking of the clock, the softened murmur of a city's breathing, and the heavy beatings of his heart. This heart, burning with passion, seemed about to burst the iron frame incasing it.

"Fool, fool!" He laughed in bitter scorn at his own weakness, and, dashing from his brow the heavy beads of sweat, leaned out in the cold night-air.

It was December, and very cold; but he seemed suffocating. Tearing open his collar, while every object whirled before his blood-shot eyes, he clutched for support at the window-sill as he fell panting beside it.

Where was all his greatness now? Where his vaunted strength?

A child crying for the moon was not weaker than he. Tears, actually tears, were in his burning eyes, that for years had looked calmly on a people's degradation. He who had supported laws that lower humanity, who had gone into distant lands, and hurried thousands to their own despair, without one pitying throb of the calm, cool heart, the machine of his magnificent physique, he now was grovelling in the dust because of one weak woman.

CHAPTER XXV.

INJURY REQUITED.

AND she? Closing the door, she fell as one dead.

The little maid, who had been waiting up for her gentle mistress, was enjoying a doze. Startled by the closing door, she awakened, and, putting down the pictures she held in her hand, ran to open the door leading to the hall, expecting to see Christine. The hall was dark and perfectly still.

"Was I dreaming?" said Maggie. Then, going back into the bright little sitting-room, she brought out a light, and screamed with fright when she saw Christine lying on the floor, apparently dead.

Her scream called to her aid the cook, who came as quickly as she could; and together, raising Christine, they laid her on the lounge.

"Is she dead? Shall I go for a doctor?" whispered the sobbing Maggie.

"Sure, don't be a goose. She's fainted. It's her condition. I'm a married woman, and I know." And then, all the while busied with the insensible form before her, she related the experiences of herself and half-dozen friends to Maggie, who was crying bitterly.

Finally they had Christine's dress changed for a long, loose wrapper of white cashmere. This had always been Maggie's admiration.

"She looks like an angel in it, and may be one sooner than we think," she sobbed, as the cook said, —

" Not that fussy thing. Just a night-dress, you goose ! "

But Maggie still held out the robe ; and, as Christine's prolonged faint was making her nervous, Sallie dexterously slipped it over the deathlike figure, and began more vigorously to rub and shake her.

" Well," she said, " I wish her husband would come, and see for himself he is breaking her heart. Though she don't never complain, it's easy enough to see. Just six months married, and she to be a mother before six months more." Still rubbing and shaking, and still no signs of life.

" Maggie," Sallie said at last, " I do believe she is dead." And she, too, began to cry.

But Christine was not dead. For her the merciful sleep had not begun. And when Maggie, with wild screams, threw herself upon her mistress as the hopeful Sallie gave her up, Christine stirred, opened her eyes, and said, —

" I heard some one cry as if in pain."

" It was me, mum," answered the now delighted Maggie.

" Are you sick, my child ? " Christine asked in a weak voice. Then seeing, bended over her, both Maggie and Sallie, with tears still on their faces, it returned slowly to her that *she* had been the one in pain. And such pain ! It all came back to her now. Even each detail of the woman's dress, and every clustering curl on Malcolm's bright head, as he leaned towards her.

She tried to rise, and would have fallen, had not Sallie's strong arm caught her.

" Sure, mum, you're too weak. Just drink a bit of this." And she put to her lips a cup of strong coffee, which Maggie, with whispered directions, had found tucked away in the kitchen-closet.

Christine turned away her head.

" Mum, for the child's sake," Sallie said.

For the child's sake ! Most eloquent and potent pleader. If all the rhetoric of the world had been at Sallie's command, she could never have made so powerful an argument. For that precious life within her own! What would she not do for its sake? So she drank the coffee, and ate a little, while her heart was full of woe.

"What time is it, Maggie?"

"Three o'clock, mum."

"And you are both up, waiting on me! I thank you for your kindness, and I am sorry to have given so much trouble," she gently said. "And now, please go to bed, and try to sleep."

"Oh, please, mum, let me stay up till you're asleep! Please let me just comb out your hair. Sallie pulled it down when she was a-bathing your head. And indeed, mum," Maggie whispered, as Sallie's head disappeared in the hall, "I'm afraid we've spoiled your pretty dress with all the water we spilled on it."

"No matter," answered Christine. "But go now to bed. I would rather be alone."

And alone she was with her sorrow.

John Smith was right. She did not feel a trace of anger. That she was slighted and insulted did not seem to enter her thoughts. All her pain was, that *he* was false. And this conviction, like a sea of woe, covered, in its black depths, every bright hope of her life. Love and trust forever buried under its cruel waves, she did not question what the future would be. She was like one turned into stone by the great, the ever present, certainty of his untruth.

Through the long, silent hours, and the morning's wakening bustle, she still sat where the maids had left her. She did not notice that the sunlight was streaming in the half-closed shutters, and lay in broad bands over the floor, marking the growing day. She did not know that many times Maggie's head, and Sallie's too, had been peeping in the door, with tear-filled eyes of sympathy. To see her thus, her husband still away, they knew some great grief had befallen her.

" Perhaps he's been sent off on a mission," suggested Maggie.

" More like he's going to take another wife, and she's breaking her heart," answered Sallie, who had had her own troubles on this score. " Poor thing, poor thing!" she added, shaking her head. " He's a brute, or he'd waited till after the baby came. She must eat, or she'll

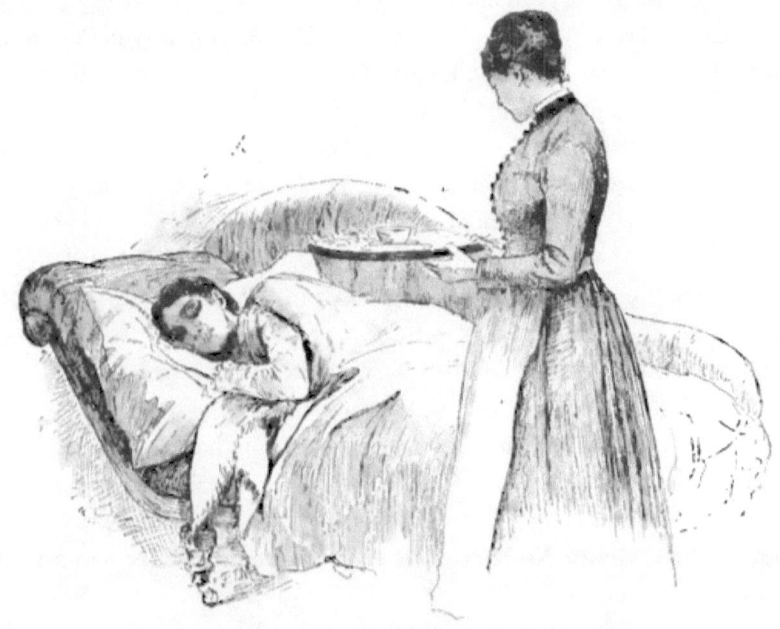

"AFTER A LITTLE, SHE RETURNED WITH A TRAY."

die," continued the kind-hearted woman, and then hurried off to the kitchen to make some toast and tea.

After a little, she returned with a tray neatly arranged, and went towards the sorrow-stricken woman. She spoke to her, but received no answer. Then, putting down the tray, she knelt at her feet, and taking the two cold hands between her strong, warm ones, began to chafe them while she spoke.

" Dear lady, look up."

Christine raised her face, and looked out from her great, sad eyes, yet looking seemed not to see.

Poor Sallie had never heard of grief like this, and began to sob and cry out of pure pity. But she, who had had in this very city the mother's sorrowful experience, spoke to the mother's heart.

" Listen, deary," she said. " Don't take on so, or you'll perhaps injure the poor baby you will have before many months. It cannot help its coming, poor thing! and its life may not be so bad, with a dear, strong mother to take care of it, and teach it right. But, if you take on so now, you might injure it for life."

At her words, a gasping sob shook the poor girl.

" The child that was coming!" God pity it! God help it!

While Sallie was in vain seeking to calm Christine's terrible agitation, the door-bell rang.

Maggie running to it, in the hope of seeing Malcolm, found Mr. John Smith.

After a night such as he had never known, he had so controlled all outward signs of the agony he had endured, as to take his accustomed place at table, and pay his accustomed courtesies to the three Mrs. Smiths. Mrs. Smith No. 1 remarked he looked pale. He had a slight headache, he answered.

" You have been overworking?" she asked.

" Perhaps," he replied, and then busied himself with the little cares of the table.

He spoke to each with his usual kindness, made his usual inquiries of each; and, while he felt as if every instant were an hour of torture, he did not show the slightest haste or impatience. When, at last, the frightful meal was over, he stood a few moments, chatting pleasantly with his wives, as if to try his own strength, and see how long he dared trifle with the raging storm within.

Once in the street, he hailed a passing carriage, and shortly dismissed it a few doors from Christine's house. He had hardly touched the bell when the door flew open ; and while those terrible, gasping sobs smote on his heart, Maggie told him all she knew of what had happened.

"We found her like dead on the floor," she said ; "and then Sallie put on a wrapper, and we rubbed and bathed her until Sallie said she was dead. And then I screamed and screamed, and fell a-kissing her ; for I loved her, and the dead don't know. But, O sir ! she was not dead, but opened those great dark eyes so sorrowful-like for calling her back to life. And then she made us go to bed. And, when we came down this morning, we found her sitting just where we had left her, and looking for all the world as if she was stone. And then Sallie said she must eat. So she began to talk of the baby that she says is to come in three months, and then those terrible sobs began ; and we believe she is going to die at any rate. And Mr. Malcolm, he ain't never come home."

Maggie had been crying and sobbing as if her heart would break, and now stood holding on to John Smith while she poured forth her story. She still clung to him, not knowing what she was doing ; for she was so grieved about her dear mistress. It was not until he put away her hand that she knew she had been so near the awful Mr. Smith.

At the sitting-room door he paused, and looked at the woman he loved. She was sitting in a large chair, her body bent forward, and her head resting on Sallie's breast ; the dark hair concealing her face, and falling like a mantle of night over the snowy robe lying in graceful folds around her ; the fearful, gasping sobs shaking her frame, and even stirring the strong, ruddy woman kneeling at her side, whose coarse red arms were holding Christine to her honest heart.

Only her cook ! But a woman, good and true, who had tasted

sorrow, and whose tears fell thick and fast at the grief of this sister-woman.

Standing an instant at the door, madly jealous even of Sallie, yet, through all his passion and pain, having a consciousness of the extreme grace of the drooping figure in white, and a desire to see her face. Then, with a step, he was at her side. Dismissing the weeping women, he took the slender hands in his as he knelt in Sallie's place.

Would she put her head on his breast, — he who never before had knelt at human feet? His very breath ceased in the half-second of expectancy.

No. She leaned her head back on the chair, showing her face, while the white lace fell away from the snowy pillar of her throat, and the gasping sobs, that had never ceased, at every instant seemed about to rend her tender bosom.

How grief-stricken, yet how beautiful, she looked to him! He smoothed the soft hands, clasped the delicate wrists, talked to her as a father to his child, forced a few spoonfuls of the warm tea between her teeth, until gradually, gradually the sobs became less frequent, less terrible ; and softening tears rained down her face, falling on his hands that were smoothing hers.

How it happened, he could never tell, and cursed himself a thousand times for his madness. But thus close to her, as he had never before been, holding her hands, feeling her soft breath, while her tears' slow stream fell down her face, and bedewed his flesh, his passion, like a furious lion, tore down its cage, and glared triumphant. The hands that were soothing hers as a father, caught her in a lover's mad embrace, and crushed her to his bosom.

"Christine, I love you! Leave this weak and shallow creature, who is utterly false to you. Say you will but be mine, and, sure as there is law in any land, I will make you legally so. You shall be made free, and so will I, from the false ties that bind us. Our marriage shall be recognized everywhere ; and you shall be the honored of men, as you are the mistress of my soul. For you I will do deeds so great, so noble, that they will raise me even to your God of goodness. We will leave Utah, whose institutions revolt your purity. We will take your grandfather and friends, and make a home wherever you shall will ; and there, in that home, that paradise, you shall feel what a man can do for woman like you."

In the paroxysm of intense passion, he had risen to his feet, raising her also ; for never once had he relaxed his fierce embrace. Standing thus, with her bosom pressed close to his own, he felt her fluttering, weak, but persistent effort to release herself. Looking into her deathlike face, the possible effects of his madness came over him like the opening of a tomb. The horrible thought that she was dying, and he had killed her, made his arms drop ; and she was free.

Weak, trembling, clinging for strength to the chair, she stood a queen. A widowed wife, an insulted woman, but a queen in the magnitude of her purity and her woes !

Even then, with his love, passion, and horror full upon him, he was wondering what she would do, so different was she always from any being he had ever imagined could exist. Was she trying to summon that faint breath to bid him leave her forever as a coward, and insulter of grieving womanhood ?

He could endure any bitterness from her, for he deserved it. If she had taken a knife, and stabbed him to the heart, he would not have lifted his hand to prevent the blow. He felt like Satan driven from the sight of God. He knew he could never more look on her face, and this pale woman was the only god he worshipped. His full crime against her, and his mad love for her, rose before him, and drove him to despair.

She raises her arms : the loose white sleeves fall away, showing to his aching eyes their perfect loveliness. Her dark eyes open wide, as if to the God she worships. Her lips unclose. His heart stops beating. Is she about to curse him? A faint whisper comes : —

"Lord, Lord, have mercy on us, poor sinners!"

She was praying for him, — for him, who had so injured her!

As the faint words died on the air, the great rush of mighty waters came in her ears, the deadly faintness again overpowered her; and before he could, or dared, stretch out his arms to catch her, she lay at his feet, a white marvel of loveliness.

"O angel! O saint!" he whispered, kneeling beside her unconscious body, and looking at her as if to impress on his heart each charm of form and feature. Then Maggie's words, "for the dead don't know," came back to him. He knew that never again in life could he look at or speak to her; and he stooped, and took her in his arms.

"HAVE MERCY ON US, POOR SINNERS!"

"For the last time," he murmured, as we do to our dead; and then he kissed her face, brow, lips. "Cold, cold, and deathlike. Have you gone, pure spirit? Is there, in the hereafter, a resting-place for such as thou? Then, pray for me once more, most lovely lips! Farewell, farewell, my first, my last, my only love!"

Again and again he kissed her. Then placing a cushion under her head, putting on his hat, and pulling it down to conceal his face, he summoned Sallie.

"Your mistress has fainted again. Attend to her, and send Maggie for a doctor. I will go for one too. But there must be more than one here. This is something serious."

And so he hurried off, his step brisk, his face showing but little of what he had passed through, but his heart full of despair. He felt like a man who had seen the grave close over all he cared for in the world. And so he ever felt.

"Man's love is of man's life a thing apart."

It was so with this man. Until his death he would love the woman who was to him a revelation of the possibilities of human nature. Yet he lived the same life he had led before he met her, followed the same ambitions, and upheld the same laws. If, for her sake, he did secret acts of charity, and sometimes mercifully shielded another woman, it was between him and the silent, watchful Power that rules over all.

On leaving her, he hastened to send a doctor : then he went to his office, and thence to his home. His friends saw no difference in him : his wives saw no change in him. He ever treated them with the same kind deference. Yet, during the next few days, he seemed to be moving, speaking, eating, in a dream, — a terrible dream, more real than all the rest of his life.

* * * * * * * * * * *

On hearing from the doctors that Christine was out of danger, and would probably soon go to her grandfather's, he made up his mind to leave at once for Washington.

He was in the midst of his preparations for departure one morning, when Malcolm called. Mr. Smith had conceived a hatred for this handsome, shallow nephew, whom he used to like. He could hardly endure to breathe the same air with him, yet he received him civilly enough.

"You are going to Washington, uncle?"

"Yes."

Mr. Smith was busy looking over a bundle of papers. Malcolm waited for a little, and hesitated, moved about the room, and finally threw himself into a chair, with an air half-sulky, half-determined. He had something of importance to say to this uncle, who had been a sort of guardian to him; supplying his wants as a child, and, when arrived at man's estate, securing for him a fine position in the Mormon banking-house. There had never been any obedience exacted from him; but he had generally consulted Mr. Smith on any matters of importance, and generally found him of great help. And now while Malcolm was very full of some subject, and showed by his manner that he had something to say, his uncle seemed to feel no interest in any thing beyond that bundle of papers, over which he was bending with knitted brows. Tired of waiting for him to look up, Malcolm said, —

"Perhaps you won't be surprised to learn I've made up my mind to take another wife."

"You have? And what of your vow?" Still busy with the papers.

"Why, uncle, you told me that would have no effect in Utah! and Utah suits me well enough to live in."

"Perhaps, sir," Mr. Smith answered in a muffled voice, "Utah may be lenient to the breaking of vows made against her institutions. But there is a stronger restraint to the weakness of men in the knowledge that a perjurer can never be looked upon as a gentleman; that no man, in whom there is a remnant of manhood, will extend to him the right hand of fellowship."

He was trembling with rage, and put down the papers, because their shaking betrayed him.

Startled and confused, Malcolm knew not what to answer. The uncle who had laughed at his vow was now confronting him with scorn for breaking it.

He had had a "scene" this morning with Christine ; and partly for encouragement, partly to ask his uncle to reason with her, he had called at his office ; and, instead of an ally, he found a foe. His face darkened, and grew dogged.

John Smith, looking at him, thinking of his youth, of his own evil influence, and, more than all, of the woman he loved, whose heart this man was breaking, stepped nearer to him, and said, more kindly than would have been possible had not Christine's face, as he last saw it in her deathlike faint, come before him, —

"Malcolm," — and he laid his hand upon his nephew's shoulder, — "keep true to your vow. It is the only way to retain your own and others' respect. I am rich, and have some power. Only keep true to this vow made to Christine, and I will pledge myself to advance you until your ambition is satisfied. It is not likely I shall ever have children ; so you need not worry about the future, for I will make you and your children my heirs."

The young man hesitated ; and his uncle, with the hand still on his shoulder, stood watching him. Then the handsome face darkened, and grew dogged again. Taking his hand from his shoulder, John Smith faced this poor apology for manhood, to whom nature had given the beauty of a sun-god.

"Be true to your vow, and I will keep my word. You shall stand foremost in Utah."

No lightening of the dogged look on Malcolm's face. Then John Smith, in tones of bitter scorn, —

"Break this vow, and never again claim kinship or acquaintance with me ; for, if I met you at the gate of heaven, I would not recognize you. I cannot consort with *perjurers.*"

"Well," said Malcolm, "I love a girl: she loves me; and her father, Mr. Mellon, is very rich, as you know. She's willing to marry me if I had a dozen wives, and I sha'n't let Christine's whining cant come between me and my happiness."

It was well for Malcolm that his uncle was a man of great self-control; for at this instant, while he was standing there in the full brightness of his beauty, speaking thus of Christine, it was only the iron will of that uncle that kept him from clutching at the handsome throat, and strangling him. He never knew that the most dangerous moment of his life was when he stood opposite his uncle, who was looking at him in quiet scorn.

"You have made up your mind to be false to every principle of honor, and break this solemn vow?"

"Well, I've given my promise to the girl," Malcolm answered half apologetically, and then added doggedly, "And I won't go back on it. Her father has agreed to give her thirty thousand dollars as dowry."

"You surely are not in need of money! You have only been married six months, and Matthew did not let his child go to you portionless."

"A few thousands," Malcolm answered sneeringly.

"Malcolm, have you spent this money?"

"That is my own affair, Mr. Smith."

Disgusted, and angered almost beyond endurance, John Smith still held himself in-check.

"Malcolm, give up this notion, and I will settle thirty thousand dollars on your first child."

"It is not a notion, Mr. Smith. I guess if any fellow could have a pretty girl, with a nice portion to do with as he chose, he wouldn't refuse. Besides, I've promised her; and a promise to one is as good as a promise to another."

John Smith clinched his teeth to keep the words back. After a moment he said, —

" Have you told your wife of your intentions ? "

" Yes."   And here Malcolm grew more like himself, the winning smile coming back to his handsome mouth.   " And I came here to see if you could not reason with her.   She refuses to live in the same town with me.   Says she will go back to her grandfather.   That she will not injure her unborn child, and all that sort of cant."

Again John Smith's fingers closed convulsively : again Malcolm's throat was in danger.

With deepening scorn in voice and eyes, his uncle said, —

" Sir, I cannot reason with your wife on a subject whereon we agree.   A vow once made should be sacred forever, and a perjurer is one I cannot permit in my apartment."

He opened the door for his nephew to pass out, looking down at him from the height of his contempt ; then, hurrying his preparations, left the city in the evening.   He dared not remain so near Christine.   He knew not at what moment he might be guilty of a madness worse than any before.   Before he left, however, he called at the bank, and deposited, settled on Christine, the same sum that Matthew had given her as dowry.   He arranged the interest to be paid to her, either personally or by letter, and gave her country address as her home.

" Beloved," he said to himself, " at least you will not be penniless ; and, though you will never know it, I shall watch over and protect you."

CHAPTER XXVI.

"FOR HER CHILD'S SAKE."

FTER her last fainting-fit, Christine was very ill, — so ill, that the doctors summoned did not leave her for hours. John Smith had told them to spare no expense. She was his niece, and the bills must be sent to him ; and, John Smith being of wealth and consequence, the doctors gave much time, and all their skill, to their patient.

After many days of illness, and faithful nursing from Sallie and Maggie, Christine crept from her bedroom to the sofa in the sitting-room, and lay there a shadow of her former self. She had been too ill to speak to Malcolm ; and he had only occasionally, and for a few minutes at a time, visited the sick-room.

Full of blooming health, he had a dread of sickness, or of any thing that alluded to death. Contenting himself with telling Sallie to "take good care of her," he avoided the room, and even the house, where his wife was hovering on the borders of the spirit-world. He had been so little at home the last few days, that he was astonished, on entering the room, to see her lying on the sofa.

"Why, Christine," he said, going towards her as she half rose, "you're almost well ! How glad I am, my love !" And, taking her hand, he kissed her.

He thought it a curious freak of her sickness, that she, who had

always so gladly welcomed his lightest caress, should have tried to
move away as he kissed her. He sat beside her for a few moments,
chatting in a pleasant way. He did not notice that she was trembling,
and trying to speak. After the first glance, he did not look at her.
Her extreme pallor and evident weakness were not pleasant to his
eyes, that only liked to rest on the fresh and blooming. But he was
doing the "duty" business, as he called it, and, at the same time,
casting about in his mind for some way of escape. He was wishing
Sallie or Maggie would come in, and afford an excuse for leaving ; but
they had seen him enter, and were very carefully keeping out of the
way. Finding no opening made for him, he concluded to make one
for himself, and, looking at the clock on the mantel, said, —

"Why, I didn't know it was so late ! I must be off, dear, to business. Don't fret, love. It will soon be over, and then we can have
more time together."

And, stooping to kiss her good-by, he thought the little chat with
Christine was well over ; but, as he turned to go, her hand detained
him. For the first time since he entered, she spoke ; and the words
were so low he had to bow his head to hear them.

"Malcolm, your uncle and I sat in the box opposite yours the
evening 'Othello' was given."

"Oh ! you did ? "

He threw himself into a chair, and waited for the "scene," as he
phrased it, to be over. As she did not speak, he worked himself into
a petty rage, trying to force things a little ; for, to him, it was becoming awfully slow, this waiting for some one to speak who looked more
like a ghost than a woman.

"And so you, the noble, the exalted Christine, condescended to
play the spy, did you ? "

"I did not see you until the close of the play. Up to that time,
I had never doubted your truth. And since then " —

She was so weak, trembling violently, and the tears were rising to her eyes. If there was one thing Malcolm hated, it was a woman in tears. It was one of the few unchanging sentiments he was capable of. Sneeringly he spoke, —

" And *now*, madam, what do your doubts tell you ? "

She did not answer : she could not, her feelings were so strong, and she was still so weak. Finding his taunt did not stir any angry reproaches, he rose, and, going over to the sofa, spoke in kinder tones : —

" Now, my dear girl, don't be silly. You saw nothing that should have made you unhappy. I was talking to a very nice young lady, whom I hope you will learn to like very much. She feels most kindly to you, — is ready to treat you like a sister ; and I truly hope you will receive her in the same pleasant manner, for I intend to make her my wife."

" Make her your wife ! *Malcolm !* "

Her weakness forgotten, the woman stood upright. How tall and shadowy she looked ! her hands clasped tight together, and the great eyes, filled with amazement, staring at him.

" Well, madam ! " The beauty of the man was almost lost in the cold brutality of his expression as he stood facing her. Did there come to them both a memory of that other time, when, under the orchard-trees, they had stood thus face to face, while he pleaded for, and won, the woman whom now, like a useless toy, he was casting aside ? It may have been so ; for, once more approaching her, he once more spoke in kindly manner : —

" Now, Christine, don't get the heroics. Be a sensible, good girl, and I will be a kinder, better husband to you than ever before. If you make a point of it, I will delay my marriage until after the child comes ; though I hope you won't be so silly. This second marriage will make no difference to you. Nellie's father will give her a house near, if you object to sharing this one with her. I find, by looking over the papers, the house is deeded to you ; and, while in Utah a man is generally entitled to his wife's estate, I will waive this right. I will do any thing in reason if you will only submit to the inevitable, and *inevitable* it is," he added, again sinking to brutality. Then, in a more usual manner, he went on, as if arguing a point of slight, and not vital, interest, —

"Why, Christine, if you're only sensible, you two young women can live together in peace and harmony, and be company for each other when business calls me away. Look at my uncle's wives, how pleasantly they get on !"

He waited a little for her to answer. As she did not, he went on, —

"And, if you really want to please me, you will try to get well and strong, so you can take the true wife's place, and give your consent to the marriage."

Until this moment she had stood perfectly still, gazing at him. Words had rushed to her lips, — pleading, earnest words, praying him, for the sake of the little one, to have pity, and be true to his vow : but, as he went on speaking, the words died before they had been spoken ; for she felt their utter powerlessness. When with this last insult, uttered with a smile, he advanced a step nearer to her, she fell back on the sofa, answering in a faint but determined voice, —

"Consent to a crime ? Rob my unborn child of its birthright ? *Never.*" Then quickly, in a nervous whisper, she went on, —

"You can have this house. I shall leave it, and never enter it again. I will go to my grandfather to-morrow." And then, for the sake of her child, her heart broke out in one last effort. Falling on her knees before him, she exclaimed, —

"Malcolm, for the sake of this baby, do not break your solemn vow ! Do not commit bigamy. Be faithful to your better self. Do not make this child of ours the child of a criminal. The law of the land may not punish the crime, but it is a crime in the sight of God and man. Have pity on yourself : have pity on your child. As you have a soul to be saved, do not violate God's sacred law."

She still knelt before him, still mutely pleading with clasped hands and upraised eyes. He looked down on her, and laughed, brutality and selfish-ness portrayed in every line of his face.

"Well," — and he laughed again, — "you are a greater fool than I thought you. Go to your grand-father if you will ; but remember, it is only my indul-gence that permits you this license : for in Utah's law, unless divorced, a wife must cleave to her husband ; and it would be rather difficult, in a land whose foremost in-stitution is polyga-my, for a woman to

"FALLING ON HER KNEES BEFORE HIM."

obtain a divorce because her husband decides he needs another wife."

Still at his feet, the silent figure pleaded for the unborn child.

"Perhaps, madam," — and his beautiful mouth curled into yet more brutal sneers, — "it is as well for you to know that a marriage like ours is not recognized here ; and, if I choose, I can proclaim your child a bastard."

Hurling this at her, crushing her under its false and cruel weight, he left the room, nor looked behind to see his work. Sallie, who had heard his loud, excited voice, had stood near the door of Christine's room, ready to rush in if he offered personal violence. At his closing words, she could hardly contain herself, and shaking her fist, hardened with honest labor, at his retreating figure, said, —

"O you brute! I wish I had a chance to spoil your beauty for you. I'd do it, so there'd never be a sign left to guess it by." Then, hurrying in to the prostrate woman on the floor, she found Christine panting, exhausted, but perfectly conscious. Relieved, for she had dreaded another of those terrible faints, she lifted her in her arms, and put her on the sofa.

*　*　*　*　*　*　*　*　*　*　*

"I must sit up, Sallie. I must write a line," she whispered hurriedly. "Quick!" she said, seeing Sallie hesitate.

"Ah! sure deary, you're too weak."

"I must, Sallie. Please!"

Sallie brought her writing-desk, and held it while Christine wrote a few tremulous words to Matthew.

"SALT LAKE.

"FATHER, — Meet me at the train to-morrow. I am going home to you.
"CHRISTINE."

Not a word of explanation. It was not needed. Matthew would know his child was in trouble, and, if alive, would be there to welcome her. The message was sent; and Christine, filled with nervous haste, was directing the packing of her trunk, — the same little trunk that stood in the corner of her maiden room, and which Tabitha had packed the last morning they were all together, when, except for the coming parting, they were so happy. Motioning aside each article that had been bought since her marriage, she took only the things she had brought with her as a bride, and a few trinkets Matthew had chosen for her during his visit. Out of these, selecting a remembrance for Sallie and Maggie, she gave them with gentle words, as one friend to another.

When all was finished, the confusion of the room made orderly, and Christine's travelling-dress on a chair, ready for the morning's journey, she turned to Sallie, asking, —

" May I sleep in your room to-night ? "

" Sure, deary, just sleep in your own bed ; and I'll draw the sofa near the door to be handy when you call me. I'd like to see any one pass over me to trouble her," she muttered under her breath.

But there was no need for anxiety. Malcolm did not come near the house, neither that day, nor for several days after Christine's departure. She left in the morning's train, Maggie and Sallie riding with her to the depot, and standing there crying long after the cars, that were bearing away their mistress, were out of sight. It was a long, weary ride to poor Christine, sitting alone, too weak and sick even to think.

When, at evening, she reached the terminus of the road, and saw the dear father's face in the crowd at the station, she staggered out, and down the steps, and fell into his outstretched arms. He blessed her, he soothed her, carrying her to the waiting wagon he had made comfortable for his darling ; and then, turning away to hide his tears, he went for her trunk.

" My birdling, my birdling ! I did not know it was so bad," he murmured to himself. He was shocked at the change in her, who, when he left her, was in the full beauty and bloom of woman-hood.

The quiet ride through the snow-covered country, the loving tenderness of her grandfather, and the home-coming, were doing wonders for the sick, heart-broken woman. And when she reached the little cottage, where she had passed such peaceful days ; when the door, thrown open, let fall on her the warm, bright light ; when the loving faces of Tabitha, Patience, and Christie in his mother's arms, hastened towards her, welcoming her with joy, she was no longer a lone wanderer, but the dearly beloved coming back to her own. Even Rex, grown as large as a lion, seemed to feel he must do his share ; and barking, and wagging his tail, he capered around the group.

Matthew had asked no explanation ; but riding by his side, her head on his shoulder, and one arm thrown round her to steady her from the jolting of the wagon, she had simply said, —

"Malcolm is about to take a second wife, and I have come back to you."

Not a word blaming her husband, not a mention of John Smith's cruel insult. Only these few words. And never again did she allude to her life in Salt Lake, but she prayed for the two who had so cruelly wronged her. Often would her lips form the words, that above the contention of politics, the merry clatter of a festive meal, the subdued hum of fashionable reception, were constantly ringing in John Smith's ears, "Lord, Lord, have mercy upon us, poor sinners !" And the friends who loved her, seeing her thus come back to them, broken in health and spirit, loved her all the more for the suffering that had left its mark forever stamped upon her face.

Christine had not dreamed it possible that ever again she could feel so near content as now, sitting in an easy-chair before the bright, warm fire ; Christie propped up in another chair by her side, looking at her in his old fond way ; Patience at her feet, with her heart in her eyes ; and Tabitha, full of motherly tenderness, coaxing her to drink some warm tea. And then the door opened, and Matthew's noble face appeared.

"Ah ! thanks for the place left for me so near my birdling." And, taking the chair Patience had placed for him close to Christine's, he kissed the hand his child extended to him.

"This is home, now we have you, my darling."

"This is home," said Patience's loving face, looking up into hers.

Christie and Tabitha took up the words, saying them softly to her. Rex left his warm corner, and came towards Christine as if about to speak, but contenting himself with a knowing wink at Christie, and an affectionate poke of his nose in the wan little hand, went back to his corner and his snooze, grunting in a satisfied kind of way, as if he had fully performed his duty.

"He says he quite agrees with us, Christine dear," said Patience, who was always translating Rex's thoughts.

The absent one rom the group of friends was not forgotten.

"Is there a day fixed for Martin's return?" asked Christine.

"No; but surely in time for Christmas," answered Paience. "He has been now working over a nonth for Mr. Marks, and gets four

"SITTING IN AN EASY-CHAIR BEFORE THE BRIGHT, WARM FIRE."

dollars per day. He is 'rigging up a little place for us' so he wrote in his last letter. We'll go early in the new year, and you and Matthew are coming too. How happy I will be!"

"Father, is this possible?" said Christine, turning to Matthew.

"This little girl has been coaxing so, that I can hardly refuse her," the old man answered, patting Patience's fair cheek. "But, darling,"—turning to his child,—"I will do about it just as you wish."

"O father ! I will be so thankful to go."

And so, with hopes for the coming year filling their hearts, and brightening even the heavy clouds on Christine's life, the quiet home-evening drew to its close.

CHAPTER XXVII.

IN THE SITTING-ROOM.

CHRISTINE had been home a week. Daily growing stronger and stronger, she could now walk around the little garden. The plants all wore their winter garb of snowy white, and were hung with icy jewels that sparkled gayly in the bright sunshine. She was sitting by the warm fire, sewing on some tiny garment. Near the window, on a large stand, were the plants love had tended for her, — Matthew's geranium and ivy, Christie's mignonette, Tabitha's hyacinths, and Patience's rose, — a large, healthy bush, but not a sign of a bud.

"Vexing, isn't it?" said the girl, when she had given it to Christine. "If you only knew how I've watched and tended it to get one little bud! But it wouldn't come." And she sighed.

"Never mind, dear," Christine had made answer. "Each glossy leaf is as fair as a flower to me, for it tells of my Patience's love."

These friends never spoke now of the past. There was too much pain buried in its graves. Their hopes and thoughts were all for the coming year. On the evening of Christine's arrival, Matthew, going to the door with Tabitha and her children, repeated to them Christine's words to him. They asked no questions; for they loved her, and respected the sacredness of a grief so great that it had forever washed away Christine's youth.

She was thinking now, as she sat alone, of what their lives would be when once out of Utah, and really under the protection of the laws of the United States ; and her heart gave a little throb of something like happiness that her child would not be born a Mormon ; when the door was opened, and Patience, brighter and fairer than the morning, stood before her, clapping her hands, laughing and dancing about, while the merry dimples played hide and seek. She was the Patience of the olden days ; for of late she had been paler and more nervous than those who loved her, liked to see this happy little maiden.

" It is the constant watching of Bishop White," she would answer, when asked if she felt badly. " It is fairly killing me. Wherever I go, wherever I look, I expect to see those wicked eyes blinking at me." And she would screw her own lovely ones, and twist her pretty face, into a comical resemblance of the bishop. But to-day she was so full of laughter and mirth, that Christine felt herself grow younger in the glow of this bright being.

" O Christine ! " — the merry voice filled the room with youth's own music, — " I've just seen something that has made me so glad. I went out to bring in some wood for the fire, when, lo ! at the gate stood that fearful Bishop White. I felt like running back to the house ; for does it not seem strange, though for months he has been popping up around me in most unexpected places, this was the first time he ever saw me apart from mother ? I felt ashamed of myself for my cowardice, and went on filling my basket with wood. Trembling like a leaf, and thankful I had all I could carry, I turned to go into the house, when — I almost screamed — there he stood, right between me and the kitchen-door. ' You silly little beauty,' he said, putting out his hand, and trying to take mine ; but I held the wood so he couldn't come near me. ' Give me your hand for a moment, and I will put this ring on it.' And he held out a golden ring, with a stone like a dewdrop sparkling in it. I drew back, and was just about to call for

mother, when hurried steps up the walk made the bishop start away
from me.   Looking up, we both beheld, whom do you suppose?   Mrs.
White!   With a face as red as a beet, and shaking so with anger she
could hardly speak, she stood glaring at the bishop and me.   I was as
thankful to see her as if she had been an angel.   But the bishop!   I

"HE HELD OUT A GOLDEN RING."

wish you could have seen his face!"   And Patience fell to dancing,
and clapping her hands, at the bare remembrance ; while her laughter
bubbled up like a clear spring.

   "Well, he looked the color of a sheep before it is washed for a
shearing.   Such a dirty white, and such a sheepish old face as he
raised to hers, saying, in the meekest voice, —

   "'Well, my dear, do you want me?'"

Here Patience gave the funniest imitation of the bishop, so that she even provoked a laugh from Christine.

"'Yes, my dear,' said Mrs. White." And Patience held her head back, and swelled herself out till she looked as near a fat, pursy old lady as any thing so pretty could look. "'I should like you to take a walk with me,' said Mrs. White. And, without a word, the bishop turned, and followed her. Now, although I did not see any collar around his neck, nor chain in her hand, I do believe she had an invisible one ; for he followed, as a whipped dog a master that he feared. And now, thank Heaven ! I don't think I will ever again be troubled with the bishop."

Christine was thankful too. Patience was such a sunny creature, making life brighter for all around, full of intelligence and impetuosity, and, withal, so loving, so dependent on those she loved. It had grieved Christine, in all her own heavy sorrow, to see the cloud that had fallen over this fair girl. And now it was gone. And the bright face, nestling on her knee, looked up to hers full of smiles and happiness.

" I, too, am thankful, dear, that you are happy."

Poor, innocent Patience ! If you could have heard what passed between Bishop White and his wife, you would have fallen on your knees at Christine's feet, and implored her to lend you the long, bright needle in her hand, that you might let out your pure young life.

CHAPTER XXVIII.

AN ARCH-FIEND.

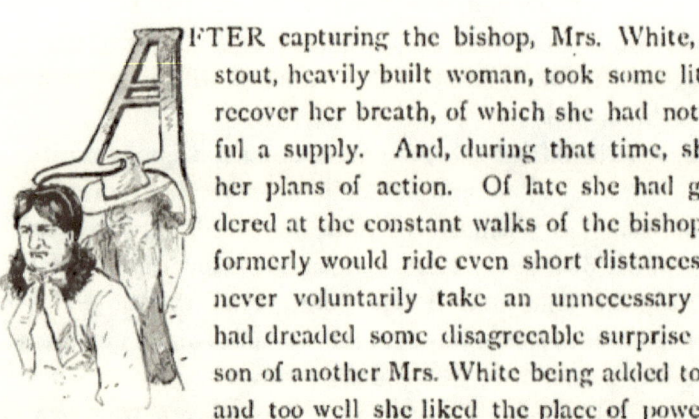

FTER capturing the bishop, Mrs. White, who was a stout, heavily built woman, took some little time to recover her breath, of which she had not too plentiful a supply. And, during that time, she arranged her plans of action. Of late she had greatly wondered at the constant walks of the bishop, — he who formerly would ride even short distances, and would never voluntarily take an unnecessary step. She had dreaded some disagreeable surprise in the person of another Mrs. White being added to the family, and too well she liked the place of power meekly to yield to an intruder.

Up to these walks, to which the bishop never alluded, she had had him under her influence; for by pandering to his every wish, by constant flattery, she had managed to get him completely in her power. It was tiresome, very tiresome, this truckling to a weak and inferior nature; but he was the sole authority in the little town: and — well, to her the game was worth the candle. So, opposing him only when he opposed her will, he rarely attempted it, finding her at other times too able an auxiliary. He had fallen into a way of consulting her; and, though sometimes he might wince when she would quietly discuss the cruel and hidden motive of his deeds, she had such a way of putting the case, that, aiding him to success, she would crush out whatever shade of remorse he might have felt. But about these walks he never spoke. Whatever the motive, — and it must be a strong one, — he kept it to himself.

Determined to solve the mystery, she had for a few weeks past begun a system of following him. He always took the same road, — the one that led to Tabitha's cabin. He generally stopped at the gate, and rarely spoke to any one. Mrs. White grew more and more puzzled. And, what seemed most incomprehensible, no one seemed anxious to attract or conciliate him. The inhabitants of the cabin came and went about their duties, without once looking at Bishop White. And even when Tabitha, and a young girl, who was, as Mrs. White supposed, her daughter, came out to work in the garden, they did not seem to notice the man leaning on the gate watching them.

"It is very curious," she said to herself. "Why should he go there? What does he want of them? Is he making up his mind to take back the house and fine garden, and then turn the woman's talents to use, and let her reclaim another bit of waste land?"

At this possibility, Mrs. White had laughed as at some huge joke. But another phase of possibilities suggested itself.

"Or" — and here she grew pale — "had he begun to desire to re-instate Tabitha at the head of his household? Not if I can prevent it," she said to herself. And so she kept on following and watching; and he, not knowing this, kept on with his constant walks, and watching of Patience.

As usual, Mrs. White had this day followed him, and, as usual, saw him stop at the fence, looking over, as if waiting or expecting something; when suddenly, and most unexpectedly, she saw him open the gate, and, more quickly than she had ever before seen him move, walk towards the house. Anxious to reach him before he could enter the door, or speak to Tabitha, and thus gain him a woman for an ally, and another antagonist for her to overcome, she ran as well as she could.

Puffing, breathless, she reached the wood-pile just as he held a diamond ring towards the young girl who drew away from him. It was a very handsome ring. Mrs. White saw it plainly, and, though too out of breath to speak, was quite enough composed to vow in her mind that she would possess the ring before she slept that night. She saw more than the ring : she had caught the expression of the bishop's face.

"Artful jade!" she thought, as she looked at Patience. "She thinks she'll get more out of him."

Just then, looking up, and beholding her, the bishop meekly followed at her bidding, as Patience, with merry laughter, had described to Christine. The crestfallen bishop walked behind Mrs. White. He supposed she was enraged, and rather dreaded one of the hysterical fits to which she occasionally treated him when he proved obdurate. They walked in silence, until, well out of sight and hearing from the cabin, she surprised him by turning around, beaming with smiles, and then saying, in her blandest tones, —

"What is it, my dear, you wish of that young girl ?"

In spite of his threescore years, the bishop stammered, hesitated, blushed. Those fat-hidden eyes sought the ground, looking for words that he might make some satisfactory explanation. But the bishop was not quick of thought. For a moment this partner of his secrets and his joys looked quietly at him, ill concealing her scorn for so low and weak a creature, and then laying her hand on his arm, and thus holding him at her side, began to waken his ruling passion, — avarice.

"I know what you want, — I who always willingly serve you as my bishop as well as husband, dear both in affection and religion." And she raised her eyes to heaven, while, looking at her in perfect amazement at her sudden increase of piety, the bishop wondered what she intended to do and say.

"Dear bishop," — she grew affectionate, — "you want to bestow your lovely daughter on the greatest dignitary of our church."

The bishop started. This idea had never suggested itself.

" You want " — she went on — " to give to that great man this fair maid, to warm into youth his declining days. Ah ! what would not that holy man give you in exchange for this rare jewel? And remember that this year your crops and dairy have not yielded well. Your income has been diminished one-eighth. What will be the result if like misfortunes should continue ? "

The bishop paled a little, and looked nervous.

" But they will not. God protects the righteous. To you, true bishop of his true church, he sends this pearl of beauty. Give her to enrich the heavenly crown of our holiest, greatest brother, even while her charms engage his earthly sight." And then, leaving the elevation of pious fraud, she said in a quick whisper, as though even the air might hear, —

" It will be worth thousands and thousands to you. She's very fresh and pretty, will be a thorough novelty in Salt Lake, and sure to please the old man's worn-out fancy. Then, while she is in power, make her get from him just what you want."

Quite her slave now, his eyes eager with the desire of gain, the bishop, also whispering, stepped closer to Mrs. White.

" Make her ? How am I to make her ? I — I've been watching her since July, and this is the first time I've ever seen her alone. It would be useless to speak before Tabitha ; and — and I fear the girl has something of her mother's cursed obstinacy. You see, my — my *dear*, in Salt Lake she'd have to *seem* pleased and willing to enter in polygamy. I would get no — no favor if she were not amiable."

" Amiable ! " Mrs. White sneered. " Leave her to me. I'll make her amiable enough."

The bishop looked at her a little doubtfully, and then, still hesitating, went on. For months, fascinated by Patience's beauty, and piqued by the difficulties that surrounded her, he had watched her patiently. But now, under this new motive, this greatest passion of his life, he could not act too quickly. The possible gain of money made him eager and anxious : —

"You — you see, there's not much time to lose. Others have pretty daughters ; and, if a new wife is taken by the old man, he — he may not very soon feel like having another. And — and the girl has been left so long with her cursed mother, I'm afraid it won't be easy to make her do as we think she should."

The thousands he would gain, for barter and sale of the purity of his child, were very, very strong arguments with the bishop. In his eagerness to devise some immediate plan to force Patience to his will, he lost sight of every thing else. The slight awe he had felt for Tabitha vanished, and he stood ready to follow any suggested plan.

"You — you see," — for Mrs. White had not spoken, — "I'd have to show her how much better off she'd be if she'd only — only hold her tongue, and obey her — father."

He could hardly say the word. Even his dead conscience raised its voice, and, from the grave of many sins, called aloud at this outrage to that holy name ; but Mrs. White would permit no such "weakness."

"Accursed of God is the sin of disobedience, and, above all, disobedience to a father," and Mrs. White raised both hands and eyes, expressing her horror of such deadly wrong. "But, my dear bishop, there shall be no such sin. The girl is young, pretty, and vain. Once get her away from her mother, and she'll be only too pleased, with jewels and finery, to object to any thing. That was a very pretty ring you offered her. Let me see it."

He took it from his pocket, handed it to her, and, though he half put out his hand as she placed it on her finger, said nothing. She had awakened a new desire in his mind ; she had touched the motive-power of his life : and, while he had every willingness to accomplish the proposed end, he was, just now, waiting helplessly for her to suggest the manner.

"There!" said Mrs. White as she pushed on the ring, and after surveying it for a moment or so, as if, having received payment, she was now ready to act, went on : —

" First get the girl away from her mother."

" How am I to do that ?" asked the bishop. " She won't come."

" She won't come ? Ha, ha !" And Mrs. White laughed, as if the bishop had said something very amusing. " Ha, ha !" she laughed on. Suddenly changing her expression, "*Make her*," she said, in cold, cruel tones. Then returning to blandness and smiles, " Why, my dear," — and she gave him a playful tap on the fat cheek, — " you, a bishop, ask me how you're to do what you wish! Do as you have done before. Use the power of your office. You know the men in the town, and how far you can rely on their obedience. Take two of those most in your control. Ride down with them to the cabin. Walk in. First ask, then demand, your daughter's company, just for a little visit. If her mother consents, all is well. If not, all is yet well. You have but to call the men, and tell them to put the girl in the carriage."

" But, my dear," interposed the bishop, " should they resist ?"

" And, my dear," replied Mrs. White, " cannot you take two men strong enough to overpower one woman, one girl, and a helpless cripple ? The eldest son is away," she added ; " so two strong men will be quite enough. Once the girl is at your house, let me manage her, and I promise I'll break her will. Once humbled, — and following my plan a few days will accomplish this, — take her to Salt Lake, show her its attractions, let her feel the value of her beauty, and your daughter will be as dutiful as you could wish."

She had watched the fat face at her side as thus she played upon his worst passions. She saw the sharp, cunning look come to the little eyes, the cruel set to the coarse mouth, and knew that she had made this man her slave.

"Do you think you can do this in two days?" he asked eagerly, his fingers nervously closing, as if they already held the price of his daughter's sale.

"Yes, if you leave her to me." They walked on, talking in low tones. The passers-by, seeing them thus together, thought how united were this goodly couple.

And thus they planned the destruction of those who had never even wished them harm, who had borne with injustice for years, and uttered no reproach.

*　　*　　*　　*　　*　　*　　*　　*　　*　　*　　*

The next day, while Tabitha was preparing dinner, and Patience, sweet song-bird, was laughing and singing as she had not done for months, a rap came at the door. Patience opened it, and paled to ashen white as she saw her father, all self-possession and smiles, and, down at the gate, two men, standing by the open door of a carriage.

"Mother!" she called, trembling so that her teeth chattered, dreading she knew not what. Tabitha, with one bound, stood beside her child. She, too, saw the cruel, wicked leer on her husband's face, and the carriage, with the two men standing near. An agonized prayer rose from her soul to God, "Protect my child, protect my child, or strike her dead at my feet!"

Why it is such prayers are not answered, no human power can understand. Perhaps this terrible suffering, these frightful human sacrifices, are needed to wake to protective action a slothful, selfish world. And, alas! the innocent and the guiltless are always the victims.

Throwing her arm around Patience, who trembled and shivered like one in an ague, Tabitha said to her husband, —

"What do you want?"

"Nothing much, my dear. Only a short visit from my daughter, Patience."

"You must excuse her to-day, Bishop White," Tabitha answered, she, too, beginning to shake with this terrible excitement. "She is not well. She cannot go to-day."

"Well or sick, go to-day she must and shall," he answered, all the cruelty of his nature showing in his face.

Patience clung closer and closer to her mother; and Tabitha, her throat and mouth hard and dry with the horror of the moment, said, —

"Bishop White, more than ten years ago you drove us from your door, poor and friendless. I took my children, and, obeying your will, uttered no complaint. Take every thing I have, — this garden, the result of ten years' labor; this house that shelters us; make me your slave, — I will swear to work for you day and night, — only leave me my children, and I will fall on my knees, and kiss the ground you stand on."

The scalding tears rose in her eyes, and poured down her face; and, as she stood with her arms tightly clasped around the pale and frightened girl, she seemed imploring for her life. But she implored one who had no heart to pity or to spare.

"I have no time for tirades," he pettishly answered. "Only say, will Patience come willingly with me?" And he tried to catch hold of her arm. Shaking him off, wild with fright, the girl sprang behind Tabitha.

"Mother, mother, save me!" she shrieked. And Tabitha, her eyes flaming, and her hands clinched, stood a lioness at bay. Christie, huddled in the corner, with clasped hands and horror-filled eyes, was praying for help. Rex, before his little master, stood growling angrily.

A motion of the bishop's hand brought the two men to his side, and they stood three to three. But what unequal warfare! Three strong men matched against one woman, a terrified girl, and a dog. Poor, helpless Christie could only bring his prayers as aid.

"That girl is my daughter. I command her to go home with me, and she refuses. Take her to the carriage."

It is a curious fact of the power of Mormon government, however vile the crime commanded, there is never any hesitation in the obedience. These men were not absolute brutes. They knew something of Tabitha's history ; and, though it was not an uncommon one, it was pitiful enough. Yet at the command of Bishop White, a hard and cruel man, they instantly advanced towards Patience, and would have carried her off at once, but that Tabitha, snatching a knife from the table, stood between them and her child.

"Come, now, missus," said one of the men, "let the girl go with her father. She's willin' enough if you'll only let her."

"No, no!" shrieked Patience. "I am not willing. Kill me. In mercy, kill me, but don't take me to that man!"

Fairly grinding his teeth with rage, Bishop White called out, —

"Will you men do my bidding, or do you refuse to obey me?"

Without a word of reply, they closed on Tabitha, overpowering her. Rex, with a growl, sprang on the nearest man, and, fastening his teeth in his arm, forced him to release the woman.

Once more free, once more Tabitha rushed to her child. Rex's antagonist, a man famous for his strength, clutching the dog around the neck, called to the other man, —

"Take off the girl. I'll manage the dog."

The noble brute fought long and well ; but finally, almost strangled, while blood streamed from his nose, and oozed out even from his eyes, was flung, as if dead, at the feet of his little master. Freed from the dog, the man turned to help his less powerful confederate, who had found it no easy matter alone to overpower the infuriated mother.

Grasping her knife, ready to strike, her lips drawn away from

gleaming teeth, and eyes starting from their sockets, she stood between her child and the two ruffians, — between her child and whatever horror fate held in store for her. For an instant the two men
paused as if awe-struck at this frenzy of maternal love. Then, the

"TAKE THE GIRL."

brutal overcoming the moral, the stronger flung his uninjured arm
around her, holding her powerless, and said to his companion, —

"Take the girl."

Resisting with all her strength, and shrieking wildly, Patience was
borne along the garden to the carriage. Her father followed, and,
motioning the man to retain hold of his daughter, the three drove off.

In the bright daylight, within sight and sound of homes where dwelt mothers and their children, this shrieking girl was put in a carriage, driven off, and not one human face appeared, even in curiosity. Bishop White was the representative of the Mormon Church, and the people were all good Mormons.

Meanwhile, the man holding Tabitha so tightened his grasp that he stopped her breathing. Feeling her struggles cease, and that she became a dead weight in his arm, he put her in a chair, and looked around. Desolation where, a few moments before, was a home, — humble and poor, but a home, neat and cheerful. In one corner, a helpless heap, poor little Christie lay, more dead than alive. Close to him, covered with blood, was stretched the huge form of Rex, perfectly motionless. And Tabitha, on the chair, with glazed eyes, and half-opened mouth, from which the red drops were slowly falling.

"Poor critter!" said the man, "you fought nobly for your chick. I didn't mean to give you such a hard squeeze, and I'm sorry I was in this business at all. But I just had to do it."

Then he took a little water, washed the blood from her mouth, and, seeing her about to revive, turned to go, shaking his clinched hand at Rex as he went, muttering, —

"You ugly brute! I'd have killed you outright, had it not been for the pale face of that wee laddie in the corner. Somehow he jest brought back my little brother. Dead these twenty years, but I grew soft-hearted." Then, with a glimmer of a tear, he went out of the cabin.

Strange contradiction of human nature! The man, who, a few moments before, had brutally overpowered a mother defending her child from worse than death, was ready to weep over a little brother dead twenty years ago.

After a few moments, with a shudder, Tabitha came back to the consciousness of her desolated home. Staggering to her feet, she looked about her. Misery everywhere! She raised her hands, and called aloud, —

"God protect my child! *God!* There is no God," she wildly cried, "or this crime would not have been permitted." Yet, even as she uttered this mad cry, there rose a protest to it from her inner spirit, barely listened to, yet felt in every fibre of the quivering, suffering heart. To each intelligence there is a necessity that somewhere there must exist a beginning and an end, — a righting of wrongs, a repayment for existence, an explanation of that, the least understood, — life.

Standing there, with dry and stony eyes, amidst the ruins of her home, despair clutched her heart with iron hands. Wild plans to rescue Patience chased each other through her maddened brain. She seemed to have forgotten all else, even Christie, until his voice called her to his side. He looked frail as a snow-wreath in the dark corner; and, catching him to her bosom, she almost prayed he would die.

"Then he will be safe," she thought.

How thankful she would feel, if, at this moment, she could close the coffin-lid over the dead face of her Patience!

"Mother," said Christie, "let us go to Matthew."

"Matthew!" At his name her faith rose triumphant from its ashes. Lifting up Christie, she nearly fell over Rex. He was still lying motionless.

"Is he dead?" whispered the child.

She put her hand over his heart. Finding it still beating, she dashed water on the faithful fellow, and waited a little until he moved.

Christie called him by name. At the loved voice, the dog struggled to rise, and, weakly walking, followed his little master, as, in Tabitha's arms, he was carried to Matthew's.

CHAPTER XXIX.

IN DEADLY PERIL.

CHRISTINE and Matthew, in the sunny parlor, were planning the moving of their little colony to the mining-camp where Martin was at work. The greater points had all been settled, and written to Martin; and now they were discussing some minor details. Christine had just said, "Tabitha, I am sure, will be content, and Patience delighted," when, looking up, she saw Tabitha, with Christie in her arms, hurrying towards them. Her pallid face, dishevelled hair, and blood-stained lips, told of some fearful excitement. Following at a little distance, hardly able to crawl, was Rex.

At Christine's exclamation, Matthew had looked out the window. Starting to their feet, some faint conception of the horror dawned upon them, as they both exclaimed, —

"Patience!" It was some evil to her, they knew. But what?

Matthew and Christine rushed to the door; Christine catching Christie in her arms, as Tabitha, breathless, staggered forwards. Matthew put out his arm to steady her, and tried to understand the disconnected words she gasped out : —

"Quick — help — Patience — carried off — her father !"

The old man turned white and faint. Was it possible for such depravity to exist? Then forcing the exhausted woman in a chair, and telling her to recover breath, and speak more clearly, so he could help her, he waited, with his hand pressed on his heart, as if that heart could not endure its pain at such inhuman wickedness.

"Christie, dear," said Christine, "tell us what is wrong, so we can do something to aid you."

Raising his eyes to Christine's face, he told the sad story of Patience's abduction ; and Tabitha's excitement, Rex's weakness, and his own failing strength, told the rest.

"Christine," said Matthew, "we must have a power greater than Bishop White's to force him to give up the child. I will write a telegram to John Smith. I believe he will come ; and without scandal, delay, or enraging the Mormons, he can manage it."

Christine knew the truth of this. She knew personal influence was their only hope. For a moment they discussed the sending of the message. They both knew Matthew was the only present help of the poor girl. His presence might be some restraint on Bishop White. He could, at least, watch if she were sent away from the town. He dared not leave. He dared not trust the message to one of his hired help. Some one must take it in whom they could trust. Where was that one ?

"Father," — and Christine stood with her hand on the door, — "I will drive the buggy to the station, send the telegram, and wait for the answer."

He looked at her in doubt. So lately recovered from illness, and still feeble, dared he let her go ? She smiled back at him a brave, determined smile, and went quickly for her hat and cloak while he wrote the message. It was only a few words : —

" *To* Hon. JOHN SMITH, *Salt-Lake City.*

"In great trouble. Can you come at once ? Answer.

"MATTHEW KLEIGWALD."

When he had harnessed the horse, and brought him to the house, he found Christine waiting at the gate.

"I've the message in my pocket, father. Don't worry. I may have to wait some time. Indeed, I am quite strong enough," she said, answering his anxious look.

It was not a moment for hesitation when one who was helpless stood in deadly peril. So he kissed his darling, committed her to God's care, and stood for a moment looking at the vanishing buggy, and the figure sitting so bravely upright. He did not imagine what an effort his child was making, and that she was trembling, and her head swimming from weakness. Coming back to the house, he told Tabitha to attend to Christie, and that he would see if he could accomplish any thing with Bishop White.

"You know where every thing is kept. Eat something. Keep up your strength, or you will be a hinderance, and not a help, to the poor child who needs us all."

Tabitha's tears were falling fast. This friend who had never failed her, this noble, uncomplaining Christian, who now took on his shoulders the burden of her woes, was a silent reproach to her own wild despair.

Taking his hat, Matthew started, but, turning before he left the room, came back to Tabitha, as if divining her need.

"My sister, your trouble is great; but, terrible as it is, there is a God above us, — a God who loves us. Why he permits such bitter woe, we cannot understand. But suffering, dying, we must believe. Could my old life be taken for thy child's, I would gladly offer it. If we save her, or if we lose her, even though our hearts be breaking, we must say, 'Thy will be done.'"

He laid his hand on her bowed head; and then with a loving look for Christie, whose great eyes were watching him, he left them, and hastened down the road to Bishop White's.

In their hearts, both Tabitha and Christie were praying. The child seemed daily fading away ; and, since the horrors of the morning, he looked more spirit-like than ever. Lying on the lounge, the blue veins showing through the white, transparent skin, the large gray eyes upturned in prayer, and the wan hands crossed on his breast, he was nearer heaven than earth.

Seeing him thus, as she looked up through her tears, Tabitha remembered, with a pang, that he had not tasted food since sunrise ; and now it was afternoon. She hastily brought some nourishment for him, but the little fellow could hardly take a mouthful. Earthly nourishment was not fitted for one so near the gate of heaven, that surely stood ajar for him. Suffering more than one in health could imagine, he lay quiet, uncomplaining, praying for his mother, his sister, and the other dear ones, whose sorrows lacerated his loving heart. And yet those holy prayers seemed unrewarded. Were they unrewarded ? Will not they, like heavenly germs, fall on those who have the power to right the wronged, and, taking root, send out healing balm ?

Watching, praying, the hour wore away ; and, after a little, Matthew came back — alone.

" Where is she ? " asked the mother ; even in her own anguish noticing that the old man looked worn and feeble, and, half falling into a chair, passed his hand over his head several times, as if to steady his thoughts before speaking.

" My sister," he answered, " I have seen both Bishop and Mrs. White. They told me Patience was in the house, and had fallen asleep after a good lunch ; that she professed herself quite contented to remain with her father."

" It is a lie," said Tabitha, rising in her wrath.

" Yes," said Matthew, " I am afraid it is. But — and I tried to take comfort in this — Mrs. White followed me to the door, and assured me she would look after Patience as if she were her own child."

"And did you believe her?" asked Tabitha.

"I wish I could say I did," answered Matthew sadly.

"Matthew, that woman is the cruellest, the falsest, in the world. I have known her to torture animals, and be amused by their writhings. I have known her to laugh at, and enjoy, human misery that would have moved a heart of stone. I have known her, with a lie on her lips, call God to witness her truth. Oh that my child should be cast upon the pity of such as she! I must go to her. I must see my child."

"My poor Tabitha," said Matthew, "I fear you will not move her. Wait until Christine returns with Mr. Smith's answer. If he comes, her prison-doors will open. Bishop White dare not oppose one so much more powerful than he."

In almost utter stillness the three sat waiting, while the hours dragged their slow length along. Darkness, like a pall, covered the most miserable day of their lives. It was quite late when the faint sound of wheels told them Christine was coming.

"Take me too," said Christie faintly, as, unable to wait longer, Matthew and Tabitha started to meet the approaching succor. It was Matthew who took the child in his arms, motioning Tabitha to go first.

They stood at the gate, straining their ears to catch the faintest sound. The night was very dark, — so dark they could hardly see each other's faces, — and it was bitter cold. Waiting in breathless anxiety, the howling wind seemed to mock them. They could no longer distinguish the approach of wheels.

"We were mistaken," said Matthew.

And a fresh anxiety crowded in his aching heart. Perhaps his child, overpowered by weakness, had lost control of the horse. Perhaps she now lay helplessly perishing on some lonely wayside. At this thought, beads of sweat rolled down his face. One fell on Christie's hand, that clasped the old man's neck. The child thought Matthew was crying, and his own tears rose in sympathy. Then, leaning his head against the loved face of this more than father, Christie heard him murmur, —

" ' Thy will be done.' "

It echoed in the child's pure heart, and seemed to quiet the incessant pain of the poor little body. Standing there in the darkness, while the sweat of his agonizing fears rolled over his face, and froze in drops upon his breast, Matthew was tenderly sheltering in his arms a helpless lamb, was meekly bowing his soul in submission to God's will.

Presently Rex, who had followed them from the house, and who seemed quite restored by his day's rest, began to bark. And now, through the howling of the wind, they heard the distinct sound of a rapidly approaching vehicle. Nearer and nearer it came. Brighter and brighter grew their hopes. As the buggy came in sight, Matthew, wrapping Christie warmly, gave him to his mother, and stood ready to help Christine.

She needed help. With a face so white it gleamed in the darkness, stiffened hands still grasping the reins, she was powerless to help herself. Strengthened by his mighty love, Matthew took her in his arms as if she were still a child, and carried her into the sitting-room. He poured a little wine between the purple lips, chafed her cold hands, and tried to bring back some strength to the exhausted girl. Her eyes seemed the only living members of her almost frozen body. And those eyes, so utterly sad and pitiful, told them, before a word was spoken, that the errand had been fruitless. Pinned to her breast was the answer to the telegram. Long before she could speak, Christine's eyes had directed their attention to it.

"Read it, Matthew. I cannot," said Tabitha.

"Matthew Kleigwald, C——, Utah.

"J. S. in Washington. Telegram forwarded.

"T. WARD."

Poor Tabitha! She hardly knew how much she had hoped until now. And the others of this sorrowful little band, in whose hearts each throb of the mother's anguish found echo! They looked at each other in blank dismay. Eight days must pass before Mr. Smith could reach them, even if he came; and the chances of his coming were very weak. What was to be done now? There was no law in the town for them to appeal to. In the person of Bishop White was vested all the law thought necessary for the protection of life and safety. They could hope nothing from their neighbors. Though they might die at their feet, there would not be one brave enough to extend the helping hand, and incur the curses and punishment of the Mormon Church. What was to be done?

"Matthew, Matthew! I must go to the house where my child is hidden. What may she not be suffering?"

And the poor mother started to her feet, as horror upon horror rose before her frighted fancy.

"Then, Tabitha, I will go with you. I may not be able to protect you from insult or injury, but I can share them with you."

So Christie remained with Christine, Rex keeping guard, while Tabitha and Matthew made the sad pilgrimage to Patience's prison.

The night was still very cold; but the wind had blown away the clouds, and a wintry moon was looking down upon the sins and sorrows of the world. It was a goodly residence, the house of Bishop White, with its well-built out-houses and large grounds. There was not a glimmer of light anywhere to be seen. Every thing seemed peacefully sleeping.

God in heaven! could they be sleeping, while, out in that freezing cold, a mother was seeking her child, — a mother whom they had robbed? Tabitha walked to every window, calling, —

"Patience, Patience! Answer! I am here, — your mother!"

And, at her side, Matthew, listening as she listened, looking as she looked, for some faint sign in answer. Nothing but the moaning of the wind.

All around the house, to every out-house, she went with the same sad call. And no answer came to her. Not a sound to tell there was a living creature in the whole place.

Finally Matthew, taking her hand, led her away.

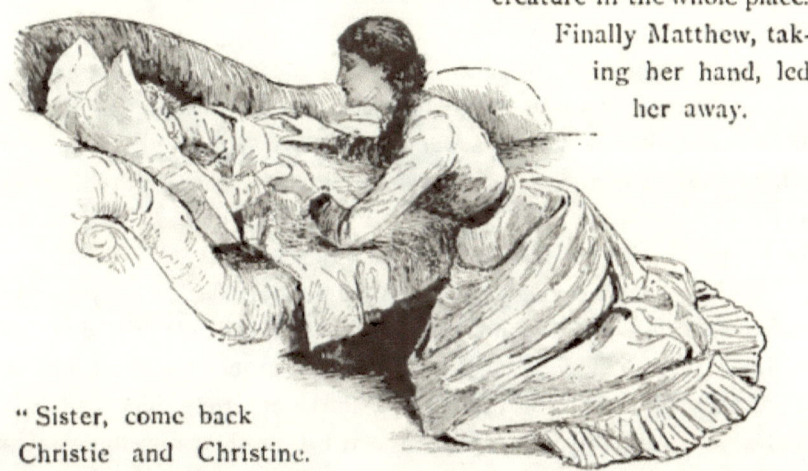

"CHRISTINE WAS KNEELING AT HIS SIDE."

"Sister, come back to Christie and Christine. I fear to anger Bishop White to more cruelties if we continue here to-night. To-morrow morning we will return again."

So back to the other two watchers toiled these weary pilgrims. They found Christie still on the sofa. One could see the sands of his feeble life were running low. Even these few hours had made a change in him.

Christine, holding his hand, was kneeling at his side; and her eyes were full of tears. He had been telling her his "vision," and his face shone with the glory he had been trying to describe. She had

read the vision word for word. Matthew kept it as his mark in the
Bible.   But to hear Christie tell it in his low, sweet voice ; to watch
his eyes dilate, and grow more and more like angels' ; and to know the
hot little hands, nervously clasping hers, would soon be stilled in death,
— made his vision seem a real thing.   And feeling he was every hour
nearing that beautiful place of his dream, made her cling to him with
all the more tenderness.

"O Christine, if you only knew the comfort that vision has been
to me !   When I see my mother frantic with grief, and know Patience
is in some awful danger ; when I look into your face, dear, and read
the story of your sorrow ; even Matthew, like as he is to the Saviour,
suffers equally with us ; and my dear, absent brother." — here the
faint voice faltered, and then went on, — "when I think of each one
whom I love, my vision comes before me, and I seem to hear God's
voice saying, ' Be patient, Christie.   It is not for long.   Soon you shall
be happy, and all you love be with you.' "

While he was speaking, his face became glorified.   His eyes seemed
looking at the world beyond.   The nervous little hands grew quite still ;
and Christine, believing he was dying, fell on her knees at his side.
Thus they were when Matthew and Tabitha entered.   The child's face
looked so unearthly, that, with a cry, his mother ran towards him.
She, too, thought he was dying.   But, smiling at her, he kissed her
hand, that was near him, then lay quite still again, while his face shone
with the light of heavenly peace.

CHAPTER XXX.

MERCY! MERCY!

OW the night passed they could hardly tell. None went to bed, and none could sleep. Tabitha started up again and again, saying she must go home. Perhaps Patience was there waiting for her. But each time Christie would say, —

"Take me, too, mother. I cannot let you leave me."

And she would remain. She feared to take him out in the bitter night, and back to the cold cabin. She could not shorten his life by one moment. Pitiful as life was, she was a mother, and would not part from her child.

The morning came, and found them still keeping their sad vigil. With the morning hope arose. It is wonderful the hopes the morning brings. Things that look dark and hopeless during the wakeful hours of the weary night, lose half their terrors under morning's shining. So it was with Tabitha. Thankfully taking a cup of tea, she kissed Christie, and started off once more to Bishop White's.

All along the road she was telling herself over and over again what she would say to him. She would try to look pleasant, and ask just to see Patience for a few minutes; and then, once with her arms around her child, she would plead with him as father, as man, so that he could not resist her. Tired as she was, the bright sunshine, tempering the cold air, invigorated her ; and, by the time she had nearly reached the house, she felt she had been needlessly miserable, — that, in a few moments, all would be well with her. Filled with these hopes, she hurried on, and reached the gate as Bishop White was coming out. Her heart stood still for a moment, and then gave a great throb.

"Courage, courage !" she whispered to herself, and then said aloud, —

"Good-morning."

She tried to smile ; but her face worked convulsively, and her voice sounded hollow and unnatural. The bishop, redder, fatter, wickeder than ever, looked at her for a moment ; his cruel little eyes gloating over her excitement.

"What do you want here ?" he said gruffly.

Another sickening throb of the poor mother-heart, another ghastly attempt at a smile.

"I came to see our daughter Patience, just for a moment."

She was determined to conciliate ; and, though the "our" nearly choked her, she said it bravely.

"Our !" sneered the bishop. "I'm glad you recognize she is not wholly yours."

"Forgive me if I ever seemed to forget it," answered Tabitha.

She had begun to shake with nervousness ; and black spots, moving before her eyes, almost hid his cruel, sneering face. She put her hand on the fence to keep her from falling, as trees, earth, and sky seemed whirling around in a mad dance.

"It's a pity," said the sneering voice, "that you've not taught ' *our* ' daughter Patience to obey her father."

"Forgive me. I will do better, only let me see her."

She could scarcely articulate, her throat was becoming so very dry, and her tongue fairly cleaving to the roof of her mouth.

"How meek and humble we've grown!" the sneering voice went on. "But meekness won't answer, my sweet Tabitha. I cannot just yet permit you to see 'our daughter Patience.'"

And he chuckled to himself as he said it.

"Not see her! Oh, surely you will not refuse me that!"

He turned to go. She tried to catch hold of his sleeve to make him listen to her; and, as he stepped back, she fell in the snow at his feet. She could see nothing now. All was black before her eyes, and a roaring sound in her ears made even her own voice indistinct; but she had caught the edge of his coat, and held it fast.

"Hear me." She spoke very loud to be heard, for the roaring was so great. "Only let my child go free, and I swear never again to look upon her face. If you are keeping her away from me because you hate me, will not that satisfy you?"

He did not answer. Then, in a frenzy of despair, she raised her face, and, looking at him with eyes that saw nothing, she shrieked out, —

"Tear me limb from limb, put out my eyes with burning coals, torture me to the utmost of your will, only spare my child, and, while breath is left, I will bless you."

"Stop your twaddle, you old fool!" said the bishop. "Do you suppose I want any thing of you? I was tired of you long ago, and I won't be kept out here in the cold to listen to you. Let go!"

And he tried to pull away his coat; but she held on tight, and crept closer to him.

"Listen," she gasped. "Injure that child, and, sure as there is a God above, I will haunt you to your dying day. You shall never know a quiet sleep. Between you and your every comfort will rise the face of the woman you are killing."

She looked terrible as she crouched there in the snow, clutching his coat until every bone in her hand seemed about to break the skin;

her wild eyes staring at him, her face ghastly, and upon her lips a red froth, while her breath came in gasps. He was a superstitious man, and might have yielded to the fear, that, as he gazed at her, seemed to strike to the marrow of his bones; but just then the door of the house opened, Mrs. White appeared, and his hellish impulse was re-enforced.

"Fool!" he said. "Do you suppose you can frighten me? You shall not see the girl until I choose to let you. If, however, she is at all like her mother, I think you may count upon having *your* daughter Patience very soon. A week will let me see enough of her."

And again he chuckled, as, with a twist and jerk, he pulled himself free; and Tabitha fell upon her face in the snow. The cold seemed to revive her; for she staggered to her feet, and stood repeating his last words.

"What did he mean?" She pressed her hand upon her head to stop its whirling. She needed every faculty now. She took a little snow from the fence, and put it to her mouth; and she noticed, when she took her hand away, there was blood upon it. She felt so dazed, that, as she tried to step, the snow-covered earth seemed rising to strike her in the face. But she must get to the house.

There was a woman there, — a false and cruel one, she knew; but perhaps a woman, though a cruel one, would easier feel for a mother's agony. Like one half blind, she staggered up the walk, and, breathless, sank upon the steps. Up, up. No time to waste. She must save her child. Half dragging, half creeping, she reached the door, and, grasping the knob with one hand, with the other raised the knocker. It fell with a feeble clang, the door opened wide, and Mrs. White stood blandly smiling down on the woman she had hated for years.

Hated for what? Because *she* had injured her. She had come to this woman's home, had robbed her of her rights, had driven her to a toilsome life, but never yet had she been able to make her bow before her, or yield one jot of her pride. Now she was at her feet. And the bland smile on the ruddy face widened as she looked on the picture.

"Upon whom did you call?" inquired Mrs. White, enjoying her own irony.

"I want my child," gasped Tabitha.

"I regret to refuse your modest request; but, really, you can't have her."

"Mercy, mercy!" moaned Tabitha. "As you have a soul to be saved!"

Her strength was almost gone. She could not speak; but, with a last effort, she threw out her arms, and clasped Mrs. White around her knees. It was a feeble clasp; and, easily shaking it off, Mrs. White stepped back; and, as Tabitha fell, she called in a loud voice, "Thomas! Fred!" and then, "My gracious, that blood will stain the porch!"

She pulled off her apron, putting it at Tabitha's mouth, from which the blood was slowly oozing. Then, calling louder and more impatiently, two heavy-looking lads came to the side of the house. They had evidently been eating, and moved slowly as if not relishing the interruption.

"Here, you lazy things! Take up this woman, and put her outside of the fence. She's had a fit. But wait a minute," she said, and, going into the house, returned with a little brandy. Wiping away the blood with the apron, she tore off a little piece, soaked it with the liquor, and forced it in Tabitha's mouth. "Now take her."

The two boys picked up Tabitha as if she had been a piece of wood, and obeyed the directions of their bishop's wife.

Mrs. White watched them until they returned whence they had come, and then, shivering with cold, and saying to herself, "It would be very unpleasant to have her die here," went into her comfortable house, and shut the door. She had not one pitiful thought for the poor creature out on the snowy road.

After a little, revived by the few drops of brandy and the bitter cold, Tabitha came back to consciousness. What should she do now? She had no hope of the slightest mercy from either the bishop or his wife. She could not force her way in the house, and take away her child.

Perhaps Matthew, who had been so good to so many, perhaps he could raise a few men, and they, moved by her misery, might free the innocent girl; for, if any thing like public sentiment could be made in her favor, Bishop White would be forced to give up Patience. If any man could rouse the Mormons against their bishop, it would be Matthew, who had spent years in serving them. And at this hope, forlorn as it was, she struggled to her feet, and tottered towards the road that led to her cabin.

CHAPTER XXXI.

A HERO.

EFORE starting to Bishop White's, Tabitha had asked Matthew and Christine to meet her at her own house; and they concluded, under any circumstances, she would be more comfortable there. Matthew walked to the cabin, made the fire, and, as best he could, removed the signs of yesterday's desperate struggle before going for Christie and Christine.

As soon as they arrived, Christine prepared a simple meal, and kept it warm for Tabitha's return. Growing anxious as time went on, and she did not come, Matthew started off to seek her.

He had not gone very far, when, with ghastly face, and tottering as if every step would be her last, came Tabitha. Forgetting his years, forgetting the growing feebleness that had so increased these last terrible days, Matthew ran towards the unhappy woman, and put his arm around her.

"Don't try to speak. When we reach your cabin, you can tell me easier and better."

And tenderly as a mother with a feeble child did he guide her staggering, uncertain steps. They reached the cabin exhausted. Christine had the door open, and two chairs near the fire; Christie watching her wistfully. How he longed to help in this time of trouble!

As he entered, Matthew looked so very pale that Christine brought him something warm.

"Tabitha first," he said.

Putting the cup of tea on a chair near him, Christine went to her. Tabitha took eagerly what was given. She forced herself to swallow

food. She was anxious to gain more strength, that she might help her child.

When Tabitha felt a little stronger, and could control herself, she told the result of her visit.

"O Matthew! Could you not raise a few men from among the many you have helped? With their backing, we could go to Bishop White's, and demand my child."

"Sister," Matthew answered sadly, "on my way to seek you, I stopped at two cabins, and asked the help of men, who, when last I saw them, told me they would answer with their lives if ever I needed

"TENDERLY AS A MOTHER DID HE GUIDE HER STEPS."

them. They were both very sorry, but said they could not battle against the Mormon Church. And when I assured them no power under heaven could uphold a man in forcing from her mother a girl of eighteen, as this unnatural father has done, they answered, even should we go and represent the case to the Mormon authorities, we would not be believed. The bishop's word would outweigh our testimony with these authorities, who appointed, and would uphold, him.

"The only way I can see to help the poor child, is to go to Salt-Lake City, and lay the case before the United-States court. The daily train leaves every morning. Keep quiet, and husband all your strength for the trip. Together we will go to the judge, and pray for immediate help. I will call for you at six o'clock. We will be away only a few days. Christie, dear, you will stay with Christine. Whatever the consequences may be, we must free Patience."

Convinced that this was the only way, Tabitha promised to rest most of the day, and to take all the nourishment she could. Then at her own desire, first doing all they could for her and Christie's comfort, they left them.

Matthew concluded time would be saved if a clear, written statement of the case be prepared, and presented to the judge. In all his life he had never been in a court, and was ignorant of the processes of law. Moreover, having lived so many years among the Mormons, he had seen numerous instances of the almost absolute power of their government. He knew of the existence of this United-States court. He knew any appeal to it was bitterly resented by the Mormons, and the instigators relentlessly pursued. He had heard of rare instances of Mormons being forced to appeal to this court, and, while the objects of the appeal were generally protected from Mormon vengeance, the instigators *never* escaped. Their fate had generally been mysterious disappearance, or found dead; or, by some strange accident, their house would be burned, and their family cast penniless upon a community forbidden to succor them. Matthew knew full well the risk he was running, the dangers he would incur. But duty commanded, and he obeyed. He was ready to stand as instigator. He was ready to bear the persecutions ; and, while he earnestly prayed they might not take the form of injury to his child, he still pursued his duty, and uttered his never faltering prayer, " Thy will be done."

And this man did not know he was a hero.

CHAPTER XXXII.

THE ESCAPE.

WHERE was Patience during these miserable hours?
Torn from her mother's protecting arms, she was
borne, half crazed with fright, to the waiting carriage. Held tight in the strong grasp of the ruffian,
the tool of the monster who sat opposite her, she
still struggled to free herself, still sent forth those
piercing shrieks for help.

"Hold your tongue, you young minx!" And the
bishop, beside himself with rage, desired nothing so
much as to shake and beat the girl who had been so
unfortunate in awakening his admiration.

"Can't you stop her screams?" he said to the man.

"Yes, if I had a handkerchief," he answered sullenly.

The man was beginning to tire of holding the struggling girl, to
whom fright had given strength. And, when the bishop handed him
his own handkerchief of finest silk, he passed it tightly over her
mouth, fastened it securely, and poor Patience was mute.

The rapidly rolling carriage soon reached the bishop's house ; and
there Patience was carried to an inner room, the gag loosened so she
could remove it, she was laid on the floor, and the door was locked
on her.

Once free to move, she tried to explore her prison. It was a small
room, used as a clothes-press, whose only opening being the door,

when this was closed left it in darkness. As she passed her hands around the walls, and felt the shelves, the remembrances of her childhood came back to her. It was in this very closet, telling frightful tales of ghosts and goblins, that Mrs. White had thrust her for some childish misdemeanors. Here, after long hours of searching, her mother found her, and took her thence, trembling with fear of the supernatural. How clearly, as she sat in the darkness, there came back to her each little incident of that time! — the nervous sickness following her too severe punishment ; and the dreams, that, weeks afterwards, would awaken her, wet with the sweat of terror, and send her weeping to her mother's bedside, — that mother whose never-failing tenderness had made her the strength and comfort for every ill that had fallen on her children.

Alone in the darkness, she was again the helpless child. And again the cry of " Mother, mother !" came from her poor heart, while tears like a flood of sorrow poured down her face. But the mother she called was as helpless as she, and this knowledge made her tears fall all the faster.

Slowly the long hours passed away. Through the cracks of the door she could see the glimmer of lights. She knew the frightful day had gone, and the more frightful night had come. She called again and again, imploring to be freed. But to her cries there came no answer. She could hear the sound of movement in the house ; and she beat her hands against the door, hoping to attract some human being to speak to her. But, for only reply, always that fearful silence.

She was so hungry, so thirsty ! She begged just for a little water. Nothing but the same silence. No one noticed her : no one seemed to hear her. Then as the lamps died out, and the quiet of night hushed every natural sound, cold, hungry, and forgotten, she seemed left to die. In despair she dashed herself against the cruel door, that resisted her every effort. She had heard of wonderful escapes, and tried, with her soft fingers, to force the lock ; but bruised, wearied out, and so miserably lonely, she threw herself upon the floor, and sobbed until merciful slumber fell upon her.

How long she slept she knew not : but, when she awoke, the light, peeping through the cracks, told of the dawning of another day ; and the moving of persons, of an awakened household.

Sitting in the dark closet, thinking of her mother, of Christie, of dear Matthew, Christine, and of her big, tender brother so far away, the sorrows of poor Patience broke into fresh sobs and tears.

It was thus Bishop White found her as he opened the door, and let the daylight stream on as lovely a picture of grief as ever met human eye.

Her long, fair hair, half loosened from confining braids, falling all around her ; her skin paled to pearly whiteness ; the large blue eyes, brimming over, with great tears dropping from the long lashes, were pitifully raised to his ; and her mouth — her rosy, quivering mouth — imploring mercy with its every tremor.

He had opened the door to bring her some food : for, since midnight, there had come no sound from the place of her confinement ; and he nervously dreaded to find her dead.

He had passed a wretched night, had heard Tabitha's piteous call ; and, alarmed at the possible consequences of Patience's abduction, half regretted the act. But the master demon he had called to his aid now held him fast to crime. With ridicule for his fears, and contemptuous words for the suffering he had caused, she conquered his "weakness." She convinced him he had gone too far to retreat, — that now to free the girl would only increase the odium he dreaded might fall upon him. But once conquer her obstinacy, once win her consent to his wish, and, in gratified vanity, she would soon forget her country life, and then he could get his reward. Thus argued this minister of evil, and, with the powerful logic, self-preservation, crushed out weakening misgivings. She had urged a longer interval without food. "Starve the young jade, and she won't be so uppish," she had said, while eating her own comfortable breakfast. But to this the bishop would not agree. He decided he would give her something to eat, and, filling a plate from their own table, took it himself to the closet.

"HE OPENED THE DOOR."

He was very nervous, every thing was so still. Dreading to see, extended at his feet, the girl's dead body, he could hardly unlock the door. But when he succeeded, and beheld Patience looking well, and lovelier than ever, he felt angered with her because of his own fears.

Yet, in spite of anger, her beauty affected him. She was so young, looked so gentle. One day was already gone : surely now he might begin and try to coax her to consent to his plan for his own aggrandizement. Mrs. White was wise, but she didn't know every thing : and, if this confinement was too long kept up, the girl might fall sick, die, or lose her beauty ; and then she'd be worthless. He put down the plate, and saying, " Patience, my dear daughter," put his hand on hers, and tried to draw her near him.

Innocence, though it knows not sin, has, as guides, its own true instincts. It is the fairy mirror given to the child, whose silvery white was marred by the mere approach of evil. Patience, free from guile, and with no more knowledge of sin than has an infant, felt an irrepressible shudder at the approach of the man she knew to be her father.

In nature he was her father. Yet when, from her earliest memory, had he ever been natural to her? When had he ever been less than most cruel, most unkind? Thus, despite her desire to be dutiful to him, as he touched her, impulsively she sprang into the farthest corner ; while the feeling that a snake was creeping over her made her tremble with mingled fear and horror.

Too angry to speak, Bishop White went out, closing the door with a bang ; and, turning the key, he cursed under his breath, as there standing in the hall, and laughing at his discomfiture, he saw Mrs. White. He had rejected her advice, and she was exulting over him. Passing her with a frown, and without a word to any one, Bishop White left the house ; when, meeting Tabitha at the gate, he was glad of an object on which to vent his spleen.

Wearily passed the day for Patience. She became so faint for want of food, that, chancing to touch the plate the bishop had brought, she ate its contents hungrily, and, with the cold tea, quenched the thirst that had added to her pains. Then, stronger, she once more began to try for some way of escape. She knew, that, between this closet and the house-door, there were only a few steps. If only she could open that door! Fleet of foot as she was, she could be out of the house and at her own home before she could be overtaken. But that door she could not open, try as she might. Again tears of despair rose to her eyes as she felt her own weakness.

Sitting there in the darkness, listening to every sound, she tried to imagine what motive induced the bishop to pursue her as he had done for the past months. Now that old age was creeping on, and he had no young faces around him, did he really begin to feel a longing for the affection of his children? As there came to her mind this explanation of his conduct, the poor girl wept, and rocked herself to and fro.

"Oh, if this be true, then will he never forgive me!" she cried, as she thought of how she had this morning repulsed him. But the more she thought of him, the more distinctly came before her each feature and expression of his cruel face, the more impossible she found it to associate any thing like fatherly affection with Bishop White.

"God help me!" she sobbed, half distracted with grief and loneliness. "I would rather feel myself in the power of some wild beast than have those creeping, fat fingers close around mine as they did this morning. When did he ever seem like a father to any of us? Even Christie, baby as he was, never had a smile from him." And then memories of past slights and unkindness their childhood had received from this so-called father rose from the buried forgetfulness of the past ten years.

Again her grief became *wildness*. Again and again she threw herself against the door, praying just for one little creak of encouragement that she was weakening it a little, just a little. But no encouragement was given her. Hope grew more hopeless, as afresh the homesick, miserable girl sobbed, and called for "Mother, mother! Darling mother! If I could only escape from this fearful place! If I could only once more be at home with mother!" She did not stop to reason that the power which had brought her here could again tear her from her mother's arms. She only longed to rest her head on that mother's faithful breast, to look on the dear faces of her home.

"The longest day will draw to a close." And so once again poor Patience saw the glimmering lamplight fade into blackness; and once again, after weary, weary wakefulness, welcome sleep wrapped her in unconsciousness.

She was lying on some blankets that were in a corner on the floor; still in her gingham working-dress, torn in the struggles of yesterday morning, and her hair forgotten in the abandonment of her grief; yet now so fast asleep, she did not hear the opening door. She was smiling in her dreams, — smiling even while her cheeks were wet with tears.

What wakened her? Perhaps an angel guarding sleep's holy rest. Whatever it was, with a shudder and suppressed shriek she started up, and sprang to her feet, as, terror-struck, she beheld Bishop White. A lamp from the shelf gleamed brightly, and showed her his face with an expression incomprehensible to her, but which made her shake with strange fear. He had talked it all over with Mrs. White, had sent to Salt Lake, and this evening had received an answer. So if on the morrow, or as soon thereafter as possible, he could bring his child, there would be an opening for her in that high household, whose head would honor this girl — if she pleased him. But time was of great value.

"Time." The bishop kept repeating the word, and seeing his coveted gold melt into uncertainty. Of her pleasing, he felt no doubt. The beauty of the girl would fire a stone. But would she go? Could he coax her to consent, or terrify her, if only to pretend to willingness ? Then they could start on the morrow, and "time was of great value." He could not sleep for thinking of it ; and after a while, by her snoring, being assured that Mrs. White, sleeping sound, would not be aware if he were again unsuccessful, he lit a lamp, and, like a thief, stole to Patience's closet.

Looking at her sleeping purity, he felt only the power of her charms, and his determination to barter them for gain. Not one atom of humanity, not one glimmer of pity, held him back from the sacrifice of this young lamb. Even while he cast about in his mind for rea- sons to convince her, or, failing that, for motives to terrify her, starting up with wild eyes she gazed at him ; and each moment from her parted lips he dreaded to hear the scream that would bring Mrs. White to see and ridicule him.

ESCAPE OF PATIENCE.

"Don't be an idiot !" he whispered. " I want to befriend you.

Would you like your freedom, and plenty of money ? Would you like to be powerful, and give your mother all she wants ? Would you like to be the greatest lady in Utah ? Then just say you'll go quietly with me to-morrow, and, before the next night, you'll be the wife of the head of the State. Will you go ?"

Patience shuddered. Her eyes grew wilder, but she did not speak.

" Will you go ? " and, fearing every minute to hear the voice of Mrs. White, he hurried on, each instant his face growing more cruel, —

" If you don't go, I swear I'll persecute your whole family. Your brothers shall suffer for it, — that miserable little cripple shall suffer for it ; and, as for your mother, you shall live to see her die in torture."

Again he waited, but Patience did not speak. Her every faculty was absorbed in horror. With hands clinched until the nails pressed into the flesh, and eyes gleaming with incipient madness, she confronted this fiend who was her father. Mistaking her continued silence, thinking perhaps he had conquered her, a look of triumph came into his eyes ; and, advancing a step nearer, he tried to put his arm around her.

" Patience, I " — But he said no more. Quick as a flash, one little hand, like an avenging angel's, struck at the hideous phantom that was glaring at her. It fell ! She was free ! With a bound she cleared the prostrate figure, leaped through the doorway, rushed down the hall, and out of the house. Staggering a little when the cold air met her, she soon recovered, and, swift as the wind, flew straight to her mother's cabin.

Tabitha was resting, trying to sleep, when she heard rapid footsteps on the frozen ground. Expecting she knew not what, she started up as Patience, with a wild, hunted look on her face, opened the door.

" Quick, quick ! " cried the girl, the wild gleaming of her eyes showing even in the dimly lighted room. " Up ! I've killed him ! They're after us ! Escape ! Escape ! "

She caught Christie in her arms, and, had not her mother prevented, thus unprotected would have taken him into the biting nightair. Warmly wrapping up the child, Tabitha threw something around Patience and herself, and then, not knowing what else to do, started for Matthew's.

CHAPTER XXXIII.

THEIR PARTING.

MATTHEW and Christine had passed a quiet evening together. They had written a clear and concise statement of the abduction of Patience, and a synopsis of Tabitha's hardships, and labors for her children's support during the past ten years. And Matthew, in his own writing, had added these words : —

" Although these facts are known throughout the village, if witnesses are called they will probably swear to their falsity, so thorough and complete is the subjection of the Mormons to their government, or any of its representatives. If insured of their personal safety, and the safety of their property, I might be able to secure two men, who, at such a crisis, may respond to a call. But of this I am not certain. I can, however, refer you to the Hon. John Smith for my character, as being strictly truthful. And I solemnly swear, before Almighty God, that the above statement is true in every particular."

He then affixed his name.

Christine, knowing full well the consequences to them both, asked to put her name also. The old man hesitated. For himself he would willingly brave every danger, every persecution. But for her, the darling of his life! And, looking down into the face raised to his own, he smoothed away the dark hair, and felt he could not let her bring fresh sorrows upon herself.

" Father," said her earnest voice, "if it is your duty, is it not mine also? You will not keep me from your side in right-doing?"

He kissed her tenderly, and said, "It shall be as you will," then wrote, —

"To the truth of the above statement I also solemnly swear, the facts occurring between my fourteenth and twenty-fifth year."

And Christine, in fair, clear characters, signed, "Christine Kleigwald Smith." Then Matthew put the document carefully away in the satchel he was to take with him to Salt-Lake City.

The evening grew later, and still they sat together. Neither thought of sleep. The parting of the morrow was full of sorrow to them. That their sorrow was chiefly for the dear friends whose afflictions had so deepened these last few days, did not lessen its sadness. They knew, too, that once their names were given as principal and voluntary witnesses in this case, they would be under the Mormon ban ; and what form of punishment and persecution would be meted out to them, they could not foretell. So the morrow was a crisis in their fate. If it might be any thing but separation for them so closely united! And somehow, Matthew could not explain or reason it away, he felt a great impending change was coming to him. He found himself grown suddenly feeble, and he longed to prepare his child for what becomes more than a possibility when threescore years are long passed.

He was sitting in his arm-chair before the fire ; and Christine, on a stool at his feet, leaned her head against his knee, while his hand caressed her brow. How often, from her babyhood upwards, had they sat thus together! They were both of them looking into the past years, and their hearts were filled with love for each other. Then Matthew's thoughts turned to his darling's future. And there came to him, with a fresh pang of sorrow, the time when she would no longer have his tender shielding from the world's storms. Oh, to protect her after he was gone! to save her from the great loneliness, the bitter consequence, of her blighted life.

"My darling," — his voice trembled, — "when God wills to take me out of this world, do not think I shall be away from you. I will ask him, in his mercy, to let me always be near my birdling. You shall feel and know, though your eyes can no longer see my face, I am with you, watching over you, and loving you with a love more tender, more exalted, than I can feel now, weighed down with the imperfections of the flesh."

At his first words, Christine fell on her knees before him, her arms clinging around his neck as he bent over her. Her tears were falling fast, but she would not lose one word that came from those revered lips. To part with him for one day was now to her a bitter grief, who had no other than him. But to part with him, and live on weary years without him, who was father, friend, guide, every thing, to her, seemed a misery beyond bearing to the sad woman at his feet. He saw her tears, he felt her dread of the lonely future coming to her. Closer he held her to his heart, and said, —

"My child, whom I would have shielded from the sadness of a life alone! But God has willed it otherwise. We cannot understand; but mayhap thy woes are sent thee, my birdling, that the sorrows of thy soul may move to pity human hearts. Perhaps the soil, wherein lie hid the seeds of that tree of justice that will shelter the children yet unborn from the cruel laws and crueller power of this unhappy State, needs tears as pure as thine to quicken it into growth. It may be his will that you and Patience, two innocent victims of Utah's institutions, shall live as blessed memories in the hearts of hapless women and children. I would I could bear the troubles that have fallen on ye! Helpless lambs, helpless lambs!"

For the first time in her life, Christine beheld her grandfather yield to grief, and sobs shake his grand old frame.

" Father," she cried, her lips blanched to whiteness as she saw him thus, " don't weep. Listen to me while on my knees before you, — you who have ever seemed to me, alone of all men, made in God's own image. Should it be my sad fate to live alone, should there not be left me this little one to cheer my weary days, I will keep before me your holy life. I will try to make mine as if your eyes were watching me, your love cheering me. I will try to take up your duties as you have laid them down ; and living thus, for God alone, surely he will let me feel the mercy of your nearness to me."

Her tears still fell ; but, like the sun through the summer's shower, shone the holy light of those deep, dark, unfathomable eyes. He blessed her, he kissed her, and clasped her to his heart ; and there came to both a moment's lull of peace, — a peace that was forever broken by hurried rapping at the door, and the whispered call of " Matthew, Matthew ! "

Tabitha's voice ! What new horror ? And horror it was. Without a word of explanation, they saw this in Tabitha's face, and Patience's gleaming eyes. In Tabitha's arms was Christie. He did not speak. He looked too weak, too near the Eternal Gate to ever speak again. On their way to Matthew's, in frightened whispers, Patience had told her mother, —

" He was forcing me away, mother ! He was forcing me away ! And then I raised my arm : I struck and killed him."

She muttered this over and over again, shuddering as she said it. And to Matthew, Tabitha repeated the girl's words, while Patience stood near, shivering and jabbering, — so unlike their own sweet girl, that but for her beauty, which even in this horror shone out like a star, they would have doubted her identity.

" She has not killed him," said Matthew. " So don't break your heart over it, my poor child. But there will soon be raised a hue-and-cry, as if she were truly a murderess ; and there is nothing for us but escape. We must not let her fall into the power of Mormon justice."

O noble brother! Faithful friend! In this their hour of supreme woe he stood beside them, shoulder to shoulder. Tabitha felt his greatness; and, without a word, her heart, breaking as it was, turned heavenward.

"Christine," he said, "get what money there is in the house, and hide it on their persons. Get warm wraps. Put wine and food in a basket, and be ready as soon as possible."

Starting to go, and seeing Rex with his knitted harness on, he turned his head, and said, —

"Secure as much money as you can inside of Rex's harness. It will be least suspected there. And we dare not leave the dog," he said to himself. "They might use his affection to track us."

In an incredibly short time, Matthew, with his swiftest team harnessed to the light buggy, stood waiting for them. Quickly, with hurried kiss of this perhaps eternal parting, they took their places. As Christine bent over Christie, she knew he was dying. They all knew this. But who could part him from the agonized mother? Who could loose the tight clasp of those little fingers holding fast to her hand?

"God bless you, my angel Christine," he faintly murmured, as she kissed him.

Then Matthew, taking his child in his arms, said, —

"Don't wait in the cold. Go into the house quickly. I fear you may be ill. We will hasten to get beyond the Utah border, and then, for her safety, obtain a trial for Patience. She has not killed her father; but we dare not remain here an instant, and let her meet the mob, that, before morning, will be raised against her. And now, my darling, good-by. Keep up your courage. God bless you, my child!"

One more tender kiss; and then, with a spring, he was in his seat, and the horses dashed off.

She was alone! Even Rex was gone. As in a dream she had seen him in the bottom of the buggy, Patience huddled close to him; while her mutterings, "I've killed him, I've killed him!" sounded even now in her ears. She stood like one dazed, and then, feeling some dampness upon her face, knew it was snowing.

"Thank God! it will hide the tracks," she murmured. And then remembering Matthew's words, and his tender care of her, she went in. Closing the door, and lowering the lamp, she threw herself on the lounge. She could not sleep. She was breathlessly listening for the slightest noise.

The gray of earliest dawn was showing through the windows, when the dreaded sound of many footsteps startled Christine to her feet. She blew out the lamp, and listened.

Nearer and nearer, quicker and quicker, they came. She fell back on the sofa, with clasped hands pressed against her heart to quiet its wild tumult.

"If I can but gain a little time for them," she said, as she tried to compose herself.

Presently a rap at the door, and a voice she knew calling, —

"Matthew!"

It was the voice of a man, who, a few weeks since, unable to pay his tithes, had come pleading to Matthew.

"They will take my horse and wagon," he said tearfully; "and I shall not have the means to earn bread for my little ones."

Then he had covered his face with his hands, and cried like a child. And Matthew, going to his desk, took out the needed sum, and, giving it with a smile, said, —

"Take it, my brother, and God bless you!"

How grateful the man had seemed, as he told Matthew this goodness had saved him from desperation! And now this man's voice was calling Matthew, to meet what? Again the voice: —

" Matthew, I come as a friend. Open the door."

O human treachery ! As a friend !

Stilling the bitter rising of her heart, in memory of his holy patience, who, often deceived, yet never

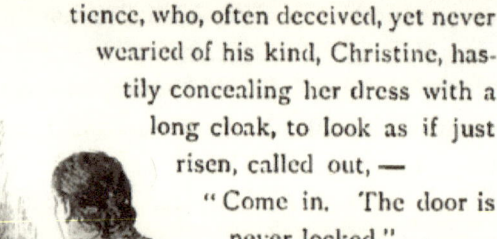

wearied of his kind, Christine, hastily concealing her dress with a
long cloak, to look as if just
risen, called out, —

"Come in. The door is
never locked."

With a white, scared
look the man en-
tered. He did not
speak, but just
looked at her.
A pitiable
coward, come
to betray his
best friend !

"What do
you want,
James?" she
asked, trying
to speak nat-
urally, but
trembling in
every nerve.

" WHAT DO YOU WANT, JAMES?"

" My child is sick. I want Matthew to come to see her."

Pale as he was, he blushed as he uttered this lie.

" I will go to her." And Christine, rising, walked to the door.

" O miss, miss !" the man cried, as he caught hold of her cloak, "don't go out there as you value your life. Where is Matthew?" he added.

Then, pushing past her, he went from room to room, and, before she could prevent, had gone out of the front-door. A slight return of that deadly sickness had come over her as he had caught her cloak, and pulled her from the door. With a great effort she overcame it just in time to see him leave the house.

She hurried after him. In front of the gate was collected a crowd of people; while galloping off, in the direction Matthew had taken, was a band of horsemen. She tried to count how many, but could not. She was so dizzy she could see nothing distinctly. The crowd seemed to fade away on the road the horsemen had gone. She half ran, half stumbled, trying to follow, feeling she must shield her grandfather, or die with him, when once more that deadly sick feeling, once more the rush of waters in her ears, and, senseless, she fell on her face in the middle of the road.

CHAPTER XXXIV.

A TERRIBLE RACE.

IN the brief moment that Matthew, pressing Christine to his heart, bade her farewell, there came to him the greatest temptation of his life. He was leaving her so utterly alone to face the possibilities of her darkened future. Again she seemed to him a little child, and the baby fingers kept tugging at his heart-strings. She was so helpless, looked so ill, that his great love for her, rising triumphant over duty, made him hesitate. Could not they guide the horses, and leave him to his darling? He turned, and looked at the buggy.

There sat the exhausted mother, holding her dying child; at her feet, poor Patience, muttering and trembling; and Rex the dog.

Back, back, Love, tender, sorrowing!

And to the fore, Duty,—his ever constant guide!

In that moment's temptation, Matthew suffered his death-agony. He felt that never more would he behold the child of his old age,—never more could he temper the bitter wind to his ewe lamb. Yet, crushing down the pleadings of his love, he sprang to the buggy, took the reins; and the horses dashed down the road, leaving all of his life behind him. He was the sole succor of these poor human waifs. Either he would guide their frail bark out of this dark sea of trouble, or he would perish with them.

He felt the snow, and he blessed Heaven for it. But it soon stopped, cruel traitor that it was, and only served to make their tracks distinct. Matthew knew this. He knew their only chance was to put as many miles as possible between them and the sleeping village before their pursuers could start. So he kept the horses at their full speed. On, on they dashed in perfect stillness, except the ringing of the horses' hoofs, and the whirring of the wheels.

At last Patience, lulled by the motion of the carriage, fell asleep. Ever watchful, Matthew noted this, and hoped good results for the girl from this repose. She was chiefly on his mind. Her wild eyes, her mutterings, and, except these, her most unnatural stupor, all told that reason was tottering on its throne.

"Poor lamb!" he had said to himself again and again, as he had watched her sitting in the bottom of the carriage, her large eyes fixed on vacancy as she muttered to herself. But when she fell asleep, and her regular breathing told of her real rest, his anxiety for her became less pressing.

They had travelled seven hours, had made nearly sixty miles, and the first faint streaks of gray were dappling the black of the winter sky. Matthew could see in the distance the mountain range near the boundary. Once beyond that, they were out of Utah. They were free! On that line, ever nearing, were fixed his hopes for the safety of these unfortunates. Like Moses, he was gazing on the promised land.

As this came to his mind, there followed the thought, Like Moses, was he never to reach it? "If it be Thy will," he said in his heart, and, while struggling as man might struggle, was ready, like hero, to endure his fate.

On, on, the horses dashed. They were all flecked with foam, but responded to their master's voice, urging them onwards, while their veins, like whip-cords, rose on their sides and haunches. Noble

beasts. They went as if they knew that human lives hung on every
rod they gained.

The hours advanced. Over the earth now hung the light of dawn.
The sun would soon be up. Matthew hoped, before its light made
bright the day, he would have landed his bark into a safe haven. He
was thankful; for he felt that within, which told him the cord of his
life's bow was stretched to its utmost, and it would take but little
more to snap it.

He had pointed out the border-line to Tabitha. Every now and
then she would raise her eyes from Christie's face, and look longingly
towards their destination. Oh, if they could but reach it before
Christie's little soul winged its flight to God! If only he could have
a few peaceful hours of rest before he died! And that in peace she
might catch his parting words, and treasure them as comfort for the
time, alas! so near, when she would have him no longer.

Patience still slumbered quietly. In the gray of morning her face
looked calm as a child's.

"She will wake from this rest her own self," Matthew said to
Tabitha, as he looked at the sleeping girl.

Each moment hope grew stronger. But Matthew knew the value
of each moment, and still urged on the tired horses.

What was that?

A hardly perceptible sound, but one that fell on Matthew's ears
as the knell of death. His heart contracted in agony. These unfortunates! After all, would he not be able to save them?

Had they heard it?

No. Tabitha's eyes were fixed on Christie; and over the storm-
tossed soul was falling a sad, a holy calm. It shone in the tired face,
and seemed a reflection of the look in the dying eyes gazing at her.
And Patience was smiling in her sleep, poor lamb! The tears started
to Matthew's eyes.

That awful sound! Nearer, nearer! The clamp, clamp, of horses' hoofs. Not one, but many.

Tabitha heard it now. She did not speak; but her face turned a ghastly white, and closer to her aching breast she pressed her child.

Matthew looked behind, still urging on his horses. Faint, dark objects approaching, told of their coming fate. Unless their horses could more swiftly carry them past the border-line, which for them stood between life and death, they were doomed.

"Up, up!" called Matthew, now urging the noble brutes with voice and whip, his heart aching as he did so; for he saw blood mingled with the foam that fell from their mouths. Yet they put forth new strength in these last moments of the terrible race.

Nearer, nearer, came that fearful clamping.

More livid grew Tabitha's face, her eyes still fixed on her dying boy. His were glazing fast with death. He could hardly see his mother bending over him.

"On, on!" cried Matthew. And the horses, panting, exhausted, still responded, still pushed onwards. Nearer, still nearer the horsemen came, — so near the noise awakened Patience from her long, refreshing sleep. She seemed quiet and calm.

"Matthew," she said, "I know they will kill us if they catch us; and they are gaining fast. But, if I can die with you and mother, I will not be afraid." And then, facing the death that she knew would be hers, the girl actually smiled. She was weary of her life, this bright young creature. Frightened at what had passed within these last few days, she was glad to lie down in the quiet of death.

"Poor lamb!" Matthew's lips kept repeating. And, giving all his attention to the now staggering horses, he still tried to urge them forward. A fruitless effort! He knew the race was lost. Each instant brought their pursuers nearer. They could hear the snorting of the horses, and the voices of the riders urging them forward.

Matthew felt on his shoulder the hot breath of a panting steed. In another moment the rider was beside him, and, pointing a pistol at his head, cried, —

"Halt!"

Turning, Matthew saw a man with a covered face. He had not yet pulled in the rein. The horses, seeming to gather fresh vigor

"HALT!"

from the close approach of pursuing horses, were once more gallantly striking out. There was no other rider within several yards. Perhaps the other horses were not much fresher than his own. At all events, a few moments more, and Christie, at least, would be asleep in death, beyond the power of mortal harming.

From this band with hidden faces, Matthew knew full well neither age nor innocence could hope for mercy. In less than a second did these thoughts rush through his mind; and, as the click of the pistol made ready for firing, he raised his right arm, and, with something like a return of youthful vigor, dashed from his horse the cruel enemy.

Once more they were ahead!

"On, on!" called Matthew, urging the exhausted beasts, forcing them to still greater effort. Then in this fearful moment, without taking his eyes from the horses, on whose waning strength depended their lives, he said, —

"If we should escape, it is God's will. If we die, it is still his will. Let us submit to his decree with all our love."

They listened in silence, and in silence waited their fate.

Patience was sitting so that she could see their pursuers. Paler and paler she grew, as the horsemen, in a furious gallop, were coming nearer and nearer.

"They are upon us!" As she said the words, two riders dashed past to the horses' heads; while two others, on each side of the buggy, enforced their uttered "Halt!"

In a moment more they were surrounded by a number of men, whose faces were covered with something like black masks.

No one living in Utah but has heard of this mysterious band. But no one ever tells of seeing them. Their witnesses are the silent dead; for, except in rare instances, only those that are doomed to death, or fate more awful, ever behold these avengers.

What had they now to avenge?

A girl's defence of her purity.

And on whom did their vengeance fall?

That girl, her mother, and an old man, their protector!

As the buggy stopped, there came over Christie's face the awful change of death. His eyes cleared and brightened with joy; and his voice, grown fuller and stronger, exclaimed, —

"Mother, my vision! I see God!"

An instant, and the light had faded. As two men, grasping Tabitha, dragged her from the buggy to the ground, in an agony of grief she was bending to catch her child's dying gasps.

"What have you there? A young viper?" said a gruff voice.

"In mercy leave him! He is dying." But even as Matthew, with loud voice, cried these words, cruel hands snatched the child from Tabitha's breaking heart, and roughly threw him on the ground. With one faint moan his life went out.

The two men guarding Matthew saw this brutal act. Perhaps it was the dead body of the child lying at their feet; perhaps they owed some gratitude to the old man, and thus were moved to pity, — they loosened their grasp on his wrists. Finding himself free, unobserved by the others, Matthew stooped, and felt Christie's heart. It had ceased to beat. He looked towards Tabitha. But the poor mother was beyond help or sympathy. Her head had fallen on her breast, her face grown ashen white. And only by the strength of her guards was she held on her feet.

Rex was close to Christie's body. The dog had not made a sound, and now stood sniffing around his little master. Seeing him, Matthew raised the little body, laid it on the faithful animal, slipped the cold hands in the dog's harness, then turned him towards the way they had come.

"Home, Rex!" he whispered, and saw the dog start quietly away with his precious burden.

It was all done in a moment. Before any one had noticed the mercy shown Matthew, he stood as before, between his two captors, each with a hand on his wrists and shoulders.

Patience, refreshed and invigorated by her long sleep, stood quiet and calm between her two guards. They had their hands on her shoulders, and grasped her wrists as Matthew's were grasped. But the girl, feeling the exaltation of martyrdom, uttered no moan of complaint. She had seen Matthew take from the ground the dead body of her little brother, and Rex bear him quietly away. She saw her mother's unconscious face, and was thankful for each moment that she was spared the waking to fresh sorrow. She felt that life was closing for her, and in her youth and beauty she was glad to lay down its burdens.

Matthew and Tabitha were placed near together, Patience nearly opposite to Matthew. She was better so, she thought, than at their side, where she could not touch their hands. Here, at least, she might look at their dear faces. And she seemed to catch some of the strength of Matthew as she gazed on him. She did not feel grief at Christie's death. She knew she was soon going to him ; and she thought she would not be such a stranger in heaven, now his dear little face would welcome her. She hoped she would be killed first ; for then she would keep her eyes fixed on Matthew, and not see the knife or pistol that would make her death-wound.

While she was yet thinking, the rest of the band came from the buggy. When the last one left his place at the horses' heads, he gave them a blow ; and, exhausted as they were, the frightened animals started off at a gallop ; the carriage swinging from side to side, as it vanished in a turn of the road. Patience watched it all, and the men, as they walked slowly back, and formed a circle around them.

" They will kill us now," she thought ; and she began to tremble nervously. But her heart was undaunted, and her face calm. Except the few brutal ones when Christie was killed, not a word had been spoken since they had been dragged from the buggy. And now, in silence, these men, with covered faces, stood in a dark circle around their captives.

The silence grew so awful and oppressive, Patience could hardly breathe ; when it was broken by a voice, calling, —

"Stand forth, thou hoary sinner, thou Gentile priest, thou insti-gator of rebellion to wives and children! Stand forth, and hear the doom which an avenging angel pronounces against thee."

Matthew's guards pushed him forward, and he stood alone in the centre of the circle. A prisoner; but he looked a king, with his noble head erect, and his tall frame drawn to its full height. For himself he feared not death. Calm and undaunted by this mysterious circle, he looked beyond their cruelty to God's throne. And yet, even now, exalted by his faith, his heart was filled with tenderest human pity for these two helpless ones who must share this terrible doom. Again the voice : —

"Brothers, what does this wretch merit?"

Silence! Awful silence!

And then many voices hiss out one word, —

"Death!"

Matthew's guards advanced, and, grasping him, once more pull him back.

"Woman, stand forth!" said the voice.

But the woman, half fainting, could not stand. Her guards pushed her to the middle of the circle, and she fell on her knees. Barely conscious, she weakly raised her head, and gazed in the direction of the voice.

Again it spoke : —

"Thou rearer of a brood of vipers; thou traitor to Utah's sacred laws; thou spy, that, escaping from our boundaries, would tell hideous tales of our holy church, — hear the doom an avenging angel pro-nounces against thee!"

As before, silence for an instant; and then that awful whisper of many voices, —

"Death!"

Tabitha still gazed around, as if not understanding what was said.

But, in a moment, her guards had raised her to her feet, and dragged her back to her place.

Once more the voice : —

" Girl, stand forth ! "

Patience's guards did not need to push her, so willingly she ran to the centre of the circle, standing just where Matthew and Tabitha had stood.

" I feel the blessing of their footsteps," she said to herself.

So fair she was, so young, and her sweet face radiant as an ancient martyr's ! Matthew, looking at her, felt his eyes grow dim with the dew of pity.

" Thus might have looked St. Agnes," he thought, as he watched the girl, quietly standing, awaiting her sentence. And the voice went on, —

" Thou would-be murderer of a fond father ; accursed of Scripture, thou thankless child, — listen while an avenging angel pronounces thy doom."

Silence for a moment ; and, in that moment, Patience's soul sang a " Te Deum" that her father yet lived. She was spared the sin of murder. While even this thought ran through her mind, the awful whisper began.

What did they mean ? It was not "Death !" No. God help her ! Fate more awful.

" She shall be given to that father to do his will, — to become his lowest handmaid. And, if ever she divulges any particular of this meeting, her tongue shall be torn out, and her eyes burned with hot irons."

All her peace and calm deserted on the instant. With a wild shriek of horror, she fell on her knees, and, before her guards could drag her back, had poured forth words of piteous pleading.

" In mercy kill me ! Do not send me to him ! Pity, pity, pity !"

she sobbed, as weeping, trembling, struggling, she was forced back to her place opposite Matthew and Tabitha. Matthew's voice rose on the air, and reached Patience's heart.

"Be patient, dear child. God will have pity on " — Ere he finished the words, a shot rang out ; and the old man fell dead.

A shriek from Patience, and again the light of madness flashed from her eyes. She looked from the dead Matthew to her living mother, and trembled and shivered. Her chin began to shake, and again she began that fearful muttering.

Tabitha was only partly conscious. She started at the shot, but did not know that Matthew lay dead at her feet. She thought he was bending down, looking for Christie.

"He's not there, Matthew," she whispered. "He's gone to God."

A smile came over her worn face. Another shot ; and she, too, fell dead, — dead beside him who had given "even his life " for her and hers.

Patience heard the shot, and saw her mother fall. Silent and rigid she looked on the two motionless bodies. And then, with a wild shriek, with eyes starting from her head, —

"Dead! dead ! All dead !"

Shrieking, laughing, struggling, she was no more the tender Patience, but a raving maniac!

And the morning sun, bursting through the clouds, shone over all.

CHAPTER XXXV.

"SEEKING, THEY FIND."

WHITE-COVERED wagon coming slowly towards the village, and a merry whistle waking up the winter's sun, as lazily he shone over the mountain tops, — a merry whistle, and Martin's happy face looking lovingly towards his home. It was not yet in sight ; but he knew where it stood, and was watching for the first glimpse. In fancy he already saw the mother's loving face, dear little Christie, and heard Patience's merry greeting. He laughed outright as he thought how Patience would jump and dance when she saw what he had brought her for Christmas. He took out something from his pocket, and looked to see if it were all safe. Yes : there it lay in its many folds of paper, — a little box, and in it a golden ring. He folded it up again carefully, and put it in its hiding-place ; giving the pocket a little pat of satisfaction.

"I'll make her keep guessing what it is, and then won't give it to her until Christmas morning. She'll be half wild with curiosity if I make her wait two whole days."

Thinking of Patience's golden ring, he sighed. The one he had brought for Christie to give Christine came back to his mind.

"Poor, dear Christine ! How I long to see her and Matthew ! What a brute Malcolm must be, to want another wife when he had won her ! I wish I could have a lick at him." And he doubled up his strong fist, and struck out from the shoulder in a way that would have been rather fatal to Malcolm's beauty if he had been before him. "Well, never mind. We'll all be happy yet, when we leave Utah, and are settled in the camp. My, how I miss the pounding of the mill!" And then he began to think of the cabin, which, in leisure hours, he had built for his family. It was all ready for them. He had even put a carpet on the floor of the large room. This carpet was a source of great pride to Martin. It was his Christmas gift to his mother, and he was wondering if she would like the pattern. He'd have to tell her of it: or should he say nothing about it, — leave it for a delightful surprise when she reached her new home, and, for her Christmas, just hand her all the money he had saved? He could not quite settle this serious question. Decided he would consult with Patience, and get her opinion.

He was growing impatient with the slow progress his horses were making, and began to crack his long whip, and start them up a bit. He was feeling very anxious about Christie. Patience's last letter had mentioned his increasing weakness. She wrote he could no longer use his crutches, and only moved about in their arms, or on Rex's back. And then she added, "Good Rexy is such a comfort to the dear boy! He acts just like an elder brother, always ready to give his strength to our little angel." These words had troubled Martin sorely, and now came rising before him, clouding the joy that was filling his heart. But he dashed away the tears that came to his honest eyes, and said, "The little man'll be all right when he gets a good doctor. And, please God, he'll have one, if I have to pledge a year's work for the money. Come, get up, you lazy boys!" he called to the horses; and, with much noise and rattling, the wagon took a brisker pace towards Martin's home. Matthew's house came first in sight. How white and peaceful it looked! "But not so white as his soul," said the young fellow. "If they knew I was so near, both he and Christine would be peeping out, just to say ' Welcome.' " And he smiled a great, broad, happy smile. How happy he was ! He had worked so hard, and now was about to taste the fruit of his labors. It had been arranged, that, immediately after Christmas, Martin was to take his mother, Christie, and Patience back with him in his wagon. They would take nothing but their clothing. The furniture of the cabin was both poor and old ; and, besides, Matthew, not feeling quite secure of Bishop White's approval, thought their chances of safe departure would be increased if they went off quietly, as if just for a trip of pleasure. A few days after they left, he would follow with Christine, and, until every thing was settled, rent a house for them. Then, towards spring, he would return to G——, and get his fields ready for the sowing, when, he thought, with the help of John Smith's influence, he might be able to bargain off his house and ranch in exchange for cattle. He did not anticipate any difficulty about his departure ; as he had paid in full both principal and interest on his lands, and owed no debts. They had talked all this over ; and Patience, the family scribe, had written it to Martin. He had partially secured a nice little house for Matthew. The bargain only waited his approval, and the young fellow was quite proud of the business ability he thought he had shown. He was longing to have Matthew say, " Well done, my boy," and feel the loved hand on his shoulder. The wagon was nearing Matthew's house. Now it stood before the gate, but there were no dear faces looking out ; and, stranger yet, the house-door stood open. " What can be the matter ? Has Christie been taken ill, and both Matthew and Christine, hurrying to him, in their anxiety forgot to close the door ? " A surge of hot blood rushed all over him as this fear arose. He gave the horses a sharp blow ; but, with a jump, they came to a stand-still. There was something black lying in the road. It looked like a woman, and he had nearly run over her. Catching the reins on the brake, Martin jumped down, and ran towards the long, black object. It was a woman, lying like one dead. He raised her up. Good God, it was Christine !

Pale, deathlike, but faintly breathing. He lifted her in his strong young arms, and laying her gently on her back, as he had seen his mother place Christie when he fainted, rushed to the wagon for a flask of whiskey. Mrs. Monk had given it to him, "to use in case of necessity," she had said. And surely there never could be a greater need than now. He rubbed some on her face and hands, wet her lips with it, and, as she began to breathe a little stronger, put a few drops in her mouth. Slowly the dark eyes unclosed, and looked at Martin. It did not seem strange to see him there. She felt as if their griefs must reach the whole world round, and they

"IT WAS CHRISTINE!"

had brought him to her. But to him, just dreaming happy dreams, to find Christine, the pearl of womankind, lying fainting in the public road, what could it mean? Where was Matthew? What had become of all humanity, that this should occur? When she grew stronger, and, leaning on her arm, looked eagerly up the road, he helped her to her feet. He held her fast in his arm, and tried to lead her back to the house. He himself was in a daze. A thousand eager questions rushed to his lips; but he did not speak, waiting for her to tell the frightful facts that had brought her where he found her. Half lifting her, he turned towards the cottage; and she whispered faintly, —

"Not that way. This road. We must follow them. Help me to your wagon. O Martin!" she wailed, as she sat by his side, held up by his strength, "either we must find and die with them, or we are left utterly alone in this weary, weary world. Drive on your horses. Lose no time. This was the way they went; and, as we go to them, I will tell you what will break your heart as it has mine."

In whispers, often interrupted by her tears and his bitter grief, the story of these terrible days was told to him. The morning greeted him a happy boy: the noon looked down on a man filled with wild revenge.

"When I meet that wretch that drove my sister to despair, I will kill him, and exult in his death-agony. He is not my father. He is a fiend incarnate."

And murder looked out of the blue eyes that ever before had beamed kindly on every living thing. Christine, while she felt even in her tender heart an echo to his bitterness, remembered her promise to Matthew. Stilling the rising of human nature, she talked and pleaded with the poor fellow at her side as Matthew would have done, until, feeling her ills were as great as his own, and her life more piti-ful, he said he would try to keep from crime for his mother's sake. The horses were not fresh, so they made but slow progress. It was a lonely road. Travelled mostly by grain-teams during the summer and autumn, it was little else used; and there were but few cabins to break its loneliness. They dared not stop at any of these, even to

hire a fresh team, that they might travel faster ; for they dared not
let it be suspected who they were, or whom they were seeking.   They
were on the right road ; for the tracks were plainly visible, — horses'
hoofs in great numbers, and every now and then the mark of a light
vehicle.   They were frantic with anxiety to push on, and learn the
fate of those dearer than life.   But, urge as he might, the horses could
not go fast ; and the afternoon found them only forty miles on their
way, with the necessity of stopping to feed the team.   The horses
must eat, or their strength would not last to the end of this terrible
journey.   For over an hour these two, their hearts bursting with their
dreadful uncertainty, must wait, must hear the grind, grind, of those
slow teeth ! would they *ever* finish ?

It was maddening !   Martin built a fire, and, making Christine sit
near it to warm her half-frozen feet, gave her some of the contents of
the little flask.   She did not know she was cold, — was not conscious
she had been shivering for the past two hours.   Her every thought
and feeling was merged in the one desire to find her grandfather and
her friends.

At last the horses had eaten their grain.   Martin was putting them
to the wagon ; and Christine, pale as death, but composed and determined, stood ready to mount to her seat, when, looking up the road
where they longed to be going, she saw, coming towards them, an
animal, large and dark.   As it came nearer, she saw it was a dog.
She called, —

" Martin ! "

He had just finished hitching up the team, and was coming to help
her in, when her voice hastened him to her side.   She pointed to the
advancing dog.   " Rex," he said.

She bowed her head.   She could not speak.   She saw he carried
something on his back, and her heart told her it was Christie.

The dog had seen and recognized them.   He began to whine ; and while he walked rather than trotted, as if he were bringing something very carefully, he seemed to increase his speed.

"Christine," said Martin, "he is carrying something. Can it be Christie?"

Again she bowed her head. Her lips seemed glued together. Speech was impossible. Dashing more bushes on the waning fire, Martin ran towards the dog.

Faithful creature! His eyes were bloodshot, his tongue hanging out, and he panted as if each breath would be his last. Yet he walked on until Martin reached him, and stood quietly while Christie was taken off his back. When he was safe in Martin's arms, Rex ran, as if half maddened by thirst, to the stream where Martin had watered the horses. And Martin, with the dead body of his little brother held close in his arms, came to the fire, and began to rub the icy cold limbs.

Even with death's awful mark on the brow, mouth, nose, the half-opened, glazed eyes, the pulseless breast, and the limp, hanging limbs, Martin would not believe him dead. He called him by every endearing name, kissed him with all the fervor of his loving nature, rushed for water to bathe his head, chafed the little hands and limbs that nothing could ever again warm back to life. He would not listen to the weeping Christine striving to reason with him, — would not hear her say he was dead. But dead he was; and, pure angel as he had ever been, there came even from his sweet lips the awful moisture that death alone can bring.

When he became convinced that the little brother he had loved so fondly was gone from him forever, Martin threw himself on the ground beside his body, and the sobs of manhood rent the air. Can any one, once hearing the weeping of a strong man, forget it? It seemed to Christine as if his sobs took actual form, and peopled with grief their lonely resting-place.

"Martin," she said, as time went on, and his grief showed no abating, "see, the day is going ; and we may have many miles yet to travel before we find father, Tabitha, and Patience." At her words, Rex, who had been whining beside Christie's body, licking his hands and face, ran to Martin, and pulled at his coat, darting down the road, and back again, as if he could show the way. "Come, Martin, come, or we may be too late."

Martin rose slowly to his feet, his face all swollen with his bitter weeping, and his bosom heaving with heavy sobs. Christine had Christie in her arms. She wiped his lips, and kissed his holy, sleeping face.

"Little angel, come to take this journey with us. Show us the way, and, oh ! help us to bear what may yet be in store for us," she said, while her tears fell fast. She smoothed back the clustering curls that hung over his brow ; and, with a heart-ache so violent that it dried the tears on her face, she saw on one temple a fearful bruise. He had been martyred ! Quickly she hid the cruel mark with the beautiful hair, and prayed that Martin might be saved this pang.

Holding the dead child in her arms, with Martin's help she climbed to her seat. Still weeping, Martin took his place beside her ; and Rex, jumping in, lay at their feet, looking up the road. So the wagon started on.

The day had sunk to rest amid glorious golden clouds. There had followed the short interval of a clear twilight ; and now the moon flooded the earth with her silvery rays, lighting their road almost with the brightness of day. They still followed the tracks, as clear now as when the sun shone on them. Their hearts were heavy with dread ; for they knew that escaping Mormons, if pursued and caught, met with most fearful doom. And that they had not been caught, they could no longer hope, since this sad messenger had come to them. Martin shuddered as he remembered a tale told him by a young Mor-

mon he had met on his second trip out of Utah. It was of a woman
trying to escape with two little children, — a boy and girl. They were
caught ; the woman cut to pieces before her children, and her limbs
thrown in different directions. The two little children, both under
five years, were turned adrift on the country. "It was believed," he
had said, "that they would perish, and that they were too young, in
any case, to remember. But they *did* remember, and would avenge
whenever there came a chance." And such a strange look had passed
over the fellow's face, that, for a moment, Martin thought he must be
of kin to these unfortunates. But he did not like to ask. He had,
indeed, driven the circumstance out of his mind. Being naturally
happy and hopeful, he tried to believe the best of every thing. But
now there seemed no best. He felt that for him there never could
come a best.

He began nervously to look along the road, watching, yet dreading,
to see some member of a human body. He knew he should go
mad if the wagon were to run over and crush any part of those they
were seeking. He was half tempted to tell Christine. But, when he
turned towards her, he feared to disturb her. She was watching little
dead Christie, and looked so holy, she seemed an angel guarding his
brother. His tears flowed afresh as he saw the peaceful little face.
But, despite his sorrow, he was thankful to know his sacred body was
saved from violation. Again he watched the road, filled with that
awful dread of seeing a mutilated body. Again he looked back at
Christine. She was so still ! Was she dead ? He began to feel his
head whirl, his senses slipping away from him. To save himself from
madness, he put out his hand, and touched her arm.

"What is it, Martin ? "

Her gentle voice, her sad and holy eyes, brought him back to
reason and to grief.

Suddenly Rex, who had never ceased his watching along the road, began to grow uneasy. He commenced whining, and then, with a bound, sprang out of the wagon, and ran in front.

"Martin," gasped Christine, "whatever it is, we are near it. O God, give us strength!" And she took his hand in hers. They could almost hear each other's heart beat. On the wagon moved, until they were near to Rex, standing over something in the road. The dog was howling and whining, and, every once in a while, putting down his head as if listening. Martin, handing the reins to Christine, said, —

"Wait here."

"No, Martin," she answered. "We will go together."

Tenderly she laid Christie in the wagon, folded his little hands over his breast, and, covering his face, left him. She took Martin's hand. Ill as she had been, weak as she now was, she was ready to share, to its bitterest dregs, the sorrow in store for them. She seemed gifted with supernatural power of endurance that rose to every emergency. Side by side they advanced upon their fate.

Alas! too soon they found it.

On the ground, lying close together, the bodies of Matthew and Tabitha, cold and dead. Their sacred dead! The moonlight fell full upon their faces in their calm, their awful, sleep. A smile on each face, as if in peace they had left this world of sorrow. Just a little bullet-hole, in the region of the heart, had let out their lives, and opened heaven's door.

Christine knelt beside her father. She rested on his bosom, and despair seized on her soul. Despair! She raised her head, and looked on his face. The demon fled abashed. Kneeling at his side, the tender words of their last evening came back to her, one by one. Like stars they lighted the blackness of her life; and, before her holy dead, she renewed the promise made to him. There seemed to come a fresh smile upon his lips. She kissed them, and took its blessing on her heart; and then she turned to comfort Martin. Without a sob, without a tear, in deep and silent grief, he was bending over the body of his mother.

"Martin, we must take them home. We could not leave them here."

Without a word, he arose. Together they raised their beloved

"COLD AND DEAD."

dead, and placed them in the wagon. Christine's weakness turned to strength, and she took her part in this sacred duty.

Suddenly they missed Patience. Where was she lying? They looked in every direction, but no trace of her. Here was uncertainty more awful than death.

With faces bent near the ground, they scanned every track. Here was a slender footprint. Here she stood, but there was no mark of a fallen body. Here was her track again, and then two heavier lines, as if she had been drawn backwards. These marks stopped at the place where they had first seen the footprint ; and there, as if she had stamped one foot on the ground, there remained a deepened mark. But no further tracks. What had become of her ? They called Rex to their aid. He sniffed around, then ran a little way, and then stopped. Following, they saw no tracks of Patience ; but just where the dog had stopped, and was, with head bent down, trying to recover the scent, they found, on a brier, a shred of blue gingham. It was a piece of Patience's dress. Just here, there was a great tramping of horses' hoofs ; and, from this point, the tracks seemed all going in different directions ; but no further footprint, — no further shred of cloth. Nothing to tell of Patience. Rex, too, seemed puzzled. Coax him as they might, he would not stir farther away than the bush where they found the piece of gingham. He seemed to tell them all trace of her ended there. And to this they finally had to submit, after hours of searching. The moon, which had favored them, was now setting in the west ; and, before many moments, darkness would cover the earth. They must return with their dead. They must bury them away from sacrilegious hands, and then their mission would be to find Patience. Dead or alive, they would find her.

Slowly, slowly, they made the homeward journey with their awful load, dreading each instant some cruel interruption to this most holy, most sorrowful, funeral.

Towards evening on the next day they reached Matthew's ; and after night fell, and the village-lights went out, Martin dug their graves in the front-garden. Side by side they buried their holy dead, their graves unmarked, save by the eternal sorrow of two hearts. As the last sod fell on her beloved grandfather, Christine lost all power of speech and motion. She who, in all that time of trial, had taken her full share of awful, of sacred, duty, now, helpless as an infant, fell upon the resting-place of him who had so loved her. Martin carried her in his arms, and put her in bed. There was no woman near to help her. No one came to inquire; though that day was succeeded by others, and she still lay in a burning fever, perfectly unconscious; while Martin, ignorant how to help, but most tender, watched beside her. There was no one left but him. Even Rex was gone; for, two days after Christie was buried, Rex was found dead on the earth that covered the child. Faithful friend, he could not outlive his master!

CHAPTER XXXVI.

MR. JOHN SMITH.

IT was the fifth day of Christine's illness. There had been no change. The same fever, the same unconsciousness, and Martin at her side, moistening the hot lips, and cooling her burning head. He looked haggard and ill. There was the sound of wheels stopping at the gate, a rapping at the door ; but he heeded it not. His whole attention was given to Christine. His heart was full of anxiety for her, grief for his dead, and torturing fears for Patience.

He did not even hear the steps through the house, nor ascending the stairs. Even the opening of the door was unnoticed. It was not until a voice exclaimed, in tones of horror, "Great God!" that he turned his head, and saw John Smith.

He was looking at Christine. Even in that instant, when he thought her life was ebbing fast away, he loved her to madness. He touched her slender wrist. It almost scorched his finger, and the pulse was so weak and rapid he could not count it.

"She is desperately ill," he said to Martin. "Where is the woman waiting on her?"

"There is none," answered Martin.

"Has she seen a doctor?"

"There is none in the village." And Martin added bitterly, "If there were one, I doubt if he would come. Look!" he went on, "that poor girl lying there, and her old grandfather, have, for eleven years, nursed the sick, and helped the poor, of this village. Yet they see him pursued by a murderous band, suspect he is killed, know she is ill, and never one has called to say, 'Can I assist her?' It is not that they do not love her. How could they help it?" And his voice faltered. "But it is that they are afraid to succor one whose friends and kinsmen were murdered by Mormon justice."

"Hush, boy!" said John Smith, looking quickly around to assure himself they were alone. He knew the truth of every word the poor fellow had said. But they were words not to be spoken aloud. "I will find some woman to stay with her to-night, and will telegraph to Salt Lake for doctor and nurse to come by morning train. I will go at once, and return here from the station. The latest news I have is this." And, as he started off, he handed Martin an open telegram. It was the one Matthew had sent.

" In great trouble. Can you come to us? Answer.
"MATTHEW KLEIGWALD."

These few words had outlasted that noble life.

Telling the driver to reach the station as quickly as possible, John Smith sprang into the carriage.

Matthew's telegram had reached Washington ten days ago. It was handed him just as he was receiving some guests. He had invited a small party of influential men to a most elegant dinner. Those living among the intrigues of any great capital, know the value and effect of select and elegant dinners. John Smith understood how to give, and how to make them effective. As a host, he was inimitable; and, giving entertainments only to gentlemen, these gentlemen, in the enjoyment of his princely hospitality, managed to forget he was a Mormon and a bigamist. Entertaining was one of his greatest accomplishments. He never allowed any thing to disturb him when once he had undertaken the *rôle*. And yet, as he read this short message from a simple country farmer, he felt the very ground slipping from under his feet. Something was wrong with Christine, and she had told her grandfather to telegraph him. Or perhaps she was ill, and the old man thought he could direct him to the best doctor. Perhaps she was dead! And John Smith turned so pale, that the guest with whom he had been talking as the telegram was brought in, asked, with some alarm, " Is any thing wrong with you ? " and recalled him to himself.

He knew there was no train going West within three hours. At that time he would make some excuse, and leave his guests. Up to that time he must play the charmed and charming host. To his aid he called every gift and power of pleasing he possessed. He made his listeners laugh and sigh at will, and never seemed more absolutely fascinating than during those three hours that were to him more horrible than a nightmare.

To every word he uttered, there was an undercurrent in his mind. " Christine! She was in trouble, and called on him." He had thought of her every day and hour since he parted with her. But he had thought of her as one dead to him forever. Loved passionately, madly, but, like a star in heaven, far, far beyond his reach. And now she had called on him, — or Matthew had. And, even if she did not want him, he would see her again, — again press her slender fingers, whose lightest touch he could never forget ; and, with this inward flame scorching his soul, he smiled, talked brilliantly, and charmed the guests, who, at that very moment, he was hating, as the chains that bound him to the rock.

The clock struck the hour. In twenty minutes the train would start. They were only in the sixth course : there were three more to come, and wines of the finest. Rising from his seat, Mr. Smith, their host, begged for a moment their kindest indulgence.

"Gentlemen, three hours ago I received an important business telegram, calling me West immediately and imperatively. All men are slaves to business, and I must obey. But every slave may have

"MR. SMITH BEGGED THEIR INDULGENCE."

his memories and dreams of pleasures past, and brightest among mine are these moments when I have been honored by your company. I must take the train that leaves in fifteen minutes. But may I, before departing, ask the favor that you will remain until the little dinner is over, and keep in your memory a place for him whose greatest trial is having thus to leave you?"

The words were few and simple. But his manner and his look had that great personal magnetism which made of his lightest spoken word a power.

Amid a murmur of applause, acquiescence, and regret, John Smith, bowing and smiling, left the room. Giving a few words of direction to his secretary, who was writing in the ante-room, he threw an overcoat over his evening-dress, dashed out of the house into a carriage, and was off, before the astonished secretary had fully realized what he had heard.

"What's up now with the old man!" said that irreverent gentleman. "Is the president of the church dead, and is old John going to strike for it? Or have all his women perished at one foul blow, and is he off to play chief mourner, and replenish his harem?" And the young fellow, himself a Mormon, gave a laugh over the picture he had conjured up.

John Smith reached the depot just in time to catch the train. He was alone in the sleeper. Thank God for that! No need for further acting to-night. He telegraphed ahead, and engaged the drawing-rooms to Ogden, so he would not be needlessly tortured by troublesome acquaintances.

After days and night interminably long, he arrived at Salt-Lake City. It was evening. There was no train for G—— before the morning. So he drove to his house, astonishing and delighting the three Mrs. Smiths. They asked no questions, — were quite satisfied with the "important business" which gave them the society of the husband whom they held in "*shares.*" He was obliged to leave them early in the morning, and would not then disturb them, he. said, but would hasten back as soon as he had settled his matters, and steal a few hours from Washington to enjoy with them. And they seemed not only satisfied, but pleased. Marvellous women! Was it all acting? John Smith did not stop to question. He was anxious only for the morrow.

Carefully dressed, and apparently most calm, he was at the depot in ample time for the train. It seemed to his impatience that the stations had increased wonderfully since last he travelled this road. He knew a good many of the country people getting in and out at the different stations; and he pulled his hat over his eyes, that they might not see and speak to him. He was in no mood to receive their almost worshipping admiration. At that moment he was like a leaf in a storm, tossed hither and thither by a thousand ever changing fears.

At last the terminus was reached. At the station he inquired for Matthew, and was told that Matthew Kleigwald had left G—— some days ago. "It was a night journey," said the station-master, who knew John Smith, and was anxious to give him any information he desired, as well as to enjoy the chance of a gossip. "It was a night journey. The old man took off one o' the wives o' Bishop White. P'r'aps it was a 'lopement, for they do say as how the bishop is clean tuckered out about it."

An elopement! John Smith clinched the hand in his coat-pocket, and felt like knocking the man down. But he said nothing, looking as if it were of slight import to him, and then, quietly walking up and down the platform, waited for the carriage he had ordered, and longed, *longed* to ask for Christine. But he dared not. He feared her name on his lips would peril his self-control, and betray his carefully guarded secret. The station-master, however, delighted to speak to so distinguished a fellow Mormon, joined Mr. Smith as he passed the door of the little office.

"You knows Kleigwald pretty well, Mr. Smith?"

"Very well," Mr. Smith answered.

"Wal, they do say as how his granddaughter is mighty ill."

Christine ill! The cold heart of the distinguished Mormon gave a heavy throb; but his voice, as calm as ever, made reply,—

"Mrs. Smith, the granddaughter of Matthew Kleigwald, is my

niece. I have heard of her illness, and am now on my way to see she has every attention."

One of the strongholds of the Mormon leaders is the semblance and pretence of good-fellowship which is kept up among the brotherhood. Questions are asked, and seemingly answered with frankness, that, in another community, would be treated as impertinence. The power this gives is remarkable, having as its auxiliary the vanity of the masses. But, at this moment, John Smith was thinking less of political power than of shielding Christine under his acknowledged protection.

Flattered by the frankness of the great man, and changing his tone somewhat, the station-master said, —

"I do hope you'll find the young ooman better," as he thought, "Oho! she's not so bad off if the Hon. John Smith's a-lookin' arter her."

Just then the carriage drove up; and, bowing graciously to the station-master, John Smith stepped in, saying to the driver, —

"Go as quickly as you can."

She was ill, and he was in a fever of anxiety. The carriage stopped at the garden-gate; and, hurrying up the walk, John Smith knocked at the little door, first softly, then louder and louder. But, no answer coming to his summons, he opened the door, and entered. There was no one in the hall, nor in either of the lower rooms, which were in strange dust and disorder for the neat little household. With anxiety growing greater, he walked quickly out to the kitchen, to send his card up by the servant. But there was no servant to be found, and in the kitchen only the same dreary disorder. More and more anxious, John Smith, no longer considering life's conventionalities, went quickly up-stairs, and, first rapping at a door standing ajar, pushed it open.

"Great God!" He spoke unconsciously, as with horror he looked on Christine. He saw nothing but that figure on the bed.

How ill she was! How near death she seemed with the black hair all about her, the half-closed eyes, and fever-flushed face! How she had suffered since he saw her! What great hollows in the checks he thought so perfect in their soft oval! Yet, robbed of her freshness and her beauty, looking at her through a strange mist that obscured his vision, he still loved her madly.

He had no thought for any one else, until a voice, hollow and unnatural, said, —

"Well!" And then he looked

"HE SAW NOTHING BUT THAT FIGURE ON THE BED."

at the face of the boy at her side. He knew him as one of Matthew's *protégés;* and, in spite of his extreme youth, he seemed prematurely aged. But there was no time to waste on him or any one until Christine was succored; so, after a few hasty words, thrusting in his hands Matthew's telegram, John Smith, commanding speed, rode off to the station. He took off his hat to let the country air cool his head, but the air brought no peace.

He had seen her whom he had travelled so many miles to see, of whom he had thought through so many weary days and nights. He had touched her hand, had called her name, and had not gained even one glance from her unconscious eyes. For all his power, for all his wealth, this man was pursued by his Nemesis.

He reached the station, and telegraphed for the immediate attendance of Dr. ——, who stood at the head of the profession in Salt Lake. Then he sent a message to his clerk, to find at once, and send by morning train, Sallie Brooks, who had been cook for Malcolm Smith's first wife. This woman he remembered as having been particularly fond of Christine. Poor girl! she needed all affection, and should have the services of the woman.

"She shall have every thing I can give her. My darling," he said under his breath, with a painful contraction of throat and chest. The telegrams sent, he drove back to Matthew's house, where he found installed beside the unconscious Christine the woman he had sent from the village.

Martin was pacing up and down the floor of the little sitting-room. The boy looked ill and worn; but he was only a boy, and must get used to hard knocks. It was the lot of man, and in general was of little consequence to John Smith, who shutting the door, and telling Martin to speak in whispers, heard the story of the sufferings and death of Matthew, Tabitha, Christie, and of the disappearance of Patience.

While Martin was speaking, John Smith had shielded his face with his hand, and, through all the terrible recital, was listening to every slight sound from the room up-stairs. He was sorry for the boy: he knew the truth of all he was saying, and rather deplored these terrible retributions. But he also knew that the power of the Mormon Church depended on the fear it inspired in its believers; and he had risen, was upheld, by the power of that church. Ha! was that a moan from Christine? No. Had he been in Salt Lake, he could have prevented the mur— the punishment of the good old man and his friends. But now it was too late, and the less said of the matter the better. Matthew was a good man, but old men must die. Surely that was a call from above! And John Smith half rose from his seat, then, convinced of his mistake, made it seem only a change of position, as he went on with his thoughts. It was a pity that Matthew should have sacrificed himself. But the deepest regret of John Smith was, that all this had caused grief and illness to the woman he loved.

Martin, walking excitedly up and down, with a dry sob every once in a while breaking through his hoarse whisper, hardly looked at the quiet man with shaded face, until, with a " There, you've heard it !— God, I wonder you don't send down fire, and burn up such cruel devils ! — Well, can you help us ? " by his abrupt question he forced an answer.

" I will do my utmost, and think I will be able to find your sister." Then he assured the boy of his deep sympathy, and then, for a moment holding his arm, cautioned him to quiet and patience. " We can easiest work if we work quietly. I will at once call on Bishop White."

" He is not in town. As soon as the woman came to stay with Christine, I went to his house. It was closed. The only person I saw was a boy about the stables. He said the bishop was away, and would not be back for some time."

" Then, my dear boy, I will find him, and speak to him. If possible, I will find where your sister is, and let you know. But again I caution you to be patient and quiet."

The night dragged through somehow. Towards morning, Martin, exhausted, fell asleep on the lounge, the nurse dozing in a chair at the foot of Christine's bed ; and John Smith, at her side, moistened the hot lips, and smoothed the burning hands and brow. Thus near her, serving her, unconscious as she was, he passed the happiest, saddest moments of his life.

The next day came the doctor and Sallie. How the good woman

wept when she saw Christine so ill, so changed! She told Mr. Smith that her own children were dead; and, if he would arrange it so she could be free from her husband, she would never leave "Miss Christine." This John Smith readily agreed to do, settling on Sallie a handsome annuity so long as she should stay in Christine's service; and this was to be unknown to any but themselves.

The doctor found his patient very ill, her case much complicated by her delicate condition. For three days she hovered between life and death.

While she was still unconscious, her baby was born before its time, — dead. Sallie lovingly laid it beside the place Martin showed her as Matthew's grave. He had no headstone save his noble life, and that seemed forgotten by the people he had served.

Martin told Sallie all of their griefs, and she wept over him and petted him as if he had been her son. For three days Christine's life hung in the balance. For three days, at John Smith's request, the doctor, neglecting all his other practice, remained to attend her; and John Smith, forgetting all the world outside that sick-room, watched beside Christine, and helped Sallie nurse the love of his life.

At last the turn was made; and Christine, broken-hearted, lonely Christine, came back to life. The first conscious dawning of the dark eyes drove John Smith away. Learning from Martin how Matthew's property stood, he bought at a liberal price the farming lands and stock. The money he placed, settled on Christine alone, at the same bankers who had charge of her dowry. He showed to Martin the letter he had written. He said he had taken a fancy to do a little farming. But if Christine, on growing stronger, would like that care, she should have the property back again. And, having settled her affairs so that she would have an ample income, John Smith bade her farewell one day while she slept, and the next morning was on the road to Washington.

CHAPTER XXXVII.

SALLIE'S LETTER.

ONTHS had passed. It was now the last of March. The weather had been cold and rainy. A new sorrow had fallen on Christine. One morning, desperate from their long and fruitless search, despite her pleadings, Martin had gone to Bishop White's.

"Villain," he had said, "tell me where my sister is. Give her to my care, or I will make you rue the day you ever wronged a helpless woman."

He looked so tall and resolute, that the bishop promised, if he would come on the morrow, he would give him his sister. In triumph Martin hastened back to Christine. That evening, for some slight cause, he went out to the front of the house. Christine, alarmed at his absence, ran out in the rain to find him. He lay prostrate by the gate, — dead, with blood running from a wound under his left shoulder. She knew he had been killed by the same fell power that had murdered her grandfather. Again there was a midnight burial in that little front-garden. The grave was made by Sallie and Thomas, — a man sent from Salt Lake by John Smith, and warranted by him as trustworthy ; and Christine, whose heart had seemed full to bursting with sorrow, had now a fresh one. In his youth and strength, in the noble promise of manhood, Martin was stricken down because he sought to protect a young and helpless sister. And now Christine was left alone to seek Patience. Where was she? This question came to her at the dead of night, in the earliest dawning, and all through the long hours of the day.

Father, Tabitha, Christie, Martin, her little baby that she never saw, all dead, all gone! But this trust left to her, — to find Patience.

When Christine recovered from her illness, and heard from Sallie of some of John Smith's kindness, she wrote him a few lines of thanks, and then added a piteous postscript, telling of the lost girl, and imploring in her search Mr. Smith's influence. . He wore this little note next his heart, and never parted from it. He answered it by a kindly one, assuring her that he had not been idle in the interests of her friends, — that he thought he had a clew, and hoped to be able to give her some reliable tidings erelong; that he would return to Salt Lake by the middle of March, and would make the finding of her friend his first care. This note came the very morning after Martin was killed. Christine was too broken down to think of any thing for days and days after this cruel blow. Had it not been for Sallie's care, she would again have fallen into illness.

Sad as was her life, she dared not even wish to die while poor Patience was among the missing. She knew that Bishop White could unravel this mystery; and, as soon as she was able to go out after Martin's death, she went to see this cruel man. He looked nervous and ill at ease. But he received her politely; and he swore, with the most solemn oaths, that he knew nothing of Patience since she had left his house, — that the sorrow and death that had fallen on her friends were as much of a mystery to him as to her. Sickened at his falsehood, she left the house so weak that she could hardly walk to the carriage waiting at his gate. Sallie was looking out for her. She ran down the walk to give her her strong arm to lean on, and then again, for several days, nursed her with a mother's tenderness. As soon as Christine grew a little stronger, Sallie wrote to Mr. Smith, and told him of Martin's death.

"It has almost killed Miss Christine. She does look that pitiful and miserable, that my heart is like to break. For days she was too weak to stand. I nussed her like my own baby. If she was, I couldn't love her better nor I do. When she was able to move, she had Thomas hitch up the carriage, and drive her to that Bishop White's. What the ole varmint said to her, I don't know. But she comed back a-looking more ill than ever. And when I just riz up, and called him a devil, — begging your pardon, sir, that's jest what I sed, — she, a-looking so white and sick, jest answered, 'Let us pray God to forgive him, Sallie.' Well, I guess I ain't no Christian; for, while I prayed jest to please my deary, I thought if I had God's power jest for a little, I'd make him suffer a lot afore I'd forgive the wicked ole wretch. And now Miss Christine's only been up and on her feet five days, and what do you think these miserable critters did? Some on 'em fell sick, and sent for her to doctor them. I tried to stop her when I seed her puttin' on her bunnet; but I couldn't say nothing when she looked at me with them great sad eyes, and said, so soft-like, 'Sallie, would you keep me from helping the suffering? It is all the comfort I have.' So, sir, I jest whipped on my bunnet: and sez I, 'If you go, Miss Christine, Thomas shall drive you in the little close carriage Mr. Smith sent down; and I shall go with you, to see you don't a-tire yourself out.' She didn't want me to go in the house with her. She said it was something the matter with the throat. Dip something, she called it. But, indeed, while I don't like to be sick no more than nothing, I thought if it was catching for me, it was catching for her; so I jest goes in. The smell was somethin' orful. I put the camfor to my nose my dear Miss gave me, and then I could hardly stand the smell. But I looked at her pretty nose that had no camfor to it, and she looked so sweet and angel-like, that I jest felt ashamed of myself. But I held on to the camfor all the same. And now, for the last three days, she's jest been a-goin' and a-goin' to the sick ones. There seems to be a new lot every day. And there's no doctor, and they all send for my dear young lady; and she jest goes, and gives her medicines and her care, and don't even get no thanks. It jest keeps my blood a-bilin'. She told me last night perhaps she might hear from some on the sick and dyin' what's become of that poor little Miss Patience, who seems orful dear to her."

So Sallie's letter went on. She used often to send letters to Mr. Smith. She would take great pains with them, and look for the spelling of all the hard words in Christine's largest dictionary.   And, as answer to each letter, she would receive a handsome present.   John Smith knew she was a true, honest woman; and he liked to think Christine had so good and capable a servant.   And Sallie felt quite at home with the great Mr. Smith.   Of all the world, this poorly educated woman, this servant, was the only one who had guessed his secret.   She was really honest and true ; for she carried it to the grave with her, and never, by look or word, betrayed it.   But she would think of it, and like him all the better for the love he could not control.

CHAPTER XXXVIII.

GOOD FOR EVIL.

THE rains fell, the winds blew, and diphtheria became an epidemic in the little village. Christine, out of her own purse, sent for a doctor. She wrote to John Smith, saying she would pay all expenses, and asking him to send one immediately. There came to her aid a clever young fellow, Dr. Grey.

He worked faithfully ; and, when she asked his terms, he said, when engaged by Mr. Smith, he had already been most liberally prepaid. With the ill, dead, and dying around them, Christine had no time for argument or explanation. She was kept busy, — even more so than before the doctor came ; for the disease was on the increase, and there was no time for either to rest. The little close carriage was constantly in motion.

One night, quite late, there came a summons at the door.

"Mrs. White is dying, and sends for the doctor and Miss Christine."

Hurriedly throwing on his coat, the doctor ran for the carriage while Sallie wrapped up her mistress. The faithful creature would not go to bed during these terrible nights when the knocker was kept going, and messages came from the ill and dying, calling upon Christine. She never refused her help. Yet, as Sallie put on her warm wraps, she looked so frail and shadowy, that the good woman began to cry.

"I know you'll be sick yourself, my sweet lady," she sobbed. And Christine leaned down and kissed her as the carriage-wheels sounded on the road.

They drove rapidly to Bishop White's. Christine thought of the only time she had entered this house. She thought of Patience, and shuddered as all the poor girl had here suffered rose before her. And, thinking these thoughts, she went quickly up the stairs, to serve with all her ability her bitterest enemies. She entered the sick-room. The room of death, she thought it soon would be, when the face of the woman lying on the bed met her gaze.

Mrs. White was dying. She knew it. She was no weak sinner, ready to cry and bewail her past wickedness. She motioned away the doctor, saying, "I am past your help," then, beckoning to Christine, spoke to her in husky whispers, sometimes hardly articulate.

"I am dying, — I know it. I sent for you, — for I have deeply — injured you and yours. Can you forgive? Will God forgive? I have always — said there was no God. It suited me to believe it ; — and I succeeded when — I was well — and strong. But I've been ailing some time ; — and I've been watching you, — never tiring in — serving the people, — who, when — you needed them, — turned away. You have — helped every one — who called on you. There must be a God — to teach such forgiveness. I have suffered — greatly for — two days. Would not send for you — till I knew — I was near — death. Pray for — me, — and tell me how to pray. I have a sin, — a fearful sin upon — my soul. Patience White — she is living — but insane. Is confined in " — And here her voice completely failed. She was trying to speak ; but the awful choking, that in diphtheria often precedes death, prevented Christine from catching the words.

"Where is Patience?" she whispered in the dying ears, and then bent over to listen. But the woman was already in the throes of death. She could only say "Bishop White," and then, imploringly,

"Pray." And Christine, putting all other thoughts aside, prayed for the dying. Imploring mercy for a sinful soul, her voice rose and fell on the still air of death's chamber.

Mrs. White seemed trying to pray; but with a few gasps, a choking effort to get her breath, she was dead. Gone to face her Maker, and the woman she had so injured praying at the side of her dead body.

As Christine joined the doctor in the hall, a door opened, and out came Bishop White. He was ghastly with fright. He shook as if he had the palsy.

"Is she better?" he said.

"She is dead," said the doctor.

"My Lord! Dead! Is it catching? I've not been near her since she was taken sick. I kept down here. Do you think I'll have it?" And then, "Doctor, look down my throat. It feels a little queer."

Holding a candle, the doctor looked. Yes, there was already the inflammation that preceded the dread disease.

"Am I all right? Is any thing wrong?" he asked, as the doctor did not reply to his first question.

"Well, Bishop White," the doctor answered, "there is a little inflammation. But we'll take it in time, and I hope you'll be well in a few days."

"O God, O God!" cried the bishop, his face turning almost green with fright. "I'm going to die, I'm going to die! Doctor, I'm a rich man. If you save me, I'll give you a thousand dollars. Two thousand, three thousand!" he shrieked, as, seeing the doctor turn towards the door, he thought he was going.

Doctor Grey only went to his case to get some medicine. Selecting some powders, he put one in the bishop's mouth, and said quietly, —

"I will save you if I can, Bishop White. But, if you want to get well, you must keep calm. Your nervousness may increase your disease."

He gave him the powders to take during the night, and went to the door, holding it open for Christine to pass out. For the first time, Bishop White saw she was there.

"DOCTOR, LOOK DOWN MY THROAT."

"Don't go! For God's sake don't go, and leave me here!" And he ran, and caught Christine's cloak.

In all her life, she had never felt such a repulsion for any created thing as she did for this man. Yet she gently pushed him back, and said, —

"Keep out of the draught, or you will grow worse."

"Oh, then, stay with me ! Take care of me, and make me well."

He was sobbing and crying as he shook with fright. Christine hesitated. This man knew where Patience was. He alone could tell her. She would make a compact with him. For, once well, he might once more be the same cruel, unnatural father.

"Come, madam," said Doctor Grey. "You are tired out, and need repose."

"Stay, oh, stay with me !" cried the pitiable coward at her side.

"Bishop White," she said, "I will stay with you on one condition, — that you will tell me in what asylum you have put your daughter Patience, and write me the order for her release."

As soon as she said "condition," some of the old shrewd cunning came into the bishop's eyes. But he started when she asked "in what asylum."

"Who told you she was in an asylum ?" he asked.

Christine answered, "Either do as I require, or I go." And she moved towards the door.

"Stay ! For God's sake, stay !" he cried. "I will do as you wish if you promise not to leave me."

Christine took off her bonnet and cloak. She asked the doctor for paper and pencil. Handing them to Bishop White, she said, —

"Write the order for release."

Tremblingly, but clearly, he wrote, —

G——, April 10.

DOCTOR Y——.

My dear Sir, — Please deliver into the care of bearer my daughter, Patience White, whom I put in your care December last. Any unpaid charges the bearer will settle.

Yours,

T. C. WHITE.

A miser to the last! But Christine was content, and, taking the paper, gave it to the doctor's care.

"Doctor Grey," she said, "hand this to Sallie, and tell her for me, should I die before she sees me, she must go direct to Salt Lake, ask Mr. John Smith to accompany her to this asylum, and take away Patience White. Tell her to ask Mr. John Smith, for me, to have my property settled on Patience, and to make Sallie her guardian until Patience shall recover her reason. This is my last will and testament."

It was a solemn moment. They both knew she was offering up her life for her friend; for, in her exhausted condition, to keep to the confinement of the sick-room of that terrible disease was almost sure death.

Doctor Grey took the precious bit of paper, and, raising Christine's hand to his lips, kissed the tips of her fingers as he would have done to a queen.

"Good-night," he said. "I will call to-morrow."

He entered the carriage, and drove to Christine's house. He was actually afraid to meet Sallie's wrath when she would find him alone.

She did truly rave and storm. And he went off to bed feeling very much like a whipped school-boy.

CHAPTER XXXIX.

THE LOVELIEST WOMAN.

BISHOP WHITE was dead. After two weeks of most faithful nursing, Christine watching beside him day and night, he fell into delirium and convulsions; and, in one of these spasms, he passed from this world, which had been every thing to him, to that other for which he had so illy prepared. True to the last, she knelt by his side during these awful moments, praying, as she had never before prayed, for this wretched sinner who could not pray for himself.

Doctor Grey had called daily, doing all in his power for the sick man, and giving strongest tonics to the delicate woman who was tending him.

Sallie wanted to go to her mistress, but Christine had sent word imploring her to keep away from the contagion; for on Sallie, should she die, depended the future of Patience. So fuming and fretting, making the doctor's few hours at home very far from comfortable, Sallie passed the two weeks of Bishop White's illness.

The disease was on the wane now; and the village, except for the many fresh graves in the little cemetery, seemed much the same as before, so soon are the dead forgotten, and their places filled, even in this little world.

Sallie was all bustle and preparation; for the doctor had sent a boy running up, to tell her that Bishop White was dead, and he would shortly drive home with Mrs. Smith. So the good creature was flying around in a terrible flurry to make things look even neater than usual for the "poor deary."

She saw the carriage, and rushed to the door, as red as a peony, and as warm as if it were July. She fairly lifted Christine out of the carriage, talking, laughing, crying, as she helped her up to the house. She had feared to see some great change in her dear mistress after these weeks of fatigue, and she was so thankful to find her much the same. Frail and delicate as it was possible for a woman to be and live, yet she did not seem any nearer death than when Sallie had cried over her the evening she started for Bishop White's. And now, in that sad, sad face, there was a look as if the sun were shining on it.

"Sallie," she said, "to-morrow we will start for Patience."

And then Sallie knew the meaning of that look.

"O my sweet lady!" Sallie answered, "you are not strong enough." But when she saw the mouth sadden, and the large eyes look as if tears were in them, she knelt at Christine's feet, and said, "You shall go, deary, if I have to carry you in my arms."

So, the next morning, Christine, Sallie, and Dr. Grey all went to the city. Dr. Grey was returning to resume his practice. At the station they parted. Christine had told him she was going to take Patience from the asylum, and asked him to call at the hotel in the evening to see her. He readily promised. He was glad to be able to do any thing for Mrs. Smith. During their many weeks of working together, he had been amazed at her intelligence, endurance, and tender sympathy with suffering. Never in his life had he met, or even heard of, such a woman. So grand, so noble, and so womanly, she seemed to him as if set apart for the worship of mankind; and he dreaded never seeing her again. He was thankful they would still have a bond between them in the disease of the young girl who was only a name to him.

He called a carriage for Mrs. Smith, and, helping her and Sallie into it, stood looking smilingly after them. He no longer felt so desolate. He was no longer a poor young doctor hunting up a practice. He felt that he had been honored by the respect of the loveliest woman he could ever know.

CHAPTER XL.

THE LOST IS FOUND.

HE carriage drove to John Smith's office. Mr. Smith was very busy, — had denied himself to all visitors; but when his office-boy, putting his head in the partly open door, said, "There's a woman, and a sickly-looking lady in mourning, who wants to see you. Shall I say you are out, sir?" he sprang up from his writing, and nearly knocked the boy over as he brushed past him.

Yes, it was Christine, looking like a fair spirit in her black robes; and Sallie, all smiles and courtesies.

When Christine asked if he could go with them to the insane-asylum in charge of Dr. Y——, he was as pleased as a boy off for a holiday. He locked up his papers, and, saying he would not be back before morning, started off at once with Christine and Sallie.

On the road, Christine showed him Bishop White's order for the release of Patience.

"But, as it is a Mormon asylum, I knew this, or any doctor's certificate, would be less effective than personal influence."

She spoke so gently, looked at him so calmly! yet this was the first time, since his mad avowal of love, that she had been conscious when he was with her. And that love was at this moment eating his heart out as he gazed at her, and saw she was fading away.

She did not refer to any thing that had ever occurred in Salt Lake.

Could she have forgotten those moments when he bared his soul before her horror-struck eyes? If she had, and he could once more resume the part of a tender uncle, he would ask no greater boon of life. But, no: that was impossible. Never again could he enter that paradise, for the angel with the flaming sword stood at the gate.

It was quite a long ride to the asylum. Whatever difficulties stood in the way, John Smith's name and power pushed aside.

Dr. Y—— himself came to see his distinguished visitor. He desired to have the patient sent for. But Christine declined. She wanted to go to the cell herself. She believed the sudden surprise of a familiar face would have a good effect.

She was pale as marble, perfectly courteous to the doctor, but very determined; and John Smith, willing in all things to please her, seconded her wish with unanswerable arguments. The doctor felt vexed enough to have confined this obstinate young woman in a cell of her own; but he only smiled affably, and led the way.

"I warn you, madam," he said. "This young person, though seemingly gentle, is one of our most dangerous lunatics. We are forced sometimes to put her in one of the garden-cells, she grows so much more violent when in a close room."

Christine simply inclined her head. Her gentle heart ached with pity at the sight of so many unfortunates. As she glanced at them in passing, their cells seemed small, badly ventilated, and badly lighted. The air was close, and had an unpleasant odor; and, although the weather was cold and damp, she felt relieved when they passed out of the house into the "garden," as the doctor called it. A strange garden, and awful flowers! There were a good many iron cages around in different places; and in them, oh, horror! exposed to the sun's heat, the cold wind and rain, were confined human beings. Some were men, and some women like herself. They were all perfectly still as the doctor approached, and stood looking at him with terror in their wild eyes.

"Poor things!" Christine murmured, while tears of pity sprang to hers.

The doctor was a little in advance of them, and was hastening his steps, increasing the distance between them. Why, she could not tell, Christine quickened her steps almost to a run, until, standing beside him, out of breath, she laid one slender hand upon his arm, as if for support. John Smith had kept pace with her, and stood at her other side. It was the sight of him there, as if guarding her, that changed the doctor's baleful look into a smile. As they stood a moment, Christine heard a voice that chilled her very blood, — a sad, wailing cry, —

"Dead, dead! All dead! Oh, kill me too! In mercy kill me too!" And then a man's rough voice, —

"Be still, you little devil, or I'll make you."

At this, Christine, who had stopped, and gasped for breath, hurried on. A path opened on her left. Patience's voice, still wailing, coming from that direction, she turned in time to see a heavy whip, in the hand a burly fellow had thrust through the bars, descend with a "whiz" on the shrinking shoulders of her dear girl. She gave one scream, and ran towards the iron cage.

Patience, who had cowered down at the blow, when she heard Christine's voice sprang to her feet. Pale, thin to emaciation, her large eyes wildly staring, and the wasted arms, showing through rags, extended as if for an embrace, she stood, the pitiful ghost of herself. She seemed to see nothing, but appeared as if each faculty was absorbed in listening. In her madness she had heard a dimly remembered voice; and now there were coming quick footsteps, nearer, nearer, and then some one calling lovingly, "Patience, Patience!"

The madness brightened into intelligence, as, with a glad cry of

"Christine!" she rushed towards the friend coming to meet her, and, striking her head against the iron bars, fell stunned on the floor of the cage.

Tenderly they took her up, and put her in the carriage. They had reached the hotel, had said adieu to Mr. Smith, and were safe in Christine's room, before Patience spoke to any one. She had soon recovered from the shock of the blow. Only a red mark on her brow told of the accident. But she seemed afraid to move. She would open her eyes, see Christine, and then close them as she whispered to herself, —

"Another dream! Alas! I'll soon awake." And then she would shiver and moan.

Christine, keeping back the tears that rose to her eyes at this pitiful sight, put her arms around her, kissed her, caressed her ; but still she was unchanged, and answered not. When, however, she and Christine were alone in the room, she grew more restless, watched every motion Christine made ; yet, every time her eyes met the poor girl's, Patience would shiver, and then cover her face.

She was lying on the sofa, and seemed too weak to move. She had been very still for the last few moments. Christine was leaning over her, gazing at her. She was so emaciated that every bone was visible, and her face showed evidence of terrible suffering. Sallie had gone out to procure necessary articles for the poor child ; and these two friends, so sadly parted, so sadly re-united, were alone. Suddenly Patience opened her eyes, and saying, "Christine, dear Christine!" they were locked in each other's arms.

Dr. Grey called in the evening. He found Patience quiet and gentle, but she seemed sane only so far as Christine was concerned.

He told Christine, when she followed him in the hall to learn his opinion, that he believed Patience's mind would strengthen when her health improved. She was in a terribly reduced condition ; but her youth, and absence of local disease, were in her favor. Christine's desire that he would, when he could arrange the time, come, at least once a week, to G——, and take Patience under his medical care, made him so happy, that, instead of saying he would try to manage to oblige her, he grasped her hand with a hearty "Thank you."

The following morning Christine, Sallie, and Patience went back to G——.

CHAPTER XLI.

PEACE.

T was spring-time once more in the valley of the Jordan. The blossoms were filling the air with the same sweet perfume, the birds making it musical with song. But there were no young lovers under the apple-trees. Only a pale, sad woman holding tenderly the hand of a girl, who, no longer a child, was yet childish. Patience had gained in health and strength, and her beauty was almost as remarkable as ever. But in mind she was still a child. She seemed to have forgotten every thing in the past. Even her alphabet had to be relearned. Beyond Christine, every event in her life was a blank. She lived as a child in the present, — as a child loving her new friends. All her memory dated from the hour in Christine's room at the hotel. Thus she was always, except when her melancholy fits would come on, and she would not know Christine. Then she would repeat, over and over again, the incidents of that terrible race, and the death-scenes of Christie, Matthew, and Tabitha. These moods were now becoming fewer and fewer, and it was well they were ; for as her pathetic voice would dilate on each detail, and her large eyes, distended, seem again to behold them, Christine's tears and sobs would exhaust her strength.

And Christine now had very little strength to lose. She was fading away to the " Land o' the Leal." The most casual observer saw this. She would, in her moments of rest, lie quietly on the sofa, with her dark eyes fixed on the sky, as if she saw the spirits of her beloved ones stretching out their arms to her. And yet she was spared a little longer to watch over Patience. Dr. Grey came regularly. He had, from the first, taken a great interest in his patient. And as she improved so much beyond his expectations, as her beauty bloomed back into life, and her sweet nature shone in every look and gesture, he had grown to love her.

Christine and Patience were expecting him this evening, while they walked under the apple-trees towards the house.

"There he comes," said Patience, gently smiling.

And, springing from the carriage, Dr. Grey came quickly to meet them. The bright color rushed to Patience's sweet face, but faded when she saw he looked pale and nervous.

"Mrs. Smith," he said after a little, "may I speak with you for a moment?"

"ONLY A PALE, SAD WOMAN HOLDING THE HAND OF A GIRL."

And then, turning to Patience as if she were a child, "Will you wait for me under the large tree yonder?"

Her answer was a smile, as she ran towards the tree he had pointed out.

How sweet and fair she looked, standing under its blossoming branches! Yet so unlike the bright, impetuous Patience of other times! Christine's eyes had followed her; and she noted, with a sharp pang, that it was the very tree where she had stood, that beautiful spring-time, when Malcolm won her heart just a little year ago.

It was the first time she had thought of him for many, many days. He was like one dead. Truly was he dead to her. And yet, in this soft evening-light, he seemed to stand before her in all his beauty. Then, remembering that Dr. Grey was waiting, she turned her head with gracious gesture of attention.

"Dear lady," he said, "I want first to tell you something of myself, and must, or you may think me a traitor."

She did not speak, but that sweet half-smile encouraged him more than any words; and he went on, —

"I find I cannot help loving Patience, she is so gentle, so sweet; and I really think her mind will come all right. I notice, every time I see her, how her intelligence develops. Yet, in her affliction, she is but a child; and I seem a mean-spirited fellow to even think of trying to win her affection from you, who have done so much for her, and should keep her growing strength to care for and tend you. So I thought I'd just tell you what a fool I am, and to-night say 'good-by' forever, lest I turn knave."

He was so earnest and manly! Not handsome, but with a true look in the clear gray eyes, a true ring in the deep voice.

"Doctor," — Christine's voice was very low and faint, — "you have lifted the last of this world's cares from off my heart. I have not long to live. I feel my strength waning day by day. See how wasted I am!" And she held out one thin hand. "But I felt I could not die in peace, and leave my dear girl to an uncertain future. I am quite content now. I can trust her with you."

He kissed the hand she extended to him, and thanked her. But, man and doctor as he was, he could not keep back the tears when he looked at the noble woman before him, and knew she was speaking the truth.

"A martyr! A glorified martyr! Sacrificed to the cruel Moloch of Utah," he muttered to himself.

He was still looking at her, when she said, —

"Go to Patience." And then she turned up the walk to the house.

Dr. Grey had almost forgotten the other matter. It was a note from John Smith to Christine. She took it, saying gently, —

"Give my love and blessing to Patience."

As she turned, her steps were uncertain. Seeing this, Dr. Grey wanted to walk with her to the house; but she shook her head.

"No, no. Go to Patience. Tell her I shall hope and pray for her happiness." Then she turned once more towards the tree where Patience was waiting, and kissed her hand to the sweet girl.

"God bless her!" she said, and then walked slowly to the house. Dr. Grey did not move until she had taken several steps. She seemed stronger; and then, with a few hurried strides, he was with Patience.

Slowly Christine walked up the little path with the unopened letter in her hand. She would not read it here: she was on sacred ground. Here were the unmarked graves of those she loved, — father, baby, Tabitha, Martin, and little Christie. These were her sacred dead.

"And Rex, faithful friend!" she murmured.

Sallie ran out to meet her dear lady. She looked even paler than usual. But she smiled as Sallie helped her to a chair; and her smile was a rare, rare thing. Sallie was ready to forgive her bitterest enemy, she was so happy at that smile.

"I have a letter to read, Sallie. I'll sit here on the porch, and read it, while I wait for supper."

"All right, deary," said the delighted Sallie, and was going off to hurry up the supper, when again her mistress's voice : —

"Sallie, will you always live with Patience, even if I should die ? "

"O deary, deary, don't speak of dyin'!" And poor Sallie straightway began to cry. "But indeed I'll live with Miss Patience, or any one, to please you."

Again Christine smiled.

But Sallie's gladness was all washed away by her tears. She went in the house quickly, so her sobs might not disturb her "deary."

Christine opened the letter, the smile still on her face. Before glancing at it, she looked towards the great apple-tree, and saw Patience in her lover's arms. The smile deepened ; and murmuring, "God bless them !" she began to read.

"DEAR CHRISTINE, — Your will, in favor of Patience, has been duly registered. It seems to me a wise provision, — making Dr. Grey her guardian. He has greatly benefited her, you say. I have made wide inquiries, and find he stands high in the opinion of the older men in the medical profession. His being a Gentile will not occasion any difficulty. I will give the matter my particular attention, being only too glad to be of any service to you.

"There will be a great many items in the papers about Malcolm " —

Here Christine paused for a second, and put her hand on her heart. The bare name of him she had so loved awakened such intense pain. Then she read on : —

"Malcolm that may distress you. He is safe out of the country, with enough money to give him a fresh start in Brazil, where he has now gone. I attended to this, thinking you would so wish it. He really has robbed the bank, where for years he held a responsible position, and is defaulter to a considerable amount. But he promised amendment ; and he is young, so he may begin to lead a better life. Don't grieve over it. And, for God's sake, take care of yourself ! With your permission, I shall run down to see you and Patience next week. May I ?

"Sincerely your uncle,

"JOHN SMITH."

She read it through to the last word. And then such a strange feeling came over her. She tried to call Sallie, but could not speak. Suddenly there stood before her her grandfather, holding her baby. Her own baby! She knew it at once, with its dear little hands held toward her. And her grandfather, how happy he looked!

"CHRISTINE FELL BACK IN THE CHAIR, DEAD."

"Father!" she cried, her voice ringing out as she sprang to her feet.

Sallie heard the clear tones, and stopped work, listening in amaze, then, with a sudden fear that sent the blood to her head, rushed to the porch. She reached the door just as Christine fell back in the chair, dead.

There she rested, joy upon the still face, smiles on her parted lips.

Sallie, at her feet sobbing, dared not touch her, lest she disturb the blessedness of her rest.

In peace at last, sweet soul, in peace!

www.ingramcontent.com/pod-product-compliance
Lightning Source LLC
Chambersburg PA
CBHW020931030726
47496CB00005B/1141